"Race you!" A... digging her spurs into Jenny's flanks and slapping her neck.

From behind came the thunder of Graybob's hooves on the dry prairie.

"Go, go!" she shouted at Jenny. Annie loved the chaos of the gallop, her hair tumbling free, tears in her eyes from the impact of the wind, her body tensed to join with the power of the horse. Something inside her loins detached itself, drifted upward, carrying with it the knotted bud of her desires. With it came a premonition of how things would end.

The gray horse ran even with Jenny now. She must win. If she did not, Quent had the upper hand. Graybob pulled ahead, and in one flash her eyes absorbed the rider. Hatless, his blond hair flapping wildly, his blue eyes squinting against the self-generated wind.

He will win, her heart said, *and he will not leave, and you will accept him.*

Dear Reader,

Rae Muir's first book, *The Pearl Stallion,* one of our 1996 March Madness promotional titles, earned a 5★ rating from *Affaire de Coeur,* whose reviewer placed the book on her "top ten" list for 1996. This month we are delighted to bring you the author's second book, *The Trail to Temptation.* This wonderful Western takes place on a trail ride from Texas to Montana and features a heroine struggling to overcome her past and a hero searching for his future. Don't miss this warmhearted tale.

Another March 1996 author, Tori Phillips, returns this month with an unforgettable story, *Silent Knight.* Despite *his* vow of silence and the fact that *she* is promised to another, a would-be monk and a French noblewoman fall in love on a delightful journey across medieval England.

We are also so pleased to welcome back award-winning author DeLoras Scott with her new Western, *The Devil's Kiss,* a romantic comedy featuring two misfits who discover love, despite Indians, outlaws and themselves. And from award-winning author Margaret Moore, *The Wastrel,* the magical story of a disowned heiress and a devil-may-care bachelor, introduces her new series of Victorian romance novels featuring a trio of "most unsuitable" heroes that she has aptly named MOST UNSUITABLE....

Whatever your taste in reading, we hope Harlequin Historicals will keep you coming back for more. Please keep a lookout for all four titles, available wherever books are sold.

Sincerely,

Tracy Farrell
Senior Editor

Please address questions and book requests to:
Harlequin Reader Service
U.S.: 3010 Walden Ave., P.O. Box 1325, Buffalo, NY 14269
Canadian: P.O. Box 609, Fort Erie, Ont. L2A 5X3

RAE MUIR

THE TRAIL TO TEMPTATION

Harlequin Books

TORONTO • NEW YORK • LONDON
AMSTERDAM • PARIS • SYDNEY • HAMBURG
STOCKHOLM • ATHENS • TOKYO • MILAN
MADRID • WARSAW • BUDAPEST • AUCKLAND

ISBN 0-373-28945-6

THE TRAIL TO TEMPTATION

Books by Rae Muir

Harlequin Historicals

The Pearl Stallion #308
The Trail to Temptation #345

RAE MUIR

lives in a cabin in California's High Sierra, a mile from an abandoned gold mine. She is, by training, an historian, but finds it difficult to fit into the academic mold, since her imagination inevitably inserts fictional characters into actual events. She's been a newspaper reporter, wrote and edited educational materials, researched eighteenth-century Scottish history, ran a fossil business and raised three children in her spare time.

She loves the Sierra Nevada, Hawaii, Oxford and San Francisco. Her favorite mode of travel is by car, and she stops at every historical marker.

To Jane and Jeff
and the Native Texans

Prologue

Washington, D.C.
November 1882

"The tall gentleman," said Ted, pointing with a shrug of his shoulder, "is our host, Senator Wise of Texas."

Quent stared hungrily. Even New Yorkers had heard of the legendary Texas cattleman, now a senator. He felt immediate disappointment. In his dress clothes, the senator resembled every other man in the room.

"I do not," Ted continued in a whisper, "see any representatives of President Arthur's cabinet. Other than myself, of course."

Quent smiled at this bit of braggadocio. His cousin was an under secretary in the War Department, hardly a member of the president's cabinet.

"Senator Wise is already wise to the ways of Washington," Quent said flippantly. "He's found out who spends the money, and does not invite the figurehead secretary, but those who award the contracts."

Senator Wise wandered through the crowd, greeting his guests. His gray eyes picked Ted from the crowd, and he strode to his side, grasped his arm and steered him in the direction of a table covered with whiskey bottles. Quent knew no one else in the room, so he tagged along. The senator walked tall, with the loose, rolling gait of a man accustomed to being on horseback.

"Who's your friend?" Senator Wise asked Ted, spinning around so suddenly Quent nearly stumbled into him.

"Senator Wise, my cousin, Quentin van Kelson," said Ted. "Quent, Senator Wise of Texas."

"Another New Yorker come to rustle his fortune in the capital." The senator had not learned the gentle tones of diplomacy. He spoke as though his voice must be heard through a storm, over the thunder of cattle stampeding across the largest ranch in Texas. He grinned with one side of his mouth. He gripped Quent's hand tenaciously, as if he were clinging to the tail of a rambunctious bull. "Nicholas van Kelson's your father?"

"My uncle," said Quent, flexing his numbed fingers. He understood the reason for the question. Uncle Nick had his finger in every railroad pie; Senator Wise supported all the railroad bills before the Senate, *if* those railroads headed toward Texas and the stockholders made significant donations to his coffers. "My father is Claude van Kelson," Quent added.

"Who?" bellowed Senator Wise.

"Claude van Kelson. My father practices law in New York. Lowell, Paige, van Kelson, van Kelson and McCormick," he added lamely.

"Never heard of him, but I'm sure he's a bandicoot if he's Old Nick's brother." He punched Quent's shoulder playfully. Quent grabbed at Ted to stay upright. "Should move out to Austin, where there's proper work for lawyers who can nose their way about the statehouse." He winked. "You come from a large family, if I'm to believe your name. Quentin, the fifth child!" His words and grin made leering comment upon the virility of Claude van Kelson.

"I have two sisters and two brothers, all older than myself," said Quent. "And a younger sister."

"Which one you favor?" the senator asked.

"Pardon me?" asked Quent, astounded at this strange comment upon his siblings.

"You take after your father or your uncle?" demanded the senator, prodding Quent by digging an elbow sharp as a chisel into his ribs. "Railroads or the law?"

"Neither at the moment," said Quent. "I have yet to make a final decision on the course of my life."

"My cousin aspires to be an artist," Ted said mischievously, getting even for the remark about his position in the War Department.

"Artist!" Wise sneered. "You best come to Texas, put your rear on a horse that knows his way through a herd, swallow a peck or two of dust, learn to live on beans and bacon. That'll knock the artist foolishness out of you. The country's not in immediate need of picture painters." He turned away, his gray eyes searching for more stimulating and useful company.

"Why did you say that?" snapped Quent. "No one in Washington cares about artists."

"But it's the truth, I dare say," Ted replied. He did not look at Quent as he spoke, but examined a group of young men and women entering the ballroom through a side door. "Look at the redheaded one, will you, Quent. I've never seen her before. Perhaps *she* is fascinated by artists."

"Young ladies quite often are intrigued, but their fathers are not," said Quent. "I've found, to achieve serious attention from a young lady's family, I must pretend an overwhelming interest in the stock exchange or speak knowledgeably about the latest case before the state supreme court."

"A strange set of attitudes we have in this country," said Ted. "I've always thought you had more nerve than the average man, daring to pull out a sketchbook. You wouldn't catch me with paper and pencil.... I mean, those stevedores this morning laughed at you."

"To most people, I fear, art suggests a man of weak hands and idle mind," Quent acknowledged sadly.

"Perhaps if you concentrated on society ladies, instead of forever looking for men with bulging muscles heaving crates, or plowing or splitting...."

The redheaded woman and her escort stepped beyond the entry. Another couple stood just inside the door. A tall man blocked Quent's view of the second woman momentarily, then stepped aside, as if unveiling a sculpture. Quent gasped.

"That redhead *is* spectacular," said Ted. "I thought you'd appreciate her. Perhaps you could offer to paint her portrait. That would bring her to the house regularly for a few weeks. Sittings, you know."

Quent kept his mouth shut. Let Ted think it was the redhead who attracted his attention. From the behavior of the young woman's escort, he had competition enough already. The tall fellow bent over her possessively, making a very obvious claim. But, at a party of this sort, partners might change.

Nothing spectacular about her eyes. He could not see, from this distance, what color they might be. Her hair was brown; not golden as a wheat field, not red as flame, not black as the raven's wing. Simply brown, neither dark nor light, yet it draped as gracefully as the cloak on a Grecian statue. She knew precisely how to arrange it, in soft wings, framing her face. High on the back of her head she wore a small cluster of flowers. No overwhelming headdress of feathers and ruffles to distract from her beauty. His fingers itched for a pencil.

Her face, a delicate composition of light and shadow, reminded him of a saint in an Italian fresco. From the deep-set eyes to the curves of her mouth, perhaps a bit more angularity than usually found in a female, but perfectly balanced. Her beauty flowed from the total composition of all her features.

"I must meet that redhead," said Ted. "Let's catch up with the senator." He pulled on Quent's arm. "I'm getting an introduction to that strawberry filly."

"You go," said Quent.

Her grace contributed more than half her loveliness; he doubted his ability to capture her spirit with pencil or paint. All the other young women had a stiffness about them, either from nervousness at attending a Washington party or from the steel bands in their corsets. The object of his desire floated, and her arms, bare almost to the shoulder in her evening dress, lifted and fell with the grace of flowing water. But strength lay close to the surface, the strength and weight of falling water. A stream, gliding languidly, until it crashed headlong over the lip of the flume, taking the mill wheel with it, turning an entire world with its power.

"A goddess," he muttered. "A water nymph." The liquid imagery touched his blood and sped his heart. Somewhere, beneath the silk, her tall, muscular body flexed. He surveyed the dancers already on the floor, searching for the most convenient way to her side. He must find a mutual friend and obtain a proper introduction. Did he know any of the men on the opposite side of the room? Probably not, for this was his first visit to Washington as an adult. He must wait for Ted. No hurry. Simply watching her gave him great pleasure.

"Hellfire," muttered Ted.

"No introduction to the flaming-haired beauty?" asked Quent.

"She's that cove's wife."

"Hard luck. Who's the girl at the door?"

"She's some ramification of Congressman Meechem of Texas."

"Introduce me," Quent commanded.

"Can't. Haven't met the girl myself. She looks quite taken up with Lampman, anyway," Ted said uneasily.

"Lampman? Of the iron-and-steel family?"

"The same."

"I want to meet her," Quent insisted. "Introduce me to Lampman—to be polite, he must introduce his partner."

"Lampman's father has been all over me about the horseshoe contracts for the western posts," said Ted, his voice sinking with embarrassment. "I don't want to get near him. You see, the secretary says they won't get the contract, no matter how much they spend. Something to do with not supporting President Garfield."

"So there are disadvantages to being an under secretary of the War Department?" asked Quent, laughing.

"Not at all," said Ted. "I simply avoid the people I can't look in the eye. Why should you want to meet her? There's nothing special about the girl that I can see. And she's got on the same dress she wore at Cady's ball, so there's no fortune there."

Quent looked about frantically, searching for a familiar face. Senator Wise could introduce him, but the man had vanished. He must make a move. Some man or woman who knew Ted would know Miss Meechem. She turned toward her escort, lifted a slender hand and took Mr. Lampman's arm, and the two of them disappeared through the doorway.

"The Dodsons ask if we'd like to join them on a hunting trip into the mountains," remarked Ted over breakfast the next day. "Bear, deer at the very least, and perhaps a panther."

Quent dropped his fork, ignored the ham and eggs. Tramping through the November woods, the leaves crackling underfoot. The smoke of the campfire, the aroma of boiling coffee, of roasting venison. The parties he would miss, the parties where he eventually would find Miss Meechem.

"The weather?" he mused. "Isn't it a bit late...?"

"Dodson says perfect."

The holiday season arrived before Quent found an opportunity to again inquire about Miss Meechem—at the Christmas tea of a senator's wife. The lady believed—Quent saw the flash of disapproval—that Congressman Meechem's niece had gone home to Texas.

Beyond the French windows the trees bent under wet snow.

Chapter One

San Antonio, Texas
April 1884

Bob Linares gave the man standing before him only a cursory glance. His stomach hurt—whether from too many chilies or too much whiskey, he didn't know. Maybe it hurt because he had worked from dawn to dusk for weeks, putting together eleven cattle drives.

The news that Linares needed trail hands had spread like a creek in flood, and now, when he should be buying supplies and finding more than a thousand horses for the remudas, when he should be checking the condition of the chuck wagons stored since last fall—all the cursed details—a dozen times a day men hassled him, seeking work. Every time he sat down in the hotel saloon, he found some cowboy standing over him, pleading with soulful eyes. Or scared eyes. Or flashing eyes, daring him to say no. Those were the ones he dreaded, the ones who argued; his stomach burned after the stormy confrontations.

He took a slow sip of whiskey, lifted his eyes to the stranger for a better look, gaped in astonishment. The man took off his bowler hat. His silk suit very definitely had been made special for him by some city tailor. His shirt, that part visible above his vest, was snowy-white linen, and most amazing of all, his collar was linen, too. Not paper. A tall fellow, maybe an inch over six feet, but the slim, formfitting lines of the suit made him look even taller.

Good God! Would he never be quit of these eastern dandies who thought a cattle drive some kind of extended picnic?

"Can I be of service?" he asked, knowing already what the dude wanted.

"Mr. Bob Linares?" Linares nodded. "I've been told you're organizing several cattle drives this spring."

"You've heard right." Let the young fool have his say, Linares thought with resignation. He could trail back to Baltimore or Boston or New York, and be able to say he'd talked to a man about going on a trail drive, and leave out the part about being turned down.

"I'd like to apply for a position, sir."

Sir! Not so arrogant as the majority of the eastern crowd. Most of the young puppies simply handed him a letter of recommendation from the president of some bank, or the chairman of the board of a railroad, and assumed they were going to lead the left point to Dodge City. One fellow had come with a character reference from Chester Arthur, the President of the United States!

"Sit down, young fellow. What's your name?"

"Van Kelson. Quentin van Kelson." He placed his hat and a leather folder carefully on the table, extended his hand for a shake, sat expectantly on the edge of his seat.

"And what's your experience, Mr. Kelson? In the cattle-driving way, I mean?"

"I can handle a horse. I've been on horses since my second birthday."

From the looks of his suit and the finish on the leather folder—Florentine, certainly—he handled dainty-legged Thoroughbreds.

"Cattle-drive experience. I don't hire green men."

"Then how, sir," asked the young man without a hint of sarcasm, "does one gain experience?"

His cultured accent grated on a Texas ear. Linares glanced uneasily around the saloon. None of his friends would join him for dinner so long as this greenhorn sat at the table. He saw Perk and Stack across the room, leaning against the bar, strangling on their laughter at his predicament.

"You get experience by riding drag on someone else's herd for a year or two. You ever been to Dodge, Mr. Kelson?"

"No, sir. I came through St. Louis on my way to Texas."

"I meant, have you ridden from Texas to Dodge City?"

"No, sir."

"Why are you in Texas?" asked Linares, knowing what the answer would be. Another eastern family wanted to get rid of an embarrassing son, while at the same time make money in the booming cattle business. Of course, the young man would not say all this right out in plain daylight, but Linares had become quite adept at listening between the lines.

"I've been unable to decide on my future, sir, whether I should follow in the family tradition and become a lawyer, or perhaps enter banking. Last summer my father sent me to Europe, thinking it would help me settle on one or the other. This summer I intend to make my own way, learn what it is to work." Linares looked anew at the young man. Not the answer he'd expected. He warmed, unwillingly, to the overbred slicker. A Texan had to feel sorry for men like this crazy Kelson. After all, the poor young fool hadn't chosen to be born in Boston or New York instead of Texas. So young, doomed to a boring life sitting at a desk. Linares glanced at the leather folder.

"You one of those easterners planning on writing a book about the west?" he asked, nodding at the folder.

"No, sir." Linares kept his eyes on the folder, forcing Kelson to speak of it. "I do some sketching, sir."

"Let me see." Kelson opened the thing slowly, like he was ashamed of what he had done, and revealed a sheaf of loose papers. The top sheet showed nothing but drawings of the legs of horses in various positions. Linares lifted it, glimpsed the sketch beneath. A picture of Stack, no question about it, working with his new mare. He'd just got the hackamore on her. Linares could almost hear Stack's singsong muttering as he calmed and comforted the horse.

"I like it. Wish I could do something like that. You study drawing in school?"

"A bit. But I drew long before I went to school. Mostly, I've taught myself."

"And I suppose, judging from your clothes, you've time to sit about doing it. You ever have to work for a living?"

"No, sir," said Kelson, a bit shamefaced.

"Then why in a blue norther do you want this kind of a job? It's just about the hardest work God ever set a man to do, and you want to start with that?"

"It's because it's hard, sir. You see, that's why I didn't go to Europe again. I want to do real work. I believe honest work will help make up my mind about my future better than sight-seeing in old cathedrals."

"Most of the cowboys in Texas would be glad to change places with you," mused Linares. He straightened the picture of Stack and the mare with his index finger to get a better look at it. He'd drawn a saddle hanging on the corral fence, and tucked into the curve of the saddle were the words *van Kelson*. Seeing it written, Linares realized it was one name, a double-barreled eastern name. And that brought to mind the gang of strutting, silk-hatted men who'd been in San Antonio last fall, getting everyone excited about a railroad to run north out of central Texas.

"You related to that railroad fellow?" he asked.

"Nicholas van Kelson? My uncle."

"You're from a fancy family, then. Back in...." Linares couldn't remember where the fast-talking old buzzard had been from.

"New York."

"Old-time family, I understand."

"My ancestors settled New York in the time of the Dutch, when it was New Amsterdam," said van Kelson, but he didn't say it with pride to knock a man down, so Linares forgave him his pedigree. Poor kid! Born in the wrong time in the wrong place. If he'd been one of those Hollanders who sailed across the Atlantic into the American wilderness, he'd have been faced with plenty of work.

"Now look here, Mr. van Kelson. I admire your pluck, but I don't hire aught but the best men. Many a cowboy who's ridden point for another outfit comes to me and finds he'll be on the swing or eating the drag dust of a Linares herd. I don't saddle my trail bosses with greenhorns or boys, because both are prone to excitement. Bossing a drive of two or three thousand steers is hard enough, without giving a man help he can't depend on. It's got nothing to do with you, personally. Just rules."

The young man stood up, picked up his folder and hat with his left hand, extended his right.

"I'm sorry to have put you to bother, Mr. Linares."

"No bother at all. I'd think less of a man who didn't come straight up and ask. Some just hang about the saloons, bragging in loud voices how good they are with a rope. I know they're waiting for an offer, but by damn, if a man hasn't the nerve to ask, he hasn't the nerve to drive."

"Thank you. Do you mind that I loiter about the corral, sketching the cowboys?"

"Not at all. Next time you see Stack, show him that picture. He'll like it."

"That's the man's name? Stack?"

"Nickname. Tell him you're a friend of mine."

"Why, thank you, sir."

"And, if any of your friends inquire if I'm hiring," said Linares as the man turned away, "just remember, no greenhorns, no boys and no one-eyed cows in my herds."

"No one-eyed cows?" van Kelson asked, turning around, wide-eyed and innocent. "Why not?"

"If you have to ask, you're not fit to be on a trail drive," Linares said scornfully.

After the greenhorn left the saloon, Perk and Stack joined him, carrying their whiskey and beer from the bar.

"He's a wet one," said Perk. "'Nother eastern fellow?"

Linares nodded. "Knows nothing, but he's kin to one of those railroad magnates who came through last year."

"Rich, then," said Perk with respect. Indiscriminate admiration for men with money was Perk's one weak point.

"No, his pa's rich. There's a big difference between a man who's made money through honest labor and a man who had it dumped in his cradle to keep it rocking. He wanted to go on a drive."

Perk and Stack both laughed contemptuously.

"He made a picture of you, Stack, working with the mare."

"Why didn't you call me over to see it?" asked Stack.

"I didn't want you to get any bigger in the head than you already are," said Linares. "Your hat's got to fit all the way to Montana or you'll get sunstroke."

A gangly young man stood in the door; he squinted, stared into the shadows until his eyes adjusted from the bright, sunlit hotel lounge to the dim interior of the saloon.

"Mail, Mr. Linares. I thought you'd be here."

Linares threw him a quarter, but frowned as he did it, to show he didn't like receiving his mail in public. "Next time, just leave it at my room," he said quietly.

"But I thought, sir, seeing as how one came all the way from Montana, it might be of importance to you."

"Probably is, but I'd get around to it just as fast if you'd left it at my room, because I don't read my mail in a saloon. See? Don't do it again."

The kid escaped back to the lounge before he hit him with a stronger reprimand. Linares tucked the flat packet of mail under his vest, with the tail ends of the letters beneath his belt. A letter from Elam Brownell. No hurry to read it, for Linares knew what it said. He grinned to himself, wishing he could be a fly on the wall watching the tantrum Annie Brownell was going to throw when *she* got *her* letter from her pa, ordering her to take the train to Montana and forget about cattle drives.

Elam's daughter, Anne, had been living in Louisiana, going to school or some such foolish thing, and was now visiting friends in San Antonio. He'd seen her on the street, a tall girl, twenty-two or twenty-three, stubborn, and maybe a bit wild. She had written her father, and let Linares know, too, that she intended to ride north with the herd, rather than take the train to Montana.

No greenhorns, no boys and, it went without saying, no women. Who ever heard of such a thing? In this letter Brownell would be letting him know he'd put his foot down on his daughter's crazy scheme.

Three more men looking for work found Linares in the saloon. The sun had dropped to the horizon before he made it to the privacy of his room and opened his letters, most scrawled notes from cowboys who'd heard he needed hands. He ripped open Brownell's letter, hoping the rancher had no last-minute changes he wanted made in the herd. Three thousand head were already gathered outside town, and Perk planned to turn them north in the next day or two.

Dear Linares,
May be you have heard Anne wants to trail along with the herd to Montana. Seeing she has been cooped up a year and a half down in New Orleans, I don't see the harm of it. I figure she will probably give up about Dodge, certainly by the crossing of the Union Pacific tracks.

Enclosed is a draft. Buy a small, sturdy wagon for her gear and bed, so she can sleep away from snakes. Get two or three teams of tame mules, none of those wild Mexican critters, to pull it, and a man to drive, and make sure it and Annie stay with the chuck wagon.

Also, get a responsible gentleman from a good family to ride along and look out for her. None of your damn cowboys! I will pay all his expenses up till Annie quits the drive or gets to Montana, whichever comes first. Tell the whole crew if any man touches her, I'll skin him personally, then let McCann feed him to a panther.

You remember Hugh McCann? He and Annie are engaged, and you and Perk and the trail crew are invited to the wedding if she makes it all the way to Temptation with the cattle.

I would appreciate if you would include half a hundred good, stocky two-year-old heifers in the herd, even though they are hard to drive. But only if you can find some with . . .

Linares no longer followed the meaning of the words. Anne Brownell on the drive? Damn that indulgent old man! He'd refuse to make the delivery, by God! No one could order Bob Linares to deliver a woman. . . .

The cattle were waiting. Perk had his crew together.

Well, he'd lie. He'd tell Brownell the herd had started ahead of schedule, they were on the trail when his letter arrived. He would not—could not—make Perk take Anne Brownell along! That was that.

Linares had made his second traverse of the eight-by-ten-foot room before he realized he was pacing. Sweat started out on his brow. Only April, but already over ninety. He had to get Perk's herd started, because four more were within a hundred miles of San Antonio, on their way up from the south . . . no way to stop the flow, any more than he could stop the Rio Grande from heading to the Gulf of Mexico. But he could refuse to let Anne Brownell ride along with Perkins, no matter what her old man wanted.

He glanced at the letter once more, unable to believe the message it contained. "None of your damn cowboys," Brownell said. How did he expect him to locate this "responsible gentleman from a good family" in just a day or two? The drive would take all summer. All the men of good family in Texas had their own business to tend to.

Linares stopped at the window. His stomach burned. Down the side of the building he saw the rounded fence of the corral, half a block away. A dark figure perched on a post, bent over, concentrating on the paper on his knee.

"I will not do it, curse all indulgent fathers to hell!" he snarled at the same time the plan formed in his head. He ran down the hall, found Perkins at the bar, washing the dust of the corral from his throat. Linares motioned him to a table, outlined the situation.

"Damn Brownell to a closed box in the corner of hell," said Perk.

"Look, we can't go against Brownell," said Linares, feeling a little feverish on top of his stomach hurting. "He took three thousand cattle last fall, is taking another three thousand this fall. I can't afford to sacrifice his business, particularly over a little thing like Miss Brownell going on the drive."

"So?"

"There's a man hereabouts who's frantic to get on a drive, but you and I know he isn't going to stick on the trail more than a week or two. When he gives up, Annie will have to go to the closest railroad. And her daddy can't say we didn't try."

Perk smiled, then frowned. "You're not the one who's gonna have to put up with her for that two weeks. You'll send the greenhorn who sits out there drawin' pictures?"

"Exactly. He's from a good family. His uncle is that railroad man."

"Who's to say he won't hold out longer than a week or two?" Stack asked cautiously. "He's been sitting all day, in the sun, drawin' pictures."

"Swing close to Dodge. I'll come up by train, meet you, and convince them both to give it up. But I don't think they'll make it that far."

"He can't go dressed like that," said Perk, his eyes shifting about as he hunted for obstacles.

"He can get himself an outfit in two, three hours. Brownell says he'll pay all the fellow's expenses."

"I'd rather try to dig a well in Brewster County," snapped Perk. "I don't like this."

"Neither do I, but I don't like losing Brownell's business, either. If I refuse to send her along, the next letter might tell me he doesn't want the cattle. You'd have to shift the herd to Dodge...."

"Quit talking, Linares, I know. We got to take her."

"And the greenhorn. His name is Quentin van Kelson."

"Three names?" asked Perk, curling his lip. "Why can't these easterners be satisfied with just one?"

"I'm sure you and the men will come up with just one in the space of the first day. We'll get even with Brownell by not getting him fifty stocky heifers. Now, you come out with me to the corral and we'll tell him. Look pleased, Perk. We're going to give a young man exactly what he thinks he wants. He's going to be happy for maybe eight, ten hours."

Annie stood defiantly in front of the full-length pier glass and stared at Mrs. Moultry's uncertain reflection.

"It looks very practical, my dear," said Mrs. Moultry after several seconds, "but do you really think it wise to appear in public in that...skirt?"

"There's nothing improper about it," said Annie. "With the panel buttoned across the front, not a soul would suspect it's split. And the bustle covers the back."

"But you can't ride with a bustle," protested Mrs. Moultry.

"It unties. See?" Annie pulled the end of the wide bow at her waist; the bustle came away in her hands. "I just tie it to the saddle when I'm on horseback. And it's most practical. Mrs. Laurie suggested, instead of putting in useless stuffing to make the bustle stand out, that it be pockets." Annie triumphantly pulled a light woolen jacket from the largest billow, bandannas, handkerchiefs, scarves and gloves from the smaller ones.

"Mrs. Laurie has already made herself a skirt like this. By summer, it will be the rage of San Antonio."

"Saints preserve us!"

"It's terribly practical for any woman who must ride in rough country. Sidesaddles are so unsafe."

"Most of my friends don't bother riding," Mrs. Moultry said. "We find buggies more ladylike."

"Women should not be prisoners of their wardrobes," said Annie.

"Anne," Mrs. Moultry said hesitantly, her voice low, warning Annie she was edging toward an unpleasant topic. "I really wish you would give some thought to the consequences of this trip. It's not my place to say yes or no, so I've not interfered, but I *never* expected your father to agree to such a thing. It's my fault I didn't speak earlier, you being motherless—and men, knowing so little of the realities of life, they're apt to make wrong decisions. I'll say it bluntly. You must take the train, meet your betrothed as soon as possible, and have the summer to embark on your... uh...future."

"Why should a few months make a difference?" objected Annie.

"Anne, it's best for marriages to begin in the spring."

"What?" she exclaimed, startled. "Why?"

"Because then the first babe—I'm sure you understand this—comes in the winter, when a man isn't so busy and he can take you to the nearest town and stay about. If you wait until fall to be married...well, he'll be terribly busy in the summer, and you'll be left alone, with naught but strangers to help." Her voice died away, nothing left but the pleading on her strained, flushed face.

A year ago I was left with strangers, Annie nearly blurted out, but caught herself in time. Instead of the bitter accusation, she said, quite calmly, "I have no intention of giving up this chance to spend a summer on the trail. I haven't been out with a herd since I was a child. Mr. McCann's written me but one letter, and he didn't express any need to hurry our wedding. It's not a question of love between us, you understand.''

''I realize that, Annie, but Mr. McCann must be anxious, nevertheless. And the sooner the matter's commenced, the sooner love *will* come to the both of you.'' The clock downstairs chimed eight.

''It's time I met Mr. Perkins at the corral. Mr. Linares said he'd found a gentleman to be my escort. Daddy insisted I have an escort.''

''Quite rightly,'' said Mrs. Moultry.

''Has José brought round my horse?'' She asked the question as she leaned out the open window. Below, waiting for her, José held the bridle of her horse, Jenny.

''Annie, please. What would your mother, God rest her soul, think if she knew I allowed—''

''You're not allowing. You have nothing to say about it,'' snapped Annie. She immediately felt guilty, speaking so harshly to an older woman, and one who had been kind to her. ''Please, don't worry about me,'' she begged. ''I'll be just fine. I have a gentleman to accompany me on the trip, and this fall I'll marry Mr. McCann.''

''What if something should happen to Mr. McCann?'' Mrs. Moultry whispered fearfully. ''It's bad luck, I know, to anticipate evil, but this summer, months in the saddle, out on that horrid northern range, anything can happen. You should not take any risks with this marriage. It's difficult to say this Annie, but there may be no other offer. Your reputation...after what happened in Washington—'' Anne cut off the words by throwing her arms about the woman.

''My reputation is worthless, Auntie Moultry. Most people are not so kind as you—they don't forgive and forget babies. I love you so for being understanding, for taking me in when I needed a friend. Now, I shouldn't want to be late in meeting my escort.''

"Who is he?" asked Mrs. Moultry. "I hope he doesn't think he can take advantage of you, just because of what happened in Washington."

"I don't know who he is. Mr. Linares said he comes of a very good family and is a true gentleman."

Anne ran down the stairs, patted Jenny while she examined the bridle and saddle. The saddle was new, made especially for this trip weeks ago, when she was not certain she'd be allowed to go. No flowers or birds stamped in the leather; just her initials on the saddle skirt, plain and strong, to last through a long summer's drive, from San Antonio to Temptation, Montana.

Chapter Two

Annie rode away from the center of San Antonio. She wore her new hat, black, wide-brimmed, with fringe all around that danced with the horse's gait. Viewing the world from beneath the brim was a bit like looking through a window, with the edge of the curtain above her eyes. She breathed easier as she joined the trail along the river. The trip for the very first time seemed real, not an impossible dream. She wished her father was here, so she could throw her arms about him.

In all directions the sky rose to a cloudless blue dome, an arch of celebration. For so long she had been confined, seeing the sky in patches—from a window, or the zenith visible from the courtyard of the convent where she took her daily walk. But never the matchless sensation of a blue bowl inverted above her, touching the earth on every horizon. She wanted to shout, to lift her hands to the liberty this azure exaltation symbolized. Men and women hustled by, walking and riding. They would not understand her excess of emotion at so simple a thing as a sunny day, so she kept silent. For now. But once alone on the prairie, she would yell her delight, gallop her horse, dance a private heathen dance under the furnace of the sun. Perhaps under the moon, as well.

Men clustered about the corral and squat adobe hotel where Linares established his headquarters each spring. She saw no other woman. Perkins waited near the corral, astride his big chestnut horse, whose name she dared not pronounce. A lady, particularly one careful of her reputation, must pretend she did not know the words men used, but she had heard Perk call the gelding Hellcock.

"Good morning, Miss Brownell," he said quite formally. He smiled with his mouth, but not his eyes. Linares had warned her: Perk did not want her on the drive. Well, she had expected that, and she intended to change his mind. She would give Perk no trouble at all, and once she got back into the routine of trail life, she'd pull her own weight. At least she could help the cook. And once Perk had overcome his prejudice about women on trail drives, maybe he would let her ride drag, pushing the laggard steers and the cows and calves.

Annie glanced about the corral, searching for a second mounted man, her unknown escort. Perkins gestured toward the corral, where a slender man sat on the top rail, his attention riveted on a paper on his knee. Perk caught his eye, and he snapped shut a folder, stabbed a pencil into a pocket and jumped off the corral fence.

"Miss Brownell, I'd like you to meet Mr. van Kelson."

She felt awkward, meeting a man on foot when she was mounted, so she threw her leg over and slid off Jenny's back. She had not anticipated the dilemma her skirt created. Politeness dictated that she greet Mr. van Kelson immediately, which meant she had no time to button the panel. Without the panel, he must see she wore trousers. Full ones, but trousers, nonetheless. And fussing about, untying her bustle from the back of her saddle, tying it about her waist, was a bit like dressing on the street.

"Good morning, Mr. van Kelson," she said, eyeing his painfully new clothes. The pants and shirt showed the creases they had acquired on the shelf in the store. His 5X Stetson advertised the fact that he had money, but no sweat stained the base of the crown. A greenhorn.

"Mr. van Kelson is from New York," Perk said, with too obvious a pleasure. He licked his smirking lips, enjoying her shock. Anne struggled to catch her breath. Not just a greenhorn. An eastern greenhorn. Linares was saddling her with a shavetail, a man she'd have to take care of, a man...a man you couldn't trust. Perk's happy voice droned on with the introduction. "Miss Anne Brownell."

"I'm very pleased to meet you, Miss Brownell," the greenhorn said, bowing over her hand, almost touching her gloves with his lips. She nodded, aware the smile frozen on her lips had turned to a grimace of disgust. His words brought echoes of that other smooth voice in Washington, cultivated, false, traitorous. She turned to Perk.

"Mr. Linares, where—?"

"He's rode south, Miss, to meet the herds coming up from the Rio Grande and hold them until we get ourselves off the grazing ground. Mustn't delay. We've got to be gone early day after tomorrow."

No chance to see Linares and swear at him for this dirty trick. A greenhorn would not survive on a cattle drive. Linares must know... He had picked this man, this Mr. van Kelson, intentionally! Hoping she'd give up!

"That," continued Perk, "is your wagon, over yonder. Linares said for me to send it by the Moultrys' today, so you could load your truck into it. He asked, please, would you keep it light?"

"Mr. Linares should be aware I'm quite accustomed to traveling light. Most of my things will be sent to Montana by rail," she snapped. She strode across the dusty yard, taking the long steps permitted by her unfettered legs, forgetting until she was nearly at the wagon that the two men would see she very definitely wore pants.

"Damn, Linares," she muttered with every breath. Linares would see who gave the trip up, and it wouldn't be Anne Meechem Brownell!

The canvas top of the small wagon stretched over hickory bows. She poked her head through the flaps at the rear, where the puckering strings hung limp. Blue calico lined the top. Nothing inside except a mattress. Annie reached in, patted it. A feather bed on top of a cornhusk tick.

When she turned around, she found that Mr. van Kelson and Perk, still astride Hellcock, had followed her across the yard and waited only a few feet away.

"What's to pull it?" she asked.

"Two teams of big mules. Linares got them from a teamster here, Brenerd's the name, who's to come along as driver."

She nodded her agreement. "Have Mr. Brenerd take the wagon to the Moultrys' right away. My things are all packed. I can join the herd before evening." She turned to van Kelson, who clasped his leather folder to his chest. Papers stuck out at odd angles. He stared at her like a half-wit. If she and Bob Linares ever met again, she'd kill him for this!

"Do you ride, Mr. van Kelson?" she asked, with a sweetness not nearly thick enough to cover her sarcasm.

"Yes, Miss Brownell."

"You have a string of horses? I expect to be in the saddle all the way to Montana, not in the wagon."

"There's four or five in the remuda not yet taken by the hands," said Perk. "He can ride those."

"I can imagine," she said, hiding her smile, knowing full well the sort of nags and outlaws remaining in the remuda after all the cowboys had made their choice. Why was van Kelson staring at her this way? He had not taken his eyes off her since Perk made the introductions.

Is he some kind of rattlebrained idiot? Linares is trying to scare me off the drive, damn him! She wanted to shout curses, but instead she stamped her feet in fury. She ran to Jenny, still standing by the corral fence. Linares, the snake, had hired this wide-eyed New York calf, hoping she'd turn tail. She'd show them what kind of woman she was!

She mounted her horse, ignoring van Kelson, who rushed to help her. Van Kelson still gaped as if he'd not seen a woman in months. She'd get rid of him, send him back to San Antonio after two or three days. Her father wouldn't know of his departure until the herd reached a telegraph office, where Perk could send a wire. By then she would be indispensable to the cook, or the horse wrangler. Mr. Brenerd would be escort enough. A good steady mule driver.

"Goodbye, until this evening," she said, hoping she sounded gracious.

Quent kept his eyes on Miss Brownell until she and her horse became a speck on the road. There was no doubt, no doubt at all—unless the young woman who had spoken with so much animation to David Lampman had a twin sister. But how had Miss Meechem become Miss Brownell?

"Ready to ride out?" Perk asked impatiently.

"Yes," Quent said absently. He had never been introduced to her. Had he simply assumed her name was Meechem? He strove to recall the words he and Ted had exchanged in the ballroom, but could remember nothing concrete, except for the crisp memory of her lovely face, her graceful body.

Through more than a year she had remained in his mind. And often, from memory, on his sketch pad. But he'd never succeeded in catching the vibrant charm, the spirit.... She had stretched her legs walking to the wagon, determined, but elegant. Her clothing—what a strange skirt—accented every movement.

"Your gear?" asked Perk, this time tapping him on the shoulder with his quirt.

"I put everything but my saddle in the chuck wagon early this morning."

"Good. You can ride my spare mount out to camp. That black'n there." Perk pointed at the horse in question, standing near the middle of the corral. Quent removed his rope from the saddle. If the beast would only stand still, he might snag it. He'd practiced at home on stumps and fence posts. He made the loop, swung it over his head, let it fly. It landed five feet short. The black horse eyed the limp rope, shuffled off to the other side of the corral.

Quent circled around the corral, gauging the horse's position, avoiding looking at Perk. He climbed upon the corral fence, made his loop. Just as he flung it, sure this time of an easy catch, the black bolted, sprang into the air and landed ten feet beyond the loop.

Perk's sigh could be heard from the other side of the corral. While the horse focused red, angry eyes on Quent, Perk's rope settled around his neck. He bucked twice in protest, then let himself be saddled.

Quent saw Perk's lips move silently. He didn't think the man normally prayed before setting out for camp. Well, he hadn't expected this to be easy. He'd be disappointed if it was. He hadn't come to Texas for easy, but for hard work and some sense of direction in his life. And now another reason had materialized, in the person of Annie Brownell. A reason that overwhelmed and made him forget the first.

Perk rode the first miles in silence, giving Quent a chance to think about Miss Brownell. Her hair, beneath her broad hat, had been just as he remembered, medium brown, unremarkable, except for the softness that tempted a man's hands to an experimental caress.

He'd been drawing her nose too broadly. Not by much, but it was definitely narrower than he'd portrayed it. He should have remembered, a face of slightly angular features. Her eyes, though, he'd gotten exactly right. Deep beneath arching brows, and now he knew the color, brown, with a golden wash. And her figure, marvelously akin to the rolling countryside. She moved with an elemental, primeval grace, as the goddesses of the ancient world had moved....

The yellow-green of the new grass called his attention. He should be looking at this country. Here were alien sights to be analyzed by his eyes and set down by his fingers. Low trees marked the lines of streams, flowing in graceful curves. Almost as graceful as Miss Brownell. Here and there were

rambling adobe houses, radically different from the familiar farmhouses of the Hudson Valley. The adobe buildings
beckoned to him. He imagined riding up to one of those
doors, meeting the lady of the house. In his daydream, Anne
Brownell stood framed by whitewashed adobe. She smiled.

"I suppose this country ain't nothing like where you're
from," Perk interrupted innocently.

"No," said Quent. "Nothing at all."

Two miles beyond the last shanty, three thousand Texas
longhorns spread across a thousand acres of grass. Quent's
fingers bent around a nonexistent pencil, longing for his
paper, for easel and paints.

A square object on the horizon turned out to be a wagon
on a low hill. Below it a stream flowed from a squat cliff
covered with moss and ferns.

"This here's Sid," said Perk, dismounting. Quent interrupted his study of the picturesque embankment to meet a
short, stout man. "Sid's our cook. Best cook on any trail
drive. This," said Perk, assuming an air of importance
bordering on ridicule, "is Quentin van Kelson. Today, at
least, that's his name. I expect the boys will come up with
something better shortly."

"I expect," said Sid.

A dozen or so men trailed up the hill. They must have
been bathing in the creek, for none wore more than long
underwear between hat and boots.

"This here's Stack, he's *segundo* and on left point. Rolf,
Heady, Coleman, Broadbrim, he rides right point, Lucas,
Huzzy..." Perk's voice droned as he pointed to one man
after another. "...Soto, Lash, and Johnny Snitter, our horse
wrangler," he concluded, indicating a young man with dark
hair, a dark mustache, hands and face burned mahogany.
The rest of him was white as a baby.

"This here's the gentleman who'll take care of Miss
Brownell," Perk announced. "Quentin van Kelson."

A chorus of "Howdies."

Quent had been unable to follow the speedy introduction, and could put no names with faces, except for Johnny and Broadbrim. The latter man was obvious, with a huge hat trimmed with gold and silver braid in the Mexican manner. He was of indeterminate race: high cheekbones, black hair straight to his shoulders, skin the color of strong coffee.

"Johnny'll show you the horses in the remuda no one's put their claim on," Perk said.

"Where's the lady? Miss Annie," asked one of the cowboys.

"She'll be here tonight, to get her bones accustomed to sleeping out in the open before we hit the trail."

Johnny approached Quent, lifted his hat, which, except for a brief pair of white flannel drawers, constituted his wardrobe.

"I'll get dressed, if you don't mind, and we'll go see the horses."

"Fine. I could use a drink," said Quent, pointing toward the stream. He walked uphill to the bank where the water seeped out of the limestone hillside, not so much because he thought the water would be purer there, but because he wanted to see the garden nook. He passed a cow and calf sampling the green shoots bordering the stream. A low stone wall held back a small pool at the foot of the cliff. He followed a path of stones to the reservoir. Quent stepped up, onto the stone wall topped with metallic green algae, stringy and slippery beneath his feet.

The water ran down the embankment in a myriad of steady small cascades, wandering around a patchwork of mosses. The limestone strata formed minuscule shelves, and on each ferns had taken tenuous hold. He would sketch the grotto in the level sunlight of evening, when the shadows grew long.

Quent inched along the wall until he stood almost against the embankment. He bent his knees to scoop up a handful of water, had a fraction of a second to wonder at something large and soft pressing against his back. He twisted, heard the cow's soft snort as his feet slid out from under him and the green water came up to meet him.

He first thought of the ignominy of drowning in a spring, before the drive had progressed one foot toward Montana. A fascinating liquid, crystalline world distracted his mind from the immediate threat of death. An explosion of dark specks raced before his eyes in random dances, as if he'd fallen into one of those glass domes, where a twist of the wrist set the snowflakes spinning about a miniature Swiss village. Except these flakes were black. He longed for his sketchbook. Then he remembered he'd never sketch again, because he was drowning.

His hands and knees touched bottom. He lifted his head, sputtering, shaking water from his hair.

The cow snorted and jumped backward as the arc of water caught her full in the face.

Quent pulled himself to his feet. Water ran from his sleeves. He stepped over the stone wall. Water streamed from his pants, overflowed his boots. He reached up to check his hat. Nothing there. He searched the tank, expecting to find his hat floating. The hat had cost him twenty dollars, the most expensive part of his outfit, except for the boots and saddle. He stirred the roiled water with his toe to bring the hat to the surface.

The cow snorted again, and Quent turned and snarled back at her to show his disgust at her part in this performance. The calf's front feet were centered on the crown of his new hat.

"Shoo!" he yelled, swinging his arm, letting loose another arc of water droplets that reflected in the sunlight like the fragments of an exploding silver dollar. The cow took fright, bounded away from the tank, followed a second or two later by her calf.

Quent retrieved his hat, beat it against his wet leg to shake off the dirt, pushed the crown back out. Only then did he hear the gales of laughter from down the hill.

The half-dressed cowboys cavorted about the chuck wagon like savage dancers, their red-and-white underwear contrasting flashes of war paint. Some bent over, holding their stomachs, while others held their arms up and howled at the sky. One fellow rolled on the ground, like a mule recently relieved of a pack. Nothing to do but join their merriment, Quent thought ruefully. Resentment and a sour face would not win their regard.

He loped down the hill as lightly as he could with water squelching out of his boots. He shook his arms and loosened his cuffs to spill the water from his sleeves.

"Lord, but that cow did dunk you fine," choked Sid the cook. He hung on to the side of the wagon to keep himself upright. "I hope you didn't rile the water overmuch, since that's what's used for the cooking."

"Riled for a while," said Quent, exuding good nature. "Everyone will have to wait for coffee until it settles."

One of the cowboys—Quent hadn't the slightest idea what his name might be—came up, slapped him on the back, causing new, hurried rivulets to slither down his spine.

"Baptism by cow. You're sure enough a trail hand now."

"Baptized," cried another. "What's his name?"

"Wet behind the Ears," came the caustic answer.

Sid held up his hand, stilled the crowd. "As cook, it's my duty to baptize everything what gets wet on this drive, willingly or not." He held up a long spoon. Quent, realizing this was some sort of ritual, removed his hat. "I name thee Dunk," Sid intoned, touching the spoon to Quent's head, "in honor of the first great hilarity we've had on this trip."

Dunk, thought Quent. Well, it was better than Greenhorn, certainly. Better than a horde of names they might have bestowed upon him. "I'm honored," he said. He bowed to Sid, again to the cowboys.

Johnny came around the wagon, still buttoning his shirt. He stared at everyone, puzzled. He looked at Quent and his eyes opened wide with shock.

"What happened to you?" he asked, setting off the roars of laughter anew. Someone finally found voice enough to tell him the story.

Johnny nodded wisely. "Well, Dunk, you ready to go look at them horses, or you want to change out of them wet clothes?"

"They'll dry," said Quent, afraid the cowboys might think him overly sensitive if he insisted on dry clothes. From what he'd read of trail drives, he'd be wet often enough in the coming months. Besides, in the heat the bath had been rather pleasurable. If he'd been able to take off his boots before going in, he would have enjoyed it. "Just let me empty my boots." He sat down on the grass, pulled off his boots and rid himself of two pounds of water.

"Mr. Perkins," he asked, "might I ride your horse out with Johnny to see the remuda?"

"Of course, and my name's Perk. On the trail it's best not to get too formal."

Quent remounted the horse, felt new streams of water on his hips and legs from the pressure of his saturated pants on the saddle. He followed Johnny at a trot across the small stream and up a long, low rise. At the top grazed the remuda, a hundred and fifty horses. All wore the Tall X brand, which designated this trail herd.

"That pinto there, no one picked her," said Johnny. Quent knew of the cowboy prejudice against spotted horses. The horse in question did not look very big. "And that bay, the one on the left." Quent started to object, shaking his head furiously, then stopped, for fear he might insult Johnny. "I like to see horses start off a bit fleshier than that," Johnny said doubtfully. The bay's hipbones stuck out at uncomfortable angles.

"There's a chestnut," Johnny continued, "but I don't see him nowheres."

"In the same condition as this bay?" asked Quent.

"Just about. I'll show you the pinto twins."

Johnny slapped his horse with the end of his reins, jogged along for a quarter of a mile before stopping.

"See them two pinto geldings? Twins, I'd say. Spots the same. Never see one without the other."

"So if one's ridden, the other tags along?" asked Quent.

"Yes, I guess so. But no one's managed to stay on one nor t'other for more than five seconds, so we ain't sure," Johnny said flatly. "Every bunch of horses Linares buys, always some spoiled ones. You want me to rope one so's you can try?"

"No. I don't think so," said Quent. Johnny looked disappointed. "Is this all? The three pintos and the bay and the chestnut?" He tried not to sound appalled.

"Sure is. But they should be enough, since all you'll be doing is riding along with Miss Annie."

"And what if there should be an emergency?" Quent persisted.

"Emergencies, that's not your worry," said Johnny. "Them's for Perk and Stack to take care of."

"If something should happen to Miss Brownell, I'd need a better mount than you've shown me." He touched the black horse's neck with the rein to turn his head and ride back to the camp hidden beyond the lip of the hill. "I'd better go into town and see what's available."

Perk knelt by the creek, rinsing out a sweat soaked horse blanket.

"Sir," he began.

"The name's Perk," said the foreman, without removing his attention from his task.

"The horses in the remuda," began Quent, "the ones not claimed anyhow, I don't think are suitable. Miss Brownell, to judge by the horse she rode this morning, is well mounted, and to keep pace with her—"

"Linares won't pay out more money for horses," said Perk. "He brought the remuda up from the border, and a good one it is, and that's it. Now, maybe Brownell wouldn't mind, for he did say he'd pay your expenses, but he said nothing directly about horses for you...."

"I'll buy them myself," Quent said hurriedly.

Perk considered this a moment. Quent thought he saw respect in the man's dark eyes, then decided he had simply dropped his eyelids against the glare of the sun.

"You'd best get back into town, then, and get to haggling. Johnny!" Perk raised his voice. "Get Dunk another horse. I don't want that black of mine all beat to hell, riding back and forth in this heat, before we even get going."

Twenty minutes later, Johnny returned with the small pinto mare. Quent thanked his lucky star he had not roped one of the twins.

Chapter Three

Annie rode sedately beside the wagon, forcing herself to keep the pace set by Mr. Brenerd. She wanted to gallop full speed to the camp, yelling like a wild woman.

"It's a beautiful day, isn't it?" she marveled, lifting her hat so she could view the sky without a border of black fringe. Mr. Brenerd, slouched on the wagon seat, grunted. His mouth had a permanent droop at the corners; his sad face discouraged another inquiry.

"I hope your business won't suffer, with you being gone so long," she said.

Brenerd muttered a sentence. The only word Annie caught was "woman."

"Beg pardon?" she said, leaning toward Brenerd. The man did not deign to repeat himself.

When she had camped with her father during roundup, she had been left alone, playing near the chuck wagon, while the men worked. Loneliness had never bothered her. After her mother's death, her father had taken her everywhere, the only child in a world of men. Looking back, she realized she had seen and heard things not fit for a child. Not only around the campfire, but dozing in the corner of many a bunkhouse and saloon while her father played poker.

Until she was twelve or thirteen. Then everything changed within a few months. Her father shifted her into the care of a succession of female relatives and friends. No more ecstatic mornings on horseback, no more coffee around the evening campfire.

She was back on the range, she exulted. Five months of freedom. And, at the end, a husband. Hugh McCann. Her memories of him were four years old. She had never looked at him very closely, aware of him only as her father's friend, ten years or more her senior. She had never regarded him with any romantic interest. Hugh McCann would, however, make a very suitable mate for her. A good cattleman, willing to overlook a woman's shadowed past so long as she possessed the makings of a sturdy ranch wife.

"Have you been on a drive north before?" she asked. Brenerd muttered a few words that she translated as meaning "No." Whether the mule skinner would talk or not was of no consequence whatsoever, she thought gaily. During the past year and a half, speaking and silence had been predetermined by the clock. She had been so accustomed to silence that Mrs. Moultry and her friends had used up her entire store of chitchat in two days. Silence, voluntary silence under the cloudless sky, would be a pleasure.

Far down the road, a lone horseman rode toward her. After her firm resolution to enjoy her own company, Annie was somewhat displeased to find she anticipated meeting another human being. Travelers always exchanged a few pleasantries. He would ask what was new in town. She would inquire about the condition of the road.

The dot resolved itself into a man riding a pinto horse. He was tall, rather too tall for the small horse. His body moved easily with the irregular gait of the pinto. She identified the dirty clothes of a cowboy, one who'd been out on the range for several weeks. His Stetson had cost him a month's wages, but now sagged from exposure.

"Good afternoon, Miss Brownell," he said, lifting his battered hat. She gasped, reined Jenny to a halt. Brenerd, seeing her stop, yelled at the mules. The wagon came to a halt ten feet down the road.

"Mr. van Kelson?" she exclaimed, not believing the apparition. What had happened to the shiny, brand-new outfit? He has already been engulfed by disaster, she thought happily. She would have jumped up and down in the stirrups, except she might confuse Jenny. He's giving up! He's heading back to San Antonio!

"You're going back to town," she said, not even bothering to make it a question.

"To buy horses. The ones left in the remuda aren't likely to get me to Montana." His hated accent made her head spin and her heart pound. *The wahns left in the rahmuder.* She nearly mocked him out loud, but caught herself and kept the words tucked in her mind for later use.

"If that's a sample, I agree," she said, examining the pinto from head to tail.

"And she's the best, except for the twins," said the greenhorn.

"The twins?"

"Two pintos, alike as two beans, who refuse to be separated or to allow themselves to be ridden."

"That could be awkward," she agreed, looking now at the man. Handsome, in a citified way, with short blond hair combed sleekly from a center part. The hair on the crown of his head, the part covered by his hat, gleamed darker than the back and sides. Wet? He sported no beard, not even a mustache. His eyes might be dark blue, or was that a reflection of the sky? His full lips turned up a bit at the corners. She leaned forward, enticed in spite of herself, then jerked back. Lips like that, with a faint permanent smile, marked an untrustworthy, lying cad.

A breeze snapped the canvas on the wagon; the pinto danced sideways. He reined expertly with one hand, clasping his hat in the other.

"The day is still young," he said graciously, bowing in the saddle. "Would you care to accompany me on my search?" Brenerd leaned around the front of the wagon, the corners of his mouth sunk down to the vicinity of his chin.

She would go to town with van Kelson, she decided quickly. She would determine what misfortune had destroyed his bandbox appearance, console him, express her sympathy, tell him of further horrors certain to occur before they got to Montana. He would abandon the trip.

"I'm going to accompany Mr. van Kelson to town," she shouted at Brenerd. "You go ahead to the camp and have the wrangler put the horses in the remuda." Brenerd said nothing, simply shook the reins. The mules stepped out, the wagon wheels lifted a bit of dust from the road, the ropes tightened on the bridles, the horses plodded behind.

"Your string?" asked the greenhorn.

"Except for the black one. That's Brenerd's."

"A fine-looking one, too."

"He has a nasty temper," Annie said.

"Which has the nasty temper? Mr. Brenerd or the horse?"

"Both. Do you mind my asking, Mr. van Kelson—"

"My name's Quentin. My friends call me Quent. The trail hands have christened me Dunk."

"Dunk?" What had he done to get a nickname so quickly?

"I fell into the tank at the spring, less than ten minutes after I arrived at the camp." He grinned at her, amused at his own misfortune. His dark blue eyes smiled, too. She smiled back, unwillingly. He laughed, and the delight of it brought an echo from her own throat. She resolutely stifled it in her chest. Laughing at him was acceptable, but laugh with people and they pulled you in, convinced you they were loyal friends, devoted lovers. She must not think of that.

"What shall I call you?" she asked.

"Anything but Mr. van Kelson. To make things consistent, perhaps Dunk would be best."

"And I'm not Miss Brownell, except to father's oldest, most traditional friends. Everyone calls me Annie."

His eyes studied her more minutely than she thought proper. She should feel threatened by the look, but instead, a shrunken little bud at the center of her stirred, gave promise of becoming a blossom. She had the impression of rain falling upon a land parched by months of drought.

At first she tried to shove the feeling away, but on second thought she welcomed it. If she could react to this silly New Yorker, then she had nothing to fear when she became Hugh McCann's wife. She relaxed, enjoyed the leisurely pace set by the pinto.

Her only fear when her father suggested—ordered?—the marriage had been the wedding night, and all the nights to follow. Without love would she be only the quiet object of her husband's passion? No, she almost shouted with relief. Van Kelson's smile had tickled some fragment of romance remaining inside her. If he, a damned Yankee, could arouse her a trifle, what would tall, strong, handsome, vibrant Hugh McCann set tumbling? Might she once more trust a man enough to love him?

Dunk pulled back on his reins so quickly he almost unbalanced the pinto. "Look at that horse!" he cried.

A dozen horses stood at a saloon hitching rail, but she had no doubt which animal Dunk referred to. Amid a crowd of mediocre horseflesh stood a gray, about fifteen hands high, presenting his broad, muscular rear to the street. The horse tossed his fine head, rustled his thick mane and moved restlessly, as if he knew people admired him. Three men pushed their way through the swinging doors, into the shadow of the trellis above the boardwalk. Annie recognized Mr. Weiss, an old friend of her father's. He approached the gray horse. Dunk leaped off his pinto.

"Pardon me, sir," he called. "Might that horse be for sale?"

Weiss's companions had paused near the saloon door. They burst into mocking laughter that did not bode at all well for Dunk's chances. Weiss would make a fool of him.

"You want to buy this horse, cowboy?" Weiss asked derisively.

"Yes, sir. If it's for sale."

"Everything's for sale, cowboy. Haven't you learned that? I'll sell Graybob at a bargain price. Eight hundred dollars."

"Can I look at him?" asked Dunk.

Weiss barked an impatient laugh, flipped the reins over the rail and climbed the steps to rejoin his companions. "Help yourself," he said with a sneer.

Annie edged Jenny to the other side of the street, hoping a bit more distance would disassociate her from Dunk. She would not step in to save him from making an ass of himself on a public street. Graybob was undoubtedly a good horse, one of the best she had ever seen, but *eight hundred dollars!* Dunk examined the horse, gentling him with a pat on the neck and a smooth imitation of a horse's nicker. He ran his hands down the gray legs, removed a slight tangle from the luxurious mane, patted the broad chest. Then he shouldered his way through the horses, walked, spurs ringing, to the saloon door.

"If you will accompany me to the bank, sir, we can settle this quickly. My letter of credit is quite in order, and I can arrange either cash or a deposit to your account, whichever would be most satisfactory."

"Now, wait one hellish minute!" yelled Weiss.

"Eight hundred dollars, I believe. . . ." began Dunk.

"What I meant was..." Weiss's eyes darted to his friends, appealing for help. "Get this mangy rascal off my tail!" His companions, who a few seconds before had laughed at the "mangy rascal," now laughed at Weiss.

"You told him eight hundred dollars, Weiss," said one, slapping his leg. "A bargain's a bargain. I won't lie."

"I don't ask you to lie, damn it, but I don't intend to sell Graybob!"

"I believe, sir, a verbal offer, if accepted in the presence of witnesses, can be, in a court of law, considered a valid contract."

Good gracious! Was Dunk a lawyer? He certainly sounded like one. A New York lawyer. Annie shivered at the implications. Did her father have an agreement with him, a written contract she could not wiggle out of? Was she legally tied to this man, in something like a temporary marriage?

"I think he has you, Weiss," said one of the men.

"Look, young fellow, I don't know who you are, but I've got horses back at the ranch. I'll give you four—no, five— of them, good horses, for eight hundred...."

"I believe, sir, I have indicated my intent to purchase this one. If you have others, we can engage in further negotiations, for I need a string." He turned to Annie. "How many would you recommend for the trip, Miss Brownell?"

Annie nearly fell off Jenny. Never in her life had a man asked her opinion of horses or the ranching business or a trail drive. Dunk tempted her to speak on topics that did not involve women. She searched his eyes to learn his sadistic intent, but found nothing but an earnest appeal for information. He really wanted her advice!

"Four, perhaps five," she said, knowing he was spending his money in vain. She would have him scurrying home within a week. A tiny shadow of doubt floated across her mind. Would he scurry? Of course he would. A trail drive was no place for a lawyer. A New York lawyer.

"Since we won't be doing any of the active work," she continued, "simply keeping up with the herd, four should be plenty." The little shrunken bud in her solar plexus opened a trifle, disturbing her stomach.

She gazed into the window of a milliner's shop while the men went into the bank; Weiss was smiling broadly when they emerged. Amazing, she thought with scorn, how a thousand or fifteen hundred dollars could raise a man's spirit. Affection be damned; only money counted with men. Even Hugh McCann. She did not like that thought, and suppressed it.

They set out for the headquarters of the Lazy W, five miles out of town. While the men gathered at the corral, she sat on the veranda with Mrs. Weiss, telling her about the journey to her father's new ranch in Montana and her engagement to Huge McCann. Dunk appeared, riding the gray horse, with three bays trailing behind. Weiss shook Dunk's hand.

"May I ask you why you need the horses? And where you'll be taking them?" asked Weiss. "So maybe, if there's a chance, I could buy Graybob back."

"I'm escorting this lady to her father's ranch in Montana," Dunk said. Annie looked closely at Weiss to see his reaction to Dunk's eastern accent. She waited for a grimace. Weiss showed nothing but good humor.

"Annie's going home—that is, to her new home," explained Mrs. Weiss. "You know her father moved to Montana."

"We're accompanying the herd Mr. Linares put together for Mr. Brownell," continued Dunk. "I rather doubt I'll be coming back to Texas, on horseback at least. Would you like me to send Graybob home by rail?"

"Send me a wire when you get there," said Weiss. "It would cost a pretty penny, but for Graybob. . ."

"As soon as we arrive, as I understand, in late August or early September."

"Thank you. Give your uncle my regards."

His uncle? Weiss knew Dunk's uncle? Maybe he wasn't such a greenhorn as he looked. Was his uncle a rancher who knew Mr. Weiss? She gulped, trying to dislodge the flutter of fear in the base of her throat. An untrustworthy Yankee, with a relative in Texas. That complicated the picture considerably.

Dunk turned on the fork of the road heading for San Antonio.

"We don't have to go back into town," Annie protested. "We can ride to the camp cross-country."

"I need to see the blacksmith," said Dunk. "I believe it's customary here to brand horses, although to my eyes it's rather disfiguring. I must get a branding iron."

"What's your brand?"

"I don't have one."

"Your uncle?" she asked.

"He doesn't have a brand either, I don't believe," he said, laughing. "Perhaps it's RR. What would you suggest?"

"Some ranchers use their initials."

"QVK. How do I find out if it's being used?"

"You register the brand. But I doubt we have time."

"Then I must pick something unusual. Has anyone used an artist's palette?"

"Not that I know of. Very few artists have ranches in Texas."

"Then that's what it shall be."

Who was this man, Dunk? Quentin van Kelson? Annie wondered. He showed a great deal more self-confidence and spunk than she had ever imagined a greenhorn might. She did not want a caretaker, particularly a lying New York lawyer caretaker. She had trusted a New Yorker before, and the disaster...

She straightened in the saddle, clinging to her resolve. She was going to Montana. Dunk was not. She would make sure he skedaddled back to San Antonio tomorrow.

The blacksmith worked under Dunk's direction, twisted a small band of iron into the proper shape, welded it to a long handle. The sun was low before they rode away.

"Who's your uncle?" she asked.

"Nicholas van Kelson."

"How does Mr. Weiss know him?"

"Uncle Nick is a railroad promoter. He's planning a railroad from the Rio Grande, north through San Antonio. Weiss thinks straight across the Lazy W might be a good route." He smiled at her knowingly, waiting for her reaction. She nodded. Who wouldn't welcome a railroad crossing his ranch?

"Is he the one they call Old Nick?" she asked.

Dunk laughed, a friendly, easy laugh. "That's what he's called throughout the country, wherever he does business. You've heard of him?"

"In San Antonio, the businessmen talk about the railroad."

She had not been included in the conversation, of course. In fact, she had eavesdropped shamelessly, listening to her uncle and his friends speak of Old Nick, and how they might bend him to their way of thinking and bring the railroad through San Antonio.

She studied Dunk's lithe figure in the twilight. An artist. That was what the men around the corral had said. She'd not expected determination beneath his New York courtesy. A lawyer, whose uncle was Old Nick, here to settle something, secretly, about the railroad. Lawyers, as a general rule, were not to be trusted, but a New York railroad lawyer! Ye gods! What had Linares done to her? Was she, Anne Brownell, tied into this scheme? A pawn in some railroad swindle? Had Mr. Moultry been involved, giving her to this man—?

Stop being silly, she told herself. But all her suspicions and fears molded into hard little nuggets that rolled around her brain at random, making it impossible to think logically. But one thing stood out plainly. This van Kelson might have the same determination as his uncle. He might ride, on his eight-hundred-dollar horse, all the way to Montana. She had to, absolutely had to, get rid of him as soon as possible. Ridicule! That would send a proud easterner back home, where he belonged.

After supper, after the campfire glowed in coals, the cowboys rode out with Perk to make a final check on the cattle. Dunk tagged along. Annie searched out Sid and made her proposal.

Quent lay beneath Annie's wagon, fighting drowsiness, waiting for the waning moon to rise. He wanted to see the grotto by moonlight. The wagon bed creaked as Annie shifted on her mattresses. He longed to compare his sketches with the living woman, but they were in his trunk, bound by rail for Temptation, Montana.

Annie's hair, her face, her hands, her movements, were exactly as he remembered them. Her personality, however, didn't fit. He had imagined her gentle, happy, acquiescent. Instead, hostility lurked in Miss Brownell's eyes, much of it directed at him. And beyond the anger, he had caught glimpses of bleakness, of a patiently endured sorrow and, sometimes, of fright.

Sitting on Jenny while he talked to the blacksmith, she had gazed blankly at the horizon, her lips trembling. She had closed her eyes and bowed her head, clutched at the saddle horn as if she suffered great pain. Had some dreadful sorrow fallen upon Annie in the past year and a half? Perhaps an unrequited love, a sweetheart in Louisiana her father had forbidden her to marry?

Then again, he had not spoken to Annie in Washington, had not even learned her name. Perhaps, if he had become acquainted with her there, he would have noticed beneath the radiant smile the ghost of sad experience.

The eastern sky lightened. Quent slid from under the wagon when a notch of brilliance pushed above the silhouette of low hills. When the misshapen orb hung a handspan in the sky, he walked to the grotto, pad and pencil in hand.

The shadows of the ferns created black goblins against the irregular wall, specters in violent contrast to the tiny streams of sparkling water. The wall seemed built of silver, set with jet and diamonds. At the lowest point of the tank, a notch overspilled in a sheet of quicksilver that disappeared into the miniature canyon it had carved for itself in the hillside.

Below him, the moonlight reflected from the white top of her wagon, gave long shadows to low mounds, the bedrolls of the cowboys clustered about the dead fire. The curve of Annie's wagon moved, ever so slightly, amid the shadows. No wind stirred, not even a suggestion of a breeze. He watched carefully, awaiting another shift in the white arc.

An arm lifted with smooth grace through the rear opening, followed by a leg, partially obscured by white fabric. She balanced for a moment, half in and half out, then jumped lightly to the ground. The white nightdress whirled about her like the full skirt of a French ballet dancer. He would have thought her the nymph of the spring, except for her prosaic emergence from the wagon. She took three steps beyond the wagon, away from him, lifted her face to the sky, spread her arms in a gesture of exultation.

His pencil moved automatically, catching in a few lines the arch of her body, the thrust of the triumphant limbs, the extended hands. She celebrated a victory? Or did her heart carry a primordial memory of moon worship?

Her steps ceased to be anything so mundane as walking and became the movements of the dance. She leaped into the air, her arms stretched out toward the moon, as if to clutch at the magic of it, draw it into her body. She raised her arms higher, over her head. The hands drew in on themselves, formed fists. Then suddenly, the white figure collapsed, bent as if in agony. From triumph to frustration.

She staggered back to the wagon, climbed in clumsily, snagging her nightdress on the tailgate.

He waited until the moon rode high before returning to his bedroll. He did not sleep immediately, for above him hung a sound like the crumpling of tissue. Annie wept.

For the first time, he wanted to do something more than study her, analyze her face and figure. He ached to put his arms about her and comfort her, brush away the tears caused by whatever disaster had encompassed her since that gala night in Washington.

Chapter Four

Quent peeked sleepily from under his blankets. The sun lay below the horizon, but Perk's horse stood saddled, ready to take the trail boss to his last meeting with Linares. Sid was repacking boxes and barrels in the chuck wagon, laughing quietly with the cowboys standing at the breakfast fire. Quent rolled out of his bed, pulled on his clothes. He found a tin cup in the chuck wagon, poured himself a cup of coffee from the large pot kept warm at the side of the fire.

He had never seen any vehicle like the chuck wagon. In the front it was much like any other wagon, with hickory bows arched to receive a canvas top, although in this fine weather Sid did not bother with the cover. Here were stowed barrels of flour and cornmeal, slabs of bacon, sacks of sugar, beans and dried fruit.

A tall chuck box took up the entire rear of the wagon. This box was fitted with shelves and cubbyholes to hold pots and pans, spoons and forks, tin plates and cups, plus all the small food sundries the cook would need, from salt to cinnamon. The rear of this cupboard folded down to make Sid's worktable.

"Dunk," said Stack, who as *segundo* was in charge when Perk left the herd, "I want to see your gear. See you got everything you need."

Quent unrolled his blankets and emptied his bundle of possessions. Every cowboy in camp stood behind Stack.

Two or three mouths twitched into grins, then turned down in rehearsed, exaggerated frowns. Quent had not spent half his twenty-four years observing human faces, trying to catch their soul-spirits on paper, without learning to read concealed mischief. Something was up. Stack looked over the pile of ropes, extra bridles, picket pins, horse blankets, gloves, bandannas, shaving gear.

"Where's your horn pike?" he asked gruffly. Quent studied Stack's fingers; they scratched nervously at the side seams of his denim pants. Quent darted a quick glance at the men standing behind Stack, faces unnaturally subdued, bodies tense with anticipation.

"Horn pike?" he asked innocently.

"Yeah. Horn pike," said two of the men simultaneously.

"What's it used for?" Quent asked, disciplining his own mouth so he sounded unsuspecting.

"Dull the horns of the most rambunctious steers. Of course, greenhorns don't know things like that. Without dulling the horns now and then, the steers cut up something fierce." Quent didn't know the name of the man who spoke. Small and wiry. Huzzy, perhaps?

"Particularly when they're fighting over the cows?" asked Quent, striving mightily to keep sarcasm out of his voice. He must let them have their fun. If he foiled their practical joke, if he became insulted and hurt, they would grumble over his presence even more than they probably did now. They likely resented him, and rightfully so; he had everything they did not. They could not move into his world, but he could blithely make a claim upon their time and company, for no other reason than money in the bank.

"Yeah," said Stack. "The steers do fight something awful over the cows." A thin sound drifted from the front of Annie's wagon. For one second she had been unable to contain her giggles.

''Well,'' said Quent, exaggerating his serious demeanor, ''I best ride into town and buy one. At which store do I find a horn pike?''

''Why, where you outfitted yourself,'' said Stack. ''I'm surprised old Hank didn't say nothing about you needing a horn pike when you bought your gear.''

''So am I,'' said Quent, nodding. ''He was most helpful. He assured me I had everything.''

''He'll be helpful today, I'm sure,'' said Broadbrim. His voice wavered from the laughter bottled up in his chest.

Quent went in search of Annie. When she saw him, she ducked her head and concentrated on the row of buttons down the side of her skirt. Today she wore a brown skirt, and the buttons looked like water-washed tan stones.

''Miss Brownell, I find I must ride into town today, quite unexpectedly. This will leave you without my protection, unless you'd be pleased to join me.''

Her mouth opened, closed without saying a thing. He had taken her by surprise. She would come, of course, to watch him make a fool of himself in front of Hank and any customers who might be in the store. She would not pass up the chance to report firsthand the success of the joke.

''I'm flattered that you ask,'' she finally said. She leaned around the front end of the wagon so she could see all the hands. ''Johnny, please rope Lily for me, before she wanders too far from camp?''

''Yes, Miss Annie. You want Graybob, Dunk?''

''No. The number three bay this morning.''

Quent stowed his gear in the wagon while Johnny got the horses. He lifted Annie's saddle from under the wagon, watched, from the corner of his eye, while she repositioned the front panel of her skirt, untied the bustle. He had never seen an outfit like hers before, but it seemed to work.

As they set out toward San Antonio, he kept his eyes on the horse, the road, anything but Annie. Twice he caught her smirking. No doubt she was in on the joke. Perhaps had instigated it.

"Your initials, on your saddle," he said evenly, to change the subject and keep his mind busy. "AMB. You have a second name?"

"Meechem," she said. "My mother's maiden name. Perhaps you've heard of my uncle, Ronald Meechem. He's a congressman from Texas."

Should he tell her about Washington? About falling in love with her at Senator Wise's party? He decided against a confession. If she were a gentle, sympathetic woman—possibly. But would Annie not jest about such a distant obsession? He could bear the joke of the horn pike, but not one that touched his emotions.

At the outfitting store, she lingered near the door, not wanting, he judged, to be too close when the joshing started. A Texas woman would naturally hesitate to be identified with a New York tenderfoot when he revealed his abysmal ignorance. Two men lounged on empty water casks.

"Please, sir," Quent said directly to Hank, the owner. "Stack says I don't have all my gear for the drive. He said I need a horn pike, and he's surprised you didn't suggest one when I bought my gear two days ago."

All heads twisted in his direction. The loungers grinned. Hank grinned, then frowned and snorted in exasperation.

"Damn Stack—them cowboys never consider their tricks waste my time."

"Horn pike!" snorted one of the strangers. "I didn't know there was anybody in Texas over the age of twelve who could be caught with that mossy joke. Where you from, fellow?" After this question, he laughed and slapped his knee.

"New York," said Quent. The gentleman's laughter became explosive. Tears started from his eyes. Quent waited for the second man to break into gales of laughter. He grinned, but not at Quent. He was looking toward the door, and Annie.

"Horn pike!" yelped the first man between spasms.

"I'm sorry, but that's one of the little jokes the boys are fond of," Hank said seriously. "They like to send new men on a wild-goose chase, after a tool that doesn't exist."

"Doesn't exist?" Quent protested, making sure to widen his eyes in surprise. He looked back at Annie to see how she enjoyed his embarrassment. Her fingers covered her mouth, and she was staring down at her skirt. The panel was swept to the side for riding. She had been so intent on seeing him make a fool of himself, she had forgotten to rebutton it. All the men in the store saw she had on trousers. She raised her eyes to the man who leered at her.

"It doesn't exist," Hank said firmly. "The cowboys meant for you to look silly, and I guess they've succeeded. Miss Annie, didn't you tell this gentleman he was the butt of a joke?" Miss Annie paid no attention to Hank. She turned her back on the men, edged into the corner by the door under the pretext of studying a display of ribbons. Her right hand touched a bolt of ribbon, while the left struggled with the little tan stones. Her uncoordinated efforts caused her bustle to shift. It rested grotesquely on her left hip.

"Doesn't exist," said Quent with disgust. He strode to Annie's side, grabbed her arm.

"Don't bother getting proper," he said in a wounded voice. "We're leaving."

She turned her face away from him as they left the store, and when she took his hand to mount Lily. She shifted uncomfortably in the saddle.

"You forgot to take off your bustle," he said.

"Leave me alone," she snapped.

"Your father hired me to take care of you," he said, reaching up to untie the bow on her right hip. "Stand up in the stirrups. I can slide it out from under you." She glared at him, then did as he suggested. "Now, I believe a pot of tea is in order. Can the hotel provide us with such a thing?"

"I don't know," she muttered. "I've never heard of a man who drinks tea."

"Greenhorns," he replied. "Greenhorns drink tea. The pleasant climax of a summer's afternoon, on the lawn behind the house after a game of croquet. Mother has a beautiful tea set she brought from England—"

"Shut up," she snapped.

He stood patiently by the hitching rail in front of the hotel while she, barricaded between Lily and Number Three, settled her bustle around her waist, buttoned the panel.

"Beautiful!" he exclaimed when she emerged from the impromptu dressing room. "Did you design this very charming outfit yourself?"

She glared at him. *She thinks I'm making fun of her,* he thought sadly. He offered his arm, which she took after a moment's consideration, led her up the stairs into the dining room. Only a scattering of late breakfasters still lingered. The table in the bow window overlooking the street stood empty, so he claimed it.

"Tea," he said to the waiter, "and cakes, if you have them." He removed his pocket notebook from inside his coat, a pencil from his vest pocket.

"Now, Annie—are you sure I may call you Annie?—what does a horn pike look like? Stack seems to think it's a very important part of a cowboy's gear. You must have seen one."

"No." She stared vacantly at the dusty lace curtains covering the lower panes of the bow window, her mouth a thin, insulted line.

"Never seen one," Quent marveled. "Then we must make some deductions. Do you read Edgar Allan Poe?"

"Yes."

"Then you're familiar with the process of logical thinking. Take what facts are available and use them to reveal the whole. Now, the name, horn pike, tells us very clearly the size of this implement. A pike. 'Plain as a pikestaff.' A weapon that cannot be concealed, because of its size."

"How do you know the size of a pikestaff?" she hissed.

"I saw them in Europe. The Swiss Guards in Rome carry pikestaffs. But I can't imagine a horn pike being that large. Stack implied it might be carried along on the drive, and unless it functions in the manner of a lance, I can't see it being truly as long as a pikestaff."

He drew a straight line on the paper before him, then a second parallel to it, and shaded the edge to turn it into a rod.

"Now, its function—to dull the horns of a cow. Not cut the entire horn off. Simply dull it. That implies removal of the very tip. Do you agree?" She stared at the drawing. A flush of pink accented her cheekbones. The rosy tint complemented her eyes; she was lovely in spite of her frown.

"I don't know. I suppose so."

"So the business end of this pike must contain a file or, better yet, a sharp knife. How is this knife to work, when the operator's hand is two, perhaps three, feet away?"

The tea arrived, along with a plate of cakes so stale the frosting on top had cracked. The waiter banged the cups onto the saucers, poured the tea.

"Perhaps this gentleman knows," said Quent. "Have you ever seen vaqueros using a horn pike?"

The waiter's mouth widened slowly into a grin. "So, they've taken someone else in with that old joke," he said happily.

"No, indeed. We seriously need a horn pike. The joke, so I've been told, is well-founded in old Spanish custom, to dull the horns of the cattle before they set out on a long drive, so the steers . . ."

"Really?" asked the waiter. His grin relaxed into serious interest.

"According to the records of the expedition of Vásquez de Coronado, there was even an office of *vaquero picador*, cowboy of the horn pike. It must have been a position of honor, for the *vaquero picador* rode before the general himself, along with the bearer of the royal flag." Quent caught himself and stopped. Was he overdoing this?

"I didn't know, sir," said the waiter, awed. "Wait until I tell Simpson, because he caught me with that joke the second day I was in town. Made an absolute fool of myself down at the outfitters'."

"You might also consult some of the early histories of Baja California— Ouch!" Annie had kicked him in the shin with her pointed riding boot. Her lips pulled back, revealing her small, perfect teeth; her chest puffed up with retained breath, so her lovely bustline... She let the breath go explosively when she had his attention.

"Shut up!" she mouthed, but she might as well have shouted the words.

"I'm sorry. I bore you," he said to the waiter.

"No indeed, sir. This is all most interesting. Wait until I tell Simpson," he said excitedly.

Annie caught the waiter's eye by sticking her hand under his nose. She jerked her thumb at a distant table, where a group of ladies were gesturing at an empty teapot.

"Thank you very much, sir," he said proudly. "It is a joy to meet a gentleman of refinement and education in this desert of ignorance." He turned and strode haughtily toward his other customers. Quent congratulated himself on boosting a fellow human being's opinion of himself.

"What do you think you're doing?" whispered Annie, her eyes blazing.

"Solving a problem and settling the future of a hoary old joke."

"You're lying. You're showing off. Why should you make sure the whole town hears about this? I've never met a man who wants his ignorance exposed to public ridicule."

"But a joke like this, it isn't funny unless everyone hears about it," he protested. Annie said nothing. "Or wasn't it meant as a joke?"

"Of course it was."

"Thank you for the confession. But there. We still haven't settled the problem of operating the knife from a distance. Perhaps we can learn something from that great French invention, the guillotine. If we provide the pike with a trigger mechanism, with a spring—'' he sketched as he talked ''—with a flexible cage on the business end, in which the horn is caught...'' He drew the cage, with elegant spiral arms, before he turned the book to face Annie.

''Do you think that will work?''

''Why are you doing this?''

''For the fun of it. The same motivation you had when you set up this jolly escapade,'' he said, making sure his voice betrayed nothing but pleasure.

''Why should I be behind this? Cowboys always send newcomers after a horn pike.''

''Just a natural suspicion on my part. Why don't you want me along?''

She glared at him. When she compressed her mouth, squinted her eyes, the charm and vitality drained away, even the hostility evaporated, and there was nothing left but the hurt girl. ''I don't want to be bothered taking care of you,'' she snapped.

''If I demonstrate today that I can take care of myself, will that ease the predicament in which we find ourselves? Has my behavior in the matter of this joke been appropriate? I don't want to disappoint the cowboys the way I've obviously disappointed you. Why were you crying last night?''

She had been lifting her teacup from its saucer. She dropped it, splashing tea over the lip of the cup, into the saucer, onto the tablecloth. Her face blanched. He was sorry he'd asked.

''Spy!'' she hissed.

''I'm very sorry. But Linares made it plain I was to stay close to you, sleep beneath your wagon. I'm dreadfully sorry if I've intruded on some private misery.''

''I thought you were asleep.''

''I sleep lightly. Particularly when the night is bright and nymphs dance among the moonbeams.''

Her brown eyes darkened almost to black. "I hate you," she said firmly. "You should leave the drive now, before things get worse."

"What things?"

"The taunting, the jokes . . ."

"Your dislike?"

"That, too."

"Your father said nothing at all about you liking me. He said I was to accompany you, protect you from improper advances by uncouth males. It is completely beside the point that you hate me. Also beside the point that I find you an incredible, totally fascinating maiden."

He expected her to be surprised. Or angry. Instead, she dropped her eyes, twisted her hands on the tabletop.

"Please don't make fun of me," she whispered.

"I'm not making fun of you. If you're finished with your tea, we had best make our way to the friendly blacksmith and get this implement, which Stack so desires, manufactured."

Annie watched from her wagon while Dunk opened her folding chair with a flourish and placed it near the smoldering fire. All the men not riding herd sat nearby, drinking their last cup of coffee. She had avoided the cowboys since she and Dunk had returned to camp. The entire crew had played games with the "horn pike" in the late afternoon. There had been nothing for her to do but stay out of the way, on the seat of her wagon, while they roped steers to test the sharpness of the knife, then dared one another to ride into the herd, close enough to a steer to catch the tip of a horn in the basket. There had been a great deal of backslapping and beating on shoulders, in the quaint male rituals of friendship.

When she and Dunk rode into camp, when he gravely presented the implement for Stack's inspection, every eye in camp had popped out in surprise. The horn pike had not made Dunk ridiculous, but had opened the possibility of friendship between him and the cowboys. The men were impressed by his good humor, and by his ingenuity in turning the joke on them.

As she climbed down from the wagon, Perk walked into camp, much to her relief. Without the strong hand of the foreman, the men frolicked like a bunch of wild boys. Boys—the awareness flooded over her—who could be manipulated by Dunk's city wisdom. Stack might be a good second-in-command, but he did not have the steadiness needed to be a foreman, nor was he smart enough to see the troubles Dunk might cause by simply talking.

Perk collapsed wearily beside the fire. Immediately Stack launched into a description of the horn-pike joke, showed Perk the instrument.

"Strange," said Perk, examining the tool. "Linares and I had dinner in the hotel, and the waiter there claimed a horn pike isn't a joke. Some famous Spanish general invented the thing, brought it to Mexico with the Conquest." Annie feared for a moment that she might choke. "Might not hurt to try it, I suppose," Perk continued cautiously, "just so you don't rile the cattle. I hope—" he spoke to Stack "—you haven't been running the herd trying out this thing."

"Not overmuch," said Stack, very subdued.

"That's one of the rules," said Perk, looking around at the faces of the men, shadowed in the firelight. "No exciting the cattle unless absolutely necessary. I want it understood, you carry your six-shooters, but no shooting without very good reason. More stampedes are started by fools blazing away at shadows than by lightning.

"And if the cattle do start to run, everyone but me and Stack and Broadbrim stick around camp. Stampedes peter out quick, usually. Doesn't do any good to have a whole regiment of men out yelling and waving their coats. Only scatters the herd."

"You mean we all just sit and let the herd spread itself from here to Montana?" asked one of the younger cowboys.

"No. Cattle, once they're accustomed to each other, stay together. This herd's shown no tendency to run. I'd rather have the herd ten miles away, all in one clump, than have it five miles from camp, but in a dozen different directions, no man knowing where the others are. If the herd runs, I take care of it, along with the point men. And if I catch a man with his six-shooter out, or waving his mackintosh, I'll dock his pay."

Perk turned to Dunk. "You'll stay out of the way. You and Miss Annie ride with the chuck. Brenerd, I know you like to favor your animals, but they're Brownell's mules now, he paid for them, so you'll keep up with Sid."

The taciturn man said nothing, simply nodded.

"Next rule, nobody talks politics or religion. I know your pappy—" he jerked a thumb at Stack "—died on the Chickahominy, fighting for the southern states, and I know the same war freed you and your folks," he added, turning to Broadbrim. "But it's just a sore boil on the gum, and there's no sense rubbing your tongue over it, keeping it raw. And everybody's road to heaven ends up at the same place, so forget preaching." Perk stood up. "And no whiskey, except for the bottle Sid's got in case of snakebite. I find whiskey in any bedroll, that man's off the drive."

"What about cards?" asked a voice from the twilight.

"If you're fool enough to play, it's no skin off me. But the moment there's a fight over a deal, every deck goes in the fire. Everyone got their night horse saddled?"

A chorus of deep, subdued voices replied, "Yes."

"Then let's ride out and check, see if the cattle are settled down for the night."

The cowboys walked into the darkness, and Sid disappeared in the direction of the chuck wagon. Annie heard the clatter of dry beans in a kettle, a splash of water. Brenerd heaved himself up, vanished on some private errand. Only she and Dunk were left, she in the folding chair, Dunk sitting cross-legged on the ground. From now on, she would not use the chair. She felt silly, lifted so far above everyone else, like a criminal on the gallows, ready to be hanged.

"Who are you?" she asked quietly.

"What do you mean? Quentin van Kelson. Of the New York van Kelsons."

"I know that," she said, impatient at her imprecision. "What I mean is, why should you want to ride to Montana? It can't be a comfortable experience for a—" she searched for the least pejorative terms "—a man accustomed to luxuries. For an educated man."

"You have deduced I'm accustomed to luxuries and am educated," he said. "Quite correct. I see you, too, learned from reading Poe."

"It's not necessary to read Poe to see the obvious. Why are you doing this?"

"To try something new. To see if I can do it. And if I can, I'll have something to brag about when I get home." His voice strengthened. "I want to paint pictures of significant things, things that have some meaning in the history of this nation. Not just society ladies drinking tea and college friends sculling on the Hudson. This is the last frontier outside the frozen North."

"With your money, you could explore in Central America, come back with pictures of the ancient cities in the jungle. Or sketch elephants in Africa or tigers in India. Why pretend to be a cowboy?"

"I've read too many dime novels, I expect."

"I don't believe you've ever read a dime novel," she said, snorting. "Where did you go to school?"

"At home, until I went to boarding school, then Harvard." Annie groaned, imagining the conversations that would, in five months, expose the paucity of her own education. She had hardly gone to school before she was twelve, when her father gave up hauling her on every cattle-buying trip.

"Did my father send you to San Antonio?"

"I don't think your father knows who I am or that I'm here. Your father stipulated that your escort must be a responsible man of good family. That put Linares in something of a spot, since your father also said he couldn't be a cowhand. Then he remembered me, the man who sat on the top rail of his corral, sketching cowboys and horses—a respectable man, possibly. Most certainly of good family. Linares met my uncle last year."

"So your being here is pure happenstance?" she asked, doubting he would tell the truth.

"Pure chance."

"I don't believe it," she snapped.

"What don't you believe?" asked a voice from the darkness. Perk came into the circle of firelight, trailed by nine cowboys. Annie searched hastily for a topic that would not betray her conversation with Dunk.

"I don't believe he likes his nickname." It was the first thing that came to her mind.

"Any complaint, Dunk?" asked Perk.

"Not really. It might have been much worse."

"If something worse happens, we can change it," said a cheerful voice. "I mean, maybe we should change it to Horn Pike." Annie gasped involuntarily, envisioning herself, next winter, speaking to her father or her husband about her gentlemanly escort, Horn Pike. The word bordered on the improper. Too much suggestion of length and strength.

"No," she said forcefully. "That's not a name that can be spoken in society, at least in mixed company. Mr. van Kelson wouldn't be able to tell his family his nickname."

The cowboys grunted, sat down. No one said a thing. The conversation had died, and she had killed it. By raising the specter of "society," which few cowboys knew anything about, she had made them shy of speaking before her and Dunk.

"And how he got the name Dunk is such a wonderful story—" she chattered on, in an effort to lighten the atmosphere "—it would be a shame to limit his telling of it. There are so many great tales about how men got their names. For example, how did you get your name, Stack?"

Two or three men guffawed.

"I was on a drive to Dodge," Stack said unwillingly. "The cattle ran, and we had nothing to eat for a whole day while we gathered the herd. The cook made flapjacks as a special treat, and I ate a quantity of them."

"The way I heard the story," said another man, "you ate every flapjack in sight, and the next men who came in had plain old biscuits."

"How can that be true?" Stack asked angrily. "Sid, you ever hear of a cook that stopped frying flapjacks when the men were coming in hungry?"

"Just once. My friend Dinty, he ran out of flour on a trip to Dodge," Sid said mischievously. "I do believe he once told me about a cowboy who ate every flapjack in the place."

"That's nothing but a barefaced lie!" Stack erupted. "How you fellows can believe such buzzard sh—" His face changed. He shot a hurried glance at Annie. "I can't sit here jawing all evening. I got things to do." He strode away, pretended to search for something in his bed.

"I think I'll retire," Annie said very meekly. Dunk jumped up, offered his hand as she climbed into her wagon. A solid hand, but not callused with work. Its warmth crept into her own palm, and her fingers tingled. She jerked away as soon as she got her legs over the tailgate.

"Thank you," she said under her breath.

Annie considered the disasters of the day. Her joke on Dunk had rebounded to his advantage. Instead of making the cowboys contemptuous of him, it had gained him a measure of respect. And her innocent question about the source of Stack's nickname had ended with Stack's anger. Dunk had reacted to joshing much better than Stack; the men could not help but notice the difference. Not good for discipline. Stack was *segundo*. If the men lost respect for him, would he be able to control them in an emergency?

From now on, she had better keep her mouth shut.

Chapter Five

Quent discovered that when clustered together the cattle
appeared as a mass of horns, not a herd of whole animals.
Their long, high horns, dancing in the air, caught his eye
and held it. His sketches of the herd became, more and
more, simply a study in curves, with only the suggestion of
the bodies beneath them.

And, more fascinating still, they were not alike. Some
sprang sharply upward, while others spread wide. Horns
drooped downward, horns twisted in contorted shapes.
There were pairs of horns where one curled in and the other
curled out. And convoluted horns the cowboys called
"mossy."

From a low rise, he caught a panoramic view of the entire herd strung out for three-quarters of a mile. Stack and
Broadbrim, the point men, rode with the leaders, half a
dozen large steers and two bulls. These animals had taken
the lead on the very first day and still retained it. Three men
rode on each side of the herd, the swing men. The remainder of the hands rode in the rear, the drag, urging the stragglers forward. A dozen cows with half-grown calves lagged,
along with several steers who were either lazy or reluctant to
leave Texas.

The two wagons drove far ahead, but still in sight. Sid
would select the nooning spot, and by the time the herd ar-

rived, dinner would be simmering. He could barely make out Annie, riding far beyond the chuck wagon.

Quent pulled his sketch pad from the protective leather case tied to his saddle. He paused long enough to sketch the view before him. Annie took no more than a few tentative lines showing the presence of a human on horseback. He no longer made detailed studies of her. While her face and body remained the same, exquisitely beautiful, close acquaintance had dulled his appreciation.

Curious, he thought, how beauty could not survive an unpleasant personality. She had told the truth when she said she hated him. In the three days since leaving San Antonio, she had spoken to him only when absolutely necessary, and what she did say dripped with disdain. She had ordered him to stay away from her, preferably far behind.

The cowboys included him in some of the evening work; they let him ride along on the final check of the cattle. Huzzy and Lucas tutored him in throwing a rope, without, he feared, making any significant improvement.

Yet Annie Brownell, the person whose acquaintance he had so desperately wished to make, Annie Brownell had faded into a distant witch. She was, he reminded himself, the witch placed in his care; he had no alternative, if he wanted to stay with the herd, but to shadow her, knowing all the time she hated being under his eyes, tried his temper. To leave was unthinkable. The dramatic countryside shouted for his attention. He must not sacrifice this chance to ride through it, two thousand miles to Montana.

Besides, he had made a contract—verbal, but binding nonetheless—with Linares. Stay with Annie, get her to Montana, whether she went on horseback or by train.

He spurred his horse to catch up with the herd. In the distance, a thin column of smoke marked the spot where the dinner fire had already been kindled. The dust of the milling remuda obscured the horses, but Quent knew Johnny had set them to graze not far from the wagons, so remounts would be available after dinner.

Perk came riding in from the north, for the trail boss scouted the way ahead. Quent spurred past the herd, turned the bay's head in the direction of the wagons. Respectful of Perk's orders, he hung back, out of the way of the real workmen. Perk saw him, lifted his arm and waved him toward the chuck wagon.

"We'll rest the herd here for an hour or two, then push on and cross the Guadalupe River before we camp for the night," said Perk. "You keep her—" he jerked a thumb toward Annie, a quarter mile ahead "—out of the way. The both of you change to fresh horses for the crossing. Wait until Johnny has all the men remounted, then ask for yours. The wagons will come over last, you and Annie with them."

Quent lifted his hat to show he understood the orders, then put spurs to the horse to catch up with Annie. She received the message wordlessly, automatically turning her horse to the noon camp. He fell in, slightly behind her.

"Can you swim?" she asked suddenly, twisting in her saddle to face him. He kicked the bay to close the gap and seize the opportunity to ride beside her.

"Yes."

"Well? I mean, are you good at it?"

"I suppose so. As a child I spent my summers on Long Island."

"Good," she said. "I'd hate to have to rescue you."

The cowboys ate in shifts, downing beef and stew and biscuits and canned corn faster than Quent had ever seen men gobble. Annie loaded her plate, carried it to the front box of her wagon and perched there in isolation.

Johnny strung two long ropes from the wheels of the chuck wagon, then drove the horses into this improvised corral. The cowboys called out the names of the mounts they wanted and Johnny roped them from the herd. Quent envied Johnny's unerring eye and arm. His loops fell effortlessly over horse after horse, so automatically it called forth no admiration except from Quent.

Annie selected the largest of her horses, a gelding named Bird; Quent had long since decided he would ride Graybob for the toughest parts of the trail—river crossings, night emergencies, waterless stretches. There was no need for Johnny to throw a loop over the big gray horse. He stood at the edge of the herd, anxious to be chosen.

"Annie, you stay with the wagons until the herd's across," Perk said sharply. He glared with downturned mouth. It was the first time the foreman had shown irritation with her. "And Dunk's to stay with you. I don't want people spread all over the countryside when we get to the river." Annie nodded. If she felt the rebuke, she did not show it.

Beyond the nooning spot, the country grew rougher, and as they neared the river the ground sloped in a confusion of gullies. The path to the ford was plain. Dozens of herds had already passed this way since spring, thousands of hooves beating the ground into dust. Annie led the way to a grassy knoll a few yards from the river, away from the main path. Sid, astride his left wheel horse, and Brenerd, driving like a coachman from the wagon seat, whooped at the mules, encouraging them up the low rise. The entire span of the river lay before them.

The lead steers and bulls ran eagerly into the stream, hot and thirsty from the day's drive. The cowboys rode in close pursuit, plunged into the river yelling, their ropes swinging. They did not allow the cattle to stop, but forced them farther and farther into the stream until, several yards out, the leaders went completely underwater. Only their heads and horns showed, undulating with the rhythm of their swimming. Behind them came the rest of the herd, crowding as more and more hesitated on the bank.

Quent knew this was the moment of danger, for if the leaders should turn, try to come back, the herd would be thrown into confusion. He held his breath until he saw the first steer jerk and heave as his feet met the rising riverbed on the far side. One after another they lifted themselves up the bank, their flanks streaming water.

"Why are most of the men on the downstream side of the herd?" Quent asked, leaning toward Sid.

"To keep them on the crossing. Below the ford, the bottom's not solid—the cattle get bogged." Sid mounted his mule, preparing to move the wagons to the riverbank. Only a few laggards, including two cows with their calves, remained on the near shore. The men hollered, pushed the spooked animals into the water. A cow reached the deep channel, tried to return to the southern shore. Quent recognized Huzzy's wiry form on a twisting horse, trying vainly to intercept the frightened cow.

It began gracefully, like a slow ballet, but Quent's throat closed when he noticed the angle of Huzzy's horse. Not one of the animal's feet securely gripped the bed of the stream. The cow regained the south bank, stood bawling for her calf to join her; Huzzy's horse struggled to right itself, pawed in the water for solid footing. For one moment, it seemed to regain equilibrium. Then it staggered.

The cowboys turned after the cow. Quent spurred Graybob toward the river, well downstream from the struggling horse and rider. No, the horse was no longer visible.

Graybob went into the water without hesitation, leaped heedlessly through the shallows in response to the spur. Quent stopped the horse before he dived into the channel where the current flowed strongest. He studied the roiling water upstream. He would be useless if he entered too soon, for Graybob would tire, paddling about in the current, waiting until the cowboy drifted by.

Twice Quent saw Huzzy's arm reach up, in the heart-rending plea of the drowning. Then he caught a glimpse of a blue shirt, the color strangely attractive against the tan of the water. Quent gauged the speed of the current, urged Graybob into the stream at what he estimated—hoped, prayed—was the proper moment. A few seconds too soon.

He snatched the expanse of blue shirt only by leaning far back in the saddle.

Huzzy, still facedown, struggled, his arms flailed to catch something. The fabric beneath Quent's fingers gave way. If the shirt ripped, there was no way he could pull Huzzy onto Graybob's rump. He dared a single glance downstream, saw that no one had galloped into position to attempt a second rescue. The fear of failure tensed his hand and arm. How much longer could he hang on? He thought of the nameless fear possessing Huzzy's mind and strengthened his grasp.

A hand, blindly thrashing, lifted out of the sodden mass of blue cotton, out of the muddy water; Quent dropped his reins, trusting Graybob to swim the river and climb out without guidance. He grabbed the hand. It clung to his in a grip made viselike by fear of death.

Graybob stepped into the shallows, water cascading in red streams from his flanks, Huzzy dangling, coughing and gagging, on his left side. Quent heaved the man across the front of his saddle, found the reins hopelessly tangled in Huzzy's legs. He leaned over, patted the horse, tapped him with his spurs. Graybob stepped carefully around the half-buried rocks, through the glistening slime, heading for the crowd of men rushing to the riverbank.

They eased Huzzy onto the ground. Two men joined hands, a third draped Huzzy, facedown, over the support to drain the water from his lungs. He gagged, vomited, coughed. The men eased him to the muddy riverbank after he managed a few shallow breaths.

Annie! He'd dashed into the river, leaving Annie with the wagons on the far bank. He must get back to her.

"How bad?" yelled a voice. Perk left his horse above and slid down the steep, sticky clay bank.

"He'll live!" yelled a voice right in Quent's ear. He jumped in alarm, his nerves still jangled.

"Dunk pulled him out," continued Stack. "He was downstream a ways."

"What the hell were you doing downstream?" asked Perk. "I told you to stay out of the river until the herd crossed."

Quent stepped back, a bit hazed that Perk should snap at him when a man's life had been in the balance. He considered his decision to ride into the river. He had, most certainly, left his place on the knoll before Huzzy was completely down. More important, he had abandoned Annie on the other side of the river. But hadn't it been justified? He looked at Huzzy, still spitting up dirty water.

"I saw Huzzy's horse was in trouble," Quent said, as mildly as he could. "I decided to get in the right position, in case he went under."

"He hadn't—" Huzzy choked. "I'd be feeding the buzzards down about Seguin."

"Stack, get the wagons across," Perk ordered. "Two of you—" he studied the group "—Broadbrim and Soto," he finally said, "go back across, get Miss Annie over. There shouldn't be any trouble. She's got a good horse. The rest of you get to the herd."

Quent turned to Graybob, irritated that his action had earned him nothing but a reprimand. He lifted his left arm to the saddle; pain shot from his shoulder, down his arm to the wrist and hand. He kneaded the shoulder with his right hand, circled the bone and sensed a settling into position. In his panic to keep hold of Huzzy, he'd nearly pulled the arm from the socket, and he had not even noticed. He lifted his hand again; the shoulder complained with a dull ache as he climbed into the saddle.

"You okay?" asked Perk.

"Yes. Just a bit of an ache. I'm sorry I didn't do as you said, but under the circumstances..."

"Usually, I make a big point about the men following orders, but I also expect everyone on this drive to do the sensible thing in an emergency. You did right. I'm sure Huzzy's mighty glad we had an extra man on the downstream side. From now on, when we cross a stream, you take that place. With that horse of yours, you're the one most able to dash out and scoop someone up. You can swim?''

"Yes."

"Good. Most cowboys can't. Some years there's not enough water in Texas to wet your whistle, let alone cover your belly button when you're standing in the middle of it.''

Quent watched the mules pull the wagons to the water's edge. He was curious about how they would be maneuvered across. The men unhitched the mules and drove them into the river. Once they had passed the deep channel, they were reharnessed, the traces attached to long ropes extending all the way across the river. With men riding on either side to keep the wagons steady in the current, the mules easily drew them across, floating on their tightly caulked beds.

Very simple, if you knew what you were doing, and had planned ahead of time. For all his education, would he have thought of such an elegant solution?

Annie stood behind Bird, wringing the water from the bottom of her skirt. Not that it would take much time to dry, in the heat of the afternoon, but she hated the flap of wet cloth against her legs. By peeking over Bird's back, she could see Dunk. He was thoroughly soaked from splashing about in the deepest part of the river. His pants clung to his legs, revealing the long muscles of his thighs and, when he turned his back, the narrow curves of his buttocks.

She shuddered, stood up straight and looked resolutely in another direction. The sight reminded her too painfully of another young man. Not that she had seen Davy's thighs, for the room had been dark. But she had learned the configuration of his body with her fingertips. Her hands had expressed her love, caressed his tight rear end, stroked his lean hips. That Dunk could revive the memory made her hate him more.

"Yankee men are all liars," she confided to Bird. "You can't trust one of them. Dunk was told to stay with me, yet he went dashing into the river."

She rubbed the horse's flanks with the edge of her palm, pushing the water down his sides. Bird stirred with pleasure, so she continued the gentle grooming. Bird shook his head, his mane grazing her hair as she leaned against him. She did not hear Graybob's approach, did not lift her head until the shadow of horse and man fell over her.

"Perk says we're going on a few more miles before we camp," Dunk said. "He wants to get the herd away from the river, for it's boggy downstream and he's afraid the cattle will get stuck."

She refused to respond, didn't even look up. Was Perk now explaining his movements to this greenhorn, instead of simply giving orders? Bird turned his head, stared at her with appealing eyes. Her hand had stopped kneading the horse's shoulder. Unconsciously she had responded to Dunk's closeness.

"Thank you," she said gruffly. She mounted Bird and headed for the wagons.

The cowboys on the right side of the herd waved, and someone yelled, "We'll change Huzzy's name to Dunk and start calling you Huzzy!" Dunk waved and laughed.

Annie's hands tightened on the reins. Dunk was still at the bottom of the pecking order, but not so far down as he had been.

When Dunk spurred away from her side, her first reaction had been contempt, for she had supposed he was frightened at the thought of swimming the river. Only when he entered the water had she noticed Huzzy's frantic struggles. For one instant, she had glimpsed the cowboy's terrified face, and her heart had stopped. In those seconds when Dunk's hand clasped the blue shirt so precariously, she had nearly flown after him, plunged into the river to help. She would have, except that Sid had noticed her impulse. His voice had cut through her nerves like a knife, ordering her to stay where she was.

Graybob. Dunk's horse. Dunk had saved Huzzy because of Graybob. His eight-hundred-dollar horse. Any of the men might have made the rescue, if he'd been in the right place and had a horse like Graybob. Any of the men could have done it, if he'd been born rich and a thousand or two thousand dollars meant no more to him than a two-bit bandanna. Very few of the cowboys would ever in their lives see eight hundred dollars, all together in one pile. That great abyss stretched between them and Dunk.

She lifted her head with sudden satisfaction. Dunk, no matter what he accomplished, would never be accepted by the cowhands. He was rich, they were not. No matter how many cowboys he pulled away from danger, he remained an outsider.

She gulped as a new thought floated through her busy mind. Dunk would stick with the drive. No weak man, afraid of hardship, had driven his horse into that river. No stupid man had timed his plunge into the current so precisely that he was able to grab Huzzy as he swept by.

"I don't want him here," she muttered to herself. She glanced around, saw him behind her, off to the side. His drying trousers had tightened on his legs, revealing more of their shape. "More than ever, I don't want him here. I can't trust him. I'm not sure I can trust myself. I couldn't trust myself with Davy, and I knew him only a few weeks. The trip to Montana will take months!" She groaned, pressed her hands against her body as if she might compress the expanding flower below her heart, strangle it, make it once more sere and dry. When Dunk dashed into the river, in that horrible fraction of a minute when the rescue was in doubt, the bud had opened a trifle more. Its petals fluttered close to her heart.

Stack waved the signal to camp, and Sid swung the chuck wagon aside toward the creek. Brenerd followed more slowly with her own wagon. If she could find a private spot on the creek, she might bathe and put on clean clothes. The muddy river water had dyed the bottom of her skirt red, and the short pantaloons she wore beneath it were stiff with sweat.

She slowed Bird to a walk as she rode beside the trees and bushes lining the upper reaches of the watercourse. She investigated each bend of the small stream. One hundred yards above the wagons she found the perfect spot, a shallow pool with a flat bottom of limestone, almost completely surrounded by a thicket. She turned Bird over to Brenerd.

"See him to the remuda, would you please?" The man made no answer, but he frowned even more than normal. She collected her towel and clothes from the wagon, released her hair from its bun and plaited it into twin braids. The camp rang with the busy noises of evening. Firewood snapped under Sid's boot; the first flames crackled; men grunted, lifting the saddles from their mounts; horses nickered with relief and rolled on the ground; the harness chains clinked; men shouted as they heaved the bedrolls from the wagon. She would be quite safe in her private pool.

The brush along the creek turned out to be much thicker than it had appeared from the back of a horse. Tough high grass grew in tangles between thorny bushes, vines climbed spindly trees. She could not be more than twenty feet from the water, yet she could not see it. Following a circuitous path through willow trees, she lifted a drooping limb to crawl over a prostrate trunk. The stream flowed a few feet away. Sunlight reflected off the water and momentarily blinded her.

"Woo—eeee."

He squatted in the center of the pool, in the midst of the brilliance. Her situation might have been tenable if he had stayed submerged. But just as her eyes focused, just as her brain told her arm to drop the branch and her legs to step backward, at that moment he stood up. He scrubbed his shoulders, his chest, his loins, with a dripping bandanna. The hair on his chest stood out, dark with moisture. He bent to rinse the bandanna; the muscles running from his body to his thighs stretched. Annie shut her eyes to keep from seeing more. A great splash and a gleeful shout. She opened her eyes in alarm.

He swam the length of the pool, powerful arms lifting and plunging, heading to the opposite bank. He turned and swam straight toward her. He pulled himself onto a ledge of rock not six feet from where she stood, his back to her. He twisted and turned beneath the narrow length of flannel.

What to do? If she moved, he would hear. If she stayed motionless, he would discover her when he left. Pretend she had only just arrived. That would be best.

He sat down, dried his feet, paying great attention to the spaces between his toes. Annie inched backward, dropped the limb slowly to screen her view of the pond.

"Hello!" she yelled. "Is anyone here?" The silence lasted only a second or two, but seemed an hour.

"Yes." Did his single word betray a bit of shock? She imagined him frantically wrapping the towel around his hips to cover what she had already seen. "I'm sorry, Annie. Did you wish to use this swimming hole?"

"It seemed to be the best spot," she said, keeping her tone as formal as his.

"So I noticed when we arrived," he agreed. "I shall be dressed quickly." Leaves rustled. A bush three feet away swayed as he lifted his clothing from it. Her hand went out to the branch separating them. She should not peek. Her hand grasped the leafy screen, even as her mind said no.

He had on dark underclothes. He stood on one leg to pull his pants on. A long-sleeved shirt flapped, then covered his arms. He sat down to pull on his boots. She stepped back, fearful of what he might say if he found her so close. The crack of twigs, the slap of limbs, warned her he had left the rock.

"May I stand guard while you take your bath?" he asked. Her legs quivered, for the question suggested that he would take her place, a voyeur, peering through the willows. Would he sketch her as she bathed?

"No, I think everyone is busy. I won't be bothered."

"I'll tell the cowboys to stay downstream," he said.

"No," she said sharply. "You might as well shout that I'm on display to anyone with an excuse to get on a horse and ride upstream."

"Then I think it would be best if I took up my position not far from here, warning the men away. Many of them must have observed this bathing—"

"You'll spy on me," she said heatedly. "Do you frequently use live models, Mr. van Kelson?" She had heard of fallen women who actually posed naked for artists.

"Seldom," he replied, without emotion. "And certainly only when the model volunteers herself or himself."

Himself! Men? She had never considered that men, as well as women, could serve as models. Did women artists observe men in their nakedness? The idea repulsed her.

"Go anywhere you want," she snapped. "Just be sure you can't see me. If I find out you've spied, I'll kill you."

"I have no doubt," he said modestly, but she did not like the lilt in his voice, as if she had said something very amusing. She watched his back as he shouldered his way through the brush.

"I'm out of the thicket, Annie. I'll sit here until you're done."

"Protecting me?" she cried derisively.

"Your father asked that I accompany you for exactly that reason. To protect you," he answered calmly. She hated that he could be so infernally levelheaded, so blasted eventempered. She longed to make him furious, fighting angry.

"So you vowed to protect me, against every man but yourself," she accused. She waited for his reply. Nothing. Not so much as a leaf trembled. She dropped onto the flat rock, unbuttoned her bodice, untied the tapes that fastened her skirt to her underclothes. She wished she'd thought to bring one of her long shifts. She might bathe in it, safe from prying eyes. But it was almost impossible to swim with fabric bunched about one's legs. And she did so long to stretch her weary muscles by swimming across the pond.

She strained her eyes, searching the path Dunk had taken through the thicket. She couldn't imagine he could come back silently. Yet it was conceivable that, by moving very slowly...

She stepped into the water, crouched at the foot of the rock, dabbed at herself with a sponge, climbed out, dried and donned her clean clothes. It wasn't the bath she had hoped to have, energetic and refreshing, but it was better than nothing. She found Dunk lounging against a tree at the edge of the brush, his sketchbook on his bent knee. She leaned over to see what he had drawn. The camp, two wagons, Sid bent over the fire.

"Turn back a page," she ordered. He flipped the sheet obediently. Nothing but a mass of horns. Horns of every conceivable kind—twisted, smooth, flaring, curled upward, curled down.

"Thank you," she said, heading for her wagon.

"What are you thanking me for?" he called. She stopped, but didn't turn around.

"For not sneaking up on me, for not making any improper pictures of me."

"I told you I wouldn't do that!" he protested, wounded. *Good, I've insulted him,* she thought. *I've hurt his silly feelings by questioning his silly sense of honor.*

"I know just how dependable the word of a New Yorker is," she said, taunting him. "You may think I'm just a little Texas girl who'll fall all over a rich Yankee. I've had more experience than you think. Eastern men are full of promises, but mighty short on the keeping of them."

She walked away, leaving him sputtering.

That night, around the campfire, she noticed a new relaxation between Dunk and the rest of the men. Always before, a barrier had existed, keeping him slightly beyond the jokes and the serious discussions of business.

"I say, Huzzy, you needn't drink so much coffee," teased Sid. "You must of drunk your fill down there in the river. You think he should have another cup, Dunk?"

"The water he took in carried quite a large quantity of mud," Dunk replied seriously, reminding Annie of a doctor giving a diagnosis. "There's a chance it will settle out in his stomach, like a mud flat. Coffee should kill off any chance grass seed, so he doesn't start a pasture in his stomach." Huzzy started in alarm.

"Be mighty hard to get even one steer down there to graze," offered Soto. "He'd have to swallow some of those little mice what nibble grass."

"Every time he burped," offered Broadbrim, "the cats would come running. I think Dunk's got a point. He'd better drink all the coffee he can hold for a day or two."

"Perk, why don't you let the cattle drink before you push them over the river?" Dunk asked.

Perk answered at some length, patiently, describing the importance of getting the leaders across before they have a chance to hesitate.

"What if the leaders hadn't been willing to go? What if they'd turned around?" Dunk asked.

Annie waited for one of the cowboys to tease him about his ignorance, taunt him as a tenderfoot. When no one laughed, or even offered a mild joke, resentment tightened her chest.

"That's why we have a few cows with calves along," said Stack. "You want the herd to go someplace none of them are anxious to try, you take a calf. He starts bawling, his mama rushes to find him, and the whole herd will follow."

"Usually it works," said Perk. "Though I remember once trying to get a herd through a narrow lane in a little town in south Texas. We took a calf to the other end, he set up crying, but the cow wouldn't go down that path. No way would she be forced into that lane. Finally, the bawling got so bad, she got crazy anxious, she tore right through a bob wire fence, took the whole herd with her. They trampled a cabbage patch and two cornfields, but she got to her baby. Linares had to pay the farmer two hundred dollars."

The stories continued. Annie climbed into her wagon and pulled her blankets over her head to shut out the flickering shadows cast by the fire. The wagon jostled as Dunk accidentally brushed a wheel, spreading his bedroll. She imagined him between his blankets, his shirt and pants rolled into a pillow beneath his head. He'd have nothing on but his dark underwear. She ran her fingertips the length of her body, caressing her silken nightdress, pretending the fabric covered his lean body, not hers. She had touched Davy in that way, but had never seen him. Now she could imagine how he had looked in those exciting, stolen moments.

Would it feel the same with Dunk? Could she trust herself to be near him for five months and not think of him as a man? Could she resist his soft words and strong hands?

Yes, because now I know the terrible results of yielding, she reassured herself. *I'm stronger now. I can wait until I get to Montana, until I marry Hugh McCann. He's a real man who will bring that wonderful excitement to me.* "Dunk doesn't tempt me at all," she whispered in a final lie. "He's too much like Davy. And Davy's a liar and a cad."

She ran her hands down her sides to demonstrate her strength, found her legs spread, harboring a small ache of anticipation. She moaned at the falsehoods she told herself. She had to get rid of this man. If Dunk would not go, she must leave herself, ride east, catch a train to Montana and marry McCann quickly. If she could not control herself, it was the only honorable alternative. She had disgraced her father's name once. She must not do so again.

She forced herself to remember all the horrors that had flowed, inexorably, from those delicious moments with Davy. The months of hiding, the pain of birth, the eternity of gossip. The pleasure had been fleeting; the ache would last forever. The memory of what she had lost caught in her throat, rose moistly in her eyes. She brutally stifled the tears. She would not let him hear her cry.

I've got to get away from him, she thought in despair. *If he will not go, then I must.*

Chapter Six

Annie swung her legs over the tailgate, dipped her head beneath the canvas, dropped to the ground and gasped in surprise. Brenerd stood only a few feet from her, half concealed by the morning mist. His long, sad face was stretched longer and sadder than she had ever seen it. He twisted his slouch hat in his stubby fingers.

"May I ask something of you, miss?" The rare sound of his voice, plus the fact that he had spoken a complete sentence, left her dumbfounded.

"Miss?" he repeated, reminding her of his presence. She coughed to clear her throat.

"Of course. What is it?"

"When do we head back to San Antonio?" he inquired.

"Go back?" she asked, then realized she spoke too loudly. Everyone in camp would hear her.

"Yes. Mr. Linares said you and Dunk, the young Yankee, wouldn't be on the drive but for a few days. That you'd give it up. When do we go back?"

"Linares said *what?*" she shrieked. Let everyone in camp hear the conversation! Brenerd must be lying. Linares could not have believed she would give up!

"Yes, miss. And my wife—"

"You have a wife?" Her astonishment, which had ballooned when he opened his mouth, now became monstrous. This old grump had a wife? But, now that she looked closely, not such an ancient as she had supposed. Thirty-five or forty, perhaps.

"Yes. Marie. And she's in the family way, and I told her I'd be gone but a few days." Annie hung on to the tailgate with both hands. Linares had assured Brenerd she would turn back. Who else? Perk, most certainly. Dunk? Was he part of the plot?

"Linares is wrong," she said sternly. "I intend to go to Montana."

"But there's more rivers, like yesterday, miss." His eyes widened, either with respect for the rivers or in panic at the thought of them. "The Guadalupe is a babe compared to the Red, and the Platte, and you saw yesterday with Huzzy, someone can go down so easy in the crossing of them."

Her arms and legs turned heavy and cold as stone. She stood alone, every man in the world an opponent, to be fought or avoided. She had trusted Linares. She had learned, bitterly, of Yankee cunning and deceit, but a Texan! She trusted Texans to be gentlemen.

All I want is to enjoy myself for a few weeks, do what men do every day, riding open and free, pursuing the horizon. Is every man against every woman? Her lungs pumped up to scream, her fists clenched to hammer into the sorrowful face. No, no! That was an irrational, feminine response, and would only prove, so far as the men were concerned, that her emotions made her unsuitable for a trail drive. She jammed down her feelings, made her eyes narrow and cruel when she returned Brenerd's plaintive stare.

"What did Linares say? Why should I turn back? Is Dunk the one who's supposed to make me go back to San Antonio?"

"Linares says Dunk's nothing but a city boy who's gonna be scared off by the first night sleeping on the ground. And you, he says ladies are too fine to stand the life, that you'll soon see it isn't suitable, that you should take the train to your daddy."

"We've been on the trail close to a week." She tilted her head so she looked down her nose at him. "Do you think Linares told you the truth?" The man stuttered, caught between calling Linares a liar and denying the evidence of his own eyes.

"I'm not sure," he finally confessed. He lowered his eyes and carefully scanned his boots. "You haven't screamed and cried, even at a rattlesnake. And yesterday, when I saw Dunk go after Huzzy, I thought, 'He ain't no city boy scared by the elements.'"

"No, he doesn't seem to be, does he?" she said, her limbs further chilled by the implications of Brenerd's statement. Dunk would ride to Montana; she would not. She would cave under the pressure as man after man lectured her. Men determined what women might do, right and wrong. What they considered ladylike, and what exposed her as a slut. Men could tempt her, seduce her with words weighted with promises. Unless...

She kept the smile inside, so she did not betray a hint of her plans. She would turn this male power to her own advantage. Men thought of women as weak-minded, unable to make plans and stick to them. Men had pride, and that pride was a weakness she could turn against them. Against Dunk.

"You may go home, Brenerd. Take your horse, ride back to San Antonio. I'll tell Sid to sack up some grub."

"But my mules, and the wagon?" he protested.

"As I understood it, Linares bought them on my father's account. They aren't yours any longer. They belong to me."

"I was to buy them back when you gave it up," he said stubbornly. "At half the price paid."

Annie stamped her feet, wished she could spit fire. Whose idea had that been? Linares's? Her father's? What dirty, low-down dogs all men proved to be in the end!

"So, the sooner you convinced me to leave, the more money you'd make from the deal?" she shouted, not caring that her self-control had vanished. "I'm not leaving.

You run on back to your precious wife, but you're not taking the wagon and the mules. My father paid for them, so they'll stay with me. Take your bedroll, your gear, and get off, before we cross another river." The corners of his frown rose slightly.

"Who's to drive the mules?" he asked triumphantly, as if that automatically swung the decision to his side. Annie allowed her smile to surface, let it become a wicked, calculating smile. She folded her arms across her chest.

"Dunk will drive. Mr. van Kelson will become my mule skinner."

"I doubt he knows the caring of mules, miss. Likely harness is beyond him. Your feather bed would be ruint if he ran into a gully or tipped over in a river."

"I imagine he's a bit deficient in driving," she said with relish. "In the East, servants take care of the carriages. But he learns quickly." Her fingers tapped nervously on her upper arms. She could hardly wait to tell Dunk of his change of duties. No longer riding free, on the fringes of the herd. Tied ignominiously to her wagon, to the care of her mules, while she galloped ahead, sneering at his captivity. How long would he stick with the herd then?

"Go back to San Antonio, Brenerd," she ordered. "Go back to Marie. Is this your first child?"

"No, miss. The sixth."

"The sixth!" she exclaimed. "And she's concerned that you're gone, when she's done this five times before?"

"Marie is most stubborn, miss. She made me promise, years ago, that I'll be around when the babes arrive. Otherwise, I'd most likely be a drive foreman. But to please her, I have my wagons and haul about town."

Annie's anger melted into a puddle of pity. No wonder Brenerd snarled and snapped at the world. He longed to ride to Dodge, maybe all the way to Montana. Become a trail boss, sit in the saloons with the cattle buyers and the horse dealers. Instead, his vow tied him to hauling bricks and hay about San Antonio.

Her pity edged into respect. She viewed Brenerd with new eyes. Both men and women took marriage vows, but men thought only women truly bound by them. Men could brush away the ties of home and family, excusing themselves because they must earn a living. Brenerd, however, had sacrificed his ambition in life. He had given up the trail to take responsibility for his family. He must be a terrible grouch to live with, but he did his duty.

Davy and Dunk, her father and Linares, all claimed to be gentlemen, but each would cast a woman aside the moment she became an inconvenience. Her father had moved to Montana without her, without even consulting her, leaving her to be shifted from relative to relative. Linares had pretended to allow her on the drive, but conspired to make it impossible for her to continue. Davy? She must not think of his dreadful abandonment. Dunk? Exactly like the others, as time would undoubtedly show. Brenerd, with his unhappy face and slovenly bearing, was twice the gentleman any of them would ever be. He stuck by his woman.

"Go home, Brenerd," she said gently. "Be with Marie when she needs you. I'll sell the wagon and mules when we get to Montana and send you the money."

"That's not necessary, miss. It would mean your father'd be paying twice for the same merchandise."

"It's the least we can do for you," she said sincerely. "Linares lied to you, and you, naturally, believed him."

"Of course I believed him," said Brenerd. "Linares is a fine gentleman."

"Gentlemen," she fired back, "are the very ones you should distrust. Remember that. Never trust a man who acts like a gentleman. He'll take advantage of you."

Quent shook his tin cup over the breakfast fire, dislodging the last dregs of coffee before he washed it and returned it to the chuck wagon. His bedroll still lay unrolled under Annie's wagon, but he delayed leaving the group around the fire. For the first time, Perk and the cowboys had included him in their conversation. They appreciated his dash to save Huzzy and respected him for it, even though they made nothing but the most jocular reference to the event. Words weren't necessary. They did not turn their backs to him.

He happily contemplated his choice of a horse. Graybob? Or one of the bays? He glanced at Johnny, far beyond the wagons, herding the remuda closer to camp. The ropes for the corral strung out from the wagon wheels. Annie came tearing around the wagon. His whole body recoiled at the fire in her eyes. She held her head high, and her right fist hammered into her left palm.

"Perk!" she yelled, still twenty feet away. "Did Linares tell you I'd not be on this drive for more than a few days? Did he lie to you, too?" Every man turned on Perk, whose face stiffened. He fingered his chin self-consciously.

"What did Linares say?" she shouted, needlessly, for she had planted herself no more than five feet from the foreman. "You might as well tell the truth, because Brenerd's let the cat loose. He thinks it's time to go home. Linares told him I'd skedaddle off at the first rattlesnake."

"Now—now, Miss Annie," said Perk, stuttering. Like any man, he searched for calming words. "He just warned me you might not want to go the whole way...that I should be prepared to swing over to the railroad." Quent had the impression Perk was keeping his hand on his chin to steady it.

"And Dunk? Is he expected to leave with me?" She spun around, her distorted face two feet from his own. "What story did they tell you? Or perhaps your job is to talk me into going back to San Antonio." Thinking on it, considering all the evidence, he realized Linares had not been quite honest about the whole thing.

"I was told to stay with you all the way to Montana, regardless of the way you made the journey," Quent said flatly, knowing she did not believe anything he said.

"Look," said Perk in despair. "Linares didn't know if you'd care for life on the trail. He just wanted to be sure..."

"He told Brenerd I'd be turning back in a few days. Not that I *might* turn back. That I *would* turn back," she cried. "Brenerd hadn't even bothered to make plans for someone to take over his business in San Antonio. Whose job was it to make me go home?"

Perk's eyes swung away from Annie and, to Quent's consternation, fastened upon him. Accused him.

"Linares supposed Dunk wouldn't make it more than a few days out on the trail. And your daddy made it plain you had to have a gentleman along to escort you. So when Dunk washed out, like we figured, you'd have to give it up, too."

Would she believe this? Or would she assume the worst of him? For the first time, he understood her hostility. Her father and Linares and Perk and Brenerd had conspired, tricked her into thinking they welcomed her on the drive. She glared at all the men in turn. Most dropped their eyes, but Quent forced himself to meet her furious glare.

"If Dunk gives up, he gives up for himself, not for me," she announced. "Daddy said I might come to Montana on the drive, and that's how I intend to get there."

Quent watched her carefully, memorized the flare of her nostrils, the hardness of her eyes, the arch of her brows, the line of her mouth, which at the moment might be sketched by a single stroke. Perhaps he had been unable to capture the vitality of her because he had never seen her truly angry—outrageously, righteously furious.

"Brenerd is going home. He has family duties."

"But, Miss Annie," cried Perk. "Who's to drive your wagon?"

"The man Linares hired to take care of me," she said with sudden sweetness. Quent saw the laughter, the derision, in her eyes. "Dunk will take care of the wagon."

"But he's gonna catch on to herding and roping real quick," Stack cried in protest. "Why, just yesterday, Perk said he's to have a regular spot when we're crossing rivers, to do just as he did for Huzzy if one of us has trouble."

"Dunk was hired on to be my escort, not part of the crew," she said coolly. She didn't bother to hide the triumph in her voice, in the set of her shoulders. Women were so openly cruel when they bested a man.

Quent turned, walked away from the fire, bound for nowhere. He must control his temper. Johnny had the remuda a short distance from camp. Quent kicked moodily at a clump of grass. Graybob, the three bays, of no use at all if he sat all day on the seat of that damned wagon. Why did she hate him so much? He had not lied to her.

She hates me and I hate her. Annie Brownell is a spoiled, strong-minded shrew. Look at the way she's dressed! No respectable woman would prance about in a skirt that's nothing more than disguised trousers. This man McCann, does he know the devil-inspired trickster he's getting? I almost feel sorry for him.

Quent considered riding back to San Antonio with Brenerd, finding a herd that needed a cowboy, not a servant for a blasted female imp. He'd rather ride in the dust at the rear of ten thousand cattle than play the fool for Annie's whims. He clenched his teeth, stooped under the wagon, rolled his blankets and tied them in a bundle. A few things—a spare bridle, his rope—were still in the wagon. He leaned over the tailgate to pull them out.

If you leave, a voice within him said, *she wins.*

"Let her win," he snarled into the ethereal blue interior.

Her blankets lay in a careless tumble, revealing the white sheet on the mattress. Her silken nightdress cascaded like snow against the dark gray of the blankets. Delicate. Beneath the fury lurked feminine delicacy, a fragility the cowboys respected. Except for two, perhaps three, whose crude comments he had heard. Stack, regardless of his herding skills, did not have the commanding grip demanded of a foreman. If an emergency called Perk away... It might happen right on this mattress. A vision of her, struggling against two of them, a bandanna muffling her cries for help. Quent's throat turned dry.

Annie might not want him around, she hated him, but he'd made the bargain with Linares and her father. He shoved the bridle and the rope into the corner of the wagon, accepting the fact that he would not need them in the days to come. He retrieved his bedroll, jammed it against the tailgate, taking out his anger on the innocent blankets. This was not between him and Annie Brownell, but between men. Men expected men to keep their word, honor their contracts.

"Brenerd," he called as he turned around. "Anything about this harness different from the usual?" For the first time, he saw something besides resignation in Brenerd's eyes. Something like pity.

"Nothing out of the ordinary. I'll show you." Quent followed him to the pile of collars and the complexity of leather straps and chains.

"She's not an easy woman," Brenerd said heartily. "Sure you don't want to ride back with me?"

"No one said it would be easy," said Quent, to convince himself more than Brenerd. "I said I'd get her to Montana, and by God I'll get her to Montana, if I have to bind and gag her."

"Possible," said Brenerd, nodding. "Possible."

Much to Quent's regret, Perk swung far west to avoid the settlements spreading out from Abilene. He'd planned to dash into the town one evening, hire a man to drive the wagon, so he could get back on his horse. Get back to doing what he had dreamed of doing. He flipped the whip lazily over the backs of the mules, aiming at the front right animal, who shirked every chance he got.

Each morning Annie lifted her wide-brimmed hat, its dancing fringe taunting him, bade him goodbye and trotted off, well ahead, sometimes out of sight. Within a few days they would cross the Red River, into the Indian Nations. Might a lone woman, riding in advance of a herd of three thousand cattle, be in danger? The Indians levied a toll on the herds passing across their land. If Indians got hold of Annie, how many cattle might they demand as ransom?

The land ahead lay flat as a table, then dropped gradually toward the next river. The Wichita, according to his map. He saw Annie as a speck ahead and to the right. Off to his left, the mile-long string of cattle plodded under the dust kicked up by their feet. The dust hung in the still air, a permanent canopy over the herd. He watched Sid from the corner of his eye, letting the chuck wagon determine the pace, letting the cook choose the moment when they would move ahead of the herd in preparation for the noon break.

"Hold up!" Sid yelled unexpectedly. "Perk's holding the herd."

"What for?"

"Darned if I know. We'll find out soon enough, I suspect." They waited, the cattle milled about, moved a bit off the trail in their search for grass. An hour passed before Perk, Stack and Annie rode to the wagons.

"Might as well get a fire going and fix something to eat," said Perk. "Stack says there's a town up ahead."

"Town?" asked Sid in astonishment. "But we came this way last year. Weren't no town."

"There is now," said Stack. "Down in the river bottoms. Houses, at least. And fields with bob wire and seeded corn just coming up."

A half dozen cowboys rode in, excited by the change in routine. They chattered, all at once, asking Stack about the town that had spread so unexpectedly across the driving road. "A saloon?" "Any women?" "Any chance of a game?"

"Can't we swing west?" asked Quent. His map of Texas showed no settlements at all between them and the Red River.

"There's no good crossing on the river west of here."

"We could just shove the herd through, show these nesters a thing or two," suggested Huzzy.

"Shut up and listen to what Stack has to say," ordered Perk. They gathered around as Sid pulled a few sticks from the rawhide slung under the chuck wagon. He placed a bit of tinder in a shallow trench, added tiny bits of wood, scratched a match into life.

"This here town," Stack said, "ain't nothing but maybe sixty or seventy people, with their fields spread along the river. I hunted up what seems to be the head man, and he says they don't want to stop the drives. But we got to be real careful, 'cause they don't want their crops trampled. They left a space for us to get through, one road, but we're to take only a hundred or so head at a time. There's a place north of town he showed me with good enough grass to hold the herd until they're all moved through."

"Not time enough to finish today, if we take only a hundred at a time," said Perk. "This will use up two days."

"More than that," Stack said mysteriously. "They won't let us go through at all unless we agree to stick around for a horse race tomorrow."

"A what?" exclaimed Perk.

"A horse race. Once we get the herd through, they want a horse race. The best of our remuda against their best."

"Betting?" asked Perk.

"I never heard of a horse race without betting."

"Well, they'll lose everything they put up," said Broadbrim, "for none of theirs could beat Dunk's gray."

Quent eyed the cheerful group. Every one of them contemplated how much money he'd tucked into his bed, how much he might win on such a race.

"No," he said sharply.

"But, Dunk... We could skin these nesters clean. They'll not expect us to have any horse like Graybob in the remuda."

"You don't have Graybob in the remuda, remember? He's mine. I have only four horses to last me all the way to Montana. The rest of you have ten or twelve apiece. I won't let Graybob be run to exhaustion in a race."

"You're not riding him at all," protested Lucas. "You're driving Miss Annie's wagon."

"Temporarily," said Quent, looking at Annie when he said it, to enjoy the surprise widening her eyes. They narrowed as she tried to work out the meaning of his remark. The cowboys all started jabbering, intent on making him change his mind, but Perk stepped in.

"Dunk doesn't have to run his horse if he doesn't want to," he said firmly. "The whole thing sounds crazy to me. Why should these farmers want to pound their horses in a race, when it's the planting and haying season?"

"Probably just want some excitement," said Stack. "Can you imagine living out here, every month of the year?"

Quent couldn't imagine it, although he tried. Cold in winter, hot in summer, the wind blowing a gale half the days of the year, filtering dust or snow through a shanty's sievelike walls. Mud when it rained, so deep a team couldn't move. Boredom and isolation might send a man to perdition.

He remembered his sisters complaining when snow cut them off from a party. He himself had snarled in outrage when a train did not run on time. How spoiled we are! he marveled.

"Douse that fire," Perk said suddenly. Sid sighed, replaced the pots and pans in the wagon. "The wagons through first. Stack, you go ahead and show Sid where we're to leave the herd north of town. Sid, get a meal cooked, and the men will come in to eat one by one. That way we get as many cattle as possible through before nightfall."

"We'll be split overnight, with some south of town," objected Stack.

"Can't be helped. We'll bring the rest through at first light, then get the crazy horse race over with."

"Dunk." Annie jerked upright in her wagon. The round hole of sky visible through the rear of the wagon cover still showed dark. "Dunk," again.

"What? Huzzy?" inquired Dunk's voice sleepily.

"I gotta go out with the others, to get the rest of the herd through town. Could you loan me ten dollars? I'll pay you back tonight. I ain't got no money to bet on the race."

"No, Huzzy. I won't lend you ten dollars," Dunk answered wearily.

"Please, Dunk. Stack looked in every corral around here last night, and these folks ain't got a horse to beat one like Hellcock, or even Stack's best."

"Do you think they'd keep their best racer on public view?" Dunk's tone exposed his exasperation. "He's probably hidden in someone's kitchen."

"But, Dunk, this is my chance to win enough to pay Stack and Lucas what I owe them."

"What you've lost playing poker in the evenings?"

A long silence before the young cowboy said, "Yes."

"Gambling on a horse race isn't exactly a sure thing, Huzzy. What if you lose the ten dollars you borrow from me? Then you'd owe me *and* Stack and Lucas. Do you have anything coming from your pay in Montana, or have you already gambled it away?"

"I still got some coming," Huzzy said petulantly. "I could pay you when we get to Montana."

Annie crawled from her blankets, stuck her head out the back of the canvas cover.

"Shut up," she hissed. "I expected to sleep late this morning." A dark figure on all fours scrambled backward, out from under the wagon.

"Sorry, Miss Annie. I didn't think I'd wake you."

"Are you lending him ten dollars, Dunk?" she asked, leaning over, risking falling over the tailgate in order to stare at the recumbent figure under the wagon.

"No. I believe gambling with borrowed money is a very bad policy, particularly if you're the lender."

"I'll sell you my six-shooter," said Huzzy with sudden inspiration.

"I've got one, Huzzy."

"You do? You never wear it."

"I don't wear my waterproof, except when it's raining," he retorted. "Get those blasted steers through town, then sit and watch the race without sending all your money to the devil. A horse race can be quite entertaining without a penny riding on a nose."

Huzzy turned and walked away. Annie saw his slumped shoulders, realized the first light of morning had spread across the land. The clatter of the coffeepot lid sent its alarm through the camp.

"If you were Chinese," she said, directing her voice to the body under the wagon, "you'd have no alternative but to lend him the money. You saved his life, so you'd be responsible for him for so long as he lived."

"I'm not Chinese. The boy's lost nearly all the pay he'll get at the end of the drive. He's an inept poker player, and Stack and Lucas take advantage of him." He said it as a statement of fact, without condemning anyone.

"Do you really think a horse race can be exciting without placing a bet?"

"Of course. I've done it myself, many times."

"What are you back in New York? Some kind of puritan?"

"An aversion to gambling can be based upon something other than religious scruples." She snorted at his pomposity. "My objection, personally, is based upon mathematics and theories of chance, an understanding of odds and how they can be manipulated."

She was interested in spite of herself. Mathematics had something to do with how cards and dice fell? If she had known that when she dozed in a corner of a saloon, she might have watched the poker games more closely.

"How can odds be manipulated?" she asked quickly, to keep him talking.

"In most games of chance, one side has better odds than the other. The gambler simply takes the side with the best chance of winning, and over the weeks and months he comes out on top. Occasionally he'll lose, and some lucky man struts around with his winnings for a few hours, certain he's discovered the key to riches. Until he gets into another game, and loses."

"But in horse racing, the best horse will win."

"Unless someone with the second-best horse has a bit of opium powder, or knows how to slide a long needle into a horse's leg, leaving him crippled with no obvious wound."

Annie slid back under the canvas top, horrified. She visualized a sneak thief, all in black, creeping up on Jenny or Bird or Lily, burying a long pin in some vital spot.

"You didn't know cheats did things like that?" he asked. She stuck her head out, but didn't answer him. "I've seen horses who, ten minutes before a race, looked like sure things. On the track, they're stumbling, falling and hurting their riders."

"Maybe that's the way things are in the East," she said proudly, "but Texans have more honor."

"I saw this in the East," he said sarcastically. "East Texas. Just before I came to San Antonio."

Annie sat back on her heels. A faint morning breeze played seductively down the low neck of her nightdress, but she ignored the tempting sensation.

"I'd been thinking of letting them run Bird," she said in a low voice.

"Reconsider. Or, if you want to see him run, have three or four men about the horse every minute. Don't let one of these farmers near him." Annie crawled back to her blankets, drew them over her. She had only the three horses to get her all the way to Montana.

Rustling sounds told her Dunk was getting up, spreading his blankets over the wheel to catch the first rays of the sun and the morning breeze. Then came a small click, the sound of the silver tongue of his belt going through the buckle. Now he would sit down and pull on his boots. Now, off toward the fire and breakfast.

The sight of his back signaled her to get dressed, not an easy chore in the confines of the wagon. Strip the night-dress over her head, pull on her short chemise, stockings and pantaloons, then a light corset, without stays, one that did not interfere with her movements when she rode. Pull the batiste corset cover over her head, then struggle into the split skirt, first pulling it above her knees, then inching it over her hips while she knelt with her rump toward the rear of the wagon. She hated that moment, when she'd not see a man peeking in the small hole left by the tightly drawn pucker-ing strings. Last of all, her bodice, with several inches of peplum to cover the top of her skirt.

Today, in the presence of the settlers, she had best but-ton the panel across the front when she dismounted. She'd grown careless around the cowboys, and she seldom tried to disguise the fact that she wore trousers. She dug around in her box of clothing, found one of the discarded bustles at the bottom. She sat on the edge of the tailgate to pull on her boots, then, after loosening the puckering strings, opened the canvas, swung her legs about, lowered herself to the ground.

"What horse for you today, Miss Annie?" asked Johnny as she came to the fire.

"Jenny." She thought of a long needle in the hands of one of the settlers. "Make sure Bird and Lily stay here, in the camp. Tie them to the wagon wheels, or hobble them."

"You're not racing Bird?" asked Lucas, obviously dis-appointed.

"No. I have but the three horses. I can't risk any of them." She spoke sharply, and the cowboys still about the fire turned away without protest, accepting her decision. Good! They were learning not all women could be cajoled into doing things their way.

The cowboys rode off, heading south to move the rest of the herd through the settlement. Perk stared after them, then came back to the fire.

"Dunk, you and Annie ride north five, maybe ten miles, find some better grazing than this." He studied the circle of the horizon. East, where the sky already brightened with the rising sun; north, where a few clouds rested like rosy pillows upon the skyline. "The settlers' cattle and passing herds have grazed all the grass down to the roots for two or three miles around. It doesn't make sense for them to want us to stay here—" he shook his head "—even for one extra day, because that takes grass away from their own animals. I can't figure what's in their minds, but to get the herd through town I had to agree to this crazy race. If you hear or see anything . . ." His voice dwindled. "You understand, Annie?"

She did not want to be paired with Dunk, and she opened her mouth to say so. The crease across Perk's eyes deepened, the folds from his nostrils to the corners of his mouth went into his chin. Perk was worried. Her protest died. She must not load on greater burdens than he already carried.

"I understand. Do you intend to drive the herd away from the settlement today?" she asked.

"Yes. Find the closest place where there's good bed ground. We'll run a few races, then shut the whole thing down as soon as we can, without making the nesters mad."

Chapter Seven

Annie could not tell Dunk to stay behind her and out of sight, because Perk had given the orders to him. Perk had made her Dunk's assistant. She ground her teeth in frustration, until she remembered Perk's knit brows and tight mouth. The boss had given them an important job; she resigned herself to doing it.

Dunk did not crowd her, but he did not keep his distance, either. An internal quake sped her heart and opened her lungs. She took deep breaths of air newly flavored by morning dew. How wonderful to be alive! How marvelous to be on horseback, on the wide prairie!

A gully ten or twelve feet deep blocked their way. During the spring melt, a stream had run in the bottom, but now it held nothing but a string of mud-fringed puddles. Instead of consulting her, Dunk rode upstream a bit, guided Graybob down a slope where the bank had caved in. The horse sank fetlock-deep in ooze.

"It's okay," he called, "but don't hesitate, or Jenny will sink in the muck."

She followed Graybob's prints, descended into a cloud of mosquitoes. She tapped the horse with her spurs, telling her to hurry. Annie clung to Jenny's mane as the mare scrambled out of the gully. Dunk waited for her, his hat off, beating the air to rid himself of the mosquitoes that had followed the scent of warm blood. Why did she smile in thanks for his having tarried?

It's his job. But a pulse throbbed in her neck, warmed her face. She snatched off her hat to cover her confusion, discovered a dozen healthy mosquitoes perched on the crown.

"More reason than mud to hurry through that gulch," she said, to distract both of them from the sudden rush of heat. *I hate him.* She brushed the mosquitoes away, slapped at her shoulders and Jenny's flanks, using the activity as an excuse to keep her face averted.

"What do you think the farmers are up to?" she asked. She must talk about something, anything, to still the flutter in her chest.

"I don't know, but I feel the way Perk does. Whatever their scheme, it's not good, for us at least."

"Can't you, by the process of logical deduction, figure it out?" she teased. "The way Edgar Allan Poe's detective does?" The teasing did not decrease the flutter, which now drifted to her throat.

He shook his head. "Nothing makes any sense. Unless they're just dreadfully bored, living way out here, and want some excitement."

A low ridge separated two seasonal streams.

"Grass," she exclaimed, pointing to a green haze in the distance. "And there's a high spot, a good bedding ground."

"Let's go," he said. She rebelled at the thought of riding tamely beside him, following his directions and decisions. If this continued, she'd be drawn into his orbit, her independence stifled.

"Race you!" she yelled, digging her spurs into Jenny's flanks and slapping her neck. She left him behind, leaned over the horse, urging her on. The wind whipped off her hat; it thumped against her shoulders, the string cutting her neck so firmly it would leave a mark. From behind came the thunder of Graybob's hooves on the dry prairie.

"Go, go!" she shouted at Jenny. She loved the chaos of the gallop, her hair tumbling free, tears in her eyes from the impact of the wind, her body tensed to join with the power of the horse. Something inside her loins detached itself, drifted upward, carrying with it the knotted bud of her desires. With it came a premonition of how things would end. The gray horse ran even with Jenny now, his muscles standing out as if they belonged to a sculpture. She must win. If she did not, Dunk had the upper hand. The gray horse pulled ahead, and in one flash her eyes absorbed the rider. Hatless, his blond hair flapping wildly. The blue eyes squinted against the self-generated wind, the long arms hugged his body, the slender hands barely touched the reins, the strong thighs gripped the horse.

He will win, her heart said, *and he will not leave, and you will accept him.* She stopped shouting at Jenny and faced the inevitable. She had tried ridicule, shame, degradation, and still he persisted. Now he would beat her at a race she had instigated. She wanted to sob in disappointment and frustration, but didn't dare.

Beyond the grassy plateau, the land fell away in all directions, taking with it a sparkling stream flowing amid low trees and brush. He stood beside Graybob, walking the winded horse to the water. She reined Jenny, dismounted, approached nearer to him than she ever had before.

"No wonder the cowboys want you to run Graybob."

"Only against Jenny," he gasped, out of breath himself. "And just this once. We both must spare the horses if we intend to get to Montana."

Montana. To Montana, together.

He knelt by the stream and scooped the clear water in his cupped hands. She followed, blinking back tears, knowing this was the sequence from now on. He would lead, the New York greenhorn, and she would follow.

"Ready to head back to that horse race?" he asked. His eyes glowed, his hair stood in tousled curls, as if still controlled by the wind.

He doesn't understand that things have changed. How ~~lo~~ng before Dunk realized his power? He held her stirrup ~~w~~hile she mounted, handed her the handkerchief she had ~~ab~~andoned beside the stream. She studied the thrust of his ~~le~~g as he climbed on Graybob, knew how it looked beneath ~~th~~e fabric. His body strained as he leaned down to retrieve ~~hi~~s hat.

"Annie." His subdued voice frightened her. What would ~~h~~e ask of her? "I'm going to find some man or sturdy boy ~~in~~ this place, hire him to drive the wagon."

Tiny flowers hid within the tall grass. She must pick some ~~an~~d press them in her diary, to remind her of what hap~~pe~~ned this day. His eyes leveled upon her, waiting for her ~~ob~~jections, prepared for the explosion of temper.

"I think that's a fine idea," she said, unable to control the ~~qu~~aver in her voice. Did he hear it? "I'd feel better having ~~yo~~u ride with me," she admitted, both to herself and to him. ~~"~~My father will be happy to pay him."

"I'll take care of that myself," he said casually. He did ~~no~~t smile in triumph. Only Sid remained in camp, so he had ~~to~~ listen to their excited descriptions of the prime grazing less ~~th~~an five miles ahead. He poured thick coffee, the last in the ~~po~~t, into their tin cups. He fried some bacon, served it hot, ~~dr~~ipping with grease, on cold biscuits. They ate leaning ~~ag~~ainst her wagon, reins looped about their wrists.

"All the cattle are through," Sid said. "Everyone's gone ~~to~~ the race." His sidelong glance swung from her to Dunk, ~~th~~en back again. A foot, no more, separated them. Sid's ~~st~~ocky body straightened in surprise. *Sid sees things have ~~ch~~anged, and in a few days everyone will know.*

"You going to run Graybob?" asked Sid, his eyes busy ~~ap~~praising the inches between them. Annie shifted a bit ~~ag~~ainst the side of the wagon, narrowed the space separat~~in~~g her from Dunk, just to convince Sid he wasn't seeing ~~th~~ings.

"No," said Dunk. "He's got better places to run than in ~~a r~~ace against some settler's ringer."

"So you think there's a ringer. So do I. They've got a horse or two stashed away that Stack missed—a horse who'll beat the entire remuda."

"Is Perk at the race?" asked Dunk.

"I guess. He hasn't been around."

"I want to see him, ask if he'd object if I hire on a boy to drive Annie's wagon. She and I both agree, she needs a driver." Sid's eyes widened, his lips curled, and his eyes sparkled.

"Linares is pretty firm about no boys on a drive, but Perk would probably make an exception here," he said. "Just so he don't have nothing to do with the cattle."

Dust and noise marked the location of the race, near the plowed fields. A large man on a tall yellow horse fell in beside Annie and Quent as they approached.

"So this is the gray all the cowboys talk about," he said heartily. He lifted his hat. "Ardisson's the name."

"Van Kelson," said Dunk. "This is Miss Brownell."

"Never seen a woman on a drive before." He shifted his reins, and his horse moved so close to Jenny that his leg nearly touched hers. She would collide with Graybob and Dunk if she moved in the other direction. Ardisson's gaze locked on her chest. He smiled without bothering to look her in the face.

The cowboys were jumping up and down, yelling, slapping one another's shoulders. One of the remuda horses must have won a heat. Annie gave Jenny a little tap on the neck, and the mare sped up and left Ardisson behind.

"What's happening?" she asked of no one in particular.

"Perk's horse just beat that farmer's nag," said Stack. "All just for fun. These dust-busters don't have no money hardly at all to bet. No more'n two bits at a time."

Annie's shoulders relaxed. So there was no sinister plot behind the race. Just a bunch of bored people, looking for one day of pleasure. She twisted in the saddle to find Dunk. He spoke with Ardisson, but Ardisson did not bother to keep his eyes on the man. They continually shifted to her.

he had heard women speak of leering men, men whose lust
ame plain through their eyes. Now she knew what they
meant. She turned away from him, uneasy.

The farm women wore faded calico dresses, the hems so
agged she could see their legs up to midcalf. Around the
attered folds hung ten or twelve children. Two of the
women cradled babies in their arms. Annie considered
oining them, but Dunk blocked her way.

"Come away from here," he said sharply. Must he make
t so obvious that he led now, that she followed? He stopped
fifty feet beyond the cluster of cowboys.

"What is it?" she asked.

"Doesn't this crowd look a bit strange to you?" She
tared back at the ragtag cluster of men, women, and chil-
ren.

"No. It's just a bunch of farmers, enjoying themselves."

"Look, Annie!" he commanded. "There are men,
women and young children. But where are the other chil-
ren? The ones thirteen and fourteen and fifteen years
ld?" Now that he mentioned it...

"The herd," she whispered in alarm. "They could send
he older children to the herd!"

"Yes. You and I, we're going to play the part of sophis-
cates, bored by this rustic play. We'll mosey away to the
orth, but circle to the south once we're out of sight. I no-
ced two sod corrals south of the fields, empty when we
ame through. I'd wager Graybob they're not empty now."

They eased away from the settlement, heading slowly
ortheast. In the protection of a gully, they managed to drift
bit south. Two hours passed before Annie picked out the
walls of the corrals, the same color and texture as the sur-
ounding prairie. Above the solid walls something moved,
writhing mass of discontent. Horns!

"How many have they taken?" she asked. "Forty?"

"Forty or fifty. We'll let down the bars and drive them
ack. We'll probably meet the rustlers coming in with forty
r fifty more."

"No need to drive them back," she pointed out. "Just open the gate. They'll hurry back to the herd on their own."

They both heaved at the heavy poles blocking the corral. As she had foreseen, the steers, released from the waterless pen, set out for the stream and their fellows at a run. They rode a quarter mile to the next corral, found it empty, but heavy timbers leaned against the walls, ready to be placed across the opening.

"They're out gathering more steers," Dunk said. "You get back to the race, use some excuse to draw Perk aside and tell him what's going on. I'll ride out and try to spot the youngsters."

"Do you think that's wise?" she asked. "Alone?" She looked at his belt. "Dunk, you don't even have your gun."

"These rustlers are children, remember. I wouldn't shoot at them in any event."

"Don't go near them. Just get them in your sight and stick with them. I'll get the cowboys out there as fast as I can." He turned Graybob west, toward the herd beyond the horizon.

"Don't take any chances," she called. He lifted his hat and smiled.

She encouraged Jenny into a trot along the lane the herd had taken through the settlement, the most direct way to the racecourse. The path headed due north, between barbed wire, jogged around an adobe barn with a gaping, unshuttered door. Someone, years before, had tried to make a go of farming in this place and had failed.

She slowed at the corner. The tall yellow horse blocked her way. Ardisson raised his hat, smiled at her—a smile so cold and threatening she shivered.

"Never seen a woman on a drive before," he said. She spurred Jenny, jerked her head, telling her to swing around the man, but the yellow horse anticipated her. The man's huge hand grabbed the reins as she brushed against him. The barn door yawned, cavernous and dark. Jenny plunged, kicked, at being so forcefully led where she did not want to

o. Annie jerked on the rein, almost pulled it from Ardisson's grasp, but he raised his quirt, slammed it down on her left arm. The pain flashed from wrist to shoulder. She cried out, cradled the limb with her right hand as they passed from the sunshine to the dim interior of the barn.

Ardisson leaped to the ground, pulled her from Jenny's back, paying no heed as she beat on his head and shoulders with her fists. He flung her aside, and she staggered wildly, fell onto a pile of hay.

He intends to rape me, she thought, amazed at the clarity of her mind. She rolled over onto her hands and knees, ignoring the pain in her arm. *Think,* she commanded her brain. She gauged the distance to the door. Ardisson extended the quirt toward her face.

"You want to feel this again?" he asked. "You be quiet and go along with what I say, nothing bad will happen to you. I'll be quick the first time."

"I can just imagine," she snapped. Something lay beneath her hand, deep within the hay, hard, small, almost round. It flaked under the pressure of her fingers. Just a clod of dirt, but better than nothing. Ardisson dropped the reins of the two horses, walked toward her, the quirt still extended threateningly, aimed at her eyes.

"Go!" she screamed, rising to her knees, lifting her hand. Jenny's head came up. The clod caught her smartly on the rump.

"Go!" Annie shrieked, scrambling, trying to reach the other horse. The man's hands seized the full legs of her split skirt. He threw her down on the hay, but she had the satisfaction of seeing Jenny leap through the doorway, the long reins dragging in the dust.

"They'll come looking for me." She gasped at the untidy beard and squinting eyes, eyes as yellow as the decrepit horse. Beyond his head she saw the underside of a thatched roof, except where a second floor had been built, about half the length of the barn. From a beam in the roof, a rope angled, the end tied into a loop.

"By the time those cowboys get here, it'll be all over," he said. His hand went to the bottom of her skirt, and he dragged up one leg, peered down, lifted himself, taking a bit of weight from her shoulders.

"What's this?" he asked in surprise.

His distraction gave Annie an opportunity to shove against his chest with all her strength. Ardisson fell sideways, took his hand from her skirt to catch himself. She rolled from underneath him, grasped at the rope, catching the loop over her arm. Could she climb, with her arm hurt? She pulled herself up with her right arm, found the left one weak, barely able to support her weight. She clamped her boots around the rope, lifted her right arm, pulled up again, carrying the loop with her.

Ardisson shouted, wasted several seconds locating his quirt in the hay. She had time to struggle up a few more feet, almost to the level of the haymow. He roared, rushed, bull-like, toward her, the quirt raised to strike. She had her arms over the edge of the mow. She gauged the strength of the blow he would deal her, steeled herself to accept it while at the same time she drew back her leg.

The quirt landed with brutal strength across her hips, but at the same moment the point of her boot caught him in the face. Much to her satisfaction, his scream, not hers, echoed about the solid walls. She ignored the agony circling her lower body, swung her legs once, twice, three times, until her toe caught on the rough timbering of the mow. She crawled into the tenuous protection of the second story, dragged the rope over the lip, just as Ardisson, a hand protecting his right eye, came snarling to grasp it. He fell, groveling in the shallow piles of hay below her.

Annie allowed herself two seconds to examine the haymow. She cried out with joy when she saw the pitchfork plunged in a stack of hay. Someone had carved the head from a single piece of hardwood, the tines tapering to sharp points that would slide easily into tangles of wild grass and

weeds. The handle rose as tall as she, with grooves carved at
he end to provide a handhold.

Ardisson staggered to his feet. From his closed right eye,
a trickle of blood rolled down his cheek. Her stomach contracted, her breakfast rose in her throat. Had she put out his
eye? She beat down her rising gorge. She must not waste pity
on him. He had none for her.

She held the pitchfork in her right hand, wondering how
he would make his attack. She saw no ladder in the barn.
Would he think about mounting his horse? From the back
of the tall animal he might seize the edge of the mow. She
would have one chance, when both his hands grasped the
edge to climb over. She must jab the fork in his face. Did she
have the nerve to aim at his eyes, intentionally blinding him?

"You bitch!" he screamed. "You're nothing but them
cowboys' whore. A honest farmer not good enough for you?
Bitch whore!"

She nearly launched the pitchfork at him to shut his foul
mouth. Just in time, she realized his shrieks helped her. No
one knew she was in the barn. She must keep him shouting,
to guide Perk or Dunk.

"Who's a bitch?" she screamed back. "Your mother, I
don't doubt, bedded every man in town! Same as your
wife!"

He roared, wordlessly. Beyond Ardisson the yellow horse
wandered out the door, grabbed a clump of grass growing
where the adobe met the ground. He reached for another,
farther around the corner, out of her sight. Go, horse, she
encouraged him silently.

"You don't know your father!" she yelled, to keep his
attention. "No more than you know who fathered your
woman's children!"

Ardisson backed away from the edge of the mow, almost
to the door. The blood running down his cheek, the squinting eye, the snarling mouth, the dark hair, upright like an
alarmed beast's, gave him a monster's face. He squatted,
ran half the length of the barn, leaped, grasped the edge of

the mow in his fingers. Annie ran forward, ground the heel of her boot against the brown knuckles. Blood started, but the man hung on. He swung his legs. She had no choice. She turned her head aside as she plunged the fork into his face.

She expected a scream, but Ardisson uttered only a huge groan, ending with "Umpf" as he landed on the hard barn floor. Then silence.

Several seconds passed before she dared look at the tines of the fork, expecting them to drip blood. Only a furring of dark hair. She leaned over the edge of the haymow. Ardisson lay, facedown, straight below her. The man pushed himself up on his elbows, moaning. Blood ran from his scalp, down his face. His bristled hair looked as if a miniature plow had engraved three furrows straight through it. He got to his hands and knees, then to his feet, staggered toward the door. On the spot where he had lain, a gun shone, half buried in the scattered hay. It must have spilled from his holster when he fell.

Annie waited, catching her breath, until Ardisson reached the door and leaned against the pillar supporting the great overhead beam. She dropped the rope slowly over the edge, ready to jerk it up if he showed any sign of turning in her direction. She slid down quickly, scooped up the six-shooter. The hooves of a horse pounded on the road. She sighed in relief. One of the men had come to help her.

"Pa! Pa!" A boy's voice. Had they caught Dunk? "They seen us. One of them seen us." The horse ceased to gallop. A cloud of dust rolled past the open door.

"What happened to you, Pa?" The voice screeched high one instant, low the next. A boy just coming into manhood.

"Yeller threw me. Damned no-account horse."

Annie edged toward the door, hugging the wall to stay out of sight of the man and the youngster.

"How many steers you get in the corral?" Ardisson asked harshly.

"Four dozen, but they let them out, and the critters went like the wind back to the herd. I said we should of moved them more east."

Ardisson's knees bent and wavered. He placed his back against the adobe bricks, then collapsed. If he had turned just a bit more, he would have seen her. He dropped his head in his hands.

"You okay, Pa?" asked the cracking voice. "Should I go get Ma?"

The noise of several dashing horses, the chatter of excited voices. The cowboys! Coming to find her! She rushed heedlessly to the wide door, afraid they'd gallop by without seeing her. She faced a motley gang of three boys and two girls, mounted on a collection of aging horses and mules.

"He's after us!" screamed one of the girls.

"The man on the gray horse?" asked the youth, who must be Ardisson's son. Fifteen or sixteen. Beardless, gangly, his hands ridiculously large at the ends of his thin arms.

"Get off your mounts," ordered Annie, raising the revolver. Ardisson reared up, his hand went to his hip. Only then did he discover the empty holster. He sighed, the way a woman does before the tears come, sank lower.

"Get over here by your pa!" she yelled. She examined the young rustlers, saw no weapons. One by one they slid from their saddles and plodded through the dust to stand a few feet from the wounded man.

"Don't you know cattle rustling's a hanging offense?" she asked firmly. The two girls and one of the boys had no shoes. The girls' hair hung in untidy braids that had not been renewed for days.

"Now, we're walking down this road, out to see the race," she said. "Leave your mounts. They're of no account against any of our horses. You don't want to miss the race, do you?" she asked sarcastically, looking directly at Ardisson. "Get up."

"I can't," he muttered. "I'm hurt."

"But not from falling off that worthless horse of yours," she snapped. She looked at the children, huddled together, staring at the six-shooter. How many of these half-nourished infants had he fathered? "He came after me, and I beat him off with a pitchfork. You can find it later, up in the mow, with his skin and hair on it. You young fellows, look at him and fix it in your minds—some women fight back." She walked to Ardisson, kicked him in the hip. "On your feet." Ardisson pulled himself up by clinging to the irregularities in the adobe bricks.

"Annie, Annie!" Dunk's voice. She didn't turn, she didn't even shift her eyes from the shambling man and the frightened children.

"I'm here," she answered loudly. From the corner of her eye she saw Graybob, followed by Jenny, wending their way through the shanties.

"I got your rustlers for you. Pretty pitiful bunch, I'd say." Why did both her voice and the gun start wavering, now? She didn't look at him, even when he came to her side.

"What in the name of Satan do you people think you're doing?" he snarled. Annie jerked her head about, stared at Dunk. She'd never heard him speak in that tone of voice. "What happened to you?" he asked of Ardisson.

The man groaned, sat down, right in the middle of the road. The two girls rushed to his side; he shoved them away.

"I hit him with a pitchfork," Annie said happily.

"Right offhand, he looks more like he's been scalped, by an amateur," said Dunk. "How often have you played this game?" he demanded of the man. When Ardisson didn't answer, he looked at the eldest of the boys and repeated the question.

"Last couple months," said the kid, digging a hole in the dust of the road with his big toe, which protruded nakedly through the side of his clumsy boot.

"Why?" Dunk asked in astonishment.

"Why, to get together a herd to sell in Dodge, naturally," said the boy, his tone of voice indicating Dunk was a fool not to understand the necessity.

"And you don't think some buyer in Dodge is going to wonder that your herd has several different brands?"

"Pa can take care of that," said the boy, pointing to Ardisson. "He's good with a runnin' iron."

"Let's walk them down to the racetrack," said Annie, feeling a bit nervous at facing children with a gun she could not hold steady. A gun she couldn't possibly use. Dunk had been right. You didn't shoot children.

"We can settle this right here, I believe," Dunk said. He walked into the road, stood over Ardisson while pointing at the eldest of the rustlers. "This is your boy?" Ardisson nodded. "He's going with me, to Montana, driving a wagon." He turned to the boy. "Can you drive a wagon, four mules?"

"Sure can," said the boy. "You say Montana?" His eyes widened, shone with sudden excitement. He pulled off his hat. "Montana?"

"He's pretty tough," Dunk said to Annie, "rustling cattle with this crew." He dismissed the younger children with scornful eyes, turned to the boy.

"You'll get thirty dollars a month, paid when we get to Montana. Then you're free to do what you want, come back here in time for the corn harvest or go looking for ranch work. But until the drive's finished, you're on the seat of a wagon, or else I tell the law you're wanted for rustling."

Ardisson stirred, started to object.

"Does he have a wife?" asked Dunk of no one in particular, jerking his thumb in Ardisson's direction. The young heads moved up and down. "You two girls go fetch her. Tell her her husband's hurt. A wild woman tried to scalp him." They leaped away like frightened fawns.

"Ardisson, don't try this game again. I'd suggest that any cattle around here wearing strange brands, you let them wander off. I'm going to report this to the first law we find. We'll also send a message back to Abilene, when we meet a man riding south. The Rangers probably will hang you, but I don't suppose they'll hang the children, particularly since their leader's vanished. Come on, Annie. Let's go watch the races, what's left to be run. You, too," he gestured commandingly at the boy. "What's your name?"

"D-D-Dan," stuttered the youngster.

"You'd best run home and get your gear together. You have ten minutes. Tell your mother goodbye and assure her I'm not taking your neck to a noose. Unless, of course, you continue as your father seems to have encouraged you."

Dunk caught Ardisson under the arms, pulled him up, steered him into the barn. He collapsed on the same pile of hay where he had thrown her just a few minutes before.

"Is there any water around?" Dunk asked her. She stared at him, wondering where this secure, firm leader had been hiding. Or had it been hiding? Perhaps she had just never bothered to look at Dunk very deeply.

"Water?" he repeated.

"Not that I've seen. There's no horse tank."

"He's got three slashes across his scalp that need cleaning. They're full of hay and dirt. His head will have to be shaved to get at them. Where's the pitchfork you used?"

"Up there." She pointed at the mow. "I climbed the rope."

"Ardisson," said Dunk, eyeing the rope, "you'd get more hay up there faster if you bolted a pulley to the beam and ran the rope through it, instead of just hauling the load deadweight. And it would be considerably more difficult," he added dryly, "for young ladies to escape your advances. The rope, as it is now, offers them a solid grip."

The pale face of a woman stuck around the door frame.

"I think help is here now. She can tend you. Good luck."

Annie wondered at some weight in her hand, realized she still carried the gun. She caught Dunk's sleeve as he went out the door, handed it to him.

"I was meaning to ask, where did you get this?" he said. "I didn't know you went armed."

"It's Ardisson's. He dropped it when he fell out of the haymow."

"We'll take it. The boy should carry something on the trail, I suppose."

"You'll trust him? A rustler?"

"He's no rustler. He wants to go on a drive. Didn't you notice his eyes when I mentioned Montana? He's no rustler, but I doubt he's a farmer, either. Probably a born cowboy."

Dunk took her hand, led her out of the barn as he would a child. Instead of placing her foot in the stirrup he held, she turned to face him, put her hands on his shoulders, leaned against him. One of his arms crept about her waist. His lean body stood firmly, as she had known it would. His hands against her back steadied her. One of his hands pressed on the spot where Ardisson's quirt had landed, but she dismissed the pain.

"It was awful," she said.

"It's my fault," he said. "I should never have sent you back alone. From now on, you're not out of my sight."

"What use can I be to anyone if I can't ride off alone?" she objected. "And I was getting away before you came. If you hadn't come, I'd have taken them to the cowboys without any help."

"Of course. You didn't need me at all," he agreed.

"But he frightened me," she admitted. "When we get to Dodge, I'm buying a gun. I'll never again let myself get into a situation like this without a weapon." She hated her feminine weakness, hated that she was on the verge of tears, for she didn't want to cry in front of Dunk, in front of the timid girls standing in the barn door.

"You can tell me when we get back to camp," he whispered, his lips in her hair. "You're very brave, Annie."

She remembered the sound of his voice as he had called for her. The panic behind her shouted name. He had been worried. He felt something for her.

Chapter Eight

"Dunk."

Quent peered toward the creek, but could see nothing beyond the greenery concealing Annie's bathing spot.

"Dunk," she repeated, appealing, begging this time. A snake? One of the cowboys spying on her from the opposite bank? He plunged toward her, but stopped several feet short of the creek. She sat on a grassy tongue of land, surrounded on three sides by the small, gurgling stream. She had on her underclothes, a chemise and short pantaloons. He averted his eyes.

"Yes. Is something wrong?"

"I can't reach…" she sputtered. "And there's no one but you to ask." She stood, her back to him, lowered her pantaloons to display an expanse of white skin, an angry red welt extending across the top of her hips.

"Oh, Lord!" he ejaculated, crashed heedlessly to her side. "How did that happen?"

"Ardisson hit me with his quirt. I can't see. How bad is it?"

Her body curved smoothly from waist to hips, her skin the color of rich cream. He bent to examine the mark, almost expecting to smell fresh milk and butter. He clasped his hands behind his back.

"A very bad bruise, but the skin's not broken," he reported. "Do you have some ointment? Sid carries some in the chuck wagon, but I'm afraid it's designed for horses."

"Goose grease and arnica." She pointed to a small jar on a rock beside her soap and sponge. "I put some on my arm, but I couldn't . . . Well, you understand."

"I understand. Your arm, you say?" She stretched out her left arm, splotched deep purple just below her elbow.

"Why didn't you tell me?" he asked angrily, seizing the pot of ointment. "I should have killed him!"

"I took care of him myself," she said proudly. "Do you suppose his wife will actually shave his head?" She looked over her shoulder, smiling. The trembling, shy maiden departed from both eyes and body. Quent regretted the loss of frightened innocence. Standing in the middle of that dusty road, she had fit perfectly in his arms. His rational self said independence was preferable in a trail-driving woman, but he yearned for clinging helplessness and the perfect fit of that body, in a more private locale.

"I'm sure she had to shave his head completely. He'll be an object of fun to everyone in town, including the dogs, for the boys are sure to chatter. They'll let the whole settlement know a woman skinned off half his scalp."

"I hope he hurts for a long— Ouch!" She shrieked as his fingers touched the swollen flesh.

"I'm sorry," he said, pulling back and dropping a dollop of ointment on the grass. "How did you ever bear sitting on Jenny to get out to camp?"

"I just gritted my teeth," she snapped. "Go ahead." He soothed the ointment over the bruise with the softest touch possible. No matter how gently he managed it, his own body reacted to the contact. The first surge of tumescence surprised him; he shuddered, bringing the tips of his fingers heavily against the hurt. She moaned; he came very close to moaning, also.

"There," he said thickly, taking a last look at the line where her hips disappeared into the white pantaloons. He turned away, ostensibly to find the lid for the pot, but really to keep her from seeing his condition.

"Do you need anything else?" he asked.

"No. I'll get dressed. Thank you."

"You're welcome," he said to a willow tree and a bush rampant with thorns. He raged heedlessly through the thicket, ripped the sleeve of his shirt, searched frantically for a place where he might rest out of view of the camp. Brush filled a dry arm of the creek. He circled it, tucked himself under a spreading bush, drew his legs against his chest and buried his face in his hands.

She behaves like a lady for one day, and I can't control myself. She did nothing to provoke me. She's quite right to distrust me.

Touching her. That was what had caused his loss of restraint. And that bruise, horrible as it looked, would need treatment for only a few days. Two, perhaps three, times, he must steel himself to doctor her. She'd have to ride in the wagon, of course, swathed in her feather bed. He'd be forced to ride close by, naturally, to make sure the boy avoided rough spots and didn't cause her pain.

The boy! He'd abandoned Dan to the mercies of Sid and the cowboys! What sort of initiation rituals might they be heaping upon the poor scared kid, while he mooned about in a thicket, thinking of Annie's back? Annie's... Lower than her back, silken, the color...

Quent raced to camp, found Dan sitting against the wheel of the wagon, his bedraggled boots beside him. When he saw Quent, the boy dropped the work in his hands, scrambled to his feet.

"I was just... I was just..." He pointed helplessly to the strips of leather on the ground, glanced about as if searching for a way to escape. He tried to step back, but the wagon stood behind him.

"You were what?" asked Quent, astonished at the terror inspired by his presence.

"Re-repairing the harness," Dan said, his voice shaking. "One spot, it'd started to rip. You weren't here to ask, so I went ahead...."

"Very good. I'm glad to find you have some initiative."

"Some in-what?" asked Dan, curiosity for a moment overcoming his fright.

"Initiative. Get-up-and-go. Good judgment. You saw the harness needed repair, you set about doing it without bothering me. That's quite right." The boy's mouth dropped open; he stared at the ground, then dared to look at Quent.

"That's what you want?" he breathed. "You want I should repair the harness, without you knowing?"

"I suppose you know more about harnesses than I do." Quent shrugged, smiled. The boy swallowed hard. Quent decided he should say something to reassure the boy. Not empty praise, for praise should be given only for success. When in doubt, speak the truth.

"This harness must last all the way to Montana. Your job is to make sure it does. You need come to me only when there's a problem you can't take care of by yourself."

The boy's mouth opened and closed, like a landed trout's. After several tries, words came out. "Them's nice mules. I hain't never had no mules as nice as them."

"They belong to Mr. Elam Brownell, the rancher to whom this herd belongs. This wagon is for the comfort of his daughter, Miss Annie. She's a lady. You will treat her as a lady at all times."

"Yes, sir," said Dan, his mouth still directed at the ground.

"Caring for the mules is also part of your job. Do you know how to care for animals?"

"Oh, yes, sir!" Yellowish-brown eyes met his briefly. "I'm good with horses and mules. That tall horse of Pa's, last winter he like to have died, but I doctored him with chicken-gizzard tea and rubbed his belly with red pepper."

"You ask me before you doctor the mules with chicken-gizzard tea and red peppers," Quent said, checking his impulse to laugh.

"Don't see as how we'd get chicken gizzards hereabouts, nohow," said the boy, looking almost bold for an instant.

"Nor do I. Get on with your repair work before it's too dark to see," said Quent in a tone he hoped conveyed an order without terrifying. The boy sank down, took up the leather, needle and palm. He crossed his legs, exposing an open running sore on one side of his foot.

"What's wrong with your foot?" Quent asked. The boy lifted the limb in question, looked at it without concern.

"Oh, that." He dismissed the flaming eruption. "That always comes when I wear those old boots of Pa's. It cures when I leave 'em off."

"We'll get you some proper boots in Dodge," said Quent as he turned away, turned straight into Annie. She was approaching the wagon gingerly, planting her feet carefully to keep her back stiff. She carried an armload of wet clothes, her sponge and the pot of ointment.

"Have him wash his feet and put some of this on the sore," she said, holding out the pot of goose grease.

"I don't need doctoring," the boy protested. "It goes away on its own when I put off wearing the boots."

"Do as she says," snapped Quent. "I hope you're not the sort who has to hear orders more than once before carrying them out. If you are, you'll never make a cowboy."

The boy grabbed the pot of ointment, fled toward the creek.

"I think you're right," Annie said seriously. "He doesn't want to be a farmer. But he seems a bit shy to be a cowboy. Are you really going to buy him boots in Dodge?"

"Yes. If he has a proper outfit, and the promise of money at the end of the summer, he has no need to turn rustler."

Annie carefully draped a wet skirt over a bush. A stocking slithered from her bundle and landed on the ground. She stared at it with dismay. Was she in such pain she could not lean over without planning the movement? He grabbed the clothes, flung them over the bushes to dry.

"Thank you. I'm going to lie down for a bit, until supper's ready," she said. She lifted her leg to climb into the wagon, winced. Quent sprang to her side, offered his shoulder to lean on.

"I shall be well in the morning," she said stubbornly, tightening her grip on his hand. He fought to keep himself under control until she disappeared beneath the canvas. He gritted his teeth, walked to the chuck wagon, where Sid was stirring a pot of dough. If he kept his mind occupied with other things, she need never learn of his outrageous lust.

"Sid," he said quietly, so none of the others would hear, "could you fellows go easy on Dan? Not play too many tricks for a few days? Until he understands a bit how a cattle drive operates?"

"Not send him back for his horn pike, is that it?"

"Exactly. The boy's had a hard life. Any man older than he is, he expects a flash of temper, then a beating."

"The man Annie scalped?" Sid asked.

"The same."

"I'll tell the boys," said Sid, "but you're not going to be able to stop them in Dodge. Cowboys love to take the young one in, get a laugh from his first try with a woman."

Quent gulped as his own disobedient body reacted to the concept. Why did Sid have to mention a man with a woman?

He spent the rest of the evening in purest torture. Helping Annie from the wagon so that she might join the cowboys for supper, helping her back in when the sky darkened and the stars appeared, each touch brought the rush of desire. He lay under her wagon, keenly aware of her every move. Her restless, pained body refused to sleep quietly.

Never had lust seized him so suddenly and so completely. From the moment she pushed down her pantaloons and revealed her white hips, he'd been afire, with a desire more intense than any he'd experienced. To worsen the ache, he

lesired a woman promised to another, a sin much greater
han simple lust. He had promised to take Annie to her fiancé. He dishonored himself if he so much as dreamed of
aking her physically. And his body did so much more than
dream.

Overhead, she turned, murmured, "No, no!" Did she
dream of Ardisson's attack? Or of the unknown disaster, the
mark of which so often crept into her eyes? He wanted to
comfort her, stop the dream. His sex leaped in anticipation.

You have sworn to protect me from all men but yourself.
Was her accusation true? Was he, not the cowboys, the
threat to her? Not poor old Ardisson, who could only lash
out and, in the end, fall to her determined resistance.

He rolled out from under the wagon, carefully avoiding
the wheels, so a bump would not disturb her. He crept to the
creek, took off his underclothes, submerged himself in the
chilly water until the lust soaked away. *Nothing I do will
bring the slightest taint to her name. She is safe from me, as
will make her safe from all men.*

He hoped Hugh McCann was worthy of such perfection.

Quent rode ahead of the wagon, warning Dan of ruts and
holes. The herd strung out far ahead, for under Quent's direction the wagon traveled a zigzag course, making a mile
and a half for every one the cattle traveled. Occasionally he
saw Annie's face over Dan's shoulder, but most of the time
he lay flat, the mattresses cushioning her ride.

She had bravely insisted she would ride Bird, but the pain
had so overwhelmed her when she mounted that she crawled
into the wagon without further objection. Her agony had
been made public, and after Quent confessed the cause,
three of the men—Huzzy, Lucas and Broadbrim—had
begged Perk for permission to ride back and horsewhip Ardisson. Quent feared their revenge would not stop at flog-
ging. To his relief, Perk ordered everyone forward before the
sun had cleared the horizon.

"No time," Perk had said sensibly. "The Red River's ahead, and we must move if we're to pass over *that* water today. Besides, we'll let the Rangers know what Ardisson was about, and he'll be strung up legally."

Ever since Huzzy had come close to being lost in the Guadalupe, the cowboys had spoken in hushed tones about the treacherous Red, the border between Texas and the Indian Nations. Wagons crossed on a ferry, Quent had learned, but the cattle must swim. And swimming cattle meant mounted men struggling in the same turbulent water.

He reined in Number Three; behind him, Dan yelled, "Whoa!"

"What is it?" came Annie's voice from the wagon. Her face showed sickly in the blue twilight of the wagon cover.

"Stack's come back," he said. "He's talking to Perk."

"Ride on ahead," she ordered Quent. "Find out what's going on. Dan's a good enough driver—he can certainly find a tolerable road between here and the river." The boy flashed a grin at this affirmation of his skill. "Besides, I think the course you're steering is taking me twice as far as need be. Ruts and bumps might be easier to stand."

"Slow," Quent said to the boy. "Keep her slow."

Quent approached the conference of foreman and *segundo* cautiously, but Perk gestured for him to join them.

"Slow the herd," Perk said to Stack. "Dunk, you come with me. We're riding ahead." As an afterthought, he asked, "Is Annie okay?"

"As well as can be expected, with her, ah . . . back swollen and bruised."

"She'll heal," said Perk without emotion. "Ornery women, they don't hurt easy." Quent kept his mouth shut, not prepared to debate the issue of ornery women with his foreman. "Stack says eight herds are waiting to cross the Red. Water's been high from rains west of here. Remember the lightning to the northwest the other night?"

"We'll lay over?" asked Quent.

"Not if I can help it. We'd have to go up- or downriver ïve, maybe ten miles, to find grass. So many herds have ·assed, the grass near the trail is almost gone, and it's only une." He waved his arm in a wide horizontal gesture to take ı the entire landscape. "Even if the river drops tomorrow, ·e'd still be three, maybe four days waiting our turn. And it should rise again..." He groaned, a sound Quent in- ·rpreted as meaning the delay might extend to a week or ıore. Ahead billowed a dust cloud larger than any he had ver seen.

"That must be the herds that ran last night," said Perk.

"Ran?"

"Stampede. One herd took off for no reason anyone ·athomed, ran smack into another and set them running ·ack down the trail, the same wispy devil nipping their ·eels."

Gradually forms took shape at the base of the yellow-red ·loud. Steers bawling and milling, cowboys riding amid the ·attle, separating the mingled herds. Perk kept well away ·rom the commotion.

The trail ran level to the edge of the bluffs, then dropped ·ff. Quent had never considered the source of the river's ·ame until he saw the red, muddy water, contained within ·aming bluffs. The green of the trees and bushes stood out ı violent contrast, reminding him of red berries on holly, ·elvet Christmas ribbons on evergreen boughs. Perk let ·ellcock pick his own way down to the muddy flats, past a ·at ferryboat stranded several feet above the stream.

A cook for one of the stranded outfits struggled up the ·ank, bent under the weight of two buckets of dirty water.

"It's dropping," said Perk. "No rain last night." He ·urred his horse toward the man. "Has anyone tried the ·rd?" he asked.

The man lowered the buckets to the sloping ground, ·raced them with his feet and mopped his forehead with his ·eeve, turning a layer of dust into russet mud.

"Foreman planned to try this evening, but now, with the cattle riled, he thinks best not to. And the ferry cable parted when a tree trunk rammed it, so there's no easy way across for the wagon."

"Which herd has the right-of-way after the two here?"

"One from clear across the Rio Grande, from Mexico, they're third, but they went five miles downstream. We sent out a messenger, telling them to come up, but haven't heard nothing."

"Come on, Dunk!" yelled Perk, sending his horse plunging down the embankment as if chased by spirits. Hellcock dived into the muddy water. An island, perhaps two, lay between them and the farther shore. Fifty feet out, Number Three's feet left the riverbed, and the horse swam almost all the distance to the island. The low, silty bar had been scoured firm by the floodwaters.

The red water flowed only a few feet deep between the two islands. The third stretch of the river, between the second island and the northern shore, required another swim, longer than before, but with a current less strong. Perk selected a slightly different route for the return, found a path with more shallow water but a muddier bottom.

"The cattle might get bogged," he mused as he rode up the bank, past the stranded ferry.

"Let's ride downriver a ways," said Perk. Past the dust drifting from the mixed herds, Perk stood in his stirrups, shook his head. "No dust. That Mexican herd's not moving this direction yet." He turned to face Quent. "You go back, tell Stack we're taking the herd to the crossing soon as he can get it here. He should drift a bit west, to keep from edging into that tangle of cattle. He's to keep the herd tight. You ride point with him, so if I'm not here you can lead them straight on into the water and show where the herd's to pass. Remember, keep to the solid bottom, even though the other way's a bit shorter."

Quent tried to act nonchalant. "Where will you be?" he asked.

"I'll find the bosses of these two outfits." He pointed at the dust cloud. "It's only polite to tell them we're making our crossing, since no one else is using the ford."

"Annie?"

"She'll wait until the herd's across and everyone can help bring the wagons over. That boy you hired is green. Get one of the hands to take charge of the mules. Now git. I'll meet the herd at the river if I find the foremen quick enough. And put your saddle on Graybob!" he yelled at Quent's back.

Quent made his report to Stack, waited impatiently as the remuda came up and Johnny roped fresh horses for everyone. No need to rope Graybob. He came out of the herd himself. By the time Quent had changed his saddle, the wagons were near, so he galloped back to relay Perk's plans to Annie and Dan. He explained the situation to her by shouting over Dan's shoulder; it was terribly unsatisfactory, when he ached to hold her, reassure her that he'd see she got across safely.

He fretted at the delay caused by the remounting, but finally Stack called everyone together. The *segundo* outlined the situation in three brief sentences, ordered an extra man on the east side to hold the cattle away from the other herds, then turned his horse calmly, as if he were setting out for an evening ride into town. Quent fell in behind Stack, hoping he looked more at ease than his stomach felt. He took off his gloves, wiped his palms on his trousers.

Would he remember exactly where he and Perk had entered the river, where they had climbed out, onto that first island? And what about Annie? He couldn't let her ride over in the wagon. Too much chance of a wagon tipping over in that stirred red water.

He sighed with relief when he saw Perk waiting by the river, glad he did not have to lead the herd to the ford. But, on the other hand, if he had done so, and been successful, what a wonderful thing to brag about in New York, from behind the desk of a banker or a lawyer. *I led three thousand cattle across the Red.*

No great loss, he decided. Few men in New York would understand the triumph.

He walked Graybob to the edge of the river, then a bit downstream, the position he'd taken at every river crossing since dashing out into the Guadalupe. He noticed very little of the complex crossing, but kept his eyes on the line of cowboys hurrying the cattle through the main channel. A cow and calf hesitated. Someone roped the calf, towed the struggling youngster through the current, left it bawling piteously in the shallows until its frantic mother swam to join it. And suddenly the first channel was empty and the island teemed with cattle. The shadows had lengthened, so an hour, perhaps two, had passed. It seemed like minutes. He spurred Graybob into the stream.

The leaders climbed up the north bank, two cowboys driving them away from the river, up the bluff. He waited until the stragglers splashed into the shallows, until Rolf and Broadbrim and Soto came trotting back to join him.

"We'll bring the wagons down," Broadbrim said. "Perk said he'd send some men to draw them across. Miss Annie's going to ride so easy, she'll think she's on the Union Pacific."

"She's riding with me," Quent said firmly. "Not in the wagon."

"You've seen us bring the wagons over rivers," said Broadbrim, his black eyes and half smile teasing Quent. *He knows,* thought Quent. *He's figured out I feel more for her than is proper for a mere escort.*

"I've seen them come near to capsizing," snapped Quent. "She's not riding in the wagon." He should let Broadbrim, the man in charge of the wagon crew, lead the way, but he dashed ahead to forestall them. Annie waited on the bluff while Dan guided the mules down the steep path to the water. Quent dismounted at the wagon, thrust his head and shoulders through the back flap, trying to keep his muddy legs away from the canvas while at the same time reaching for the sheet on Annie's bed. His fingertips curled about the bottom edge. He pulled it from underneath the blankets.

"Can you walk down here?" he called. She didn't answer, but set her boots on the footpath that angled away from the cattle trail. She passed under the trees, and he lost sight of her until she emerged at water level.

"Can you bear it if someone lifts you up behind me?"

She nodded. "What's the sheet for?" she asked, looking a bit dubious.

"To tie you to me. A rope would slide down and hurt your back, but a sheet can be spread out, like a sling."

"Just so it doesn't become a slingshot," she said, smiling at him with so much gratitude his insides quaked. She took off her boots, tossed them into the back of the wagon. Broadbrim held her about the waist, and she curled the toes of one foot about Quent's boot, lifted herself behind him. Her bare feet stuck forward and touched his legs.

"Wrap that sheet around her, from her, ah . . . seat to her shoulders," Quent ordered. "Bring it under my arms and knot it on my chest." A number of cowboys on the island, waiting to receive the wagon ropes, hooted and yelled when they saw Annie's perch.

"Can you carry the ropes across, too?" asked Broadbrim, grinning. "Or is the load you got taking all your attention?"

"Tie them to the saddle horn," said Quent. Nothing to do but grin back.

"Dan, can you bring those mules across?" he asked.

"Sure can," said the boy.

"Perk says—" began Broadbrim.

"Dan can do it," Quent said quietly. "Let him prove himself."

He guided Graybob into the river, looking straight ahead. He spoke from the corner of his mouth.

"How are you doing?"

"Better, I think."

"Does it hurt to be on the back of a horse?"

"Yes, but I'm glad to be here, not in the wagon. Sid told me they'd make me cross in the wagon."

"Not a good idea. Put your arms around me and tuck your thumbs in my belt. You'll be more secure." Graybob plunged easily into the deep water, kept the two of them afloat without much more effort than he would have exerted in carrying only his own weight. Her legs brushed his thighs as she lifted them clear of the rushing, muddy water. She leaned against him, her cheek passing its warmth into the depression between his shoulder blades. Where her neck pressed, he felt her pulse. His loins stirred; nothing he could do about it. She must notice it, considering the position of her hands. Another man's woman, and she could lead him to this!

He recalled his vow to the stars. To himself. Through his life he had made only a handful of serious moral resolutions, and so far had kept them all. He would not break his trust in this matter, either. He admired the form of the arms wrapped about his body, felt her mobility as she swayed in response to Graybob's movements. He absorbed the pleasure of her closeness. He stored away the memory of his desire for her, as he might have secreted a fine treasure.

Annie woke to the mutter of thunder. She rolled onto her back, gritted her teeth against the pain the movement cost, waited to see the next flash of lightning. Four minutes later it came, illuminating the wagon's top. For an instant, the small print of the blue calico stood out brighter than it ever did in daylight.

Leaving the Red River, the trail had climbed, ending on a ridge between two tributaries of the larger stream, the worst possible place in a lightning storm. Dunk knew it, too, although he had tried to hide his concern from her. When he thought she was busy in the wagon, he had walked the length of a gully that cut into the ridge, studying the irregularities in the landscape. He had not picketed his night horse near the wagon, as was his custom, but led the bay into the gully and looped the reins securely about a small tree.

"Up, Stack," Perk's voice said in the blackness. "It's moving this way." Annie scrambled to the rear of the wagon.

Lightning flashed across the southwestern sky, the glow carrying all the way to the zenith. The thunder rolled a few seconds behind. She sensed that Dunk crawled around the hind wheels, lifted his arm to the tailgate.

"Annie," he said softly.

"I'm awake," she answered.

"Storm coming," he explained unnecessarily. "It might be best to get dressed."

"Yes," she agreed. She struggled into the minimum of clothing, a skirt and bodice, without underclothes. She found her waterproof coat by touch, laid it over the tailgate.

Lightning slashed across the sky, no longer a sheet of brilliance, but a malevolent dagger plunging into the prairie. Dunk spun around, buried his face in the canvas to protect his eyes from the glare and preserve his night vision. The thunder rolled over the grasslands, so massive it seemed a solid object rather than sound. The wagon vibrated under the pressure. A few raindrops pattered on the canvas. Another flash.

Annie climbed out of the wagon, into the roaring blackness that followed the fantastic illumination. She felt the near warmth of him in the dark. She touched his waterproof coat at the same time his hand clasped her arm. If he spoke, she did not hear. He tugged at her, his gesture telling her he meant to retreat off the plateau, into the gully.

A sudden torrent of rain filled the air, absorbed the atmosphere so completely she wondered if they might drown standing up. His arms thrashed at the brush, holding branches out of her way, but to her the whipping limbs seemed less an obstacle than the cascade of water. She fell in behind him, let the twigs and thorns grab at her coat while she covered her face with her arm. A lightning bolt struck so near, the crash of thunder surrounded them before the hellish light faded. In the glare she saw the protection Dunk sought, a bank eight or ten feet high, where the stream, during the spring flood, had undercut and formed a small cave.

His hand tightened on her arm and he dragged her through a pool of water. He grabbed her shoulders, thrust her under the bank; she obeyed him, for the last lightning flash had blinded her. She smelled damp loam and the drifting odor of the thunderstorm.

"Curl up," he shouted, "and crawl back!" She put her palms down on the damp ground, behind her back. She lifted her hips, crawling in the inverted way of childhood games until she met rocks and lumpy roots. Something pressed against the bruise, but she ignored it.

Another lighting bolt tore into the prairie, filling all her senses with the storm. Dunk bent over her, shielding her body with his own. His lips touched her hair. He traced the texture of her braid until his mouth rested on her ear.

"The lightning and thunder are so fierce, the ground shakes!" She moved her head to place her lips against his ear, the only way she could possibly be heard.

"Not the storm!" she shouted over a new roll of thunder. "The cattle are running!"

He shivered slightly. Was it the chill of the rain? The thought of stampede? Or that he hung over her, his position so suggestive of intimacy? Crossing the river, she had felt the excitement of his willing body. The stream of his readiness had coursed into her. From their first meeting she had realized the threat within this man, but she had held him off with scorn and anger. Now, because of what had happened in that dilapidated little settlement—because Perk had sent them away together to find grass, because Ardisson had sought to exercise his puny power—there was but little space left between her and Dunk. In the days to come, that space would narrow, until she had no defense against his passion. Until she no longer even wanted to defend herself.

She moved her face away from his, withdrawing from the immediate threat of his lips. It would be so easy, in the midst of nature's violence. She lifted a hand to his chest, then touched his jaw. Smooth—only a few brittle hairs had escaped his evening razor. "Don't," he said, clearly and bluntly, and only then did she realize the storm had passed.

"There's a way out of this gully, just to the right," he said, his face close to her. "A few bushes, then a small tree near the top. Keep a tight hold on my arm."

She took his hand. His face lowered to hers until his exhalations teased the skin of her cheeks, disturbed the wisps of hair escaping her braid. How would his lips feel when they came close, when they pressed against her own? Soft, certainly, but also daring. A risky exploration, a great discovery. He pulled away. She tugged at his coat, pleading that he stay with her in the cocoon of fantasy.

"We must get out of here, Annie. The creek's rising." She acquiesced to his demand, let him pull her from under the bank, out of the gully, onto the plateau where the double arches of the wagons stood out against a sky surprisingly filled with stars. She stopped him there, still away from the camp. She must extend some thanks, make a gesture to cement the truce between them.

"What do your friends in New York call you?" she asked.

"My family calls me Quent."

"Quent," she repeated. "Thank you, Quent. Thank you very much."

Chapter Nine

A towering yellow cloud obscured the eastern horizon, dust thrown by the incessant trampling of the herds around Dodge City. To the west Quent saw the smaller cloud produced by their own three thousand cattle. Low in the southern sky hung a curtain produced by the herds behind them. Only in the north was the sky clear, and even there, once or twice, the plume of a locomotive's smoke had created a long horizontal smudge.

He could not see Dodge City, but he knew where it lay, on the bottoms of the Arkansas River. A single thin column of dust approached from that direction. It was not a whirlwind—dust devils, the westerners called them—but the trace of a vehicle rolling at constant speed. A black speck appeared at the foot of the rising dust, and then the speck fell apart to reveal a trotting team and a buckboard.

"Linares," Annie said beside him. "Perk said he would meet us here, since he has to be in Dodge to sell the herds coming behind us." A horseman broke away from the herd, rode toward the buckboard. "There goes Perk to meet him." She giggled. "How is Linares going to react when he finds out neither of us intends to give up the drive?"

"He can say very little," Quent replied, his mind on the multiplicity of things he must do in Dodge City. A telegram to his parents, assuring them of his safety. Clothes for Dan. The boy's wardrobe had been ragged when he joined the drive; he now wore castoffs from anyone who had clothes to spare. But no boots. His feet were gigantic.

"He can say and do a great deal," she said fearfully. "What if Perk tells him about Ardisson? He'll wire my father, tell him it's not safe for me to be out on the plains. What if he won't let Dan continue? You know how he feels about boys on a drive."

"Dan has proved himself," said Quent. "You're worrying for nothing. If he objects to us being along, we'll simply go on by ourselves, the three of us. It's a free country." He regarded the expansive landscape to the north, breathed deeply, taking into his lungs the amazing liberty of the plains. He could see Linares clearly now, clad in a well-tailored suit and light-colored Stetson.

"Shall we join them?" Quent asked. He had learned not to give orders, except in an emergency. Demanding obedience, making decisions for her, brought narrowed eyes and a stressed mouth, then an eruption of her rebellious spirit. Her charming, rebellious spirit.

"Certainly." She turned Jenny's head. "We'd better speak for ourselves before Perk fills him with lies."

"Put on your best smile," he suggested, "so Linares has no reason to suppose you aren't enjoying the camping trip."

"I don't think my smile can be any better than it is regularly," she said.

Her golden tan complemented her amazing brown eyes. It matched the golden streaks playing deep within them. He compared her to the girl of the ballroom and decided he liked this outdoor radiance better. Except for the moments of sadness, when he wished to give comfort, but could not.

Linares took off his hat, squinted against the midday brightness, his head lowered so his chin almost touched his chest. Jenny sniffed at the buckboard, jumped and snorted. Linares laughed.

"Looks like both you and your horse have gone native," he said. "Trail life agrees with you?"

"It certainly does."

"Perk says he's gotten well used to having you two around," Linares added laconically, replacing his hat. His eyes, now wide open, examined them sharply. Quent met the gaze, found it steady, respectful. Perk must have given Linares some details of his actions.

"Will you be coming into Dodge?" Linares asked.

"Perk intends to keep the herd nearby for two nights," said Annie. "Does Dodge have a seamstress?"

"Dodge has everything you might want," said Linares. "Put up at the Dodge House, the hotel nearest the railroad station."

"I thought the men might go into town, half at a time," said Perk, looking to his superior for agreement.

"Of course. Each of them has some little necessities or luxuries he desires, I'm sure. But warn them, the citizens of Dodge no longer tolerate wild behavior. The hands must leave their guns in camp. Saloons are open, they'll find some gambling there, but the women come in only after midnight. Now, let me see the herd." He flipped the reins and set his team on a slow perambulation around the drifting cattle.

The men gathered at the wagons to draw straws for the privilege of being first into town. Dan stood away from the group, staring at Linares in his finely tailored coat and fifty-dollar boots. Quent doubted the boy had ever seen a well-dressed man. He beckoned to Dan, led him behind the wagons.

"Here's half the pay you've earned so far. It should be enough for you to buy boots and a couple decent shirts and pants. Don't go off like a wild bull and buy yourself fancy duds. No silver-trimmed chaps, there's no need for them on the plains. Nor a Stetson with a Navajo band. I saw you eyeing the outfit Linares wears and you can't afford clothes like a cattleman or a city dude. You need sturdy things to last to Montana." Dan nodded. "If this isn't enough, come see me." What the price of boots for those enormous feet might be, he had no idea. "I'll be staying at the Dodge

House for two nights. It's easy to find, the hotel where the cattle dealers stay, near the railroad station." Another nod, but a very tentative one. Was the boy afraid of something?

"Is something bothering you?"

"Ain't never been in no big city before." Dodge? A big city? Quent came dangerously close to laughing, then remembered the shabby settlement and tried to put himself in Dan's place. His life had been a series of such "towns," moving, every two or three years, to fresh land on the farthest reach of the frontier. Each move founded in hope that prosperity lay in the West, but each in turn failing to provide even a moderately comfortable life.

"Stick with the cowboys who go in for tonight." And where might the cowboys take him? "You know there are temptations in Dodge City?" Quent asked. He hesitated to give the boy moral advice, but considering the immorality of his father, perhaps he should get a friendly warning.

Dan's mouth moved, and finally he choked out, "Women and cards?"

"Yes. A bit of a wager won't do any harm, but it's very easy to be pulled in..."

"Like Huzzy?" So! The boy observed what went on around him and learned quickly, as he had suspected when he first looked into those sharp yellow-brown eyes.

"Yes. Precisely like Huzzy, who plans on winning enough here to pay the poker debts he's made since we left San Antonio. Do the necessary things, like buying your outfit, getting a bath and a haircut, before you put two bits on the table." Quent hesitated. "I can't forbid the women to you, if you have the wherewithal left to hire one. But the women you can afford aren't safe. Do you understand?"

Dan didn't. His mouth hung open. Quent knew the boy eavesdropped on the older cowboys, men who had been planning their conquest of the bawdy houses for weeks.

"Women of that type carry... disease," said Quent. He was not explaining this very well to an innocent. He'd never had to do this before. His friends in New York regarded him as the innocent. "Diseases you get by lying with them. How old are you?"

"Fifteen. Sixteen this fall."

"I'd suggest you stay away from women for the time being." Dan nodded, wide-eyed and openmouthed. "Go into town with the first group. Get back to camp by midday tomorrow."

"Kin I take that pinto horse?"

"Yes." Quent laughed as Dan skittered away, then set about getting ready for Dodge himself. He needed to change his clothes before he rode into town. He'd take along the one decent suit rolled into his bundle. He rounded the wagon absently, deep in thought, and collided with Annie's bustled navy blue rump as she backed over the tailgate.

"Pardon me!" he said, drawing back. "I didn't know you were here." Had Annie been in the wagon when he lectured Dan on the perils of fallen women? She stepped to the ground. She wore one of her trail skirts, complete with bustle and panel across the front. She'd replaced her fringed hat with a dainty straw hat trimmed with plumes. She carried a carpetbag. For one instant she met his eyes, but then she turned away. The color across her cheekbones darkened, spread upward. She had heard.

"Mr.—Mr. Linares," she stammered, "Mr. Linares is taking me to town in the buckboard. He'll bring me back morning after next."

"Very fine," Quent said.

"You'll join me for dinner, won't you?" said Linares, suddenly at Quent's elbow. "Shall we say at dusk, at the Dodge House?" Linares put his hand beneath Annie's elbow, led her to the buckboard. Her chin trembled. She turned back once, as if she had something to say, then seemingly thought better of it and climbed into the buckboard.

What had he said to Dan? He could not remember exactly. Nothing terribly outrageous. And it *was* necessary to warn the boy about the chances a man took with public women in any city. The ones in Dodge City lay with every cowboy who came up the trail. He'd seen a few of the pox-ridden men in San Antonio, men whose lives had been destroyed by spending a few moments with a fouled woman.

What had he said? He'd upset Annie, certainly. He would apologize to her, explain the necessity of warning an innocent boy. Annie was a practical woman. She must understand that a man who had taken on a youngster had certain duties.

At the Dodge House, Quent ordered a bath sent to his room. They charged extra for not using the bathroom, but he dreamed of a long soak, not possible when other men stood in line in the corridor. He sank gratefully into the warm water, lathered himself all over, stood and worked the soap into his limbs. The thought of Annie, under this same roof, enjoying the same luxury, brought a quiver, the first since he had nearly kissed her during the storm. He slid under the water, leaned back to enjoy a fantasy of her white skin, the molded curve from waist to hip, the firm muscles—

"Quentin!" yelled a voice at the door, followed by a thumping knock. He sat up so suddenly the water slopped over the lip of the tub. It couldn't be! "Quentin! Open up. Linares told me you were here!" Uncle Nick?

Quent stood in the tub, spilled more water on the floor as he struggled to reach a towel and wrap it around himself. He left a trail of wet footprints and spattering drops across the room, opened the door a crack, peered out with one eye, identified the tall figure, slender except for a trifle of thickening around the waist. The blond hair turning gray, the bushy mustache of the same color and texture. Uncle Nick wasn't exactly the last person he'd expected to see in Dodge City. In fact, of all his family, Uncle Nick was the only one likely to turn up at this end of the earth. But he certainly hadn't expected a family visit.

"Hello, hello!" Exultant, his uncle pushed open the door, clapping his hand on his soapy shoulder. "So you're bathing. Don't let me interrupt you. How long since you've had a bath?''

"A proper one, with soap and hot water, more than two months.''

"Delighted, delighted!'' exclaimed his uncle. He'd forgotten Uncle Nick said everything twice. "What the hell are you doing on a cattle drive? Although, you must understand, I don't think it a bad thing at all, not at all. Your father has kept all his sons too much in the conservatory. And at croquet! What a lily-livered sport.''

"I wanted to do something a bit different. . . .'' Quent began uncertainly.

"Linares assures me you've acquitted yourself well. Very well,'' said Uncle Nick, not letting him finish his sentence. "Not really a cattle driver, he says, but the next best thing. Who's the young lady you're escorting?''

"Miss Anne Brownell, late of San Antonio, soon to be of Montana, where her father has taken up a ranch.'' He climbed back into the tub.

"Montana!'' he exclaimed. "Montana! Linares tells me it's a great country. Truly great, with potential beyond the rest of the West, all taken together. Too bad the Northern Pacific has already spliced it together with a railroad, or I'd be there myself.'' He stood very close to the tub, hit Quent such a blow between his shoulder blades that he nearly plunged into the water nose first.

"Pleased, that's what I am. Pleased that one of the van Kelson boys has shown some gumption. Your brothers. Hothouse flowers, nothing but hothouse flowers,'' he muttered with disapproval. "Claude, Jr., in the law firm. Paul a blasted banker, who lectures me on conservative investments. I do believe neither's been west of the Hudson. Know more about London than they do St. Louis. But you, you're different. Showing a taint of the old pirate's blood!''

Quent sank under the water to soak the dust from his hair. He held his breath. What was the old reprobate talking about? Pirates, indeed!

"Pirate blood?" he asked when he surfaced.

"Your father forbade me to ever speak of it in the presence of his offspring, but you're over twenty-one, and in Dodge City all sins are lightly regarded, so my loose tongue may be forgiven me. In 1715, your great-great-great—I'm not sure how many greats, but something like that—grandfather ended his life on a gallows in Puerto Rico for piracy. Seized a Spanish ship, but neglected to remember the war was over. Queen Anne's War, I believe. Two generations went by before a great-grandson found the old boy's treasure, secreted under the floorboards of the house in New York. Restored the fortunes of the van Kelsons. Truly saved the family from ruin."

Was Uncle Nick drunk? No flush on his face, no smell of alcohol had entered the room with him. Quent used his uncle's momentary hesitation to dive into the conversation.

"What are you doing here?"

"You know what I'm doing here," he answered scornfully. "We need a north-south railroad on the high plains. I intend to put these ridiculous cattle drives out of business. Waste of labor, walking cattle from Texas to Kansas."

"We're bound for Montana."

"Montana, as well. A railroad from Mexico to Canada, along the hundredth meridian. And now, I have someone to share my good fortune," he crowed. "My son! My good fortune!" He slapped Quent between the shoulder blades again, knocking his breath away so he had no chance to protest this amazing statement.

"You know, Millie and I wanted a son, but nothing but daughters came. She's in Paris, by the way. She's determined to find European husbands for the girls. Says they'll have a better life in France or England with a husband of the leisure classes. Of course, I had expected one of Claude's sons to fill the gap, but the first two have been hopeless, and you, with your art... But now look at you. A man, ready to take on the responsibilities of the van Kelsons. The pride of the van Kelsons." Quent stood up in the tub, bringing his uncle's lecture to a halt.

"Uncle Nick, I appreciate the offer, but Father doesn't feel speculation and too obvious an engagement in trade are the best way to augment the family fortune and influence. He believes—"

"Good God! Boy, you don't have to point out your father's foolish attitude to me. I've known him decades longer than you, fought with him when we were boys together. Snob! That's all he is. He's taken on all the worst characteristics of the British aristocracy, just as those fellows have awakened to the fact that they need the get-up-and-go of American wives and a foot in the door of business. But you! You take after old Nicholas van Kelson."

"The pirate?"

"The pirate. Your name should have been Nicholas instead of that Latin number your father insisted upon simply because you were the fifth babe to arrive. Number Five van Kelson!" He snorted. Quent wondered vaguely if his own name might be the reason he hadn't bothered to think of names for the three bay horses.

"But I shall forgive you the name, for it would be awkward to change it now. Together we'll take this prairie land in hand. Who's this girl, anyway? A charmer, I warrant, indeed I do, if she's taken your eye."

"I told you, Miss Anne Brownell."

"But you haven't said what she's like. Tall or short, fair or dark? I presume daring, or she wouldn't be here."

"I haven't described her because I haven't managed to get in ten words since you walked through that door!" shouted Quent. He stopped drying himself, shocked. He had never, ever in his life, spoken in that fashion to an elder.

"Right. Right," said his uncle. He didn't seem at all offended. "I do run on, but it's such a delight, absolute delight, to find you here. Tell me about Miss Brownell."

"Her father is Elam Brownell, of Temptation, Montana. He moved three or four years ago from a ranch in Texas.

She has yet to see her new home, having been in school in Louisiana. Her fiancé, also originally from Texas, is her father's neighbor in Montana.''

"Fiancé?" said his uncle, clearly disappointed.

"Yes. She's joining her husband-to-be. She is the most attractive, charming creature in the world. Two years ago, while in Washington, I had hoped to meet her, but—"

"Washington? What was she doing in Washington?"

"Mr. Meechem, Congressman Meechem, of Texas." Great heavens! He was starting to repeat himself. "He's her uncle, on her mother's side." Uncle Nick, who had seated himself on the only chair in the room, sprang up and paced from the bed to the door, tracking the spilled water onto the carpet.

"Meechem! I need his backing if we're to get federal support for this railroad. We'll exploit this friendship.... You and she *are* friends, I presume." Quent didn't like the suggestive leer in his uncle's voice. It reminded him of the unworthy, lustful feelings he had for Annie...Miss Brownell. And reminded him that he encouraged that lust. His legs rose in goose bumps when he recalled that, at the very moment of his uncle's arrival, he had been...

"We are friends," he said firmly.

"Is she terribly attached to this expatriate Texan in Montana, do you think?"

"I don't know," lied Quent. There was no love, of that he was certain. She hardly spoke Hugh McCann's name. Annie's eyes glowed at beautiful sunsets, she smiled when they reminisced about the night storm, she laughed with delight at herds of antelope dashing over the plains. But she neither glowed nor smiled at the mention of Hugh McCann.

"Why should it be any concern of ours?" At the last moment, he caught his use of the plural. Why was he giving his uncle the least bit of encouragement? His father would be furious if he involved himself in his uncle's schemes!

"Because, if you find her attractive, why not marry her? Then, Congressman Meechem's vote would assuredly be for the railroad, to support his nephew-by-marriage."

Quent stopped with his shirt half-on. "I will not be drawn into such a crass scheme," he said firmly. "My wife, when I have one, will be a woman for whom I feel overwhelming affection."

"Overwhelming affection needn't be deterred by money or influence," Uncle Nick said. "Speaking of women, I happen to know of a discreet house where, tonight, we might find some recreation...."

"No."

"No? So you *have* been amusing yourself with the betrothed one in your charge!" Quent pulled down his braces angrily—a mistake, for one slipped from his fingers, flipped up and caught him in the chin. He rubbed his jaw, hoping he wouldn't have a bruise.

"Of course not! I have not touched her. What sort of man do you take me for?"

"A hot-blooded one. Did you know the old pirate had two families, one in New York, the other in Charleston, South Carolina. Imagine, two wives, two broods of children! I've met the Carolina van Kelsons. Plantation owners, with advanced ideas. There may have been a third family, somewhere in the Caribbean, but I haven't been able to ascertain—" His head jerked up. "You do enjoy women, don't you, Quentin? I know your father is terribly straitlaced, but..."

"Yes, I enjoy women. And I've had more than one, if you must know." Quent's teeth hurt. No wonder, they were clenched. He had spoken most disrespectfully to his uncle, but the old buzzard didn't even seem to notice or care.

"When?"

"When I was at Harvard," he muttered unwillingly.

"College men sowing wild oats. So did I," Uncle Nick said gleefully, slapping his knee. "Lovely girl I still remember. Name was Rosellen something. And since? I presume you have a mistress stowed someplace."

"No."

"No?" Uncle Nick was clearly astonished.

"As you so crudely put it, my father is straitlaced. He reared me to have some regard for society's morals."

"There's more to morality than sex," objected Uncle Nick, but Quent ignored him and searched for his cuff links. His uncle said nothing, leaving the field clear for him. Clear for a topic he'd rather not discuss.

"At Harvard, in my final year," he finally said gruffly, "I found some of my fellows suffered from the unfortunate effects of too free an association with women." Uncle Nick laughed, amused, Quent knew, by his ponderous speech. "They contracted syphilis," he said bluntly. "I took a vow at that time to refrain, until I should find a woman to be my wife."

Uncle Nick let out a low, long whistle. "You've been away from Harvard for two..."

"Three years." Uncle Nick frowned and shook his head. Quent sat down on the bed to pull on his low boots.

"Perhaps your strain of pirate's blood has been thinned," mused Uncle Nick. "Your mother's family certainly has some watery members, although she herself is lively and bright. But," he said, rising and smiling, "it may be the van Kelson virility has merely been throttled temporarily by too nice an upbringing. After all, your father did manage to breed six of you. Together we'll knock the edges off your rounded temperament, and the best place to begin is with a kind woman."

"I made a solemn resolution," said Quent. "That cannot be changed."

"A man of his word!" exclaimed Uncle Nick. He was unable to reach Quent's back to deliver another blow, so he settled for a slap on his thigh. "Honor, the most necessary asset in business. If men believe you have honor, they trust you with amazing amounts of money. We'll at least alter your aversion to useful trade. Do you have any money of your own?"

"Of course! Grandfather was generous."

"Stowed in your brother's ridiculous bank, no doubt. We'll find some investments to jog your mind into healthy activity. Nothing like a risk to stir the juices. Now," he said, turning to the door, "I must go dress for dinner. Linares promised I will meet the beautiful lady cattle driver. I shall ascertain her attachment to this rancher in Montana, dispel it if possible, so you can make use of the remainder of your trip for the courtship. And the seduction," he added slyly.

"You will keep your mouth shut," ordered Quent. "You'll say nothing to embarrass Miss Brownell." His uncle had already slammed the door behind him. Quent sat down in despair. He'd already said something to upset Annie. He could imagine the reaction of a fine girl, schooled in Louisiana, to his Uncle Nick.

"Enchanté," murmured Uncle Nick, hovering over Annie's extended hand. "My nephew informed me you were beautiful, but I doubted the word of one so young, so inexperienced. I shall doubt no more!" Annie glowed. "I hope it is not *La Belle Dame sans Merci,"* he added, looking a bit sad. "But I am impolite. Perhaps you do not have *le Français."*

"Mais oui," Annie said proudly. Quent gulped. Two months with her, and he had not made this discovery.

"But, of course. *L'école à Louisiane!* My nephew made such a remark." Annie frowned. "You have been to Paris?" Uncle Nick continued.

"No, I've not been so fortunate," said Annie.

"Ah! But you're young. Your husband—my nephew says there is to be a husband—he'll take you." Annie frowned, indicating she had doubts. "Young ladies love to speak of the men to whom they are pledged. Who is this most fortunate gentleman?" A waiter stood nearby. "Champagne, naturally," said Uncle Nick. "Where a beautiful young woman is, there is champagne." He looked at Annie expectantly.

"My fiancé is Hugh McCann, a Montana rancher," she said.

"A handsome rascal, I don't doubt."

Annie smiled, warming to her task. "Very handsome. Tall, and blond. His hair—" she studied Quent "—is nearly as light as Quent's. And his eyes are blue, but not quite so deep a blue as Quent's. More gray."

"Ah!" exclaimed Uncle Nick. "A man of steel-gray eyes. What more could a woman ask? But," Uncle Nick continued in a low voice, "my nephew is exceptionally lucky in his physical endowments. You must not make comparisons, to the detriment of your loved one. It would not be fair. Quentin is the fortunate one in his family. His two brothers are much darker than he, and not so tall, nor so well formed. Quentin resembles a great-great-great-grandfather, Nicholas van Kelson, who grew rich in the Caribbean trade."

"Quentin," she repeated. "I like the sound of his name, as you say it."

Did he truly resemble the old pirate, Quent wondered, or was Uncle Nick making this up? He certainly looked more like Uncle Nick than he did his own father. A man inherited his coloring from his ancestors, that he knew. Were other traits, less desirable traits, immoral traits, also passed on from the family outlaw? The old goat must have been exceedingly virile, with two, perhaps three, wives. Quent broke out in a cold sweat, remembering his reactions of the past few weeks. But why just now, and not before?

Fortunately, the waiter arrived with the champagne and Quent could distract himself by taking over the drawing of the corks and the filling of the glasses.

"Now, more about this enchanting Hugh McCann," Uncle Nick insisted.

"He's a rancher, and he has built a fine house for us to live in."

"As he should. No man should marry until he has a proper home to cradle the lovely bride. Such is the tradition of the van Kelson family. Before I married Mildred—how I wish you might meet my wife, but she has taken our daughters to Paris—I built two houses, one in New York and one on Long Island, for our summer holidays. Quentin will, of course, pursue the same duty when he chooses a bride."

Quent kept his eyes on the corks and kept his own counsel. Perhaps inheritance had nothing to do with lust. Could it be Annie?

"But I have interrupted you. Quentin will tell you it's a bad habit of mine."

Linares drank the champagne without a preliminary sniff or sip, the way a thirsty man slurps up the first handful of water he scoops from the creek. Annie seemed out of material about McCann. She stuttered, and finally said, "But what brings you to Kansas, Mr. van Kelson?"

"Business. Nothing but business." He sighed. "Nothing to amuse the mind of the young and the beautiful. Ladies should not concern themselves with business. Or perhaps you're one of the new women, who think their sphere should extend over the universe. Vote, serve on juries, as they do in Wyoming Territory?"

Annie frowned as she considered her answer. Quent had never quizzed her on the issue—no politics on a cattle drive—but he supposed she supported women's suffrage.

"I'm not sure," she finally said.

Inwardly Quent sneered. *Coward!*

"Although," Annie continued, "I think a woman should take an interest in her husband's affairs, for if misfortune should occur, and he is lost to her, other men, dishonorable men who have no concern for her welfare, might take advantage of her ignorance."

"Well-spoken. Well-spoken, indeed!" marveled Uncle Nick. "You are an exceedingly wise young woman. The deplorable habit of excluding women from business has led many widows into poverty and many families into ruin. Mrs. van Kelson, my dear Mildred, she has made many excursions, some quite uncomfortable, I must confess, with me to examine the potentialities of various railroading schemes. She has keen eyes and a quick mind, my Millie does, and I depend upon her reports most heavily."

Aunt Millie probably tags along to keep her husband out of other women's beds, Quent thought wryly. The gossip about Nick's prowess had reached even into Harvard.

"How your wife must regret she isn't here," said Annie. "Is it railroad business which brings you to Dodge City?"

"Of course. Of course. Boring, I'm afraid."

"But it's not boring," she cried. "It's only because of the Northern Pacific Railroad that my father has been able to establish himself in Montana. He wrote me long letters about his search for land near the railroad. That's...one reason I've not been there before. He wouldn't let me join him until supplies were easy to come by. Food, and coal, for example."

"Your father is a wise man," said Uncle Nick, leaning toward Annie and giving her a full blast from his blue eyes. "How I should like to meet him."

Quent looked unhappily at Linares. Linares shrugged. The two of them ate the oysters, the steaks, the pudding, the fruit and cheese, while Nicholas van Kelson charmed Annie Meechem Brownell.

"When the railroad is complete," Uncle Nick was saying, "the cattle shall be put in cars and carried to the northern ranges in just a few days."

"Making plans for such a railroad, it's very complicated?" asked Annie. Her talent with leading questions had already won Uncle Nick, Quent could see. Sitting in a hotel dining room drinking champagne, she was a very different woman from the one he lived with on the trail. She knew how to behave in all circumstances, whether eating beans sitting on the ground or being served by a white-coated waiter.

"The organization of a railroad is indeed very complex," said Uncle Nick. "Consider, for example, the cars to carry the cattle. The designers must take into consideration the shape of the beasts. Cars suitable for eastern cattle do not serve here in the West, for the range cattle have very long horns. If they were shaped differently, we could get more in each car, and make the doors narrower. But the task of engineers and designers is to deal with the problems they are given."

"Change the shape of the steers," said Quent thoughtlessly, then sat up straight, realizing it was not a harebrained idea. After all, the cattle he'd seen in Scotland and France didn't have wide-spreading horns and long legs. Nor did those in New York.

Linares laughed.

"But don't you see," Quent protested, "by raising European cattle, instead of Texas longhorns... Or perhaps interbreeding the squatter, shorter-horned breeds with the longhorns, more would fit in each car. And if they're not to be driven hundreds of miles to the railroad, they don't need long legs."

"I do believe you have a notion there, son," Uncle Nick said.

"Quentin is very imaginative," said Annie. She launched into the story of the horn pike. Her story of the joke, including witty imitations of Quent speaking of the *vaquero picador,* had everyone at the table, plus the three neighboring ones, laughing by the time she had finished. Quent paid little attention, for Uncle Nick's final word, *son,* echoed in his skull. With his reputation... They did have a great resemblance.... Might his mother have been seduced? Twenty-five years ago, Uncle Nick would have been an excessively handsome devil.

Impossible! He rejected the notion out of hand.

Chapter Ten

The maids of the Dodge House had cleaned up the mess his bath had made and turned back the covers of his bed. He felt strange, clad for the first time in months in a proper nightshirt. Two nights in a real bed! He reached to extinguish the lamp, just as a knock sounded on the door.

"Quentin," his uncle said in a low voice. "I must speak to you." Quent wearily climbed out of bed and unlocked the door. He had drunk too much champagne, because his uncle had monopolized the conversation at dinner. He'd had little else to do, except stare at the enchanting Annie and think crazy thoughts engendered by the wine.

"What, Uncle Nick? I'm tired."

"The lady is not in love with this McCann. She's an only child—I imagine her father has arranged the marriage so the two ranches may be combined."

"She told you that?" asked Quent in astonishment.

"Not in so many words, but between the lines. You didn't pay sufficient attention. You drink too much. You must learn to control your drinking—it's bad for business. She finds you attractive and I should not be at all surprised if from now on she calls you Quentin. She confessed that she finds the nickname the cowboys gave you odious."

Quent sorted through the fog of recollections. Had Annie explained the source of his nickname?

"How long before you get to Montana?"

"Two months, perhaps three."

"Plenty of time, since she's in your possession day and night. Are there opportunities for seduction?"

"She has her own wag— What?" he bellowed. "You think I'd take advantage of a lone woman, one who's been entrusted into my care by her father?"

"Naturally. Her father, whom I presume to be a gentleman, would have no alternative but to inform the unexcited McCann that the girl has been deflowered. He will reject the lady as damaged goods. Father will be quite happy to turn her over to you, the man who ruined her. Only you must not think of it in those terms, since you love her."

"I do not."

"You will. We all fall in love with the ladies we seduce. It keeps the guilt from preying upon our minds and interfering with our work."

"Did you seduce Aunt Millie?" Quent asked harshly.

"Yes. Haven't you ever counted the months between our marriage and the birth of Sarah?" he asked, astonished. "I thought that was commonly done by all members of the elite." Quent sat down heavily. He'd never met a man, at least since his college days, who confessed so readily to sin. "I'm sorry to see you ready to retire. The ladies at the house I spoke of are waiting, and I had promised them a younger man would stand to stud. . . ."

Quent leaped to his feet. "Get out of here," he snarled.

"Now, now, no need to grow hostile. You don't intend to patronize the women? It's of no consequence to me." He shrugged his shoulders. "All the more reason for you to take action with the fair Annie quickly. I'm afraid the lack of release of critical body humors is creating pressure on your brain. Very dangerous, celibacy, for a man."

"Get out!"

"Not before I say something about our future business partnership. As an artist, I presume you've studied the lay of the land between Texas and Dodge City?"

"When I found it interesting."

"Made sketches?"

"Naturally."

"If you could label them, turn them over to me, it might give my partners some idea of the route, before we bring in a team of surveyors. And henceforth, keep careful track of your trail—do you have maps?—and make detailed sketches, with notes on the rise and fall of the land. You understand?"

"And then?" asked Quent, barely able to breathe. Did Uncle Nick always make such wild assumptions?

"We shall meet, discuss the information with the engineers, experts in this sort of thing. I'll telegraph you as to my whereabouts, in care of the hotel in Temptation. That's the curious name of the town for which you're bound, is it not?"

"Yes. Perk says it was a wild place during the building of the railroad, so the workers gave it that name."

"And immediately fell into Temptation, no doubt," Uncle Nick said happily. "Good night, pirate. Perhaps tomorrow night you'll feel differently about the ladies. If you're shy about visiting their house, I could arrange for one to come here. And tomorrow I must have another extended visit with Miss Brownell, for I want the pattern to the riding skirt she described. I have a friend who would find it useful."

A friend? There had been gossip about his uncle and a lady sharpshooter in a wild West show, but Quent had dismissed it. His legs grew weak.

"Good night," Quent said wearily, unable to absorb any more bombshells. He shoved his uncle out the door, turned the key in the lock.

His father described his only brother as amoral. His mother seduced? That would explain, well, not everything, but sufficient. It would explain, for instance, why his elder brothers had gone through Harvard untempted by sexual sin, while he had spent the years, not exactly promiscuously, but keeping himself well supplied. Had Mrs. Colyer approached Claude and Paul, and been virtuously rejected?

He had been shocked when it happened, she a friend of the family, thirty, perhaps nearer to thirty-five. She had invited him, a homesick seventeen-year-old, to tea. The memory was so strong he could call up the smell of the library where the china and silver had been laid on a side table: the odor of leather bindings, of hot embers on the hearth, of a room shut against the chill wind of a Boston autumn. She had laughed gently at his hesitation when she laid her hand upon his crotch. He'd possessed no strength of character. None at all! By the end of the afternoon, he'd had his first lesson in the pleasures and techniques of sex.

Through two years, she had been his loving teacher. Then she introduced him to younger women, in decent houses, warned him against satisfying himself in the waterfront cribs. For nearly two years, he had not seen her. He had turned to her for advice, however, in his final year in Cambridge, when his best friend contracted the pox.

"Quentin," she had said in her low, sensuous voice, "I introduced you to the joys of the body not to create a libertine, but to keep you safe. Before the comfort of continence can be realized, you must taste what it is you forsake. With your experience, you can take pleasure in anticipation. Marry young, Quentin, within the next year or two. Your dreams will keep you safe until you find the right one." She had touched his hand for one last time. "Perhaps some of your dreams will be of me."

He went to sleep, and it happened as she had said it would, except the dream was of Annie.

Quent found Linares, Perk and Stack at breakfast in the hotel dining room. Stack resembled a scrub rag the scullery maid had thrown carelessly on the back stoop—limp and gray. He pushed a plate of ham and eggs away, dropped his head into his hands.

"You'd think," he muttered, "with all the modern inventions, someone would come up with whiskey that didn't end like this."

"Then it wouldn't be whiskey," said Perk, whose hangover showed merely as bleary eyes.

"The ride to the camp will straighten you out," said Linares to Stack.

"Getting on a horse will probably finish me off," he moaned.

"The rest of the crew is champing at the bit to come into town," said Perk. "You'd best scrape the men off the saloon floors and get saddled up. Anyone get in any trouble?"

"Just me," muttered Stack.

"How about Dan?" Quent asked anxiously. He reached across the table, took Stack's breakfast. "Might as well not let this get cold."

"Beginner's luck, that's what it was," said Stack.

"What?" asked three voices.

"Dan. He asked about Dan. It was just beginner's luck. The kid doesn't know nothing about roulette."

"I never expected he did," said Quent with his mouth full. He chewed and swallowed hastily. "Are you saying he won at roulette?"

"Fifty dollars and more's what I heard. I left the gambling hall when I had no more than drinking money left."

"Where's Dan now?" asked Quent. Fifty dollars! The level of mischief a youngster could get into with fifty dollars! He put down his fork, because it made a tinkling sound against the plate.

"Don't know," admitted Stack.

"Get out and round up the men, get back to camp," ordered Perk. "Make sure you find Dan."

Stack hung on to the back of his chair for thirty seconds, studying the floor for obstacles. He got to the front door and down the steps safely.

"I can't deny the rest of the crew a time in town," said Perk in a worried voice. "But the grass is none too good where we have the herd grazing. I'll feel more at ease when we move on."

"How's pasture been up from Texas?" asked Linares.

"Good in places, but there's an unbelievable number of cattle on the trail. Eight herds waiting at the Red. We were lucky to get across before one of your other herds caught up. Now, of course, beyond Dodge, things should be better."

"Don't count on it," said Linares. "The grangers are up in arms about the damage the herds do to their crops. They've plowed two furrows from here to the Platte, and you must stay between them."

"How wide?" asked Perk in dismay.

"Six miles, they claim, but I've heard at places it narrows to half a mile. You'll have to time your speed so you pass those spots well before nightfall. And four herds bound for Wyoming and Montana have passed already, and that's just the ones I know about." Linares sprang to his feet. "There's Miss Brownell."

Quent spun around in his chair. Indeed, Annie stood in the lobby of the hotel, gazing expectantly out the front window. He threw down his napkin and walked out to fetch her in for breakfast.

"Don't stir yourself," she said. "I'm invited for breakfast in the home of the seamstress. So fortunate I found her. And she has a *sewing machine,*" she marveled, "so today we can take care of my mending, plus make a new skirt. I need more than three." She met his gaze with a blank face. "Tell your uncle good-morning for me, when you see him. I like him very much." Quent stood beside her silently, uncertain why she should be so upset with him, mentally thrashing through, again, the conversation he'd had with Dan behind the wagon.

"Who's calling for you?" he asked. Just as he spoke, a buggy pulled up at the door. A lean and athletic, dark and handsome man sprang out. Annie smiled, detached herself from his arm and sailed out the door.

"Goodbye, Quentin," she said. "I'll send a message if I shan't be able to make it back for dinner."

A dark beard outlined the man's broad face. His dark eyes glowed as he looked down at Annie. There was something piratical about him. An eye patch and he would look exactly like a pirate in a picture book. He helped Annie into the buggy with overmuch attention. Quent nearly rushed out, demanded that he escort her to the seamstress. The buggy pulled away.

He rejoined Linares and Perk and stared at the ham and eggs, congealed into an attractive rose-yellow-and-white design on the plate. A hollow had been carved out inside him, but not a hollow to be cured by ham and eggs. If Annie didn't love McCann, did that mean she might fall in love with someone else? Was there a chance she would throw over McCann, if a better possibility presented itself? The conversation between Perk and Linares whirled around him, while his mind struggled with threats from dark pirates. Dark, virile pirates, upon whom Annie bestowed smiles. Did the seamstress really exist? He should have pressed her, found out the location of the woman's house, taken her there himself, picked her up in time to return to the Dodge House for dinner. What kind of guardian was he, that he allowed her to ride off with a Dodge City pirate?

Images of Annie, captured by cattle rustlers who held her for ransom... Every story he had ever read of women seized by Indians, and the horrors to which they were subjected ... He did not love her. He loved her.

"Good morning, Quentin! Where is the fair Annie?" asked Uncle Nick, approaching the table. "I knocked at her door to escort her to breakfast, but she did not appear to be at home."

"She's having breakfast with her seamstress. Her clothes need attention." Why did he feel as if he were lying?

"She'll be involved in this endeavor all day?"

"So I understand."

"This boy, this Dan…" interrupted Linares. More guilt. His concern for Annie had made him forget Dan, who had been on his own for more than twelve hours, in a city more sinful than Sodom and Gomorrah together, and with fifty dollars.

"I don't like youngsters with my herds," Linares went on.

"I hired him after Brenerd abandoned us," said Quent sharply, pushing his ace into the game immediately. "Brenerd confessed to Annie that you'd assured him his duties wouldn't last more than a few days. His wife is in the family way, and needed him at home."

Linares flushed a bit below his eyes. "Perk agrees the lad's done well so far," conceded Linares, "and that he's good with the mules. But I'd rather he had nothing to do with the herd."

"He shan't," Quent said firmly. "His time's taken up with Miss Brownell's wagon and the mules. If Brenerd had not been ill informed, I should have had no need to take on a boy of that age, and quite suddenly."

"Yes, of course," Linares said awkwardly. "Well, I have duties to perform. Shall we go see what quality of cattle are arriving, Perk?" Quent was left with his horrible suspicions and his uncle.

"Since Miss Brownell is occupied for the day," began Uncle Nick, "I propose we ride out to the camp, retrieve your sketches of the trail from San Antonio. I want very much for you to meet one of our surveyors, who happens to be in Dodge."

Spend the day with railroad men? It would certainly be better than hanging about here, trying to find someone who knew the dark pirate who had abducted Annie. Should he at least inquire at the registration desk? He hesitated to demonstrate his neglect of his duties so openly, and in front of Uncle Nick. Also, his uncle might construe from such an inquiry that Annie Brownell meant something to him.

When, actually, she was merely a woman left in his charge by sheer accident.

He spent the day in confusing conversations, punctuated over and over again by his heart repeating, *Annie, Annie*. His only relief came when he found Dan safe at camp, attired in clothes so new they crackled when he walked.

"Dunk," he said in a low voice, "I need help."

Quent closed his eyes, dreading the bad news. A fight in a saloon? But Dan didn't look like a man with a hangover. A woman who had cleaned out his pockets?

"I got fifty-seven dollars and thirty-three cents," said the boy. His forehead was corrugated with concern. "I don't know what to do. I never had so much money."

"Stack said you won at roulette."

"And a feather could of laid me out on the floor. I put down my four bits, just like you told me, after I'd been to the barber and got my clothes. Everyone was being took, 'cause I think that gamblin' man's got some way to know ahead where that little ball's gonna stop. But I said my lucky number, five, and there it was, right there, so plain no one could say different."

"You were very fortunate. What did you do then?"

"Why, I snatched the cash and skulked down the street to the place where we'd left the horses. The man at that place is a robber, he took fifty cents just for me leavin' the pinto tied there, and I come out here quick as a horned toad in risin' water. I'm scaret of being robbed, I am." Quent noticed, for the first time, that the boy wore his father's six-shooter. "I aim to keep that money and take it to Ma, who can use it for the girls."

"That's very fine of you, Dan. If you'll give it to me for safekeeping, I'll write you a receipt. Then, when Miss Annie returns tomorrow morning, we'll turn it over to her, to keep in her wagon. I believe she has a box with a lock."

"Thank you..." The boy sighed, relief washing over him plainly as his face turned from gray to its normal dull brown in a few seconds. Quent tore a sheet from his pocket notebook, wrote a quick receipt for the money, noticed Dan held the paper upside down when he examined it.

Quent and Uncle Nick arrived back at the Dodge House in the late afternoon, found Annie still absent. A few minutes before dinnertime, the buggy pulled up at the front door and the pirate helped Annie carry in her bundle. Quent waited at the door, relieved the man of the package before he stepped inside.

"I can see to getting this to Miss Brownell's room," he said sharply. The man tipped his hat.

"Thank you very much, Mr. Vonks," Annie said.

"My pleasure, miss," he said. Was there contentment in his voice? He tipped his hat again, smiled at Annie in a way that might or might not reflect immense satisfaction. Quent followed Annie up the stairs, waited while she drew her key from her pocket, took it, opened her door.

"Who was that man?" he blurted out.

"Mr. Vonks?" she asked sweetly.

"Yes. Mr. Vonks." He gritted his teeth. He had no right to interrogate her in this fashion, but his ribs ached from the fear that had beat upon them all day.

"Why, Mrs. Vonks's husband, of course. The seamstress," she added, effectively telling him he was a prying bother. She tilted her head. The feathers on her perky little city hat nodded as if a breeze blew through the hotel corridor. "Why, Quentin. If I didn't know you better, I'd think you were jealous."

He locked himself in his room, so he did not have to hear anything more about railroad surveys, the water and fuel demands of steam locomotives, the number of ties per mile of track, the cost of shipping rails from the East Coast and a thousand other facts that had swamped him during the day. He needed time to think of other things. Men seducing women, women seducing men, and how he was going to bear up, riding next to Annie all the way to Montana.

* * *

Quent got to camp before the sun came up, both to avoid a morning encounter with Uncle Nick and to anticipate Annie's arrival. Behind him, in the eye of the sun, he saw the buckboard coming out from Dodge, Linares driving and Annie sitting beside him, her feathers bobbing and waving. The mules stood harnessed to the wagons, Sid scoured the last skillet, Jenny waited quietly, already saddled.

Quent rushed to help Annie down, before Linares had a chance to come around and give her his arm. He hurried her bundles to the wagon, for Stack and Broadbrim had already ridden out to take their places at the head of the herd. In less than a quarter of an hour, he and Annie urged their horses to a trot to get beyond the dust being kicked up by the cattle and the remuda. Quent pulled up when the yellow cloud hung half a mile behind them.

"Annie, I've done something to offend you, and I don't know what I did. Will you please tell me?" She regarded him suspiciously from the corner of her eyes. "When I talked to Dan. What did I say? You must understand, I didn't know you were in the wagon. But it was...well, my duty to warn him about..."

"The women?" she said, making it a definite question, so that he had to answer it.

"Yes. Young men can find trouble in a place like Dodge."

"But you, who can afford the best, there's no reason for you to abstain, I suppose, when..." She stopped. She put her right hand against her face. He could not see her clearly, but the tears had entered her voice.

"Annie!" he said, shocked. "You can't imagine that I..."

"That's what you implied," she answered, sobbing. He pulled her hand down, held it in his own, the leather of his glove spreading the sensation of her touch over his entire hand.

"Annie, I swear to you, I did not, nor do I, have any intention of doing such a thing." She looked at him, but her eyes reflected no trust or belief.

"I know who you are," she said flatly. She kicked Jenny, trying to escape his hold, but he kept up, retaining her hand.

"Who?" he asked insistently. She gave up trying to run away, stopped again and submitted to having her hand held.

"You're connected to your uncle's railroad combine, and you're on this drive to secretly select the route of the railroad. I should have known long ago you were an engineer, for you're much too clever to be what you pretend to be. A greenhorn artist, who's never been in the West before? You designed the horn pike, you told Ardisson he should use a pulley to get his hay in the mow more efficiently, you figured out the best solution to getting cattle into railroad cars. You can't hide what you really are. A hundred little things..."

Her voice trailed off, but Quent could say absolutely nothing in response to this amazing statement. An engineer?

"I'm sure you've been in many a railroad hell town," she continued. "Like Temptation. I'm afraid now it won't offer you much in the way of entertainment, since the railroad's done."

"Annie, may I tell you something which, under normal circumstances, should not be said in the hearing of a lady?"

"I suppose, but what if I faint?" she asked. The wry humor of the question encouraged him to believe the worst was over.

"You won't. If you were a fainting woman, you wouldn't be here. I have not been an angel in my life, Annie. I'm not trying to foist such a lie upon you. But several years ago, I vowed I'd . . . The sort of behavior to which you have made reference... With no woman until she was my wife. Do you understand what I'm saying?"

Her hand holding the reins opened and closed restlessly. Jenny turned her head around, puzzled by the movement.

"Yes, I understand," she said finally. "You want me to think of you as an honorable man."

"I hope I am. I hope I keep my promises, both the ones I've made to myself, and the ones I make to others."

"My experience with Yankees," she said, bitterness open and flaring, "has led me to expect exactly the opposite in men from New York. Let go of my hand."

He did as he was told, but not until after he said, "If I didn't know better, I'd think you were jealous." She struck at him with the ends of her reins.

The sweat rolling underneath Annie's corset tickled. If the days got hotter, she'd be forced to leave it off. She swatted at the mosquitoes rising from the bog before her.

"You went downstream?" Perk asked Stack.

"Not ten miles down, settlers have moved in," said Stack. "Fields of corn more than knee-high, and wheat close to ripe. They're not friendly to herds."

"Broadbrim?"

The dark man grinned as he gave the bad news. "It's like this for fifteen miles upstream, then broke-up country that I didn't head into."

"The settlers," continued Stack, intent on his own observations, "said a week and a half ago terrible storms came two nights running. The creek rose higher than they'd ever seen it. They lost the crops in the bottoms."

"There's another herd, smaller than ours, drifting upstream," added Broadbrim. "The stream curves back south, but the foreman figures they'll find a crossing eventually."

"They crossed the plowed line, then?"

"Said they had no choice."

"They'll be trapped a week or more in that badlands before they find the trail north again," mused Perk.

"Can't stay here," offered Stack, expressing aloud what everyone thought, "with 'nother herd no more than a day behind us. The grass is shy as is."

Annie's heart went out to Perk. He was the boss. He had to solve the problem. Everyone would stand by him, of course, but he had to make the decision, then justify his actions to Linares. She moved a bit closer to the man, to show her support. Quent walked away, mounted his horse and rode off. Why must he leave at the very time Perk needed everyone's ideas? She watched with disapproval as he rode down the shallow embankment, into the mud left behind by the flood. Ten feet into the stream, the horse's hooves sank fetlock deep. Quent sprang off, went in up to his boot tops, turned the horse and led him out, rescuing his boots by leaning over and grasping the straps. The cowboys hooted and laughed.

Leaving the horse and his boots on the grass, Quent returned to the bog. With his knife he whacked down two thick bushes. When he came to the mire he laid one flat, walked out on it, laid the second, stepped onto it, turned and retrieved the first, then repeated the process until he stood on a hillock in the middle of the bog.

"We're gonna look mighty funny, laying bushes down in front of the steers!" yelled Stack. Beyond the hillock, Quent repeated the process, reached the other bank, climbed upon the grass, covered with mud.

"Well, we got Dunk across," Huzzy said sardonically. "Anyone else want to try?"

"Doesn't seem significant," said Broadbrim. "He's comin' back. You wouldn't think a greenhorn would want to get that all-fired dirty."

It took five minutes for Quent to make his way back over the bog, dropping and picking up his bushes. Once on solid ground, he grabbed his boots and the reins of the horse. He looked like a mischievous child who had gone to some forbidden hole to play mud pies.

"So, what have you discovered?" asked Perk with mock seriousness.

"Let's build a bridge," said Quent.

"A bridge!" exclaimed everyone but Stack, who asked, "Are you daft?"

"The brush held up my weight," Quent pointed out.

"You're for sure a big, stalwart fellow," said Sid, shoving back his hat and winking, "but a steer weighs a bit more."

"This is the spot, not the regular crossing point," Quent continued heedlessly, "because that hillock in the middle, it gives ten or twelve feet of stable ground and shortens the distance we have to bridge. Just a little more than fifty feet is my estimate. We can cut down the cottonwoods, lay the logs on a base of brush, drive the herd across."

"I've never seen cattle willingly walk on a corduroy road," snorted Broadbrim.

Annie saw, in her mind's eye, the bridge of brush and logs. It had a smooth top.

"So? We'll cover it with dirt and sod!" she cried. "It's a marvelous idea!"

"How many axes do we have?" asked Quent.

"Just one," answered Sid. "I hardly ever need to cut firewood, let alone build a bridge."

"I didn't come on no trail drive to play Dan'l Boone, cutting down trees," said Lucas, directing his words at Perk. "You can ask anything of a cowboy to be done on horseback, but chopping and wallerin' in the brush, that ain't included."

"You'll do what you're told," snapped Perk. "Come on, Dunk, show me what you're thinking of."

The cowboys stared in disbelief as Perk followed Quent to the edge of the bog. Perk whacked down some brush; the two of them made their way to the hillock, where they stood talking.

"This whole scheme is as ridiculous as legs on a fish," said Lucas. "We're wasting time."

"No, it's not," said Annie. For the first time since the herd had left San Antonio, she dared to disagree with the men on something touching on their business. "Quentin—Dunk—he's an engineer."

"Then where's his locomotive?" asked Huzzy, all innocence.

"Not an engine driver. An engineer. The man who designs things, decides where roads and railroads should be laid out. Haven't you noticed how much he knows about mechanics? Who else but an engineer could design a horn pike?" she pointed out.

"They're coming back," said Stack, "and Perk is paying a mighty lot of attention to Dunk."

"Maybe Perk'll fall in the mud and give up this featherheaded notion."

"I don't know that Dunk has featherheaded notions," Broadbrim said seriously. Annie nearly hugged him.

Perk began shouting orders before he had cleared the swamp. "Broadbrim, ride upstream, tell the foreman of that herd we're going to build a bridge that should get all of us across this swamp by tomorrow evening. If they're willing to come back and help, that is. Stack, ride to the herd behind us. Tell them to move up as close as possible, but not to mix the cattle, then bring all their men, every ax and spade, or any other tool that cuts and digs."

Annie jumped up and down, but found herself alone in her delight. Everyone else stood stock-still, paralyzed.

"Git!" roared Perk. Stack and Broadbrim jumped, ran to their mounts.

"Sid, get the tools out of the wagon. Johnny, get the remuda up here so's we have fresh horses. Huzzy, Rolf, you go with Dunk, he'll tell you what to do. The rest of you, get the herd two miles back. Don't let them get near this place, or we'll be all summer pulling steers out of the mud."

Annie stood in the middle of a kaleidoscope, men moving about her with sudden energy. Was she to simply stand by? She strode to Quent's side.

"What can I do? There must be something."

He didn't dismiss her out of hand. In fact, to her great pleasure, he smiled. "Is Bird bearing up well?"

"Very well. I think he's stronger than when we left Texas."

"Then switch your saddle to him, get my ropes out of the wagon. You drag the brush down here as Rolf and Huzzy cut it. They'll bundle it, you tie the end of the rope on your saddle horn."

Annie couldn't remember when, in all her life, she had had so much fun. Three more axes joined Sid's when the other herds arrived; the splintering of wood, the crash of the cottonwoods as they fell, the rasping scrape of brush through the dirt, formed a background to the excited yells of the cowboys. She tied a kerchief around the lower part of her face, for the dust grew deeper with every load dragged in. Johnny snared the strongest horses from the remuda and soon they joined the brush carriers, towing logs from a quarter mile upstream.

Bird felt the excitement and danced about, anxious to run. She held him to a walk. Hours of work stretched before them. A strange cowboy caught the end of the rope she threw, bundled it around a mass of tree limbs stripped from a huge cottonwood.

"This gonna be too big?" he asked.

She pulled her bandanna down. "No, he'll manage the weight if I keep him to a walk." The cowboy's eyes bugged almost out of his skull.

"A girl!" she saw his lips say. She didn't hear the words, for a tree thundered to the ground not twenty feet away. He turned to Huzzy.

"You fellows got a girl along?" he asked.

"Sure," said Huzzy, pausing for a moment, wiping his sweaty brow with his sleeve. "Miss Annie," he added, as if having a woman along called for no extensive comment.

"But...but she's hauling and riding like a man!"

"Don't she, though?" said Huzzy, looking up with admiration. "And takes care of herself, like you can't think. When we're done here, remind me to tell you the way she scalped an old geezer who thought to take advantage of her.'' He laughed, turned back to his work. The strange cowboy, after staring for a few seconds, joined him.

It seemed a shame to make Bird walk, when she, too, would like to run, to gallop, to celebrate. Huzzy accepted her, accepted her strange skirts, her willingness to work. The cowboys no longer considered it unsuitable that she rode with them. Some had, in the early days of the drive, been tempted to try her as a woman. She'd seen the desire in their eyes. Since she'd downed Ardisson, however, there'd been nothing but respect and friendship. She grinned beneath her kerchief when she reached the end of the bridge. A gang of men untied the rope, flipped it to her.

Brush lay almost all the way out to the hillock, and logs a third of the way. Quent sank knee-deep in muck, plunging from the end of the brush layer to supervise the placing of another log. A huge white ox pulled a log two feet in diameter over the uneven surface. Where had he come from? Five men flung off the chains, wrestled the log into position, Quent standing in the mud, giving them quiet directions, moving his hands to show what he wanted done. His hat had disappeared, his blond hair showed black with perspiration and dust. *Quent is quite handsome.* Hugh McCann is handsome, she told herself loyally, but for the life of her, she could not call his face into her mind.

Quent crouched, gave the order to let go, and the log settled onto the brush foundation. The white ox climbed onto solid ground, stood while the men chained another log. She watched the animal unerringly follow the signaled commands of his driver, using no bridle, no reins, no rope. The lithe man walked beside the ox, one hand resting on an outspreading horn.

"Getting tired?" asked Quent's voice, close beside her.

"I'm sorry," she said, grasping Bird's reins. "I'm not doing my job. But I started looking..." Looking at what? The beautiful white ox. Him, Quentin. Fortunately, the kerchief covered most of her face. Dust and grime must obscure the rest, so her discomfort at being discovered as a voyeur did not show.

"Take time to rest."

"No. Huzzy and his crew have another pile ready."

She turned Bird's head to put distance between herself and Quent. When he crouched, his muscles taut, the memory of him standing in the creek had returned clearly. *Water streamed down his sleek flanks, glistening on the hair that spread across his chest, tapered down his belly.*

Someday he will be a great man. He and his uncle will build a railroad bridge on this very spot. He'll be the boss, the one who writes out the orders, the one whose words are put into action and become shining rails laid across hard oak ties. *The rails will come through Temptation, or nearby, and Hugh and I will ride over to see the workers sweating in the sun. Quentin will invite us into his railroad car for something cool to drink.*

She threw the rope down the bank to Huzzy. Her mouth, hidden by the kerchief, pouted, desired to be kissed. *I will see him and think of him naked, standing in the stream, taking his pleasure after a hot, dusty day on the trail.*

By then she would be a respectable matron, one of the women who work to bring churches and schools to frontier towns. *How many children will I have by then? How long does it take to build a railroad from Mexico to Canada?* She blinked back the tears that sprang to her eyes. She must not cry, for she dared not put her filthy hands to her face. Think of anything, but not the lost boy.

Would the memories of Quentin van Kelson last as long, and be as painful, as the memories of her boy?

Chapter Eleven

Quent kept the men at their work until it was too dark to see. Annie, out of pride, refused to stop until everyone else did. Broadbrim, thrashing about blindly to get a final log into place, stumbled into a pool of stagnant water and lost his hat. A cloud of curses exploded in the twilight, furnishing no illumination, but letting Annie know where the men congregated. She could see nothing of the white ox but a blur in the night, his driver a shadow by his side. Annie turned Bird over to Johnny, staggered toward the darker bulk of her wagon.

"Here's a bucket of water for you to wash," said Sid, materializing from the night. "I took it from one of the pools hours ago, to give the muck a chance to settle out." He poured the water into a basin, taking care not to stir up the sediment at the bottom. She found a cloth, a piece of soap, by touch alone, washed her face and hands. A layer of grit remained.

"Grub," continued Sid, "is over at t'other outfit's wagon. Their cook killed a steer, so there's steaks and cowboy stew, besides the beans and fixings."

That explained the darkness, she realized. The fire was at the other outfit's chuck wagon.

The distance seemed beyond her energy. She sat down on the ground, leaned against the wheel of her wagon, gazed toward the fire. The cutting of trees and grubbing of brush had produced an unusual amount of fuel, so besides the cooking fire in a trench, the men had built a true campfire. Figures passed between her and the glare, some gesturing like grotesque monsters, others subdued by exhaustion. She closed her eyes to blot out the light, then lifted her face to the darkening heavens to watch the stars come out.

Distance muted all sounds—the lowing of the thirsty cattle, the conversations of the men, an occasional shout, a more frequent laugh. Soft footfalls drew near.

"Here's dinner, Annie," he said, standing five feet in front of her. "I didn't know that you'd want to join the men, since most of them find your presence a bit odd."

Even in the dark he resembled a misshapen creature of the bog, someone she should be afraid of, except for his voice.

I'm afraid of his voice. His eastern accent.

Strange, it had ceased to threaten her. And the cowboys must feel the same. His accent made no difference. Quentin had proved himself. They respected him.

He squatted down, handed her one of the plates he carried. At first she merely sniffed the heavenly aroma, doubtful that she could eat a thing. Once she picked up her fork, however, the food disappeared at an astounding rate. She heard the clink of Quent's fork on his own tin plate as he gobbled silently next to her.

"We're going to do it, Annie. We're going to build a bridge," he whispered.

"Not we. You. You're building a bridge," she said, a bit startled by the insistent pride behind her words. "The idea wouldn't have crossed Perk's mind in a month of Sundays," she said firmly, unwilling to subtract anything at all from her new appreciation of him. "And Stack and Broadbrim and all the rest, you heard them ridiculing the idea. Anyone but you would have given up. As it is, if the bridge doesn't work..."

"It will work."

"But it if shouldn't, not one of them will let you forget you thought of it. That only a stupid greenhorn could come up with such a stupid idea."

"Maybe. But necessity breeds invention, so someone would have decided to try it eventually."

"I imagine every cowboy over there is bragging about how he had the same notion."

"No. The main topic of conversation over the evening fire is you. This drive will go down in history as the one with a woman along."

"No, it will be remembered as the drive that brought Quentin van Kelson to Montana. You'll be famous."

"I'm not that good," he said. "My pictures will be pleasant and acceptable, but nothing anyone will remember a hundred years from now. A few months ago my vanity imagined otherwise, but one has to face reality out here on the plains. They're so big. Human beings learn their true significance, and I'm pretty small potatoes."

"I wasn't talking about art. I was talking about the railroad you and your uncle will build. A few years from now you'll be back, right here, building another bridge across this swamp."

"If not me, someone had better do it," he said seriously. "Next year's herds, if the stream should turn boggy, won't have the choice of building a bridge. They'll have to go upstream, whether they like it or not."

"Why?"

"Annie, we're cutting down every cottonwood tree for a mile, even more. Downstream, the settlers have cut every tree for a distance of five miles for timber and fuel. Next spring's floods will carry the bridge away, unless the settlers get here first and tear it apart for the logs. What will next year's herds do? Ride two or three miles upstream to cut down more trees, maybe. But then the game's up. We— I mean everyone involved in the cattle business, and every settler moving onto the plains—can't keep on doing things in this haphazard, temporary way. We need permanent bridges, permanent roads, permanent towns.''

''In San Antonio the cattlemen got up a petition,'' Annie said. ''They want the government to set aside a trail for cattle drives, six miles wide, with improvements, like bridges over the rivers and marked lanes around towns. No fences would be allowed to block the route, so the herds wouldn't be at the mercy of men like Ardisson.''

''And where are these herds to get their food? This year we're seeing too many cattle on the trail, Annie. How often has Perk had to drive five, six miles off the trail to find grass? And we're at the head of the drive to Montana, not more than nine or ten thousand cattle in front of us. The banks of the streams are broken down, the water running in mud below every crossing and around every watering place. Each successive herd goes a bit farther upstream to water, fouling another stretch. How many herds are behind us?''

Annie started in amazement, wondering why she had not observed all these things. Now that he mentioned it... Quentin was the amateur, but he saw more than the men who had done this for years!

''In Montana,'' she said, to reassure him, ''there's plenty of grass. My father told me, after his first visit, that the grass grew so high it brushed the bellies of the horses. That's why he and McCann went back the next summer and found land. We can graze twice, three times, the cattle up there than we ever could in Texas, on a spread of the same size.''

''I'm looking forward to Montana,'' he said. ''That's a country for the future.'' He turned his face up to the stars, and their light picked out the curves of his dirty face, shone in his eyes, black as the night.

The cowboys drove the three remudas back and forth across the sodded bridge to pack the dirt. Back and forth, until Perk and the other foremen nodded in satisfaction. Quent sat on Graybob, near the northern end of the bridge, forcing himself to concentrate on the structure. He had slept little last night, his mind in a tumult of worry, fear and sudden ideas. Would the makeshift thing stand up under a string of nine thousand cattle? Was the brush foundation deep enough to carry the load of logs, sod and cattle?

When he drifted into the outskirts of sleep, he had heard soft, muted sobs. She'd exhausted herself. He must not let her work so hard tomorrow.

In the morning, he had set her to riding from man to man, group to group, offering cold coffee to slack their thirst. The swamp water stank of rotting vegetation and the bodies of creatures caught in the flood. A man could barely stand to take a drink, but flavored with coffee it became palatable.

Now, Annie sat on Lily, fifty feet behind him. He could see her only if he turned around, and he dared not do that, in case some accident happened on the bridge. The chuck wagons and Annie's wagon came across one by one, the mules not even glancing at their precarious track high above the oily black-and-green mire. The cooks and Dan drove away from the stream, toward the widely scattered camping spots that the foremen had selected that morning.

The cowboy with the white ox rode through the three thousand Tall X cattle milling a quarter mile away. His hand rested on the horn of the ox, who stalked in regal grandeur beside him. The animal knew it was special, the leader of nine thousand of its kin, and it carried its head with the pride of a chieftain. A cow and calf fell in behind the ox, then a cluster of steers. Men on horseback lined the path to the bridge, to prevent a rush to the tempting water surrounded by treacherous mud.

The first hundred cattle streamed across the bridge, carefully spaced by riders. On the north shore, another group of men took over, pushed them up and over a rise, three miles, to a stream where they might drink in safety. The ox and his master drifted away from the cattle, circled back to lead the next group assembling at the end of the bridge.

Quent's heartbeat steadied. He felt, for the first time, the scorching heat of the sun on his shoulders, the rivulets of sweat running down his body, mingling with mud and dust, forming a crust on his skin.

Again the white ox led cattle across the bridge, again the cowboys fell in line after each fifty or sixty head. In two hours, all three thousand of the Tall X herd climbed the north bank. When the last cow and calf stepped off the bridge, onto solid ground, the men began to cheer, at first just the Tall X crew, then the men from all the herds.

"It worked!" cried Annie's voice behind him. He turned, glimpsed her smile. She waved her hat in triumph.

They had little time to celebrate, for the next herd was already being pushed to the end of the bridge, and two miles beyond them, the third. He sat watching, sweating, worrying, for five more hours, until the sun had passed the zenith, until the final steer had left the bridge.

The three foremen were the last men to cross, grinning, exulting. They looked toward Quent; they intended to congratulate him. Weariness descended on him, heavier than the sultry air. He waved to them, turned his back, spurred Graybob to join Annie. His job as bridge superintendent was done; he must turn his attention to his primary responsibility.

She sat cross-legged on the ground, holding Lily's reins while the horse cropped the few bunches of grass that struggled in the parched ground. She jumped up at his approach, smiled. He slid off the horse. The glow of her eyes, the happy angle of her head, tempted him closer and closer. His own joy leaped, an inner fountain. He let out one great whoop of delight, grasped her about the waist and lifted her from the ground. Her hands rested lightly on his shoulders; he spun about, admiring the way her hat slid off her head to expose her braids, the path her full trousers traced in the air as they swung away from her body.

"I'm filthy," he said, then roared with laughter, as if caked mud were an elaborate joke.

"Is there a bathing place at the next creek?" she asked.

"I hope so, very much. Shall we go find it?" She nodded. He placed her upon the ground, only now aware of how intimate his clasp had been. His hand reached to steady her stirrup, but the extended arm fastened around her waist instead, pulled her against his stiff clothing so that he felt the dry mud shatter and fall away. She clung to him; the pressure of her palms on his back caused little pricks where shards of mud were trapped beneath her hands. She moved her hips slightly, but significantly, pressed her body against his, took the measure of the passion he could offer her.

His conscience reproached him for the openness of his lust, but his ears roared with a powerful flow of blood. Shame, it shouted, was alien in an atmosphere of celebration, in the open reach of the plains. His heat was appropriate, and her subtle admiration of it right. He stared into her cheerful face and absorbed her affirmation. A shadow moved at the limit of his vision. Perk and the other two foremen rode by, keeping their eyes on the vanishing cattle. Had they seen? Most certainly. Would they misunderstand? Also most certainly.

Perhaps it was he who misunderstood. Was it possible for this closeness to exist between a man and a woman, except as prelude to the ultimate sensuality? His thoughts must have transferred to her, for she stepped away.

"I must look a sight," she said nervously, signaling that the moment had passed.

"Annie, you're beautiful. The first time I saw you, I thought you the most beautiful woman in the world. And mud and dirt fail to disguise the fact."

"At the corral in San Antonio?" she asked. "When I was angry at Linares, because he'd picked you to come with me?"

"No. In Washington. At Senator Wise's ball." She stepped backward—a warning?—but her loveliness filled his eyes and he plunged ahead.

"I so wanted to meet you, tell you how beautiful you were, but I couldn't find anyone to introduce us, because..."

She leaped toward Lily, her face distorted with a terror he did not understand. Her foot missed the stirrup, she fell against the horse, thrust him away as he leaned over her to help, clawed into the saddle. Lily threw up her head, dashed up the embankment in response to Annie's frantic kicks.

She did not cry. Her body shrank, dry and sere, beyond tears. Quentin knew. And she had not suspected, for he had treated her with studied courtesy, as if she were a lady. And he had known all this time, and she had never guessed. When she thought back, remembering all she had shared with him, the fact that he had known her secret became doubly despicable.

One long day's ride alone, two if she stayed with the herd, would bring her to the railroad. She had no choice now, for she could no longer look him in the eye, no longer share laughter with him. He must not fetch her chair, fill her plate, get her coffee. What mistaken notions did he carry from that embrace at the end of the bridge? The glory of celebration had turned her head.

No, not her head. What she had felt in his arms originated much lower down. Her belly had mapped the outlines of his lust. A man, embracing a maiden, might suppose such a thing happened from innocent lack of knowledge. But when a man knew what Quentin knew of her, he translated that pressure of loin against loin as the suggestive act of a harlot. At the first moment of privacy, he would seize her. When? It might be tonight, tomorrow, but one day he would climb into her wagon, demand the same privilege Davy Lampman had enjoyed.

She lifted the canvas to peep out. He was not in camp. Yes. Down by the creek. He wore clean denims. His hair clung in damp ringlets to his head and neck. Along with several of the cowboys, he threw wet, sketchily washed clothes on the low bushes along the stream. She wished she could forget the old vision of him bathing, skin exposed to air and water. She hid her face in her hands as the budding flower within her unfolded its petals to reveal one sensual, curved segment of its golden heart.

He walked to the fire, the strength of his legs apparent from the length of his stride; he might as well stand before her naked. Sid ladled out beans, the men piled their plates high with golden-brown biscuits fresh from the Dutch oven. He stared at her wagon, expecting her to emerge. One corner of his mouth turned up. Had he seen her peeking beneath the canvas? She dropped the fabric. Nothing to do but go out, act as if the day were perfectly normal. She was still filthy. Perhaps he would stand guard in the twilight while she washed in the creek. No need for her to worry about who would guard the guard. He knew what she was. He might look all he wanted.

A long trail of black smoke, a screeching whistle. The rails were invisible, so the train sliding east across the yellow-tan landscape looked like a strangely intent snake. Sunlight glinted from the windows of the Pullman and day cars. She had missed today's train.

"Perk would like to avoid Ogallala, but he thinks he'd better ride in, see if there's a message from Linares," Quentin said casually. She hated his nonchalance, more horrifying than a blunt assault upon her virtue. "Most of the cowboys are itching to go into town," he added.

The lascivious descriptions of Ogallala had not missed her ears. Last night, the older cowboys—Stack and Broadbrim especially—had regaled the crew with stories of old adventures in the hell city of the cattle trail. Quent had led her away from the conversation, ostensibly to observe the stars beyond the glare of firelight. She had waited, expecting to feel the weight of his fingers on the buttons of her basque. Nothing.

A towering cloud of dust marked the location of the herd. Farther south, three similar clouds stained the blue sky, where other hands pushed herds north, to Montana and Wyoming. Tonight and tomorrow night Ogallala would be in its cups, overrun with men taking their pleasure in great gulps, drinking and whoring for a few frantic hours, to make up for the deprivation and isolation of the trail.

"Will you go in?" she asked. She did not want to go alone. If only one train ran east each day, she would be forced to spend the night in a hotel. She shivered at the thought of a night alone in Ogallala. In that concentration of brothels and gambling dens, every man would assume... Better Quentin, whom at least she knew. Once in her bed, she would not resist. His hands might caress her breasts, her legs, her loins, without obstacle.

Her father and Hugh McCann need never know. This time, if illegitimate contact begat a child, there would be no difficulty. Three, four days at most, on the train, and she'd arrive in Montana for an immediate wedding. Both Quentin and McCann were fair-haired and tall, so no nosy gossip would suspect the child had been engendered by a man not her husband. An intense picture of herself bearing Quentin's child rose from her gut, an image aswarm with both pain and delight.

"I think I'll stay in camp," said Quentin, thoroughly dashing the fantasy.

"Please," she blurted out. She couldn't bear riding in with Stack, or Broadbrim, or even Perk. Their eyes would be narrowed in anticipation of Ogallala's pleasures.

"Why should you want to go to Ogallala?" he asked.

She toyed nervously with the reins. "I must," she whispered, then cleared her throat. "I must," she said again, louder this time. "I intend to catch the train, go directly to Temptation."

"You can't!" he cried. "Another month and we've done it! Why give up now?" She shook her head, took off her gloves in a nervous gesture. Mud still stained her hands, so deeply ingrained it would take more than one hot bath to wash it away. Less permanent, though, than the sin of her body.

"Annie, what happened at the bridge . . . I'm very sorry. But you must understand, a man can't always control—"

"You know!" she shrieked. "How can I stay with you, when you know what I've done? You know what kind of woman I am!"

"Annie, what you did, leaning against me that way, it isn't wrong. Not out here, at least. The air, the sky, the land, all encourage a bit more freedom than what's accepted in a ballroom. And I swear, there will be nothing more."

"I'm not talking about what happened at the bridge, and you know it," she snapped. "Why do you torment me?"

"What are you talking about?" he asked, mystification plain in his open, questing eyes, questions implicit in the one-sided curl of his lips.

"I'm sure everyone in Washington found it very amusing," she said bitterly. "The little Texas nobody, thinking she could marry the son of Cyrus Lampman. The silly little rancher girl, who believed the tender things a New York man said to her, when he wasn't serious at all."

"Annie, what *are* you talking about?" His arm spanned the distance between them, his hand covered her tensed one. She shook it away, slid off Jenny to get away from him, even though she had to dismount on the wrong side. He was by her side in a flash, his arms around her.

"Annie, what am I supposed to know?"

"You were in Washington. You saw me at Senator Wise's party," she accused.

"Yes. Guilty. How is that incriminating?" She could not believe he lied, for his eyes and lips were wide in innocence. The only innocent part of his body, she noted wryly as he captured her waist, her hips. It was too much to bear; she strained her body to feel the generosity of his.

"I must confess," he continued, "that I fell in love with you that night, although it was, from necessity, a rather distant kind of love. But in the past few days, I've become certain.'' He removed her hat, let it hang from its restraining cord down her back. He brushed the tendrils of hair from her forehead.

''Annie, must it be McCann?'' His voice, charged with emotion, brought visions redolent of sex in a darkened room. ''Is there no hope for a man who loves you? Might I beg of you, of your father, to let me be your husband and lover?''

Her palms shoved against his chest with such quick fear he nearly toppled over. She whirled, ran to escape the torrent of hot emotion emanating from him, as a dust cloud rises from the heels of a thousand cattle. Marry Quentin? Impossible! He outpaced her, seized her arm and pulled her back to the embrace.

''Please, Annie. You say I know something dreadful about you. What I do know is I love you. I had hoped you might love me.''

''You don't know what you're asking!'' she cried.

''No, I suppose I don't, having never taken a wife before. But there's a first time for everything.''

For everything, she thought in horror. *And my first time is gone, given to a man who abused the honor.*

''Quentin, don't you know what I did in Washington?''

''What happened? Tell me,'' he said soothingly, pressing her head into the notch of his neck and shoulder.

Tell him? She must, for any man who spoke of marriage had to know. And Quentin didn't seen to have the least idea.... She gathered her strength, concentrated it in her throat, even as the sensuality spread wide within her, fully open, desiring him.

''In Washington I met Davy Lampman,'' she said simply. ''We became quite fond of one another. He asked me to marry him. I said yes. I believed ... he led me to believe it was settled between us, and I allowed him ...'' There was no way she could set words to the sin.

"You allowed him physical love," said Quentin, making it a statement, not a question.

"Yes."

"And he withdrew the marriage offer?" he asked, his voice tight in shock.

"No. His father forbade it. He said his son would not marry a Texas nobody. He said another word, but I will not repeat it."

She wished there could be no more talking, so that she could enjoy the pleasure his hand accomplished by cradling her buttocks, pressing her belly against his. But more must be said, cruel things that would take away the honorable offer, leave only the possibility of temporary passion, temporarily sated.

"There was a child, Quentin," she said, her voice hateful even to her own ears. "That's why I went to Louisiana. To a convent. I had the child, stayed a few months longer, until the gossip ceased. Or at least until it had become so old no one showed interest any longer. My father wrote with McCann's offer. I said yes." She drew back against his restraining hands, and he let her go. She saw in his face the will not to believe. It changed as the truth sank in, an arrow in his heart, brutal, cold.

"The child was a boy," she continued quietly, not sure he paid heed to her any longer. "I held him once, but my father had told the mother superior I was not to keep him. They gave him to a woman whose child had died.... I think... They told..." The last few unintelligible words ended with a sob. She could not think of the child without bringing to life the agony of that moment. Not the pain of birth, which had been erased by the touch and sight of the tiny body, but the pain of separation.

Tears erupted, her body convulsed, ripping her heart apart, and she knew she would die of the sorrow—if not today, someday. She longed for Quentin to come to her, take her in his arms. In that time of trauma, it had been the absence of human sympathy that was most bruising.

Quentin walked away.

"Get your things ready," he said gruffly, not turning around to face her. "I'll take you into Ogallala this evening."

Chapter Twelve

Quent did not understand how the hard prairie sod could suddenly turn to sponge beneath his feet. How was it that fog should so quickly blot out the golden day? Below him, in the broad valley of the Platte River, the herd leaders stood knee-deep in the yellow water. A mirage, he supposed. Surrounded by such a suffocating cloud, he could not possibly see a mile or more.

He closed his eyes to correct his vision, opened them. The cattle splashed through the wide river, the leaders now far into the middle, the water not reaching their bellies. On the north shore, the two wagons were already climbing to the heights. The mules had pulled through the shallow river without dampening the axles. Sid and Dan reined in the mules at the top of the rise. Sid dismounted; his movements showed he was unharnessing the mules. The laggards of the herd entered the water; they would soon be over the Platte, the last leg of the journey before them. Nothing to aim for now but Montana.

"Annie?" he whispered, her name a question. Was he bound by his promise to leave the drive, accompany her on the train? The woman could most certainly take care of herself, he thought angrily. A willful, corrupt woman. Must he sacrifice the last weeks of the drive, must he give up this most delightful experience of his life, give up sketches and notes for the railroad that must come to this country if its people were to survive? Was he bound to do this for the reputation of a woman who had already abandoned both honor and reputation?

He mounted, spurred his horse toward the sheet of water that spread muted in the sun, like yellow-gold satin that has lain years in a trunk. For one instant, as the horse splashed through the river, he thought of his responsibility to her. He dismissed it.

"Mister Dunk?" Quent's head jerked up, his fists loosened, as he recalled reality. Dan stood a bit to the side in his wild-deer fashion, prepared to run at the slightest displeasure. He pulled off his hat to show respect and to signal that he meant to ask a favor.

"Yes?" Quent finally asked.

"Some fellows are a-goin' in to Ogallala," he said, the statement explaining his purpose.

"And you want to go with them?"

"Yeah."

"I see no reason you shouldn't go into Ogallala," said Quent. "Just remember, the town has a bad reputation, so be on your guard. Don't wear your gun. A gun's but a route to trouble in a place like Ogallala."

"Yes, sir... No, sir. Thank you, sir. Might you ask Miss Annie for a dollar of my money? I'd be thankful." He nervously rolled the brim of his hat against the crown, cradled it in his arm like a baby. A baby! Annie had given birth to Lampman's baby. He felt sick, beat it down.

"You may speak to Miss Annie yourself. She'll not take offense at your request."

The boy raced off toward Annie's wagon, leaving the whirling fog to close in once more, but now Quent fought against it. He had decisions to make. What time this morning had they seen the eastbound train? Past midmorning, he thought. So there was no need to take her into town this evening. The place probably didn't boast a decent hotel. He could see her to the train in the morning and, riding Graybob, have no difficulty catching up with the herd by evening.

The wagon? No need for her empty wagon to trundle on up the trail. Was selling it his responsibility, or should he wire Linares? Or her father?

Dan? He'd taken the child away from his home, so he had a duty there. Barring any other solution, he'd keep him on as a personal servant. Maybe Perk would give him some minor jobs to do around camp, so the boy could claim trail-driving experience. A winter as a cowboy on a ranch in Montana, and there'd be no need for him to return to the father who had made him a cattle rustler.

"Looks like Linares don't trust us," said Broadbrim at his elbow. Everyone in camp stared toward the river as a buckboard emerged from the ford.

"He's certainly checking up on you often, Perk," commented Stack. Sid ceased feeding cow chips into the cooking fire, joined everyone else in watching the buckboard climb the dusty trail out of the Platte bottom.

"He said nothing about meeting the herd in Ogallala," Perk said uneasily.

"Maybe Brownell has changed his mind," offered Sid. "Ogallala would be his last chance to sell the herd until we cross the Northern Pacific in Montana."

"Ain't Linares," said Lucas, who had especially keen eyesight. "It's that other feller who was in Dodge with you. Old Nick."

Perk's mouth relaxed into a smile so broad it practically split his face.

"So it is!" he exclaimed. "Old Nick's Dunk's uncle," he explained. "He's checking up on Dunk."

"He's probably heard about that bridge and wants Dunk to ride back and put a sign on it—Railroad Property," said Broadbrim. "That way, the sodbusters can't haul it away."

"Quentin!" the man in the buckboard yelled. Unmistakably Uncle Nick. Ogallala must have a better hotel than he supposed.

"How are you, my boy? How are you?" exclaimed his uncle. "How long will the herd be staying?"

"Just tonight."

"No longer than that?" he asked, surprised. "I would think all the men would be anxious to taste the pleasures—"

"If cowboys stopped for every town and tasted the pleasures," Quent said wryly, "it would take two years to get to Montana."

"Then you must come with me immediately, with your sketches. McGilvery is here and champs at the bit to see what you've done."

"What are you talking about?"

"The route of the railroad, of course." He lowered his voice. "McGilvery takes care of the tentative route mapping. Something to show Congress this winter. Come, come. We still have time to return to Ogallala and dine. Where is Miss Annie?"

"In her wagon," Quent said quietly.

"Not ill, I hope."

"She's fine," lied Quent, realizing his last view of her had been one of tears. If he headed into town with Uncle Nick, he might as well find her a place to stay.

"I presume there's a decent hotel in Ogallala?"

"No. Not at all. I talked a friend into letting me use his private car. It's at the Ogallala station, not far at all from the center of town, such as it is. Miss Brownell," he called toward the wagon.

Annie's face peered out between the folds of the canvas, her eyes red-rimmed from tears. Perhaps Uncle Nick didn't notice, since her tan covered most of the evidence, but Quent saw, and was taken aback by the rush of pity he felt for her.

"Miss Brownell, you must come with me immediately, for I've planned a gala evening in town. I have spoken so often to McGilvery about the lovely queen of the trail that he demands you join us. Don't think to change your clothes here.

The palace car furnishes every convenience. The cook is preparing a dinner of the best Ogallala can furnish. I gave the orders as soon as I identified the herd.''

"Cook?" Quent asked stupidly.

"Of course. The car comes equipped with appropriate servants. I believe we're having some sort of bird a local killed on these desolate prairies, but Cook is skilled at making the roughest sort of staples into dishes fit for royalty. And after we dine, there is the theater.''

"Ogallala has a theater?" asked Annie, surprise apparent even through her voice was muffled by the canvas.

"Not a proper one. The actors have thrown up a large tent on the edge of town. Perhaps you saw it from the hill when you came toward the river. I have procured a box for every performance, tonight *Romeo and Juliet*. Last night they offered *Macbeth,* a labored production, except for the beauty who played Lady Macduff. I go this evening, in hopes she will be the youthful Juliet.''

Quent wanted to shout, "No, no, no!" He must avoid an evening of unmitigated torture, both for himself and for Annie. He envisioned dinner with Annie, where his hopeful uncle would pair them, then the theater, undoubtedly sitting beside her for hours. He remembered with distress that *Romeo and Juliet* was about love, and families who tried to separate lovers.

If he kept a distance between himself and Annie, he announced the trouble separating them. The cowboys must suspect already, for hadn't they come into camp apart? And they all must have seen Annie's ravaged, tearstained face.

How was he to explain Annie's departure tomorrow morning to Uncle Nick without betraying her secret? He had to, sometime during the evening, have a private conversation with her, so they could agree on a story. A lie. Why did he feel it necessary to conceal the truth? How was it possible that he loved her? Still!

Uncle Nick handed Annie into the sumptuous private car. The incongruity of such luxury in the middle of the prairie struck Quent immediately. Red velvet draperies accented walls papered in gold and cream. Gold leaf picked out the heavily sculptured ceiling. The furniture had been especially designed for a railroad car: A table unfolded for dining, bookcases sank into the walls, upholstered chairs and sofas, which appeared to be the equal of any in the most fashionable drawing room, were actually built slightly smaller.

Quent mopped his face with his kerchief, helped Uncle Nick open the windows. The humid heat settled into the river bottom; it had been much more comfortable in camp on the uplands.

McGilvery proved to be a fussy elderly gentleman. He raised a pair of pince-nez to observe Quent and Annie as Uncle Nick made the introductions.

Uncle Nick shoved the silver and crystal on the table aside, spread the sketches and notes out on the table. McGilvery leaned over and studied them, his nose not two inches from the paper.

"No, no, Miss Brownell," Uncle Nick objected when Annie took a seat on a burgundy velvet sofa. "You must join us at the table. You, too, have seen these places, and can offer your opinion." He pulled out the chair next to Quent. She accepted the seat, but sat stiffly and stared straight ahead.

McGilvery praised the sketches, marveled at the copious notes accompanying them. "Very helpful," he said, moving a sketch of the crossing of the Republican River beneath his myopic eyes. "Can you add anything to this information, Miss Brownell?" he asked

"No," said she. "I mean, Quentin . . . Mr. van Kelson is quite thorough."

"Ah, but Mr. van Kelson—" he nodded toward Uncle Nick "—has marveled at your keen intelligence and helpfulness. The qualities a man should look for in a helpmate, but so seldom finds in these modern days." He shook his head sadly.

Tension curled down Quent's legs and paralyzed them. His hands separated, but his fingers did not relax. Uncle Nick still expected a Meechem-van Kelson marriage. He had not heard of the scandal that made it impossible.

"I must change before dinner," said Annie with dignity, but her fingers pressed her strained cheek. The servant showed her into a corridor that Quent assumed led to the boudoir compartments.

Dinner was served on those parts of the table not covered by paper. Quent's stomach rebelled at the rich sauces, the overdressed vegetables, and particularly the champagne. It could not satisfy his dry mouth, so he finally begged the serving man for water.

"Will you send out a survey party next summer?" Annie inquired, her eyes on Uncle Nick.

"We'll not wait until summer," he replied. "Winters are mild in the south. The survey will start immediately, as soon as we can pull a crew together."

"I believe," said McGilvery, drawing out a silver watch, "if we are to claim our seats at the theater before the performance begins, we should make some haste." Uncle Nick blocked Quent's way, drew him aside.

"Have you and Miss B. come to some accommodation?" Uncle Nick whispered.

"No!" Quent whispered back. "She is engaged. Remember?"

"Don't be foolish. I need her uncle's support. She will be given one of the two private boudoirs in this car. Take the opportunity."

Annie and McGilvery were already crossing the platform. "Miss Brownell," Quent said quickly, "has ties.... A matter of honor not to make connections where..." His lips refused to form the word *scandal*. McGilvery swung to the right of the railroad station. "Where's McGilvery going? He's heading for the main street!"

Quent dashed out of the car, across the platform, only to see Annie and McGilvery disappear around the corner. He

trotted onto Ogallala's dusty, manure-spattered main street.
McGilvery offered Annie his hand as she stepped onto the
uneven boardwalk opposite the railroad station. Didn't
McGilvery see the nature of the apartments bordering that
walk? No, his pince-nez swung from the pin in his lapel.

Quent dodged the men and horses crowding the thor-
oughfare. The sultry air lay still, oppressive; the dust stirred
by animals and humans clouded the street.

"McGilvery!" he shouted. No way the man could hear
over the shouts of long-parted friends, the music of piano,
guitar, fiddle and trumpet blaring from every saloon and
gambling hall. "Hello, cowboy," said half a hundred shrill
female voices.

Women hung out the doors and windows fronting on the
main street, their charms displayed through thin garments
or, sometimes, none at all. Sweat coursed down Quent's
spine, beneath his linen shirt and lined coat. Footsteps
pounded next to him. Uncle Nick pulled even with him.
"I'm sorry," he gasped.

"How'd you like to play with this?" asked a plump
woman. She lifted her sagging breast and thrust it in Quent's
direction. In front of him, Annie shied like a startled horse.
She, as politeness dictated, walked on the inside, within
inches of the harlots.

A leering cowboy rode his horse onto the boardwalk.
McGilvery gingerly detoured into the street, lifting his pince-
nez enough to see the step. Annie stumbled after him. Quent
shoved through the crowd until he stood directly behind her.
A thumping piano tempted men into a saloon. At the open
door, a woman moved with the music, her red skirt hitched
up on one side to exhibit the dangling tassels of her garter.
She saw Annie, smirked, drew the skirt up to show that,
above the stockings, she had nothing on. Quent gasped,
grabbed Annie's arm, knowing he was insulting Mc-
Gilvery, but unwilling to allow the vile spectacle to continue. He collided with the back of a large cowboy.

Only then did he notice the mob of people, all heading in the same direction, moving at a snail's pace. The saloon, the red-clad woman still dancing in the doorway, was the last building in the town. Beyond, Quent spotted the theater tent, bright with lanterns.

"Miss Brownell should not be standing in the street," he said to McGilvery. "Ladies most certainly have priority for entering the theater." He shoved men out of the way, saying over and over again, "Make way for the lady." Annie dragged behind him, helpless as a rag doll.

"The front box on the left!" Uncle Nick shouted.

Quent did not stop until he ushered Annie into the "box," two benches segregated from the rest of the audience by dirty ropes, ropes that had probably been hanging on saddles only a few days past. He pushed her down on one of the benches, stood between her and the mass of shouting and cursing men who competed for space on the closely packed benches. Her hands covered her mouth, and her eyes were closed, the lashes standing out pale against her sun-darkened skin. Her entire body shuddered, as if she were fighting sickness. He dropped a hand on her shoulder.

"It's all right, Annie."

"No, it isn't," she whispered. "I didn't know."

"Of course you didn't know how it would be. A young woman from polite society should never be exposed to a town full of rough men."

"That's not what I mean. I didn't know how men would expect me to behave. Men who know what kind of woman I am, they want me to do the things these women do."

"Shut up, Annie," he said angrily. "You're not that kind of woman."

"How am I different?" she asked with sad resignation.

"Annie, you're not that kind of woman. What happens in Ogallala, and every other trail and railroad town, is not what you did," he objected.

"There is no difference. You're trying to excuse my behavior, but there is no way to excuse . . ."

Uncle Nick and McGilvery shouldered their way down the aisle. Quent sat down beside Annie, keeping a few inches between them, as was seemly in public. How was it different, what she had done and what the harlots of Ogallala did?

"Between you and Davy," he whispered, "love made the difference. You fell in love, and Davy Lampman promised—a solemn promise which he did not fulfill, may I remind you—to declare that love openly. Sin is the act without love, simply to satisfy physical lust."

"By Jupiter! What a mob. What an extraordinary mob!" exclaimed Uncle Nick, taking his seat on the bench behind. McGilvery stood in front of Annie.

"My apologies, Miss Brownell. Mr. van Kelson very properly removed you from a disgusting scene. I am not so...adept at blustery western ways," McGilvery said.

"Sit down," ordered Nick. "The play commences." And indeed, an elderly, bearded man walked onto the stage in front of a canvas curtain painted with a townscape pretending to be Renaissance Italy. The crowd cheered, scrambled to find seats. Some gave up and sat on the floor in front of the stage. The actor's rolling baritone submerged the chatter in the same way the tide covers a disorderly stretch of beach. He intoned the stately lines of the prologue, the opening of the tale of "star-crossed lovers."

Before the first act was well under way, Quent decided these actors were performing the greatest mutilation of Shakespeare ever perpetrated. A woman on the shaded side of forty took the part of Juliet, apparently not the young beauty whom Uncle Nick said had graced the stage as Lady Macduff the night before.

The players depended heavily upon the prompter, whose voice carried far beyond the stage. The comic lines seldom came in the sequence which the author intended, and Romeo needed a closer shave. Quent let his attention wander to the audience. Amazing, that two or three hundred rough men should sit in hellish temperatures, in such rapt silence, charmed by words written hundreds of years before. He saw Dan among the floor-sitters, transfixed by this first view into the world of dramatic fantasy.

As act l staggered to a close, Quent recalled his eyes and mind to the performance. Romeo gazed across the stage, through the meager crowd representing the guests at the Capulets' house; he absorbed his first glimpse of Juliet. "O! she doth teach the torches to burn bright," began the hero's monologue. Now came Quent's turn to sit motionless, transfixed. He'd heard and read the words many times, but tonight they carried new meaning. He relived the moment at Senator Wise's ball. He had stood, like Romeo, his heart yearning toward a girl he did not know.

Did my heart love till now? forswear it, sight!
For I ne'er saw true beauty till this night.

Romeo walked across the stage, approached the lady who had taken his eye. Juliet simpered and played coy; even the wrinkles about her mouth did not destroy the fantasy.

"It is what I failed to do," whispered Quent.

Annie's lashes dropped, creating enough movement in her classic profile to let him know she heard. Her hands lay still on her skirt, clasping the gloves she found too hot to wear. Quent thought to touch her fingers, then decided he should not distract her from the elegant words of love. Did she comprehend it was their own story being reenacted? Their story as it should have been. His heart turned over. She had smiled at Davy Lampman and left the room with him.

The canvas curtain creaked down in jerks as the rope snagged a time or two, then collapsed in a sudden unrolling. The actors came out to acknowledge the applause. McGilvery bounced up, offered Annie his arm.

"A turn in the fresh air?" he asked brightly. "I must make amends."

She studied the roiling audience. "No, but I should like something to drink." McGilvery bowed, plunged into the crowd. Uncle Nick winked at Quent, wandered toward the stage, pretending to study the painted canvas.

"Annie," Quent whispered, "did it start...with Lampman...on the night of Senator Wise's party?" She leaned away from him, would have stood up, but he laid a restraining hand upon her shoulder.

"Please, Annie. I don't mean to cause you distress, but I must know. Was that when it began?"

"Yes," she whispered. The word mangled some vital part of him. Convulsions of guilt and remorse closed his throat. "Davy was a houseguest of the senator," she continued in an unemotional voice. "He asked me to go upstairs with him." Quent clasped one of her hands in both of his, pressing it tightly to emphasize his words.

"It's my fault," he said, "what happened." She jerked around, nearly tumbled off the bench.

"Your fault! Don't be ridiculous. I didn't even know you when I was in Washington."

"But I saw you. I watched you from across the room. Then, like a fool, I wasted minutes searching for a mutual acquaintance to introduce us. I should simply have gone across the ballroom, just as Romeo did, shoved Lampman aside, taken your hand and said, 'You are the most beautiful creature I've ever seen. May I have this dance?'"

"Perhaps I would not have accepted your declaration," she said sadly. "Davy would have considered you uncouth."

"If I had done all this, you would never have gone upstairs, don't you see? If we had spoken, you most certainly would have questioned your affections for him, at least for the moment. And your virtue would have been safe with me, as it is now."

She edged away from him, peeling his hands away from hers. "Let me go," she said, her voice threatening. "If you don't, I'll scream." He released her.

"I love you, Annie. I loved you then, I love you now. I have a great deal of wrong to make amends for."

Chapter Thirteen

Quent spent acts 2, 3, and 4 contemplating his role in Annie's fall from grace. She had shown shameful frailty in yielding to Lampman's entreaties, undoubtedly, but she might not have done so if others had offered her friendship. If her father had kept her near, instead of abandoning her to a shifting cast of substitute mothers. If he himself had not been so bound by procedure, but had marched boldly across the room, she would never have gone upstairs with that man. Cousin Ted's words tumbled through his mind.

She's got on the same dress she wore at Cady's ball, so there's no fortune there.

The most beautiful girl in the world, dismissed because she appeared more than once in a dress! The injustice of it seethed in his breast.

"I was a coward," he whispered, paying no heed to Juliet, sitting alone with her terrors in her bedchamber. "I let the silly dictates of society keep me from doing what I truly wanted to do. It will never happen again," he swore under his breath.

"Is something wrong?" asked Annie, speaking from the corner of her mouth while keeping her eyes on Juliet. The actress paced the length of the stage, raving about decaying bodies and bashing out her brains with the bone of an ancestor; her speech rose in spirit and volume, until she shouted, "Romeo, I come! This do I drink to thee." She lifted a glittering chalice, pretended to drink its nonexistent contents. She staggered backward, clutching her throat, turning her head slightly to make sure she was heading toward the "bed," a platform about three feet wide and five feet long, covered with tapestry. The chalice clanged to the floor, and she pressed her freed hand to her forehead and collapsed backward upon the platform.

Splintering wood drowned out her final moan. The moan rose to a shriek as the packing crate disintegrated beneath her. Instead of a graceful swoon imitating the stillness of death, Juliet struggled in the enveloping tapestry, only her kicking legs visible to the audience. She had on blue pantaloons. Romeo raced onstage, advanced, then retreated as the thrashing high-heeled shoes came dangerously close to his legs.

"Get me out of here, you useless bastards!" she shrieked. The canvas curtain descended with blessed swiftness, but did not blot out the fluent curses Juliet bestowed upon her fellow actors and the stagehands. The audience at first relapsed into stunned silence, then started to laugh, and each curse brought more men to their feet, applauding the accident.

Beside him, Annie bent over, her shoulders quivering. She pressed her gloves against her mouth. The sight of her struggling not to laugh was too much for Quent. He guffawed loudly.

The gloves no longer stifled her giggles. She reached for Quent's hand, held it tightly, passing on her merriment.

"I should not...should not..." she gasped between spasms of laughter. "The unfortunate woman... But I've never seen...bl-bl-blue pantaloons...." She leaned against his shoulder, helpless. Quent managed to get his arm about her shoulders to hold her on the bench.

The bearded man stepped in front of the curtain, raised his hand to interrupt the yells and catcalls.

"Mrs. Suarez has very unfortunately received an injury," he said with the same intonation he used in pronouncing his lines in the play. "For the remainder of our performance, the part of Juliet will be played by Miss Sophia de Velain." The men groaned. However unsophisticated the audience, they all suspected a second-rate player was being foisted upon them. Ah, well, thought Quent. The play's nearly complete.

"The beauty! The beauty!" exclaimed Uncle Nick. "Now you shall see a Juliet!" He tapped Quent's arm, still embracing Annie's shoulders. "Good," he whispered. "Very good."

Annie kept her seat at the end of the performance, to avoid the crowd pushing toward the exits.

"I believe I shall go backstage and compliment the young Juliet," said Quentin's uncle. "Will you accompany me, McGilvery?"

"No. The poker games have now commenced in the saloons. I shall find one."

Annie allowed Quentin to steer her out of the tent, into the open air. The night breeze lay dormant, leaving Ogallala prostrate in humid heat. Quentin headed directly for the station, and the empty car.

She had no one but herself to blame. If she had controlled herself, Quentin would have been no threat. But she had laughed, shared the laughter with him. The touch of palm to palm. Had he taken her hand? No! She had grabbed at his! She, the slut!

Leaning against him, she had felt the tremors of laughter through his chest, in the weight of his arm across her shoulders. The bed in the boudoir assigned to her was quite large enough. . . .

A lantern hung over a sign advertising the Ogallala Hotel. Annie twisted to dislodge Quentin's hand from her arm, but he simply grasped it more tightly, navigated across the street, dodging drunken men and a few riderless horses.

"Let me go," she said. "I intend to find a room in the hotel."

"A woman alone in Ogallala would be so busy defending her virtue, she'd be hard put to snatch a few minutes' sleep."

"It's hardly proper that I stay with three men in a palace car."

"It's hardly proper that you're on a cattle drive with more than a dozen men. Yet not one of them has offered a suggestion of impropriety."

"Except for you," she muttered, but she could fight no longer. She fell in beside him, pretending to agree with his decision. After he dropped off to sleep, she'd creep out and find a room at the hotel.

"Watch out!" Quentin yelled. He swung her around as a horse dashed by. He pressed her face into his shoulder, but not before she saw a man and a woman, both naked, astride the animal.

"Huzzy?" she asked in disbelief.

"Yes," he said. She did not object when he shoved her rather precipitately onto the station platform. When he opened the car door, she entered it without objection, much subdued.

The car was hotter than it had been before, for two lamps had been left burning in the lounge. She sat down heavily. Nothing to do but wait; would he speak of it, or simply force her to the bed?

"Something to drink?" Quentin asked. "I believe the servants have gone into town, but I can search the kitchen."

"Don't bother. I want only to go to my room." The emptiness of the chairs and sofas frightened her. Too much like the upstairs parlor of Senator Wise's home.

"I am quite thirsty," Quentin said. Was that an edge of sensual anticipation in his voice? Thirsty for what? "In fact, I'm hungry." Was his hunger for a woman?

"I believe I'll raid the kitchen. Is there something I can get for you?" She shook her head.

He returned in a few minutes with a plate of sliced ham and bread, and a glass that might have contained cider or beer.

"Ogallala has proved to be quite entertaining," he said. "And the play quite instructive. The day began badly, but ended successfully."

For you, she thought bitterly. "Mr. McGilvery and your uncle were impressed by your sketches." The bitterness carried over into her voice. "Other people have had wonderful times today. Huzzy certainly was celebrating something."

"Probably just a skinful of whiskey."

"Even that's better..." she began, but did not finish. How to explain her emptiness, when she herself did not understand it? "Please, I wish to retire," she said with great formality. He accompanied her to the door of her boudoir.

"May I open a window for you?"

"No, thank you. Good night." She slammed the door.

Annie blew out the lamp, wondering what kind of ignorant servant left a light burning in a closed room on a very hot night. She felt around the window in the dark, finally dislodged the catch and pushed up the sash. She sat on the edge of the bed, letting her eyes accustom themselves to the dim light.

Sweat ran down into her pantaloons. She took off her hat, loosened her hair. Bodice, skirt, petticoats, corset, came away soaked with perspiration. She kicked off her shoes, peeled her pantaloons and stockings off her wet legs. She poured water from the ewer into the basin, found soap and a clean cloth on a shelf underneath. A mirror hung on the wall behind the marble-topped stand, and in its depths a dim shadow washed itself. The reflection moved in a sensual dance, caressing itself with a white cloth that caught the light. Annie turned her back. She washed the thigh where Quentin's hand had lain, the shoulders his arm had embraced, the hand contaminated by his touch. She scrubbed with extra power, but the residual warmth refused to be dislodged.

She pulled her silken nightdress over her head, stretched out upon the bed, intending to concentrate upon tomorrow. She would not remember how Quentin had turned away from her, aghast, when she made her confession. She would erase the words he had spoken in the theater, the sensual shared laughter. She would erase the vision of Huzzy and the vile woman.

What would it feel like, to be bare on a horse? To feel the speed of the wind all over one's body? With a man's arm around you, pressing your nakedness into his own? The fantasy expanded. She and Quentin on Graybob, galloping across the prairie. The harlot had covered Huzzy's manhood. She quivered at the implications of the position. Whenever she and Quentin were close—she'd known this for a long time—his member stiffened and desired her. Yet not once had he made any move to achieve the final goal. Even now, when he knew her disgrace, he had not so much as suggested ...

She sat up to drive the apparition away. Since morning, every instant of the day had overflowed with haunting reflections of sex. And tonight! The whores, getting money to do what she had given Davy for free.

Already the back of her nightdress clung damply. She got up, pulled the clammy silk away from her buttocks. She would never sleep until she was cool and dry. She listened for several seconds at the door, heard nothing. Quentin must have retired to the compartment he shared with McGilvery. She opened the door noiselessly; her bare feet made only wisps of sound on the carpeted floor of the corridor. The car's rear platform faced away from the station, so no one would see her there, savoring a few gulps of night air. The door opened on well-oiled hinges. She stepped onto the vestibule. A slight breeze stirred the night; she inhaled once, gratefully, lifted her arms.

"Annie." He stood so close to her, the whisper hit like a blow. She spun toward the sound, at the same time backed against the brass railing, as far from the man as possible.

The starlight reflected on bare shoulders and chest, sculpted in the same lights and shadows she had fantasized in her waking dream. Perhaps he was not real, but simply an extension of that dream. His solid hand reached out to her.

"I couldn't sleep," she faltered.

"Neither could I." He took two steps to close the distance between them. His hand touched her forehead. One finger traced the lines of her brows. Her eyes closed under the weight of his touch. Both hands now, studying the perimeters of her eyes, the slope of her nose, the swelling of her lips. The heat of his body, only inches away, overpowered the heat of the night.

She lifted her arms to push him away. Her palms touched his chest, the softness of hair spread across the strength of his muscles. She wished to do what she had done at the bridge, to press her hips against his.

The first link in the inevitable chain of desire, some cautious part of her reminded. Beneath her heart, the center of her longing spread its petals wide, exposing completely the golden, sensual core. Her body opened in anticipation; the dampness between her legs came from a heat not related to the weather. She swung her hips to meet his.

His fingers trembled on the row of tiny buttons between her breasts. Inch by inch, the fabric fell apart, until the delicate breeze of late night played across her left breast. He lifted the gauzy silk, drew the lace edging across her skin, caressing with the lightness of a feather. She watched, fascinated, as he stroked her fullness, his fingers never making contact, but the lace carrying the full charge of his intention. He circled the fabric around her taut nipple, as he might use a brush to lay upon the canvas the sensual image of a woman.

She thrust forward, wanting more than this secondhand caress, yearning for him to claim her as his private possession. "Quentin, touch me!" she cried.

She was not prepared for the explosion. His hands followed the fullness of her breasts, down the neckline of the nightdress; the thin fabric sighed as it parted, exposing her from neck to naval. He seized her in his hardened hands, cradled the sensitive flesh. When his fingers grasped her nipples, she cried out, arched her back, objecting and encouraging in the same instant. Her knees gave way, and she slumped to the floor of the platform. He came with her, his hands still claiming her.

She sat with her back pressed against the smooth wall of the car. Quentin knelt between her legs. No, she thought, opened her mouth to object, but found instead his lips, his tongue, his deep kiss. His hand spread her thighs, opened her, giving his searching fingers access to the core of her. A prairie whirlwind lifted her into a glittering, moist cloud, and her body dissolved in magical alchemy.

He held her close, her breasts crushed against his heaving chest, his hand still thrust between her legs, his fingers still drawing sparks from her exhausted flesh.

"No, Quentin, no," she begged. "How shall I face my father if it happens again? Don't force me to it!"

"Of course not," he whispered. "When I take you, it will not be on the platform of a palace car. Not when you're exhausted by heat. Not when you've been aroused by crude demonstrations of excess. When we come together, your desire will be for me, not simply for release from the thrall of lust."

She clung to him, acquainting herself with the form of his body, wide shoulders tapering to slender waist. She discovered the massive evidence of his own passion against her hip. Through the fabric she measured his length with her fingers.

"Don't," he said. "Not tonight, but when we have decisions to celebrate. Public declarations."

"But what you did to me ..." she protested. It was beyond anything she had felt with Davy. Such ecstasy could not be without sin.

"What I did is what a man can give a woman without forfeiting the future. A man who loves a woman, truly loves her, can forgo his own passion until the proper time. A man's duty is to resist, for when he flings caution to the wind, it has consequences beyond...consequences you know of." A gust of wind lifted a scattering of dust, flung it with a hiss against the side of the coach. "We must go in," he whispered. He pushed her hair away from her face. "I love your hair, Annie. A woman's glory, someone said, and your hair is your glory. Your halo."

"I'm not an angel," she protested. With those words, the haze of passion cleared. She sprang to her feet, suddenly aware of her nakedness. He pushed open the door of the car, then the door to her boudoir. She stood still while he stripped the torn nightdress from her body. He smoothed the satin sheets.

"Climb in," he ordered. "Sleep well." He leaned over the bed, kissed her forehead. She lifted her arms, wrapped them about his neck to keep him near.

"I love you, Quentin."

"I had guessed you did, but hearing you say it, that gives me hope for the future."

Doors opened and closed. Male voices in the lounge. Her languid body sank into the luxury of the bed. She climbed on Graybob's back, supported by Quentin's strength; a glittering cloud seized them and flung them into the sky, where they rode with the moon and the stars.

Annie looked at the omelet, ham, sweet rolls and coffee and considered a second helping, then decided against it. Trotting fifteen miles on an overfull stomach was a sure way to a bellyache. Quentin smiled at her across the table.

Last night, in Quentin's arms, her heart had melted, and now she found room only for him. She admired the way he grasped the delicate handle of the china cup. Those same fingers had urged her desire with the lambent lace, had grasped her eager sex. An undulating wave sprang from the climactic spot those fingers had energized. She closed her eyes for an instant to let the pleasure replay. How long would this blithe spirit dwell within her?

"I'll send a telegram to Temptation, letting you know where to find me," Quentin's uncle said. Quentin nodded, smiled gently. Uncle Nick smiled knowingly. Had Quentin said something to him? Or could he tell from the electrical charge in the air that she and Quentin . . .

"I must gather my things from the boudoir," she said, jumping up.

She and Quentin walked the length of the platform and found Graybob and Jenny waiting patiently in front of the station, saddled, ready to go. How Quentin had worked the miracle of their presence she did not know, but it reminded her of the miracle of the night before. Her hand tightened momentarily on his arm, bringing his smile in response.

"Dunk!" yelled a male voice.

Annie ran her eyes across the crowd gathering to meet the morning train. Who in Ogallala would call Quentin by his nickname? All the cowhands should have been back at camp hours ago. A strange gentleman waved at them.

"Annie! Dunk!"

"Huzzy?" Quentin exclaimed in disbelief. Huzzy wore a coat and vest, topped with a brand-new hat of pearl-gray felt. The woman beside him had on a traveling costume of sober gray serge, a contrast to her hat, which sprouted a garish arrangement of red and purple plumes.

"You catchin' the train?" asked Huzzy.

"No. We're just preparing to rejoin the herd. You're leaving?" Quentin asked in astonishment.

"Didn't you hear? I won fifteen hundred dollars last night at a faro bank. I'm takin' Josie back to Texas." He pointed at the woman by his side. "Josie, this here's Dunk and Annie. We been on the trail together." Annie nodded at the woman, embarrassed because she could not tell whether she had been Huzzy's partner on the wild night ride down main street. She remembered the heavy bosom, the sturdy thighs, but not the face.

What future lay in store for a gambling cowboy and a tart? She smiled. What future for a ruined woman from Texas and a New Yorker? She decided to let the future take care of itself, because she was in love.

Chapter Fourteen

Annie knew the delightful coolness of the day came from the hours of heavy wind in the early morning; her heart, however, ascribed the newly clement weather to Quentin's love. A breeze cavorted across the grass, touched her face, crept under the wide legs of her split skirt. Her loins tightened, and an internal breeze left over from his touch titillated the petals of desire until they wrapped around her heart. She had to speak to him about what they had done, but was shy because she did not know the words.

"Quentin," she began hesitantly. "What we did, on the platform of the car..."

"Our lovemaking?" She nearly sighed with relief. Was that what it had been? Lovemaking? She'd feared it might carry some ugly, condemning word, like *fornication*, or *onanism*.

"Our lovemaking, since I'm promised to someone else...is it proper? You see, inside I feel...well, joyful, like a breeze blows in and out. And it hasn't gone away."

"Why shouldn't you feel joyful?" He shifted in the saddle, and she guessed his...private part...was swelling and wanting to go inside her.

"I'm sorry, I shouldn't talk about it," she said. She pulled her hat down on the side so he could not see her face.

"No, if you feel uneasy, we must discuss it. What bothers you?"

"I'm going to marry McCann, and I don't know how much lovemaking I should do with someone else. Even though I love you, and I don't love McCann."

"You're not going to marry McCann. You're going to marry me."

"That's impossible, Quentin, and you know it. Or you'd know it if you'd just let yourself be sensible for a minute or two."

"Why impossible?"

"What would your family say? Even without Davy, without the child, they wouldn't want a Texas girl who has no fortune as a daughter-in-law. And my reputation..." He shook his head in objection, would have spoken, except she forestalled him. "Of course they'll find out. Someone will be kind enough to take your father aside. Probably Mr. Lampman. They'd most likely disinherit you."

"Uncle Nick's very fond of you," Quent said hurriedly.

"He probably doesn't know what I've done," she snapped. "'That Texas slut' is what he'll say when he finds out. I committed a grievous sin, Quentin. Now I'm paying. McCann is willing to marry me, so I'll take him. Our children will control half of eastern Montana, when we combine his range and Daddy's."

"And you're the instrument of that domination," Quent said. "What you desire, love and affection, that doesn't figure in your father's plans?"

"I'm paying for what I've done. Don't you understand? I'm lucky I'm not one of the women waiting for the cowboys in Ogallala. When I saw those women, I realized how very fortunate I am."

"And how do I pay for my sin of omission?" he asked thoughtfully. "If I'd crossed the room, been more of a Romeo, you wouldn't find yourself in this trap."

"You pay by forgetting you love me," she answered. "Or perhaps by remembering all your life."

"The punishment's too great for the crime," he said. He stopped on the brink of a depression that had been wet during the spring thaw, for it overflowed with dark green vines. A buffalo wallow. He dismounted, and as he swung his leg over the saddle she saw the evidence of his love.

"Come," he said, holding out his hand to her. She slid off Jenny, sat beside him on the lip of the sink. The horses cropped the succulent grasses sprouting between the vines. His arm weighed upon her shoulders, pulled her against him.

"You know it's impossible!" she cried.

"Not impossible, if I'm willing to carve out my own life, instead of following what's been planned for me. Of course there will be difficulties if I join the law firm, or Paul's bank, but if I make my own way, who I marry is my business."

"You can talk all you want, but when the time comes, the sacrifice will seem too great," she said. To herself she said, *No man is willing to give up wealth and security for love.*

"Uncle Nick has asked me to join him in his railroad ventures."

"You've decided?"

"Not decided. Considering." She shuddered at the uncertainty of his words. In reality—face the truth—she had him for only a few weeks. When the time came for the permanent decision, he would leave her, return to his family and all the wealth and privilege they offered.

"Quentin, you haven't answered my question. What is proper between us? I love it when you touch me, the way you did last night, but...but..." He drew her into the circle of his arms, lifted her upon his legs.

"What is proper between lovers, before they are husband and wife?" His lips touched hers lightly. "The kiss," he whispered against her mouth. His tongue brushed her lower lip, opening her mouth without obvious intent. His exploring tongue found the clef behind the lip. "The kiss *à la française.*" She lifted to him as his fingers pressed upon her hips, examining the folds of fabric concealing the secret of her skirt.

"Everything, my dear, except the final mating, which is irrevocable. As you know from sad experience."

"Please," she begged, "please don't mention it. It hurts when you speak of it."

"But to not speak of it would hurt even more. If I don't say openly that you experienced another man, that you bore him a child, it would become a dark thing lurking between us. I must say it, so you know it's of no importance to me. A marriage can survive mistakes when they're open, but not those kept secret."

"There is to be no marriage, Quentin, at least no marriage between us."

"Yes."

"You are spoiled! All your life you've gotten exactly what you want, and you expect to get this, too."

"Somehow. I'm not yet sure how it will be done, but you will be my wife. We'll go to Louisiana and find your boy, and you'll be the happiest woman on earth."

She tried to spring to her feet, but succeeded only in falling off his legs and tumbling into the vines. He grabbed her before she rolled to the bottom of the wallow, pulled her back to his side.

"Quentin, you live in a fantasy!" she exclaimed when she had recovered her breath. "You'd learn to hate me soon enough, without a child in the house whose very existence parades my sin. I never wanted the child."

"Your body speaks volumes, and it contradicts your words. When you cry at night, it's for the baby."

She gasped, wondering how he could see into her mind. "It's impossible," she repeated. She must convince him of the truth. "Everything you say is foolish."

"I intend to ask your father for your hand in marriage. Do you agree I should do that much?"

"Please don't. It will only be a great embarrassment, on both sides."

"How can love be an embarrassment? Annie, you're not a woman to love for a moment, then dismiss it. Your love is the kind that survives, that lasts a lifetime. Love is what you've wanted, needed, through those years when your father sent you to live with others. Your need for love led you to give Davy Lampman more than he deserved. The man fortunate enough to win your love can take eternal comfort from it. In the same way, you'll love the child forever. It lives in your heart, if not by your side. A man who truly loves you will help you search for the baby. I'll do that." Her breath went in the wrong direction, and several seconds passed before she could speak.

"Another man's child?"

"Why not? He's your child, more than his."

"Quentin, you're insane. My father would never allow it. He left specific instructions with the sisters. They will say nothing. They promised...."

"When I'm your husband, your father is out of the matter, and money can overawe most ridiculous, meaningless scruples. We'll find the child."

"Quentin, listen to me. Your fantasies are tempting, like a dream of a beautiful place. I'm my father's only child. His only hope for the future is through me. By marrying Hugh McCann, I can go a little way toward blotting out the terrible thing I did. I'll give him grandchildren, honestly begotten children he can take pleasure in, not one he's ashamed of. You're spinning fictions, which is just another name for lies. Your family, my father, all would be horrified by what you propose. I must go to McCann."

"There's time yet to find a way out of that engagement. We'll think on it." His fingers worked at the buttons on the front of her bodice. "In the meantime, we should take the opportunity offered us. I'll make love to you, to keep the spirit of joy coursing in your blood." She pushed his fingers away, unbuttoned the garment herself.

"Let me. You got so excited last night, you ripped my nightdress, and I don't think I can repair it. I didn't put my corset on this morning," she added shyly. "It didn't seem right, binding up all that...feeling."

"Love resists all binding," he said, pushing the bodice back from her shoulders, "as we shall resist the bonds others try to lay on us." He scarched for the tapes tying her underclothes, stripped off her bodice and chemise. She opened his shirt, tried to pull it over his head, but found it cinched too tightly by his belt. Her fingers dropped to his belt buckle. Her hands shook violently; the buckle came open only on the third try.

He stripped away her boots, her skirt, was pushing down her pantaloons when she remembered what he would see. She captured his hands and held them still.

"Quentin, I'm not beautiful under there. The baby, it left marks on my stomach."

"We shall see," he said, then exposed her body to the sunlight. He examined her stomach as a man might study a map, then lowered his mouth to the puckers and kissed them, one by one. The glow on his hair tempted her. She ran her fingers through the curls matted by the weight of his hat.

"The sun," she whispered. "The sun makes every part of you beautiful."

"And you. We'll always make love in the light."

"I should like that. When I did it . . . with Davy. . ." How did one speak of a man, when another had his fingers—?

"When Davy coupled with you?" he prompted her.

"In the dark. He wanted it dark."

"No wonder you think it a sin," he said. "Dark and secret." He said no more, for his lips and tongue played a game of kisses, everywhere, and as eternal as the light. His arms extended like the rays of the sun god, and his hand between her legs radiated the heavenly fire. She fell into the blinding light, crying out for him, at the same time aware of his noisy passion. The sun defined the climax, the falling off of desire. Its beams revived her languid limbs, and she moved to kiss him in thanks.

"Pleasure?" he asked.

"Perfect, except that you give me all, and do not do what *your* body cries for."

"That will come. When I'm your husband."

* * *

Quent lay flat on his back, ignoring the clumps of prairie sod poking him here and there. Annie sprawled on top of him, eyes closed. He didn't know if she slept, or was merely lazy from her sexual climax. Strange, to feel so fulfilled, when he had yet to complete the union with her. He needed to talk to someone about the love he felt for Annie, about his ease at delaying the final union with her, until both felt it right and proper. He wished there had been an opportunity in Ogallala to speak to Uncle Nick, even though Uncle Nick's attitudes and morals were certainly looser than his own.

Mrs. Colyer. If only she were here. But what would that Boston matron be doing in the middle of the Great Plains? He controlled his laugh so he wouldn't disturb Annie.

Had any man in his family done anything like this? Lain naked with a girl, with the breeze playing games with the most private parts of his body? He couldn't imagine his father so relaxed. More likely, his father had a schedule posted on his mother's dressing table. His brothers? They probably always did it like Davy Lampman, in the dark.

That left Uncle Nick. Of course, all his life Uncle Nick had turned sex into play, in exactly this fashion. No, not like this. Uncle Nick would have completed the act with no moral qualms at all. He pleased the ladies he romanced, but they also pleased him completely in return.

Uncle Nick, during the building of the Pacific Railroad, must certainly have found women on the plains to satisfy his urges. Had he lain in the summer sun, next to a buffalo wallow? Quent let himself envision such an embrace, jerked away from it in disgust. The woman sprawled beneath his uncle was his mother! Oh, God! How could such a thing enter his mind?

Annie put her palms on the ground on either side of him, lifted herself off his chest.

"Is something wrong?"

"Just a clod poking me in the back," he said lightly. He had to find out the truth. The next time he saw his uncle, he would ask him. Bluntly, flat out, he would ask him if he was his father.

The sun lay, a glowing ball, on the western horizon when they rode into camp.

"It's about time!" yelled Perk when they came within shouting distance. "Ogallala has messed things up for fair. Huzzy gone, two-thirds of the hands falling-down drunk. We needed you." Quent jumped off Graybob, pulled off his hat.

"I'm sorry, Perk, but I didn't know about Huzzy until midmorning, when I saw him at the station."

Broadbrim approached the fire, collapsed more than sat down. He seemed pale and drawn. How the hell could Broadbrim look pale? But he was. His face resembled the cold morning ashes of a campfire.

"Look at this," Perk continued in a loud voice, pointing at Broadbrim. "My right point man, and he comes back at daybreak, more wore out than a stud coyote trapped overnight with bitch dogs." Quent glanced at Annie. She pretended she had not heard.

"Stack, they tied him on his horse, although how men blind drunk managed it, I don't know. Everybody better look to their boot soles, 'cause that Ogallala whiskey may have eaten its way clear through."

Dan! Quent spun about, examined Annie's wagon. The mules were unhitched, but no Dan.

"Dan?" he asked.

"He's okay," said Broadbrim from the ground. He slumped until he lay nearly prostrate. "That's what started the drinking, 'cause the boys put money in a kitty till they had enough for him to see the elephant."

"They bought the boy a woman," explained Perk.

"You what?" yelled Quent. He squatted down next to Broadbrim, grabbed his collar, lifted his head so he could look him in the face. "You what!"

"Don't get excited," said Perk. "As I understand, they made sure she was wholesome. Dan musta been good, 'cause the whore kept him the rest of the night for free. Saved him from the rotgut, anyhow."

"We had to celebrate his comin' to be a man," muttered Broadbrim thickly.

Quent dropped Broadbrim's collar. The cowboy had been depending upon Quent's hand for support, and he fell over. Dan stood on the other side of the fire, poised to run if his employer offered violence. When Quent did not move, did nothing but stare, Dan's strained face broke into a nervous grin.

Quent told himself it wasn't Dan's fault. While the cowboys were enticing him into bed with a whore, where had he been? Where had the man who bragged he'd taken the child away from a rustler been? Loving another man's fiancée, that was where he'd been! And justifying his atrocious, immoral actions by avoiding the final climax.

"Now that Huzzy's gone, you'll have to ride herd," said Perk. "Who'd ever have thought the little guy would win at faro?"

"There's no skill involved in faro," said Quent, happy to interrupt his thoughts. "It's all luck. I hope he gives up gambling."

"He says he's gonna open a livery stable in San Antonio," said Broadbrim. "Wisht I'd been in on the bet, 'stead of drinking. Don't put Dunk on swing, Perk, 'cause he can't rope a stuffed cat."

"He'll be drag, of course," continued Perk. "Annie can stay with Dan and Sid and the wagons." The significance of Perk's words penetrated Quent's skull. Ride herd! Why now? For weeks, months, he had wanted nothing more than to join the hands. Now, when he looked forward to a month beside Annie, riding off to private spots where they might exchange kisses, *now* he got his chance to become a cow-boy!

"I'll ride herd, too," said Annie.

"No, you won't," said Perk. "Linares might kill me if I let a woman behind the cattle. And if he didn't, your daddy sure would."

"Sing," said Lucas as he rode by in the dark. Quent's head jerked up so quickly he thought for a moment he had snapped his neck. Asleep again. Asleep while Graybob did the work of riding herd. He and Lucas circled the bedded cattle, riding in opposite directions, keeping about fifty feet away.

Eyes like the morning star, cheeks like a rose,
Laura was a pretty girl, God Almighty knows.
Weep, all ye little rains, wail, winds, wail.

Lucas sang in slow, tremulous tones—the vocalization cattle seemed to appreciate most. Quent did not have much of a repertoire, but he remembered one song from Dodge City.

Oh, I am a Texas cowboy, right off the Texas plains.
My trade is cinchin' saddles and pullin' of bridle reins,
And I can throw a lasso with the greatest of ease,
I can rope and ride a bronco any damn way I please.

He wished he could remember the rest of the fifteen or twenty verses. He warbled the words over and over again.

Lucas stopped the next time they met. "Shut up, Dunk," he said in a low voice. "Anything so feisty, it'll wake the brutes. Keep it slow and easy. Besides, a song what brags about ropin' ain't hardly yours, is it?"

Quent remembered a quiet and draggy song. Would the herd mind that it wasn't in English? *"Mon coeur s'ouvre a ta voix...."*

Of course, in *Samson et Dalila* a mezzo-soprano sang it, but Texas longhorns probably did not know. "My heart at the sound of your voice unfolds like a flower...." Terribly personal, really, exactly the way he felt when Annie spoke. His heart blossomed.

"You have it in your power to stop my tears...." She certainly did. All she had to say was "Yes," and he would be the happiest man on earth. Standing next to her, putting a gold ring on her finger.

Lucas rode by and made no comment, so Quent presumed the herd liked French opera. Over and over again he sang about Delilah's heart blossoming like a flower at dawn, whenever she heard Samson speak. The constellations swung overhead. Lucas stopped.

"Go in and wake Rolf and Soto," he said.

His watch was over. Now to try to get back to sleep for an hour or two, before Sid began banging pans and cursing the kindling as he struggled to make a cooking fire out of cow chips. He barely touched the men's blankets, and they woke. He headed for his own bedroll, no longer under the wagon, for fear his coming and going on night duty would wake Annie. A dark figure sat by his bed. The starlight showed Broadbrim, who placed a finger on his lips, pointed away from camp. Quent followed him, mystified what this private conference might be about.

"Dunk. Couple things I gotta say," he whispered after they'd walked an eighth of a mile beyond the camp.

"Yes."

"You have it in your mind to take Annie away from McCann, don't you?" Quent started. He'd been too open with his emotions, that was plain. Lie? Not to Broadbrim. He could keep a secret.

"Yes. I love her. And she loves me. She doesn't love McCann."

"Won't do no good to fight McCann in the open. I worked for him one year, down on the Frio. When he has his mind set on the way he's goin', nothing shakes him. Well, nothing short of a Panhandle tornado."

"So I should give it up?"

"Didn't say that. Work on her daddy. He spoiled her after her mama died. He might be willing to spoil her again in the matter of who she marries."

"How can I impress him? What does he admire in a man?"

"Man who handles a crew tight, man who can skinny a steer out of the brush and corral him without callin' for help." His voice teased. "Man who can swing his rope over the proper animal in one try."

Quent groaned. "Then I don't have a chance."

"I wouldn't say that. He's also mighty taken with men who have money behind them. You got money?"

"Some. I'm not terribly rich. Not a millionaire."

"But richer than McCann. Someone said you paid a thousand dollars for that gray horse."

"What I paid for Graybob—" Quent began tensely, then realized he'd better shoot straight with Broadbrim, since the man offered information voluntarily. "No, I gave Weiss eight hundred for him, but I'm selling him back at the end of this trip."

"Not keeping him for railroad work?" Quent bent his knees, squatted on his heels. Broadbrim came down to his level. "See," Broadbrim continued, "I'm gettin' too old for this trail-driving work. A man gets over thirty, it's not fun anymore. And I thought layin' out the railroad, that wouldn't keep me in the saddle a day and a half straight, nor make me stay out in the wet and lightning. That's what you and your uncle are setting out to do, isn't it?"

Was it? Nicholas van Kelson and Quentin van Kelson, surveying the route of the railroad? Yes, that was exactly what he was going to do, and the certainty of it surprised him.

"Yes. We start this winter, in Texas."

"Well, I'd like a job. Anything you need done, I'm not partic'lar."

"I don't know yet what I'll need, who I'll need," Quent said earnestly. "How can I get in touch with you? You'll be going back to Texas?"

"I know how low the mercury drops in Montana," he said, and followed the statement with a short laugh. "Just ask for me out about Linares's corral in San Antonio. Someone there will know where I'm bunked."

"I'll be in touch," Quent said firmly.

"Thanks." Broadbrim stood up, tipped his hat. "Remember, work on Mr. Brownell. Don't start a fight with McCann, 'cause he's bigger than you, and he's walked away from many a saloon brawl leaving a man on the floor."

Quent turned east. The morning star topped the horizon, a brilliant lantern in the sky. So, he'd decided. He was not going back to New York or to law school or to his brother's bank. He had found a home that felt more homelike than the place where he had been reared.

Annie's wagon top reflected the faint light hugging the eastern sky. His uncertainty frightened her, so she must be the first to know. He'd bring her along, of course. The little boy? Why not? He'd be at least a year old by now, and come winter he'd be steady on his own two feet. A nurse along, to help Annie care for him. Broadbrim had said he'd do anything. Quent smiled at the thought of the cowboy's big hands holding a baby, lifting him in and out of a wagon, carrying the kid in front of him on the saddle.

What a wonderful childhood the little boy would have! He wished he knew his name. And there would be others, the fruit of their passion, conceived and grown under the sky.

A flicker of flame beyond the wagons, the clatter of a dropped coffeepot. The camp was up and about. Quent ran to Annie's wagon, poked his head in the flaps at the front end, where he knew her head would be.

"Annie!" She rolled over in her blankets; they fell away, and he saw one white shoulder.

"Quentin," she finally said. She sat up, bringing a blanket with her, so the shoulder disappeared.

"Annie, I've decided. I'm staying here."

"Here! Why should you want to stay in Wyoming Territory?"

"Not right here, but in the West. I'm not going home. I'm going to help Uncle Nick build the railroad."

"That's nice."

"But don't you see, Annie? If I stay out west, there's no need for you to worry about my parents, about whether or not my family approves of you. Father won't approve of me working on a railroad survey or being Uncle Nick's partner, so you as my wife, that's beside the point." He leaned farther into the wagon, puckered his mouth for a kiss. She laid her lips upon his for an instant, then withdrew and pulled the blanket higher around her neck.

"There's still Daddy," she said.

"We'll convince him together. I love you, you love me. Besides, which is the better bargain? A son-in-law who has a herd of longhorns, or one who's going to own part of the plains railroad? A small part, I admit, but it will be just the beginning."

"That's not a nice thing to say, Quentin. You make it sound like Daddy's selling me to the highest bidder."

"If money isn't a question," he said happily, "then he'll be sure to yield to love."

"Coffee in the pot, bacon in the pan," yodeled Sid.

"Got to go, sweetheart. My heart at the sound of your voice blossoms like a flower at dawn."

"My heart at the sound of your voice blossoms like a flower," Annie muttered into her blankets. The words slid to the vicinity of her own sensual flower, which these days lay constantly open. Damn Huzzy, running off and forcing Perk to put Quentin behind the herd. Just when they needed each other. The memory of his love at the buffalo wallow brought a trace of moisture, of warmth in the early-morning chill. Could it possibly be? That within a few weeks she'd stand beside Quentin, not Hugh McCann, and say the words that bound her for life?

And her son. To make her happy, he would search for her son.

The men in camp saddled their horses and rode out to take over the herd, so the night men could come in for breakfast. She spilled the blankets, grabbed her clothing, struggled into it, all the time trying to find a flaw in Quentin's logic.

Everything fell into place. If her father wanted her to marry wealth, Quentin had more promise than Hugh McCann. Of course, his wealth wasn't in livestock, the riches that impressed her father. But her father had written in his letters how important the railroad was to the prosperity of the northern plains. And if money made no difference, if he wanted only her happiness, he would give his blessing for her marriage to Quentin.

She crawled out of the wagon, picked up a tin plate and cup from the chuck wagon, snagged biscuits and bacon.

"Sid, these biscuits have black spots in them," she protested.

"See those bushes over yonder?" Sid pointed. "Well, I discovered late last night, they's huckleberries." She sank her teeth into the biscuit, fluffy as a cloud. The taste and aroma filled her mouth. Even her teeth enjoyed the sweet sensation.

"Gonna be a beautiful day," said Sid. The night herders trotted into camp.

"Twelve miles to next water," sang out Perk. "And there's a bit of a trading post there, on a road coming out from Deadwood."

Far enough north now so the temperature was perfect for riding. She no longer had the excuse of the heat to leave her corset off, but she did not bother to put it on. Twelve miles.

An easy day, and maybe a few moments alone with Quentin in the evening. Annie took another biscuit, touched her tongue to a huckleberry peeping from the top, to anticipate its sweetness.

Sweet, sweet. Everything today tasted sweet. With a trading post at the end. And spreading over the top of everything, like sugar icing, love and Quentin and the odds that she'd be his wife shifting in her favor.

Chapter Fifteen

Perk ordered the cattle turned to graze about three miles from the tiny settlement. Annie waited for Quent, but when she learned he was still with the herd, she joined Perk, Broadbrim, Sid and five other men in investigating the trading post. The store turned out to be a log cabin twelve feet square, with a brush ramada of a similar size in front. It offered a scant selection of goods—flour, beans, cornmeal, the most common sizes of cartridges, and knives of all lengths and styles. And whiskey in a barrel, with a tin cup dangling on a chain. Sid gravitated to the green patch behind the cabin, a vegetable garden.

"I can let you have cabbage and turnips," the proprietor said gravely, waggling his long beard, "but the snap beans and the beetroot, this is the end of the crop, and the potatoes see me through the winter and I can't part with aught."

"What's the trail north like?" asked Perk. The beard, dark except for occasional speckles of gray, waggled from side to side.

"You taking a herd north?"

"Yes."

"Where to?"

"Montana."

"Well, you'll not get there this year," he said with the satisfaction some men find in the misfortunes of others.

"Why not?" Perk exclaimed.

"Why, there hain't no water for fifty miles. No rain in the mountains." He made a wide, sweeping gesture toward the west, to the range of mountains that had blocked their view for two days. "All the streams hereabouts, they run down from the mountains, and since the spring thaw, rivers been dryin' faster'n a lady takin' a bath in December."

"But there's a river, twenty miles ahead," Perk protested.

"Dry, dry, dry," said the man, shaking his head, waggling the beard to emphasize his words. "Last herd that tried to cross lost three hundred head afore they hit the headwaters of the Cheyenne, and two hundred more before they found water on the Powder, thirty miles beyond that. Bad year to be drivin'."

"How's the grass?" asked Perk. He kept his anxiety from his voice, but not from his face. His forehead wrinkled.

"Best can be expected in a dry summer," the man said dolefully.

Perk walked to the door of the cabin, gazed with clenched teeth up the sloping grasslands, toward the herd. Annie heard the clink of a coin on the counter, the rattle of the chain on the tin cup.

"Leave it, Broadbrim," Perk said harshly.

Broadbrim dropped the cup so suddenly it swung in a wide arc on its chain, thudding against the whiskey barrel. His quarter had already disappeared into a box behind the counter. Broadbrim held out his hand, the owner looked at the congregation of cowboys, grimaced and shook his head, retrieved the quarter and handed it back to Broadbrim.

"Weather's cooling," Perk mused. "If any of you need warmer clothes, get something now. But no whiskey." He stepped out under the ramada and waited until the men joined him with their purchases. He did not share his thoughts until they sat around the dinner fire.

"Dunk, what time's the moon coming up?"

"It's up," said Quent, pointing to the eastern horizon, where the moon, two days from full, hung pale in the plum-colored sunset sky.

"We'll rest the cattle until it's dark. Then, we push them slowly until midnight or a bit later, depending on how they're going."

"Never been on a night drive," said Stack, pushing his hat back from his forehead.

"Neither have I," said Perk. "But there's a first time for everything. Isn't there Dan?" Dan blushed so vividly red the dusk failed to hide it. "You got lanterns in the wagon, Sid?"

"Yes."

"Broadbrim, you'll carry one in front. Dunk, you'll carry one in back. The front doesn't push ahead unless the rear light's in view. The front lantern swinging means the herd's stopped. Sid, you and Dan, and you, too, Annie, go ahead, find a spot about where we'll want breakfast. Get food fixed so the men can eat as they're able to come in. And put water in everything that's hollow."

Twice during the night, Annie woke to find herself slumped over Lily's mane, the horse plodding obediently behind the wheels of the wagon. As the moon dropped down from the zenith, she helped Sid build a fire, boil coffee, mix biscuits, fry bacon. A huge pot of dried apples had been soaking in the chuck wagon. The cowboys ladled the stewed apples over piles of split biscuits, making an impromptu cobbler.

Quentin rode in, handed the extinguished lantern to Sid and slid off his horse. Annie's breath stopped when she saw his legs waver beneath him. He had on a vest she'd never seen before, the front cut from the hide of a spotted pony and the back from a gray blanket. He must have purchased it at the trading post.

She resented the turn of events that kept them apart. She should have known about the vest last evening, should have been beside him when he bought it. At this moment, in the magic of new love, they should be together. Nature de

signed evenings of moonlight for strolling lovers and leisurely hours, not this dusty, exhausted creature who sought
his blankets at dusk, catching a few hours' sleep before he
would be awakened to ride herd.

Quentin disappeared around her wagon. When he did not
reappear, she searched for him, found him sound asleep,
leaning against the wheel. She loaded a plate with food.

"Quentin, here's your breakfast." He snapped up, his
hand clutching at the air, his eyes darting, fearing he had
neglected his work. He'd not been able to even doze, being
in charge of the lantern.

"You must eat."

"I'd rather sleep."

"Sid made stewed apples."

"I'll eat if you sit down beside me."

"I'm helping Sid."

"Sit down. You look exhausted." She began laughing,
and couldn't stop. This gray scarecrow, this hollow-cheeked
saddle tramp, thought *she* looked exhausted! He took the
plate from her hand.

"I'd better rescue this before you start rolling about on
the ground. Is it my new vest that has this effect upon you?"

"No. It's you. You don't know which way is up, but
you're worried that I'm tired."

"I worry about you every instant of the day, Annie. Or at
least I think of you every instant." His voice turned to
smoke. "Sometimes it's not worry, but something else." His
hazy blue eyes had cleared, and she saw herself reflected in
the black pupils.

"I think of you every instant," she whispered. The plate
occupied his hands, so she laid her own hand high on his
thigh. "Certainly, when this dry stretch is over, Perk will lay
by for a day and we'll have some time to ourselves."

"Don't count on it," he said between bites of apples and
biscuit. "Perk smells Montana, like a steer smells water.
He's already talking about how he's taking a train back to

Texas, with a bunk at night, and steaks and champagne in the dining car.''

"Is that what we'll do, take a train?"

"A train east to the Mississippi. Pullman, of course, for I doubt there'll be a private car available in Temptation. Then, I thought, perhaps a very civilized steamboat down the Mississippi.''

"Oh, Quentin! I've never been on a steamboat before.''

"Neither have I. I hear the accommodations are luxurious.'' She wanted to throw herself against him, to reinforce the dream with physical contact. But he had taken another large bite of his breakfast, and on the other side of the wagon she heard Perk's voice, ordering the men who'd taken the first breakfast shift back to the herd.

The sun peeked over the horizon, and the herd gathered and faced north once more. The laggards, the cows and calves, the tenderfooted and the lame, the lazy and the homesick, had to be pushed every foot, the cowboys on drag striking out with ropes and quirts. Annie felt sorry for the tired cattle; she worried about Quentin, who would not have a chance to doze in the saddle today. She considered demanding that she be permitted to ride with Quentin. But Johnny had to keep the remuda close to the herd, so the men could change horses often. Sid no longer had Johnny's help with the fire and the washing up. She had her place now, with the chuck wagon. At the beginning of the trip she had wanted to help Sid so badly, and now she resented working because it separated her from love.

Sid stopped the wagon on a little hill to prepare the noon meal. Broadbrim, on the right point of the herd, struggled to keep one of the lead bulls in line. More than once the animal attempted to cut away, head east. Broadbrim and his horse swerved, headed him off.

The foreman, riding ahead of the herd, returned to check on the food.

"Perk," Annie said after he'd satisfied his thirst at the water barrel, "that bull keeps trying to head east. Do you think maybe—?"

"He's dazed with thirst, doesn't know where he's going. The brutes get that way."

"But might he be smelling water off to the east? I remember once with Daddy, driving a bunch back to the ranch down in the hill country, and one old cow, she just wouldn't stay pointed toward home. Finally we gave her her head and she went over a ridge, to a little water hole that only filled in the winter and spring, one we didn't even know existed."

Perk took off his hat, beat it against his leg to remove some of the dust. His face was the same color as the hat.

"You want to ride east and find out, Annie?"

"I will, if you want me to. Look! There he goes again. He doesn't want to go north. He wants to head east."

Stack and Broadbrim crossed in front of the herd to stop the animals. The bull took the opportunity to dash away once more, only to be headed off by two cowboys. The first shift headed for camp, their horses walking slowly, the men drooping in the saddle. Perk still stared at the herd, in particular the feisty, rebellious bull.

"Dunk, feel like a ride east?" he asked as Quentin rode in.

"How far?" Quentin asked wearily.

"You and Annie get fresh horses. We'll turn that bull loose, let him go where he wants. You follow. If he's found nothing but prairie in ten miles, try to round him up and drive him back to the herd. If he finds what Annie thinks he's going to find, come back and let us know. Take your gun, fire two shots to say there's water enough for the herd. One shot, there's water enough for the remuda."

She should never have mentioned the bull! Now Quentin must ride an extra fifteen or twenty miles on what might be a wild-goose chase, after being awake all night. She looked at him, worried, then saw his eyes. Her heart leaped. He brought his head up, pleased, elated at the prospect of their being together, alone.

Sid shoved a sack into her hands, biscuits, bacon and two cans of tomatoes. Perk ordered the bull turned loose. For a minute or two the animal eyed the cowboys, waiting for them to dash in front of his nose. He took a few wary steps, glared back at the men again. He ran a hundred yards, then settled down into a steady walk, Quentin and Annie behind him.

The bull trotted faster than Annie wished to push Bird, for the horses had been without water since the evening before. But the bull set the pace, and she and Quentin had no choice but to keep up. The bull's tongue hung out the side of his mouth, shaking with every step.

Annie smiled at Quentin, welcomed his smile in return. She had expected a torrent of words, for they had been silent for so long. But words were unnecessary. Their bodies made the connection without even touching, and the sensation satisfied her for the moment. Four, five, miles, and the bull pushed eastward over the gently rolling plain, each descent slightly longer than the previous ascent, so they actually went downhill. The bull quickened his pace, and Annie kicked Bird.

"Let him go ahead," said Quent. "Don't run the horses." The bull led by a quarter mile when the horses themselves picked up the pace.

"Water," said Annie. "Water, I'm sure."

"How can they smell it, when we can't?" Quentin wondered aloud.

"We're poor beasts," Annie said happily. "Horses and cows, they know there's a rattlesnake in the bushes long before we do. I've seen a cow run straight to the patch of brush where her calf has strayed. Old mavericks scrunch down in the thickets, out of sight of the cowboys. They know we're out there, but we thrash about. In animals, every sense is stronger than ours."

"Every sensation?" he asked mischievously. His eyes narrowed in the glaring sun, narrowed as a man's eyes did when he thought of taking a woman.

"Maybe our sensations would be just as strong," she said, her voice a bit uneven, "if we ran around in a state of nature."

"Naked?"

"Yes."

"You don't think, seeing every inch of skin out in the open, that we'd simply be jaded and pay no heed? I mean, human beings can get accustomed to the darnedest things. Like being dirty. Right now there's a crust half an inch thick on me, and I'm not running around searching for a bath."

"And if you were in New York, you would be?" The bull disappeared into a fold in the prairie.

"I'd never let things come to this pass back in New York. If my mother could see me!" He shook his head.

"Will you take me to New York?"

"Someday..." He intended to say more, but at that moment they both saw the water, a small lake, almost perfectly round, sunk a few feet below the level of the ground. Here and there bushes lined the shore, but in most places the grass came right to the edge of the water, blue water reflecting the blue, blue sky. Annie would have thought it a mirage, except that the bull stood belly-deep in the middle of the blueness. He lifted his head, roared out a note of triumph. The horses could not be stayed; they dashed into the water, took long drafts. Annie slid off the back of her mount, landing with a splash, not caring that her boots, the bottom of her skirt, even the edge of her pantaloons, got wet. Heaven in a prairie pond! Quentin sloshed toward her, took her in his arms. Heaven pierced her, and the building internal heat compensated for the chill of the water on her legs.

She met his lips openmouthed, welcomed the exploration of his tongue. She thrust her own tongue forward to claim her turn, brushed the underside of his lips, the smooth lines of his teeth. Her body convulsed with her need for him, again and then again. He must have sensed the jolt, for he pulled away.

"I'd better let them know," he said roughly.

"Yes," she agreed. How long before the end of the trail? When they would be together, forever. She would convince her father to let it be Quentin.

"You go to the other side of the lake, a bit away from the water. There's going to be a rush when the herd gets near here."

"Yes. I wish you could stay. We could picnic here."

"A dream," he said, whispering in her ear as he embraced her again. "We'll have a million picnics when you're finally mine."

"A million. I'll keep count. Let's see, over fifty years, that's twenty thousand picnics a year. Do you want to lower the figure?"

"No. We'll just count each time I look at you and love you as a picnic. That will add up to more than twenty thousand in any year. Now, get away from the lake. There's going to be a great stampede when the herd smells the water."

He had surmounted the slope to the west of the lake before she remembered the biscuits and bacon and tomatoes. Too late. Before she found a high spot on the other shore, two shots echoed. She sat cross-legged on the ground, letting Bird graze on the dry grass.

Would Hugh McCann object to the breaking of the engagement? Perhaps her father had persuaded McCann to accept her, fearing her past cut her off from any other honorable proposal. Perhaps McCann would welcome being released from the promise he had made his old friend.

How surprised her father would be, finding out this handsome, talented young man loved her, wanted her.

Johnny came in with the remuda, including the mules, unhitched from the wagons. He let the horses drink their fill, roll about on the damp ground at the edge of the little lake. When the dust of the oncoming herd roiled almost directly above them, he rounded up the horses and drove them a mile away to graze.

And the lake suddenly filled with cattle.

They did not drink at first, but stood belly-deep, lowing, touching the liquid with their noses, huffing as if they thought it might be a trick. Then, gradually, they drank their fill, walked out of the water, searching for grass.

Across the lake the entire crew gathered, eating biscuits pulled from their capacious pockets, cans of tomatoes unwrapped from the slickers tied behind their saddles. Annie saw Quentin and Broadbrim share a can of tomatoes, having the picnic she had wanted so badly. She walked around the lake to join them.

"Annie," Perk called. "Got mail for you."

"Mail?" she asked, disbelieving.

"Right after you left, a couple hands from a herd what's already made it to Montana came through. Riding back to Texas. They asked after you, for they had a letter from your daddy." He fished about in his vest pockets, pulled out a much-worn sheet of paper folded into thirds and sealed with a glued wafer. Annie walked away from the cowboys, to a spot where a few prickly wild roses grew. Bright red hips decorated the bushes.

Dear Annie,
I left a message for you at the hotel in Ogallala, but have got no word from you. I want you to take the train and come on to Montana soon as possible. Either the people at the hotel lost the telegram or you ignored it, and I hope it isn't the last for I always thought you a better daughter than that. I know the herd came through Ogallala, for Linares wrote that his foreman wired him the herd was fine.

Come on as soon as possible. McCann and I never thought you would hold out to the bitter end with the drive and he is getting antsy about the marriage. With good reason. Some rustlers up north started altering his

Bar H brand with a running iron. Damn thing has too many straight lines to be safe. So we marked his calves this year with the Rafter B, and he is uneasy about the whole thing since there is no wedding yet. And his whole increase for the year is running about marked with my brand. He's afraid you have second thoughts and have settled upon some other man, but I told him no second thoughts are allowed in this deal and that you know better than to even consider.

He didn't have the ready cash to finish your house, so I made him a loan of enough to get glass for the windows and curtains and a few fine things. Your wedding present came last week on the train, a bedroom suite with five pieces besides the bedstead, as pretty as you could ever want, sent out all the way from Grand Rapids.

You get that man to come along with you, soon as you get this letter, and ride straight away from the herd. I have arranged a room for you at the hotel in Temptation. Stop there and send a message out to me and to McCann. No sense making the trip to my place.

There's a preacher in town now, he is working on building a church, and the wedding will happen as soon as you set foot in town. Your trunk with the pink dress in it is waiting for you at the hotel.

Her world disappeared, nothing left at all. No prairie, no cattle, no lake, no other person. Around her lay a void, empty as life without love. How much time passed before she once again saw the herd grazing, the men plunging fully clothed into the roiled water of the little lake, she did not know. Quentin, soaking-wet, retrieved his hat and new vest from a rosebush.

It has nothing at all to do with me.

Water ran down his sleeves, the streams coursing over his hands. He flung back his head, and silver spray dashed from his hair. He pulled a late-blooming rose from the bush, walked toward her, holding it like the finest hothouse bouquet.

"Annie, what is it?" His voice, his eyes, offered to comfort her in her distress. "What's wrong? Has something happened to your father?"

She turned her back on him, bent her head to see no more, held out the letter. The paper slid from between her fingers; a slight rustling as he unfolded it, the prelude to the end. She wanted to scream, then found the silence protest enough.

"No. No, Annie. I will not let it be."

"You have no choice, for I have none."

"You do have a choice. A woman can't be bought and sold. A woman is not married to someone she doesn't love, simply because the man's cattle carry her father's brand. Men make contracts, business agreements between themselves, without using a woman as the seal on the bargain."

"You don't understand. You never have."

"What don't I understand? I love you. You love me."

"My father has only one child, Quentin. Me. I disappointed him terribly once. I can't do it a second time."

"Your father is behaving despicably in this whole matter!" he shouted. "Has he no sympathy? Hasn't he ever made a mistake in his whole life, that he must destroy you for one—"

"My father is a wonderful man!" She spun around, facing him, hoping to drive him away with anger. "My father is not despicable. He never made a mistake as huge, as abominable, as the one I made."

"Stop it, Annie. I won't give you up."

"Yes, you will. Because I don't want you." He was upon her, his sodden clothing wetting her bodice and skirt, in full view of the cowboys. She looked over his shoulder in alarm. Every eye in camp was turned toward them.

"Get away from me!" she snapped.

"Annie, I can't leave you. What will happen to me?"

"You'll find someone who's worthy of your love. You'll find hundreds of girls in Texas happy to marry you, trail along with you on the railroad survey."

"I don't want just any girl who's happy to marry me. I want you."

"Haven't you been listening? I don't want you. I'm going to marry Hugh McCann. Tomorrow, as soon as the horses are rested, we're heading to Temptation. You're delivering me to my father. You promised you would."

"I will not."

She slammed her fists on his chest, furious at his foolish objections.

"You agreed to see me to Temptation. Now you'll take me there as soon as possible."

"I agreed to accompany you, along with the herd. I agreed I'd accompany you on the train, if you decided to abandon the drive. I didn't agree to hustle to Temptation, just you and me, on your father's orders."

"You talk like a lawyer," she said sarcastically. "That's what you'll end up doing, isn't it? Going back to school, to join your father's law firm."

"What I do isn't at issue here. We're going to Temptation with the herd. What would you gain, rushing off now? Three, maybe four days. McCann won't die of nervous prostration, worried over his misbranded cattle...."

"I'll have Dan take me."

"I forbid it. Dan is my employee."

"I'll have my father pay him." She shrieked it out, every man in camp heard, and she no longer cared.

"Sorry. He can't go."

"One of the cowboys..." she was struggling, knowing she could not win an argument with him. He did not understand, and he raised silly, irrelevant objections.

"Which one will Perk let go? He's shorthanded already. You've been taking Johnny's place with Sid so the remuda can be kept close to the herd. Every day the riders must change horses more often. Are you going to run off, aban-

don everyone just as they've come to depend upon you?''
If he had shouted at her, snarled at her, cursed her, it could
not have hurt more than his flat tone and the honest, cruel
words.

"Please, Quentin. Don't make me disobey him again.
Don't make me hurt him again."

"I'm not. Circumstances are the cause, and if your father is half the rancher you claim him to be, he'll understand. Would a cattleman ask you to leave now, carrying
away a man Perk needs? If McCann frets about his calves,
your father must also worry over the three thousand cattle
he's paid for, who must walk all the way from Texas."

He abandoned her, ending the argument without a settlement. They had quarreled, because she must do as her
father said. She must never rest in his arms again, because
she belonged to Hugh McCann.

Over the next four days, she canceled anything that might
ever have grown between them. Ended it with silence, with
her refusal to so much as look at him. In her wagon at night,
she replayed the great pleasure of his love, putting Hugh
McCann's face behind the sensual lips, making the roving
hands Hugh McCann's hands. Try as she might, she could
not recall what McCann looked like. She replaced the face
with a blank, blond one, but the vision easily metamor-
phosed into Quentin. He did not hear her cry, for he no
longer came near her wagon.

Chapter Sixteen

"Sixty miles," said Perk, wrapping his hands about the tin cup of coffee, the only thing warm in the early chill of the September morning. "Maybe a bit more, but nothing you can't do with your horses in a day and a half. Take Gray-bob and all three bays, to make sure. Don't drive them too hard. Every horse in the remuda needs rest, and yours are no exception."

Quent nodded, kept his eyes on Perk, but all the time he was aware of the swaying wagon. Annie was dressing. In a few moments she would climb out the back, ready for another day. As soon as she heard of Perk's orders, she'd demand that she go with him. He would not take her. He could not stand two days alone with a taciturn martyr who sacrificed herself as penance to her father. No man should be forced to deliver the woman he loved to another man.

He looked around the camp, trying to absorb every sight, scent and sound, for the last time. The drive had ended for him, and he regretted the conclusion. He had become accustomed to the prairie sun, rising on his right shoulder, baking his back, then sliding toward evening on the left; bacon and beans on a tin plate; biscuits, the best he had eaten in his life; the sketchbook awkward on his thigh, spilling over with notes about elevation gains and losses, the width of streams, the locations of settlements; spreading his blankets under Annie's wagon; falling into exhausted sleep, to wake to the clatter of the coffeepot. He cheered himself by recalling the railroad survey being assembled in Texas. A quick trip to New York to make his confession to his father and mother. He dreaded that moment, but it must be done.

"McCann's place is southwest of Temptation, south of the railroad. If you make a long ride today, you might get there tonight." Perk drew a rough map in the dust with the toe of his boot. "Just cross the high ground beyond the river—forty miles, I suppose. You'll get to a country of little streams, all heading northeast. Cross the first four. McCann's place is under a little bluff cut by the fifth, downstream. It's protected from the northwest wind. Prettiest place you'll ever see."

Quent squatted down, watched the boot build the map, shoving up tiny hills, digging out river valleys, flattening promontories grown too high.

"With things as they stand, I gather it's as much in McCann's interest to know the herd's coming as it is Brownell's," continued Perk. "Linares said McCann's already taken over managing Brownell's place, 'cause of Brownell's rheumatism. He can hardly get on a horse, is what I hear. Anyway, McCann's soon to be Brownell's son-in-law."

"Yes," said Quent, agreeing without enthusiasm.

"So, you tell McCann everything. Maybe he'll ride on to Brownell's with you. Linares said they'd all meet us in Temptation, when their hands take over the herd. If Linares sells the remuda, the men can catch the train home if they're of a mind to. I expect some will stay in Montana, if they find a ranch needing hands."

"I'll get my things together," said Quent. "You be sure to watch over Annie."

"I'll cling like a tick to a bull's neck," said Perk. "Don't worry. She's near home now. You know I wouldn't send you, but for being shy a man, what with Huzzy leaving in Ogallala. And I must send the man who's of least value."

"I know. I understand."

"Well, you best get off as soon as you're ready," said Perk, by way of ending the conversation.

Quent decided not to wait until the wagon stopped swaying; he marched to the rear.

"Sorry, Annie, but I have to get my gear. I'm riding off to let McCann and your father know the herd's on its way." A white rump faced him. He had caught her kneeling, pulling on her trousers. His breath caught at the sight. He must have her. He could not have her.

"I'll come with you," she said.

"No, you won't. Perk said nothing about both of us going. I'll probably have to sleep out at least one night."

"I don't care."

"But I care. I don't want you along."

"Please, Quentin, I want to come."

"I don't want you. You're staying with the herd. One more day won't make any difference," he said steadily. He turned away, grasping a miscellany of equipment and ragged clothes, all that remained of his possessions. He threw the clothing on the ground. His trunk, long ago sent to Temptation by rail, awaited him. The thought of wearing proper suits and city boots and hats unexpectedly pleased him.

He tied the reduced bundle and his bedroll behind his saddle, covered it with his waterproof coat. Perk had obviously told Johnny his plans, for his four horses stood beyond the chuck wagon, Graybob saddled, the three bays bridled and roped for leading. Annie's face peeked over the end of the tailgate.

"Goodbye, Annie," he said in a low voice, so no one around the fire could hear. "May I ask, once more, if you might change your mind?"

"I can't. You know that."

"Then goodbye. Until we meet again." He lifted his hat. She smiled.

"In Temptation," she said. He did not dispute her, but he knew in his heart the meeting would never take place. He would not wait around to see her marry Hugh McCann. He would take the message to McCann and Brownell, ride into Temptation, catch the first train east. Uncle Nick's message would tell him all he needed to know. New York, then to join his uncle, deliver the sheaf of sketches and notes about the landscape of the trail. He imagined a long, serious discussion of his future over port and cigars. He would stay west, of that he was certain, but he hoped the future never brought him to Temptation, to Hugh McCann's Bar H—or was it to be McCann's Rafter B now?

She waved at him, leaning from the wagon; he waved back, studying the angle of her body, the slight twist from her hips to her shoulders, the angle of her head. Any other woman in such a position would look like a cow caught in barbed wire. She seemed to be an angel leaning through some secret portal of heaven. His last vision of her was one of beauty, and he congratulated himself that he had a pleasant memory.

He was going to be sick. He dug his spurs into Graybob's side, and the surprised horse leaped into a gallop. Out of sight of the camp. Out of sight of Annie, before he had to wipe his eyes to see the trail before him.

He pushed Graybob hard until he crossed the first river, then switched his saddle to Number One. He stopped just long enough to do a rough sketch of the ford. No need to draw in the lines of running water; just occasional stagnant pools between stretches of rank mire trampled by the hooves of countless cattle. On the farther bank, a herd of forty or fifty steers rested in the midmorning sun. A dozen or so more searched for grass along the stream's borders.

Beyond the river he stood in the stirrups, looking for the promised pastures of Montana. The grass, as far as the eye could see, had been cropped short, nearly to the roots.

"We've been cheated," he said to the horse. "'Grass as high as your belly, as far as a man could see,' that's what they said. You believed them, too, didn't you?"

You'd have seen it if you had come three years ago.

He had wasted three years, caught in a dilemma, neither horn of which he wanted, not knowing a third way existed. He might have seen this world fresh and green, but he had delayed the beginning of his life.

Just as you delayed crossing the ballroom, to lay your hand upon her arm.

How much pain he might have prevented by taking action. Annie's pain. His own. Never again would he hesitate when his heart said, "Go."

He would be understanding when he spoke to his father, but firm. He could not live at home, for it was no longer home in his heart. He imagined himself amid the constricted scenes of his boyhood. He laughed at the astonishingly small distances the vistas reached, how closely crowded the tiny farms lay. No one who had lived a summer beneath the towering sky of the plains could be happy in such surroundings.

So the trip had been worthwhile, no matter how his heart ached. Astonishing . . . in two insane meetings with his uncle their lives had entwined. An unknown heritage had been restored to him, a buried talent unearthed. Was there some deeper meaning to his almost instantaneous attraction to this uncle? No one—not his parents or his grandparents— had ever remarked on his resemblance to Uncle Nick. No one had ever said, even as a joke, that they were both throwbacks to the old pirate.

Or was the pirate van Kelson a figment of Uncle Nick's heady imaginings?

Try as he might, he could not keep Annie from his thoughts. After finding her face crowning the landscape for the third time, he reveled in the memories instead of avoiding them. He reenacted their meeting at the corral, when he had behaved like a clod, staring at her in shocked surprise. The trick of the horn pike. Her hatred. The days of driving her wagon, when she had aimed to discourage him so thoroughly he would leave. The pleasant days riding together, the evenings guarding her bathing spot. Then Ogallala, and the dive into the vortex of sex. Well, nearly into the vortex.

He congratulated himself on not having made the ultimate commitment. Annie went to McCann as perfect as he had found her.

As the afternoon progressed, the wind rose, becoming a gale on the ridges between the watercourses. He turned his head away from the cold, from the sharp bits of dust and sand it carried. He dug his kerchief out from under his shirt collar, pulled it over the lower part of his face. Beyond lay the broken country of the small streams Perk had portrayed in the dust under the gray dawn sky. Quent counted the gullies he crossed until, on the fifth, he turned downstream.

Twilight changed the prairie to gray before he saw the buildings tucked into the deeper shadows of a high embankment. Barns, sheds, a bunkhouse with yellow lamplight gleaming through the window. A spring must run all year here, for huge cottonwoods thrust sixty feet high, the wind rustled their papery leaves. He had almost forgotten the sound of wind blowing through trees.

Tall posts marked the entry gate. He prepared to dismount and open the gate, but the thin poles and the twisted barbed wire lifted away in the hands of a cowboy.

"Welcome, stranger. You huntin' for someone special, or just looking for a place out of the wind to fling your blankets?"

"Mr. McCann—" Quent chocked, his parched throat gagging on the words. He hacked the dust from his throat. "I'm from the herd Bob Linares sent up from Texas. I'm to see Mr. McCann." This time he said the name clearly.

"At the house," said the cowboy, pointing to a dark bulk under the trees. "He'll be pleased to hear, for the nights are gettin' colder than a day-old pot of coffee, and he wants to get them to a pasture up north."

"Thanks." Quent walked the horses the hundred yards between the gate and the house. In the failing light he could see only that it reared two stories high, the roof peaked. One ground-floor window, at the far right, showed a light. He headed in that direction, instead of to the front steps. Here, he was a servant, and he should use the back door.

Yellow lamplight spilled down a short flight of steps, and at their top he descried a narrow door. He flung the reins over the hitching rail, climbed the steps stiffly, pushing down on his knees to make them bend after a day in the saddle. He tapped politely on the door. The man who opened it formed a bulky silhouette.

"Yes?" he asked. Quent dragged his hat from his head, remembering he must be, under any and all circumstances, polite to this man.

"Mr. McCann?"

"Yes."

"I've been sent from the Linares herd. They're two days out. Three at the most."

"Come in." McCann stepped back, Quent entered the room. It looked to be a dining room, with a long polished table down the center, but McCann, living alone, obviously used the room for everything. Off to one side sat an easy chair and a low table, next to a small sheet-iron stove. In a dim corner stood a marble-topped washstand, a wet towel looped over a side bar. Two lamps illuminated the room, one by the chair and another on the table, next to a single place set for dinner.

"You had supper?" asked McCann. The man was tall, Quent noticed first, his eyes at least two inches higher than his own. The eyes shone dark gray in the lamplight, but in the sun, Quent supposed, they were blue. His closely trimmed beard did not conceal his jutting jaw. Annie's husband was a handsome man.

"No. In fact, I haven't eaten since I left the herd this morning."

"Sit down. Nothing but bacon and beans, but I suppose you're used to that. I haven't bothered going into town lately, seeing as how I'll have to go to Temptation to receive the herd. I'd planned to pick up supplies then, so the larder is scant at present." He opened a door, leaned his head into some interior room.

"Tabby. Another for dinner."

"You're taking responsibility for the herd?" Quent asked when McCann turned around.

"Brownell will be in town, too, to sign the papers, but the summer's been hard on him. He got bucked in July, been hobbling around with a cane ever since. I'll make sure the herd gets up north to the pasture. What's the condition of the cattle?"

"Fine. Thin, but that's to be expected, Perk says." When would he ask about Annie?

"The canyons up north have good pasture. Plenty of time to fatten up before winter comes. How many made it through?"

"At last count, 3,151. We picked up some strays on the way." McCann walked to the washstand, picked up a comb. He must have been washing up for dinner when Quent interrupted him. He slicked back his blond hair. Now, thought Quent, he will inquire about Annie.

"Where the cattle from?" he asked.

"South of San Antonio. Specifically, I don't know."

McCann stared at him with narrowed eyes. "Linares manage to get some good young heifers? I had Brownell write him and ask for fifty especially for me."

"I know nothing about heifers. You'll have to ask Perk or Linares."

McCann sneered, showing what he thought of the ignorant cowboy before him. "Annie's in town, I suppose." At last! Quent analyzed the tone McCann used when he spoke of Annie, desperate to find out if the man harbored any affection for her at all. The flat voice gave nothing away.

"She's with the herd. She's fine."

"Brownell sent her a letter, telling her to skedaddle to Temptation if she knew what was good for her. She didn't get it? Shiftless cowboys probably took Brownell's dollar and threw the letter away."

"She got the letter, but Perk lost a man in Ogallala. There was no one to bring her."

"Brownell said some gent was overseeing her."

"Yes, but he couldn't be spared. He rode herd."

"Has the man behaved himself with Annie?"

"Yes." What could he say, beyond that? Had he behaved himself, holding her in his arms, doing everything a lover might do except let her soft, expectant sex envelop him?

"I thought she should have a woman along, but Brownell said no other woman would be so crazy as to go on a trail drive. He figured a man of good family, one whose reputation would be blackened by a misstep, was the best alternative. Of course, we never expected her or the greenhorn to make it all the way. Linares wrote from San Antonio that the fellow was wet as a new kitten and not likely to see Dodge, but he seems to have stuck it out. What's he like?"

"You're looking at him," said Quent.

"You?" exclaimed McCann. He leaned a bit in Quent's direction. His eyes *were* blue. "Are you joshing me? You're just a bedraggled cowpoke who's been in the saddle too long."

Quent held out his hand. "Quentin van Kelson, of New York, named Dunk for the purposes of this drive. The greenhorn."

"Hugh McCann," said his host as they shook hands. The door opened, a woman came in with a pitcher of water. She emptied the basin into a slop jar, filled it from the pitcher.

"Wash up," said McCann. The woman had fair skin and red hair. When she stood in profile, Quent saw she was large with child.

"Tabby, bring some whiskey. This man's had a hard ride. And tell one of the hands to see to his horses." She nodded, left the room. "Now, you must tell me all your adventures. I'd wanted to come south, ride with you, but the ranch takes all my attention. And what with Brownell's afflictions, there's been precious little time to do aught but get the calves in and gather some of the best steers for shipping. And the stupid storekeeper in Temptation couldn't get my orders straight for the gear we needed for the fall roundup, so I had to travel all the way to Miles City.'' His mouth rose briefly into a satisfied smile, then dropped back into a frown.

The woman came with a jug, glasses, tableware to set another place at the table. Quent paid little attention to the fire the whiskey set in his gullet. How was he to organize five months of experience into a logical narrative? And, most important, a narrative that did not betray his true feelings for the woman meant to be McCann's wife? He helped himself to more whiskey as he sorted through the tangle of memory. He spoke first of the problems the westering settlers caused, then specifically about the settlement where they'd raced the horses. Not a word about Ardisson and Annie.

''It could be a great difficulty for next year's drives,'' he said.

McCann grunted, poured himself another drink. ''The government's got to keep the grangers out of the bottomlands. They interfere with the cattle,'' he said.

''The Homestead Law as it is, I can't see they can stop a man claiming a farm.''

''The Homestead Law's got to be changed. This country belongs to cattlemen.''

Quent shifted the conversation to Dodge and Ogallala. He had no inclination to get into an argument with McCann. Tabby brought in the beans and bacon, and a platter of homemade bread that carried the aroma of heaven with it. The food furnished a welcome excuse to stop talking. Speaking of Ogallala brought memories of the platform of the private railroad car, Annie's firm, high breasts...

He described the theater tent, and the contradiction of seeing *Romeo and Juliet* in the midst of a cattle drive.

"Annie go?" asked McCann. Quent nodded, his mouth full of bread.

"I don't approve of stage plays. They put wild notions in women's heads. Annie's got enough fancy notions, from what Brownell says. Comes from spending too much time in cities. But she'll get over that when she has a couple babies to take care of."

Why didn't I walk across that ballroom?

Quent spoke of the rivers, the dry stretches, the storms, the two times the herd had stampeded, and Perk's strange but effective ways of taking care of such emergencies. The girl brought in coffee in a china pot and sweet little cakes.

"You have a maid?" marveled Quent. "I'd not expected to find women servants in Montana."

"She came out with her husband a year ago. Homesteaders. In the spring her husband disappeared, so I took her in. Cowboys found what was left of him a few weeks back in a dry wash."

He poured coffee into china cups. Quent focused on them, the first china cups he had seen since the palace car on the siding in Ogallala. Since he had torn Annie's nightdress and exposed her to his caresses.

"Brownell's health being as it is, he'll have to move in here. He's got a bright cowboy named Bryce who I figure would make a good manager of that spread. As soon as Tabby's baby's born, I'll tell him to marry her and he gets the job. Nothing like marriage to keep a man in one place."

Quent's fingers, poised to lift the cup, froze into place. He opened his mouth to object, thought better of it, rephrased his thoughts.

"This Bryce, he's fond of Tabby?"

"I don't suppose he knows her." Quent lifted the cup, put it to his lips, but did not drink. "I thought about keeping her as a maid to help Annie, but she'd be sure to take up with some drifting cowboy and leave. Might as well put her where she does some good."

Quent's stomach churned. He recalled Broadbrim's appraisal of McCann, a man who took what he wanted, letting nothing less powerful than a tornado stand in his way.

"Want to see the house?" asked McCann, pushing back his chair. "The best house in eastern Montana." Quent accepted the invitation out of politeness, not interest.

Beyond the dining room was a central hall with a stairway, and on the other side of that a parlor. Curtains hung at the windows, but beyond three uncomfortable-looking chairs, the room was unfurnished.

"Back here," said McCann, opening a door, "is what Brownell calls the library, but it will be his room. He needs a place on the first floor, for since his fall in July he can hardly go up and down stairs." The echoes of their footsteps bounced around the walls of the empty room. "Can't let him stay in that drafty place on the Rafter B this winter."

Control, control, control, the echoing sound repeated. McCann controlled everyone around him. Brownell would move into his house, the woman in the kitchen would marry the cowboy he picked, and she would be McCann's instrument to control that man. Broadbrim had not prepared him for the full scope of McCann's arrogance. He expected to move people around like pawns, placing them on the squares where they did the most good for Hugh McCann.

Annie would be placed in the square marked Wife.

McCann returned to the dining room and the cold coffee. In the lamplight, the coffee reminded Quent of foul water from a stagnant stream. Tabby came in, removed the dishes from the table. Her bleak face, her drooping shoulders, her languid movements, showed a woman resigned to her fate.

"Perhaps," Quent said after she left the room, "it's a bit soon to talk of marriage for her. The man she loved is dead, and women mourn...."

"Love?" McCann laughed. "That's foolishness. Girls read damned novels when they should be learning how to take care of a family. They moon around, expecting some knight to come galloping up with gold and jewels and silk dresses. Even that new preacher in town's been taken in by the filth. When I told him I'd soon have need of his services, he spouted off about love and the duty of husband to wife."

"After all, we *do* live only a decade and a half from the twentieth century.... Women are assuming roles ... Ladies expect a declaration of love before ..." The meaning of the words fell apart in his chaotic mind. He was babbling.

"You think Annie's a lady?" McCann asked sardonically.

"I'm certain of it."

"Annie's a lady like a Thoroughbred mare," said McCann. "Fine three hundred and sixty days of the year, but when her heat comes, not caring what stallion she backs up to. My duty, her daddy says, is to make sure, on those anxious days, she stays in the barn." McCann laughed, a broad, exultant laugh. "I shock you," he said with delight. "You don't speak the truth back east, but pussyfoot about with big words."

"Our remarks about ladies are more circumspect," agreed Quent.

"'More circumspect,'" McCann repeated mockingly. "Another way of saying damned lies."

"What if this cowboy, Bryce, doesn't want to marry Tabby?"

"He'll marry her, otherwise he doesn't get to be boss, doesn't even stay on the Rafter B. And I'll tell him if he turns her down, he'll hurt her feelings. If he says no, she'll think she's not pretty, not attractive to men, and that's a bad thing to do to a woman."

Guilt. He would control Annie with guilt. Over and over again, reminding her of her sin, of her bastard child.

McCann would most certainly use the most direct word. *Bastard.*

"So Bryce's feelings count for nothing. Nor Tabby's?"

"Feelings are overrated. We do what we have to do."

"What you want them to. Isn't that a more truthful description?"

McCann leaned back, tipping his chair onto the rear legs. He laughed, a great hearty laugh from his gut.

"I suppose you're right. I've always been a man who liked to control things."

"And Annie, you expect her to obey you in all things?"

"That's in the ceremony—'love, honor and obey.'"

"But you think love is foolishness!" McCann's eyes narrowed.

"That's preacher talk. You have to say it to be married."

"Your philosophy, then, is that women obey and men act only for their own gain?"

"That sums it up, I guess."

"How far does obedience and self-interest carry?" He should shut up. He should not say what was in his mind. "Say in two or three years, I come back to Temptation, offer you thousands of dollars in a business deal, but before I sign the contract I must bed your wife. Do you tell me to go to hell, or do you order Annie to my hotel room?"

McCann's eyes narrowed to slits. "What kind of business you in?"

"I'll be with my uncle, Nicholas van Kelson," said Quent, pleased by his certainty. "We're running a railroad, north to south, and it may come through here." McCann laughed again, leaned forward so his chair thumped on the uncarpeted floor.

"For sure, a railroad from the south?"

"The investors are not all secure, naturally, for the route must be established. Towns along the way will be asked to contribute, for a railroad guarantees prosperity."

"If you offer to put a railroad across my land, you can mount every woman on the ranch, for all I care," he said lightly. "A railroad! It would make my fortune," he breathed, just above a whisper.

Quentin kept his eyes focused on a dark corner, not trusting himself to look at McCann. His fist prickled with the need to smash into McCann's grinning face.

"You and your uncle come to see me when the time comes," McCann said confidently. "We'll find a way to make us all rich."

Quent made himself yawn.

"You're tired," said McCann. "I'll have Tabby make up the bed in one of the spare rooms."

"I'll sleep in the bunkhouse," said Quent. The idea of sleeping in the house that would contain Annie as a bride revolted him.

"As you please." McCann rose, stuck out his hand. "I'm pleased to make your acquaintance, and hope to meet your uncle soon. Just let me know what I can do, I mean, if it's a matter of bridges or trestles, I can have my cowboys go to the mountains and cut timber over the winter."

Or order your wife to entertain me in bed, thought Quent bitterly.

He nearly stumbled over a bundle on the narrow porch, then discovered his bedroll and gear, left there by the wrangler who had led the horses to the corral. He grabbed the bundle under his arm and clattered down the stairs.

It was dark. The moon, well past full, had not yet come up, and twice he came close to falling on the uneven ground; he tripped on the single step leading to the door of the bunkhouse. Four men sat around a table. They pointed to a vacant bunk, turned back to their cards.

"Deal you in?"

"No. I'm so tired I couldn't keep my mind on cards." He could not keep his mind on cards, but weariness was not his major problem. He had to think, decide what he must do. Brownell had hired him to take care of Annie. His heart would not let that responsibility end with the completion of the drive. He must continue to protect her, and that meant keeping her from becoming Mrs. Hugh McCann.

He took off his boots, lay back on the bunk, pretending an interest in the game, but really concentrating on the problem at hand. Brownell had made financial arrangements that forced the marriage, at least so far as he and McCann were concerned.

But Brownell *must* assume that McCann had some affection for Annie, or he would never have promised his only daughter to him. Brownell had indulged Annie so far as to let her go on the cattle drive. So he loved her. Quent drew a mental line beneath that conclusion. Everything logical so far.

A father who loves his daughter would not insist on a loveless marriage when another man offered for her hand. When that man loved her to distraction. Did that follow naturally?

Annie would not disobey her father in this matter, so he must convince Brownell to change his mind. Tomorrow he would ask Brownell for Annie's hand.

The poker game did not end, but simply died when one of the players went to sleep, his head on his chips. Someone blew out the lamp; the grass-stuffed mattresses rustled as the men crawled between their blankets.

Quent found the darkness filled with ghostly images the lamplight had concealed, images portraying the misery awaiting Annie in that house. McCann's none-too-gentle caresses. McCann's obsession with control, forcing a man to marry Tabby to keep his livelihood.

The ghosts darkened. Was Tabby really a widow, expecting a child by her late husband? Or had McCann taken her... the body in the wash...?

Quent sat up. He was being totally, completely unfair to McCann. No evidence pointed to rape and murder, only the imaginings of his feverish, obsessed brain. But when McCann mentioned Miles City, he had smiled ever so slightly, and Perk and Stack had once regretted the herd was not headed for Miles City and the women. . . .

Having a woman in Miles City now and then did not condemn McCann. McCann could be accused of nothing worse than marrying a woman he did not love, a woman who did not love him. McCann wanted the marriage for the financial security Annie brought him. Such unions had taken place for millennia.

Annie would enjoy her life on the plains, he told himself. He imagined her the mistress of the lovely house her husband and father provided. In this sheltered place, she would grow a vegetable garden and raise chickens. Every Sunday she and McCann would drive into Temptation to attend the soon-to-be-built church. Annie would ride Jenny for miles to meet the women who joined sweethearts and husbands in new settlements; they would talk about hiring a schoolteacher, forming a Ladies' Aid Society.

The ghosts returned. Annie, finding her husband indelicately imposed upon the wife of a homesteader. And, when she protested, McCann's crude references to her own unfortunate past.

I love her, I love her, I love her. I only imagine these despicable things because I love her. No man can possibly care for her as I do!

He would get up before first light, get the horses from the corral, head for Brownell's Rafter B Ranch. The herd might arrive in Temptation as soon as the day after tomorrow. Perk and Annie might come tomorrow, for if Perk trusted Stack to bring the cattle the last twenty or thirty miles, he would ride on ahead to meet Linares and settle the details.

He would declare his love for Annie openly, beg her father for her hand in marriage.

Brownell thinks highly of good cattlemen, Broadbrim's voice reminded him.

Quent worried his predicament as a cat worries a mouse. He made sure he got up before dawn by the simple expedient of not going to sleep.

* * *

"Leaving so early?" said McCann's voice in the dark as Quent opened the gate. Quent spun around. A sober red sky reflection, not exactly dawn, gave just enough light to see.

"Yes. I have to get to Brownell's place."

"And I suppose, a gentleman like you, you're going to tell Brownell he's engaged his daughter to an immoral man."

Quent gulped, but decided he could not dodge his mission. "No. But I'm going to suggest to Mr. Brownell that Annie might be allowed to pick her own husband, a man she loves."

McCann laughed mockingly. "Annie deserves no better, because she birthed a bastard down in Louisiana. Or didn't you know that? Talk to Brownell. You'll find out just how much weight your fine eastern philosophy carries here in the West, Mr. van Kelson. You're in love with her, aren't you?"

"My affection for Annie is not open for discussion here."

"But neither you nor that other eastern bastard will marry her, because she's not high-class enough. You pretend to be so upright, and think anything close to the Atlantic is near to God in heaven. The eastern preachers come on missions to the corrupt West, tell us we're aflame with sin. But you and the fellow who ruined her, all you want is for her to be your pretty whore. It's best that you New Yorkers leave western women alone. There's men enough out here to take care of them. I like your gray horse," he added approvingly.

Quent gaped. A woman, a horse, all in the same breath. Quent opened the gate, led the horses through, set about closing it.

"I'll have that gray horse," McCann said firmly.

"No, you shall not."

"I will, and you can't stop me," said McCann. "The day Linares gets to town, that horse belongs to me. Same day I get your precious Annie."

"You'll have to deal with me, then," said Quent through clenched teeth. He didn't know if he meant the horse or the woman. He mounted Graybob, spurred away from the ranch. He looked back once, and to his surprise found the house beautiful. Until he saw the upstairs windows catch the first reflections of the red sky to the east. The interior seemed to be ablaze, a secret hell.

"I will not let you go there, Annie," he vowed. "You will not belong to him, I swear. You're not bound to your promise, for when you made it you did not know McCann's unfeeling heart." Or had she known? Had Annie accepted McCann's proposal completely aware that he did not care for her, would never care for her? Did she regard the marriage as her penance for allowing David Lampman to bed her and impregnate her?

He came very close to riding south, intercepting the herd. He would seize her, pull her onto his horse and gallop to the train station without stopping. He would force her onto the train, take her east. No destination in particular, just east. Someplace where she would not be the instrument of two men's desire for power.

But was he clear of the same charge? Uncle Nick would defend his right to kidnap her, because he wanted Annie for political purposes. Congressman Meechem, with his niece married to a van Kelson, would support the railroad. Married to him, Annie would be just as much a pawn as she was wed to McCann.

"No!" he raged. Love made the difference; and he had not fallen in love with her because she was Congressman Meechem's niece. He loved her because she was his wonderful, dashing, clever Annie. Why hadn't he walked across that ballroom? Why hadn't he declared his intentions in that moment, derailing Lampman's seductive plans? If he, for once, had taken decisive action, none of this need be happening.

It's my fault, he thought, *and I'll get her out of this mess. And into my arms.*

Chapter Seventeen

The Rafter B's headquarters proved to be much less elegant than McCann's place. The sheds, corrals and a low bunkhouse clustered in a shallow dip in the prairie, with not a single tree in sight. Except for the shadows cast by the sod-and-plank buildings in the late-morning sun, Quent might have ridden by without noticing. He understood why the wedding had to take place immediately. No place for Annie existed at her father's ranch.

"Perk has made good time," said Brownell, leaning on a cane in the doorway of the bunkhouse. "You stop by and tell McCann?"

"Yes, I came by his place on the way here."

"How'd you like the house?" Brownell asked anxiously. "I paid for that, so Annie'd have a nice place to live."

"It's very fine, sir."

"Well, come in, come in," said Brownell, stepping aside. "What'd you say your name was?"

"Van Kelson. Quentin van Kelson."

"Why, you're the greenhorn!" roared Brownell, clapping him on the shoulder. "Get Annie to town okay?"

"Annie's still with the herd."

"I told her to get herself up here," Brownell stormed. "She got the letter, did she?"

"She did, but Perk's shorthanded. One of the men left us down on the Platte."

"She could have ridden with you."

"You said she was to go to Temptation. If I'd taken her there, there'd have been an extra thirty miles of riding, and you wouldn't have known about the herd today."

"Perk shoulda come himself," groused Brownell. "That's usual. The foreman rides in and lets us know."

"Perk sent me, as being the most unimportant person along on the drive, the man best to be spared."

"You should have brought Annie. McCann's anxious."

"Perk will bring her in today, tomorrow at the latest. If she'd come with me, you'd have gained only a day."

"I suppose Annie's tip-top," he said sadly.

"Absolutely tip-top. She thrives in the open air."

"Always did. Even as a girl. Her mama died young, you know, so I hauled her about to places most little girls didn't go, and she loved it. Been a strain on my nerves ever since. How many cattle has Perk managed to bring north?" he asked, as if returning the conversation to its proper channel. Quent repeated his information on the herd.

"Wonderful!" cried Brownell. "McCann will be taking them on north."

"Perk and the other cowboys talked about Montana pasture, about grass so high it brushed the bellies...."

"And once it was," Brownell said in his booming voice. "But a few seasons of cattle, and drought, you can't expect those conditions every year. A good winter's what we need—then you'll see the grass come back better than ever."

Quent and Brownell ate their midday meal with the cowboys, around the long table in the bunkhouse. Once again Quent discovered the almost insatiable desire of men isolated on the range for news of the outside world. Even here, only twenty miles from Temptation, they were starved for something new to talk about. He told the same stories he'd told at McCann's, while desperately trying to figure out how he'd speak to Brownell privately. If an opportunity did not offer itself, he would simply ask.

Brownell stood up. "Time we was back to work, I guess."

"Sir," exclaimed Quent, jumping up so quickly he over-balanced the bench and two men nearly went on the floor. "Might I have a private word with you?"

"Is this about Annie?" Brownell asked sternly.

"Yes, sir."

Brownell jerked his thumb toward a door leading to a separate room. He hobbled across the threshold and slammed the door. The room was not terribly private, for there were wide cracks between the planks of the door.

"What's Annie been up to this time?" Brownell grumbled.

"Annie has been the soul of propriety," he lied with an easy conscience. After all, what passed between them had been completely his doing.

"No woman who goes on a cattle drive is proper," grumbled Brownell. "But it makes little difference, under the circumstances. McCann will marry her."

"It's about marriage I wish to speak, sir." He tried to interpret Brownell's level stare, found nothing in it, and so plunged ahead. "During these months I have come to have high regard for Miss Brownell. I should like . . . Would you consider, sir, my proposal to take her as my wife?" Brownell stared. "I love her," he added a bit lamely.

"Annie made a bargain," Brownell said harshly. "I allowed her to come to Montana if she agreed to marry McCann."

"I do not believe Mr. McCann loves Annie," he cried. "I do not believe Annie loves him."

Brownell shrugged. "It's a good connection. Her children by him will come into the largest herds in this part of the country. There'll be inconveniences, of course, and things that maybe don't square up with eastern notions of marriage, but McCann will take care of her. I've already lined up the preacher, two o'clock the day after she gets in town."

"Sir, the woman who works for McCann—have you investigated her position? I do not accuse McCann of being a libertine, but..."

"Libertine?" asked Brownell. "That's a fancy word for a womanizer, I believe. McCann's not that sort, and don't you spread word he is. He doesn't patronize the women in Temptation, nor in Miles City, neither. That gal wouldn't have roof nor food but for him."

"Sir, I beg of you, consider another offer. I love her. Please, I ask you for her hand in marriage."

Brownell's heavy brows knit together, forming a single dark line below the sharp crease on his forehead where his hat usually sat. He leaned forward, his eyes steaming.

"You've seduced my daughter," he snarled. "When Linares said he'd found a fellow from the East to be her escort, I feared the worst. 'Good family' means different things in New York and Texas, don't it? Texans honor any women, but you don't feel respect except for women of your class, do you? How far gone is she?"

"Gone?" asked Quent.

"With your child."

Quent drew himself up quite erect, appalled by the turn the conversation had taken. "That is an insult!" he shouted, not caring whether the men beyond the door heard or not. "An insult to me and to Miss Brownell. Annie...Annie is as chaste as the clouds in the sky...."

"That's a wonderful comparison," snorted Brownell. "About as chaste as a twister that levels a town and hoists a hundred cattle to slam them to earth twenty miles away. I've had nothing but trouble from that pretty face. From the time she was twelve years old, men flocked about. I'd come home, find her sitting on the front stoop, hearing stories not proper for her sex or age. I thought maybe if she lived with polite womenfolks she'd reform. But in Washington, with her aunt as a good example, what does she do? She believes a Yankee's lies when he says they'll get hitched, she lets the man take what's not his due until he's pledged, comes home weeping, carrying on, until her aunt notices that little stomach pouching out. When I learn the truth, I tell her, 'Ship her off.'"

"That is not the woman I have come to know, and to love," Quent said stubbornly. "I want her to be my wife."

"I suppose you think I'm a rich man, owning thousands of head of stock and controlling miles of grasslands. And you'll get your hands on that wealth by marrying the girl, won't you? She's not told you about laying with a man not her husband and having his child down in Louisiana? That cost me most dear, hundreds of dollars to keep her in that nunnery."

"I'm well aware of her misadventure. Once she's my wife, she and I will go find the boy. Annie's not an unnatural woman, who would, by choice, leave her child behind. She longs for her baby."

"You'll leave that child where it is, damn your prying eyes."

"*He.* Not *it.* A boy, your grandson."

"It's a it, so far as I'm concerned. A bastard. I'll not have my daughter coming around here with a child whose father wouldn't marry her and won't take note of his offspring."

Brownell had taken the only chair in the room, but even with him sitting down, his wrath was overpowering. He pointed a finger at Quent, his white hair and beard giving him the look of an angry divinity.

"You've put another babe in her, haven't you, you bastard?"

Quent grabbed the man's wrist, immobilized his arm. He leaned close to his ear so the men beyond the door would have to listen hard to hear.

"I have not lain with your daughter. In five months I have carried her on my horse across rivers, slept beneath her wagon and heard her cry for her child, doctored the hurt she received defending herself against a lecher, guarded her bathing spots from the eyes of cowboys. I have watched her take pleasure in the sky and the clouds and the prairies, seen her cope with lightning storms and rain without complaint, agonize over those less fortunate than herself. She has rejected my declarations of love, for fear she will hurt you. I ask you, please look to her happiness. Let her accept me, instead of McCann."

"And your family?" asked Brownell, his eyes darting.

"I'll not speak for my family," said Quent. "But whether they accept her or not, she'll be my wife, and I refuse to be ashamed of her or the love I bear her." He dropped Brownell's wrist, alarmed by how tightly he had gripped it. Had he hurt the man?

Brownell folded his arms across his chest. "She's going to McCann. There's a man who can control her and make sure she doesn't get in any more trouble. You prattle about love, beg me to think of Annie's happiness. I do, every day. I worry that she be properly placed so nothing bad will happen to her ever again. What kind of husband would you be? Going to your city work, leaving her alone. And what do you do when you find she's strayed? That maybe the child in her womb isn't yours? You'd thrust her aside, blacken her reputation forever. McCann will make sure it doesn't happen."

Quent felt stuck in a revolving nightmare. "Please, I love her" was all he could think to say.

"Love's well and good for quick passion. Cowboys come home all the time, desperately in love with some dirty girl in Miles City. Love doesn't hold out in the long haul."

He paid no heed to Brownell's reply. He jerked the door open, ran through the bunkhouse, into the open air. Thank heavens, no one had led the horses to the stable. He should shift his saddle off Number Two, but he dare not take the time. When he'd ridden out of sight of this pesthole, he'd stop and give the horse relief.

The anger started when he passed beneath the high gate, with its weathering buffalo skull.

Quent's watch said it was well past four when he rode into Temptation, for he had walked his horses slowly, using the time to concoct a plan. He would kidnap Annie. Who among the cowboys could he count on? Broadbrim, certainly, and Stack, perhaps even Perk. Dan would obey his orders, no matter what. Too bad Huzzy had taken off, for he owed him a favor. It would have to be done in a flash, just as the train from the west stopped briefly at the platform. She'd be without spare clothes and all the brushes and powders women pack along, for he would abduct her straight from her room at the hotel, carry her to the station—would she kick and scream?—force her aboard the train. With a cordon of cowboys walking with him, her father and McCann would be helpless.

He stopped at the station to make inquiry of the agent. "Eastbound, a Pullman?"

"Daily, 1:08 p.m. You missed it for today. It's usually on time. I know half an hour before, for they telegraph from the last stop west of here."

"You have a trunk here being held for Mr. van Kelson?"

"Sure do."

"Have it delivered to... What's the best hotel in town?"

"The only hotel in town is the Continental, so I suppose it's the best."

"It will do," Quent said. "I'm expecting a message from Mr. Nicholas van Kelson. Has he left it with you?" The agent drew a few papers from a spiked paper holder on the top of his desk.

"No, nothing for van Kelson."

His steps on the platform echoed, the hollow sound of boot heels striking the dry boards, the jingle of his spurs. When next he walked here, Annie on his arm, he'd be wearing city clothes. The last day for boots and spurs, for dirty shirts and denim pants stiff with sweat and grime.

Temptation was a single row of wooden buildings across the street from the railroad station. A few houses dotted the landscape on both north and south. At the edge of town, holding pens and a loading chute straggled along a siding. Nearly all the buildings on the main street pretended to be two stories, but behind the false fronts huddled rickety shacks. The sunbaked street lay empty except for four men lounging outside the livery stable. They exchanged nods with Quent when he left his horses to be fed and watered.

The Continental Hotel stood two stories tall, the only building in town that did. Neighbor to the Continental Hotel, and leaning against it, was the Continental Saloon. A door connected the saloon with the hotel lobby. The barkeep came in when he noticed Quentin waiting at the registration desk.

"Sorry, but we don't have many people through these days," he said. "We don't keep a regular clerk about."

"You'll have a crowd soon," Quent said. "A trail herd's coming up from Texas."

"Ah, yes!" exclaimed the barkeep. "Mr. Linares has already arrived. The herd's here?"

"Probably tomorrow. Do you have a message for me, Quentin van Kelson?" The barkeep shuffled through a thin pile of papers, shook his head.

"No, no message."

Well, they were a few days ahead of schedule, so Uncle Nick had not yet sent the telegram.

"You want a room?"

"Yes. And a bath."

"Bathroom's at the back, bottom floor. You want downstairs or upstairs?" Where would Annie be staying? According to his letter, her father already had a room reserved. Upstairs, probably, so that she would be as far as possible from the cowhands and away from the noise of the saloon.

"Upstairs. In the back."

"Can give you number 5. Four, old Brownell's got a handle on that room for his daughter, arriving from Texas sometime soon, so I can't let you have 4."

"Five will be fine," Quent said, overjoyed by this lucky piece of gossip. A thumping noise on the front steps proclaimed the arrival of his trunk. He tipped the man half a dollar, carried it upstairs. Across the hall from his room, a bold *4* decorated the door. The doors had neither knobs nor locks, but fastened with a wooden latch raised from the outside by a string. He stared at the string hanging from the door to room 4, pulled it, felt the latch lift. The door swung open silently.

The room smelled of dust and of cigars smoked months ago. A trunk stood at the end of the bed, the lid decorated with brass bands and the initials *AMB*. If he found a way to warn her ahead of time, she might be able to make a bundle of things from that trunk, so that she would not be on the Pullman without a nightdress. *Nightdress*. The word recalled the night in Ogallala, and his heart rose in his throat. He shut the door carefully, lifted the latch to number 5.

Now that he saw the lay of the land, he could make specific plans for the kidnap, but instead he worried about the lack of a message from Uncle Nick. Had Uncle Nick not been serious in his proposals? All the plans for his own future, for Annie, depended on Uncle Nick. Maybe Uncle Nick had second thoughts about taking on a nephew with no experience. A nephew whose father would probably disown him when he discovered his intentions. A nephew who looked a great deal like him.

The question he could not bear thinking rose stark and plain. What *was* his relationship to Nicholas van Kelson?

Quent unlocked his trunk, found clean clothes, went downstairs to the bathroom, spent half an hour soaking in tepid water. At least he found plenty of soap and was able to get the trail dust out of his hair and most of it off his hands.

In the saloon, men argued about the consequences of the dry summer. He heard the barkeep's voice, stepped behind the counter, pulled the sheaf of papers from their cubbyhole, flipped through them, paying careful attention to the telegrams. Nothing addressed to him.

He climbed the stairs slowly, dispirited. He had counted on Uncle Nick. He wished Uncle Nick was here. He would help him get Annie out of this place, onto the train. Why did the old coot not turn up when he needed him?

Back in his room, he dumped his trail clothes in a corner, rescuing only his boots, hat and belt. His bowler had survived five months in his trunk with scarcely a dent. A bit of brushing and it looked nearly new. Where else might Uncle Nick have left a message? Was there a telegraph office separate from the railroad station?

He wandered down the street, found the crowd in front of the livery stable grown to eight. The telegraph office was at the end of the station. No, no message for Quentin van Kelson. His unease grew. Perhaps he should go back to the saloon, get a drink and dinner. Where was Linares?

As if in answer to his question, a buckboard rounded the corner at the end of the street, directly opposite where he stood concealed in the door of the telegraph office. Bob Linares held the reins of the team, and Annie sat stiffly beside him, her eyes straight ahead. Quent thought of descriptions he'd read of the queen of France going to her execution.

Much the same, the guillotine and marriage to Hugh McCann. But, unlike Marie Antoinette, Annie would be rescued. The light of that optimism immediately darkened. A spring wagon, accompanied by four men on horseback, crossed the railroad tracks a bit east of town. The driver had white hair.

Annie had slept very little, for she had expected Quentin at daybreak. She had made a bundle to carry with her on horseback when they rode away. Where, she did not know. Quentin would have that all planned.

She had wanted to ride Jenny into town, just in case Quentin planned to accost her on the trail, but Linares had insisted she join him in the buckboard.

"Your horses will come in with the remuda," he had assured her.

Now, standing in the lobby of the Continental Hotel, she knew for a certainty she had to marry Hugh McCann, that she would not escape that fate. She had given Quentin no hope; he had not come for her. He might have already left Temptation, traveling to meet his uncle.

Linares went into the saloon to fetch the barkeep, leaving her standing alone in the lobby. The registration book lay open. She bent over the counter and, by reading upside down, saw his name, the last on the page. *Quentin van Kelson, New York.* On the line above, *Robert Linares, San Antonio.*

The door to the street opened behind her. She straightened, pretended she was examining the flyblown portrait of Ulysses S. Grant hanging over the desk.

"Annie." She paid no attention to the stooped, white-haired old man in the doorway.

"Annie!" He could not be her father! Not strong, confident Elam Brownell. But he was! What had Montana done to him? His hair, which had been steel gray, now resembled a snowdrift. He limped on his right leg, and with every step his cane thumped on the floor. She rushed to him, doubting, returned his embrace, then stood aside as he exchanged greetings with Linares. She looked for shock in Linares's face, saw none. Linares, she recalled, had seen him last summer and was not appalled by the change. Linares gallantly offered to escort her to her room, so her father would not have to climb the stairs.

Which room held Quentin? She had been so afraid she would not find him here, afraid he might have already left.

"I'll have the woman bring up some hot water so you can freshen up," said Linares.

"Thank you. Ask if they can send a bath." She sat down heavily on the edge of the bed, the thoughts of escape engendered by Quentin's signature vanishing like smoke. For three years, while she flitted from relative to relative, flirted in Washington, reaped the consequences of that flirtation in Louisiana, spent a summer riding with the herd, her father had struggled to build a future for himself, and for her. And, considering the money a steer brought in Omaha or Chicago, he had succeeded. She must be one of the richest heiresses in eastern Montana.

To give her a fortune, her father had sacrificed his health. His letters had spoken of grandchildren. No wonder he was anxious to see the next generation. He doubted he would live to see the boys who would inherit the combined Bar H and Rafter B.

"Quentin, all my dreams are foolish and selfish," she said aloud. "I owe Daddy my obedience in this thing. And Mr. McCann is a very handsome man. All the women in Texas flirted with him, but he paid no attention." She ignored the tears on her cheeks. "If Quentin speaks to me, I'll pay no heed," she resolved.

She knew who came up the stairs. The hesitant steps, the solid thunk of the cane. She brushed her tears away, opened the window and stood in the fresh air to clear her lungs. His knock was tentative.

"Daddy, you should have asked me to come down. You shouldn't climb the stairs."

"We need to talk. That Yankee who rode with you, he told me he wants to marry you. Is that true?"

"He asked me."

"What did you say?"

"I refused him."

"Has he touched you?"

"Touched me?" she asked, feigning innocence.

"Annie Brownell, you know what the hell I mean. Has he lain with you?"

"No."

"Did he ask to?"

"No. He's a gentleman."

"I got worried. So did McCann, when you didn't come up on the train. You plan on holding to your promise?"

"I expect to marry Hugh McCann," she said, as evenly as possible. There. She'd said it. She had made the promise face-to-face, not simply in a letter.

"He's built you the best house in eastern Montana. You'll get used to his ways easy enough."

"I have no choice but to get used to his ways, do I?" she said sweetly. "That's the meaning of marriage."

"I'm glad you see it that way, Annie. I've been terribly fearful, you with all those men."

"Mr. van Kelson stood between me and the cowboys, and they soon learned I wasn't available."

"Perhaps I misjudged the man."

"Daddy, you didn't . . . accuse him of misbehavior?"

"Not in so many words," he said hastily. "I'll speak to the preacher," he added, very obviously changing the subject. "Two o'clock tomorrow be acceptable to you? We'd do it tonight, but McCann sent word he can't get in until early tomorrow morning at the soonest. He's short-handed."

"That's fine," she said.

"You can spend your wedding night here, rather than ride all the way out to the Bar H. Even though I'm most anxious to hear what you think of the house. Until then, I think it best you stay in this room, with so many cowboys in town. I'll have meals sent up."

"That's fine. Thank you for making the arrangements," she said, wondering if Quentin would stay for the wedding, for the wedding night. Would he be under this same roof when Hugh McCann pushed her nightdress up and took her as his wife? She did not want Quentin to be near, did not want him to hear McCann's cry of satisfaction when his seed went into her.

I want it to be Quentin, her body cried. *Always and forever, I'll want it to be Quentin.* Would McCann ever suspect she thought of another man when he lay on top of her?

The horrible truth came like a cold shower. She could not allow herself to be captured in her husband's web of passion, for she might cry another name and betray her true love. With McCann she must forever be passive, through all the nights of their marriage. To herself, when he was finished and asleep, she would whisper, "Quentin, Quentin!"

Chapter Eighteen

Quentin sat in the Continental Saloon, nervous, but highly satisfied with what he had achieved during the morning. Linares, Perk, McCann and Brownell sat with him, passed around a bottle of whiskey and signed the papers that transferred the herd. At one end of the bar lounged eight Bar H and Rafter B cowboys, ready to ride out and take over the cattle. At the other end stood Broadbrim, Dan, Lucas, Soto and Rolf, drinking slowly, with moderation.

"Don't get drunk," Quent had ordered. "Whatever you do, don't get drunk!" He had felt shamed by this implied distrust of his fellow conspirators. "I'll tell the barkeep your drinks go on my bill."

His trunk had been carried to the station, tagged for the eastbound train. At precisely five minutes to one, he would mount the stairs to room 4. Annie, he had noted, left her latch string out. Dan would enter the room with him. While Quent scooped Annie into his arms, Dan would bundle as much of her clothing and trinkets as he could into a blanket or sheet. The other cowboys would range themselves at the bottom of the stairs, then surround Quent and Annie while he made the dash for the station.

McCann and Brownell would have the greater force, of course, but he would have Annie. He dropped his hand to his right thigh, felt the six-shooter resting there. If nothing else prevailed, he would hold the gun—unloaded, of course—to Annie's head. The law would be after him if he did, but by the time Brownell got a sheriff or marshal, she would be hundreds of miles away, bedded, maybe pregnant. Would Brownell pursue the matter under those circumstances?

"...amazing good condition," McCann was saying. "Brownell, I'll drive you out after dinner in the buckboard, so you can see the herd." Everyone around the table fell silent, embarrassed at the forgetfulness of the bridegroom.

"There's a wedding," Brownell said in an undertone. A very subdued question crept in beneath the words, giving Quent hope. *Brownell wonders if he's doing right by Annie*, Quent thought. *Maybe he'll not interfere when I snatch her away.*

"Ah!" exclaimed McCann, not at all embarrassed by his neglect. "So there is. Well, soon as we can."

"One more thing, Linares," said Brownell, "I want to buy that remuda of yours. Some good horses in your herd."

"I'll sell, but the price must be high enough to cover the cost of sending my hands home by rail. Some had planned to ride back to Texas."

"You'd best remember," said Perk, "Hellcock belongs to me. The rest of my string, it goes, but not Hellcock."

"I'm offering two thousand dollars," said Brownell.

"My hands wanted me to buy the remuda," said McCann mildly. "Two thousand two hundred."

"Now why should we compete?" asked Brownell with equal mildness, but steel lurked in his voice. "Your ranch and mine, they're heading to be one and the same."

"There's always gonna be some separateness," McCann said sharply. "And my hands want the remuda." Quent recognized the bullheaded man Broadbrim had described; he heard again the determined words McCann had uttered at the gate in the faint light of dawn. *I'll have that horse.*

McCann was bidding for Graybob! Quent leaned forward to inform him that Graybob and the three bays were not part of the remuda. Then, on second thought, he leaned back to enjoy the fun. Why interfere with Linares' profit?

"Twenty-five hundred," said Brownell.

"Twenty-seven." Still a bargain, if Graybob was in the offering, which he was most definitely not.

"Three thousand," said Brownell, but he hesitated just a few seconds. If McCann made another bid, he'd take the remuda.

"Three thousand one hundred," said McCann. He grinned, certain he had won.

"Three thousand two hundred," replied Brownell defiantly. Linares looked with wonder from one man to the other.

"You—" snarled McCann, then cut off the epithet of insult. "Thirty-five hundred," he snapped.

Every eye turned to Brownell. The cowboys at the bar stopped talking. Even the barkeep stood idle, his towel hovering over a glass.

"I guess you take them," Brownell said sadly. "But there are a few horses in that bunch I'd really liked to own."

McCann turned to Quent, not just his eyes or his head, but his whole body, to put power behind his words. "Get that gray horse and the three bays out of the livery and back to the remuda, where they belong. I told you I'd have that horse."

"How much do you offer?" Quent asked. He made sure he frowned.

"I just bought him. Haven't you been listening?"

"You bought the remuda. My string belongs to me, not Linares. They wear my brand, not the Tall X."

McCann's large fist slammed onto the table. He turned a grim face to Linares. "Why'd you not tell me he owned his string? I take back my bid."

"Mr. McCann, those horses weren't with the remuda when you saw it this morning. They don't wear the drive's brand. It didn't occur to me that you might presume Mr. van Kelson's private string to be part of the remuda."

Brownell's face lengthened with new understanding, and obvious relief. So, he, too, had bid thinking Graybob part of the herd. When he smiled, some of the wrinkles smoothed out, and Quent saw Annie's eyes reflected in her father's.

"Mr. van Kelson," Linares continued, "is sufficiently wealthy to purchase a much finer quality of horse than I can provide for a remuda. I can't believe that you supposed they were part of the herd."

"Then I withdraw my bid," snapped McCann.

"There're plenty of witnesses to your offer," Perk said dryly. "When a man makes a bid in a public place, he usually expects to stand behind it." His eyes enlisted the support of the Tall X cowboys. Broadbrim nodded, the rest of the crew nodded. Dan looked on in wide-eyed amazement.

"That one," McCann growled, pointing at Broadbrim, "that nigger's not standing witness to any remark of mine. This is a deal amongst white men."

Quent's breath stopped when all the Tall X men straightened. Even Dan. "No! No!" he whispered. A fight would destroy his chances of getting Annie on the train. He pushed his open palm against the air, telling them to bottle their anger at the insult to Broadbrim.

"I'm not to blame," continued Linares calmly, as if nothing else had been said, "if you didn't bother to check the brands of the animals you purchased. In Texas it's a poor cattleman who doesn't ride out and check the brands when he's thinking of buying."

"Now, there I must agree," Brownell said loudly. Too loudly. His reprieve from paying too much for the remuda had made him bold, youthful, in spite of the white beard and hair. His cheeks flushed with his unexpected triumph. "You should have checked the brands, McCann. Mr. van Kelson—" Brownell turned to face Quent, his brown eyes more respectful "—he spent his own money on some fine horses. What's your brand, Mr. van Kelson, so if McCann wants to wander down to the livery and check, he'll know for sure?"

"An artist's palette."

"A what?" McCann erupted.

"A funny little misbegotten circle, like," explained Perk. "Dunk says it's what artists mix their paints on."

"I guess you should of gone looking for misbegotten circles," said Brownell. He laughed, slapped his knee, but stopped when McCann rose so quickly he knocked his chair to the plank floor. The big man leaned over, his knuckles tense against the table.

"You best stop directing remarks like that at me, Brownell—that is, if you expect me to marry that heifer of yours who dropped a woods calf down in Louisiana."

Quent stood up, found McCann's thrusting face at exactly the right level to meet his fist. McCann, caught off balance, not only fell, but caught his chin on the edge of the table as he went down. The table followed him over, taking the bottle of whiskey. A lesser man would have been knocked out, but McCann took one deep breath, jumped to his feet.

Quent tried to guard against the blow, but was too late. A blow to the jaw, he noted, did not hurt immediately. He hung over the table leg, saw several other fists in action. One connected with McCann's jaw; it was black.

Someone pulled him off the table leg, into the haven behind the table. The shouting, the thud of falling bodies, informed him that the melee had become general. A flood of despair weighed on Quent, kept him down. He had ruined any chance of getting Annie out of here. He had defended her against McCann's nasty comment, but at the expense of stealing her away from Temptation. He struggled to his hands and knees. His head spun. Brownell faced him.

"Is what Linares said true? You rich?" Why talk about money now? He had to get back into the fight, not let the cowboys carry the thing for him.

"I suppose." He put a hand on the table leg to pull himself erect, but Brownell jerked it away.

"Thank you for defending Annie's honor—what she's got left, anyhow. Too bad you didn't have your way with her on the trail. If you had, it'd be you next to her in front of that preacher, let me tell you."

Quent could not have been any more astonished if Brownell had claimed he pastured cattle in Siberia. Brownell would give permission for their marriage if he had done the dishonorable thing? Was the entire western United States insane?

"Well, I'll get to my feet and try to get my licks in," said Brownell. He grasped his cane, grabbed a table leg and wavered upright.

Quent dodged behind the man, trying to force his foggy mind to make sense of Brownell's remark. The door of the saloon stood open. He crawled to the opening, got to his feet by hanging on to the bench on the front walk. By the time he got that far, he knew what he had to do. His legs worked fine. He ran into the lobby, raced past the empty desk and up the stairs, taking them two at a time without touching the banister. The latch string of number 4 hung out, welcoming. He opened the door, threw himself in and slammed the door behind him in one movement. After an instant's consideration, he pulled the string in.

"Quentin!" she cried. She had on pantaloons and chemise, her hair hung about her shoulders, and she held a hairbrush. "What's going on? What's all the noise?"

"A fight in the saloon. Annie, get off your clothes and get in bed. I can't explain everything now, but you do as I say and we'll get married." He held on to the bedpost to steady himself, raised one leg, pulled off a boot.

"Quentin, someone hit you!"

"McCann. I had a fight with McCann. Get your damn clothes off Annie, 'cause I'm coming for you." Out of habit, he loosened his tie, then realized that what needed to come off was lower down. "Please, Annie, trust me in this."

She untied the webbing that bound chemise to pantaloons, began pulling the chemise over her head.

"Not that!" he yelled. "Your pantaloons! We don't have much time before your father figures out I've left the saloon."

She pushed the pantaloons down over her hips as she hopped toward the bed. Quent loosened his braces, pulled at his trousers. Something interfered. He looked down, saw the gun, hastily unbuckled the belt and let it fall to the floor. He shoved down his pants. She sat, half-naked, on the bed, staring at him, but not at his face. He took one great leap, leaving his trousers in a heap on the floor.

"Annie," he whispered as he pushed her back onto the comforter, "this isn't how I intended the first time for us to be, but I've got to move fast. Your father said we'd be married, if only I'd done...been inside you this summer."

Her legs lifted, wrapped around him. "Go in me," she whispered. "Go in me, Quentin, go in me."

In the muddle of noise and emotion, Quentin wondered what connection there could be between a horrendous crash, the tinkling of glass and his smooth, unimpeded entrance into Annie's body. She shoved her hands beneath his shirt and encouraged him with little pats and strokes. Silence wrapped them like a lowering fog.

"Annie, you're the still center of this insane world," he whispered.

"Hurry," she cried. "Daddy's coming." Slow-paced footsteps, the thud of a cane braced on stair after stair.

"I'm sorry, Annie," he said, then drove into her the way a man might plunge lustfully into the most inconsequential woman. "I'm sorry, I'm sorry...." The first thunderous knock came in the instant of his shuddering release.

"Annie," roared Brownell, "you open this door right now!" A crashing blow against the wood. "The latch string's got pulled in, Annie." His voice became even louder, which did not seem possible. "Is that damned Yankee in there with you?'' Another blow. The dry wood of the latch splintered.

"Yes, Daddy. Quentin's here with me." Crash. It would give on the next blow. Perhaps he should get off her, but Annie's hands cradled his buttocks. There was a great deal of noise, both from the door and from Brownell, when the latch gave way. Quent noted that the tone of Brownell's yell echoing about the room blended with the splintering of wood and the impact of the door against the wall.

"By God! Annie, can't you keep out from under Yankees?''

"Daddy, I love Quentin." Brownell's hand closed around his collar, lifted him away from his daughter, although not at the important end.

"By God, sir! Do you intend to ruin my daughter?''

"No, sir." Quent was choking. His collar button was still fastened. "But I should like to marry her." He wanted to point out that he had made the proposal more than twenty-four hours earlier, but the collarband cut off his windpipe. Brownell released his hold so quickly he fell heavily upon Annie. For a moment he feared he might have hurt her, until he heard her sigh with pleasure and felt her hands tighten on his buttocks.

"The first man who did this, he got away, but only because I wasn't around. Don't think you're so lucky,'' snorted Brownell. "You're not leaving this building until the preacher gets here. Whether you like it or not, you're getting hitched to a Texas gal.''

"I should like that very much," Quent whispered in Annie's ear, not bothering to address Brownell, who wasn't listening to a word anyone else said, anyway. He twisted his head, saw Brownell heading out the door.

"Please, sir..." he called.

Brownell stuck his head back in the door. "Won't do you to beg, young man. It's as certain as winter in Montana.''

"It's just that...my trunk's already at the station. Could you please see to having it carried here? And please close the door," he added as a happy afterthought. Brownell grunted, slammed the door, leading Quent to hope he would comply with the other request.

Annie giggled and moved her body beneath him in a way that suggested the unrestrained joy of jumping up and down.

"Quentin, Quentin, what happened? Tell me what happened." He gave her a breathless summary of the bidding for the remuda, the dreadful insult McCann had spoken against her and her father's remarks in the fortress behind the table.

"I'm so sorry it had to be like this," he said again. "So many times I dreamed of the pleasure I'd give you before I ever asked this of you."

"Don't worry, you'll give me pleasure the next time," she said. Her hands curled into his hair, she drew his face down to within an inch of hers. Quent decided, very happily, that the next time might not be very far distant. He managed to get one hand into his vest pocket, found his watch. How remarkable! It still ran. Yes, there was time for a next time, before they donned their wedding clothes.

Annie unbuttoned Quent's vest, slipped her hands under his shirt. "Take it off," she said. They sat up and he slid her chemise over her head, but before she had his shirt opened, he cradled her breasts in his hands and bent to kiss them.

"Quentin," she whispered, "it's wonderful, but I want you bare, too." He pushed her upon the heap of disarranged blankets, his lips closed upon the point of her breast, drawing it gently into his mouth. She tried to fondle him in return, but her hands got tangled in his shirttail.

"Quentin, please!" she begged. He sat up obediently. She shoved his vest off his shoulders, worked at the shirt buttons, while his fingers continued to stroke her breasts. She gasped when they reached her nipples, got another button undone. She desperately wanted him to expand the caress, but she had to get his damned shirt off.

"Quentin, you've got to help me." He laughed when he released her breasts, laughed when he stripped the shirt over his head, then the undershirt. He pulled her down and they lay face-to-face.

"Do you remember the wind at the buffalo wallow?" he whispered.

"And the sun," she answered. "I wish we were there now."

"We'll go back. And to a hundred other places like it, because no matter where we go, we'll always return to the plains. Where we fell in love."

He kissed her gently, held her close, and led her slowly to a new union. So different from what he had accomplished minutes before, plunging into her, unprepared. His hands mimicked the wind, his flesh the heat of the sun, and the elements entered her with him. The whirlwind joined with the breeze, and lifted them together, in a rising gale of power. For one instant she hesitated, fearing Quentin's determination and force. Then she threw herself into the heart of the storm, and let it—and Quentin—toss her sky-high.

"How fortunate," she murmured, "that you're on top of me, for otherwise I might had floated away."

"We did float away," he replied. "Together."

"You felt it, too."

"Of course. And you must forget what went before. This was our first time."

"No, Quentin, we won't forget. We'll laugh about it, that we're the only couple in history who got each other because he burst into her room and ordered her to lower her pantaloons."

"And speaking of pantaloons, perhaps it's time we got dressed," he said. He lay back upon the pillows, she rested her head on his chest. "Where's my watch?"

"I think it went onto the floor with your vest," she murmured. She reached out her tongue to touch his nipple, hidden in a tangle of hair.

"Stop that," he said playfully. "I know there's not time enough for us to dance together again."

"Where are we going, Quentin? On the train tomorrow?" His hand, which had been stroking her hair, tightened.

"To Louisiana, of course."

"And then?"

"I don't know. I'll have to find out where Uncle Nick is. He . . . didn't leave a message for me here. Or if he did, the barkeep lost it." He very nearly succeeded in sounding completely at ease, as if the message were of no importance. She thrilled at the realization that she knew he was worried. They knew one another so well, after months of living in such close proximity. And now, with this intimacy of body, would come intimacy of mind. She would know Quentin better than any other human being on earth.

"We'll find him," she said calmly. Had his uncle forgotten his promise? Were all eastern men—except Quentin—careless of their word?

"Don't worry, Annie." She lifted her head, stared at him. He had the same insight into her! How was it going to be, living with someone who could almost read your mind? She sighed and put her head back on his chest. She would learn to live with it. Better than learning to live with Hugh McCann.

"Quentin, you didn't tell me exactly what McCann said about me. You said he insulted me, but I want to know what he said."

He said nothing for quite a long time. She hoped he would not censor McCann's remark from some mistaken notion that her feminine ears could not bear profanity.

"Annie, he called you a heifer who had dropped a woods calf."

"That's all?"

"All? He said it in front of two dozen men in the saloon."

"And you hit him for saying it?"

"Of course I slugged him. A man can take only so much, and McCann had given me cause—" He stopped very suddenly. What else had McCann said about her, before he compared her to a heifer?

"What else?" she asked.

"I met McCann at your...his house. I realized he did not love you. I determined you would not marry him. It's of no importance now, but I planned to steal you away. Just before the eastbound train came, I would burst in here, carry you away."

"Alone! So gallant!"

"No, Broadbrim and Dan and some of the other cowboys offered to help me, after I explained about McCann."

"What about McCann?" Another long silence.

"Annie, he wanted nothing but the ranch. You were the price he paid."

He took her hand, and the innocence of his touch made her giggle. Holding hands, when they lay beside one another naked and he had just minutes ago made love to her. Love so remarkable she was uncertain she could stand up. She heard footfalls from the stairs.

"I think perhaps someone is coming to tell us we'd better get clothes on," he said. The steps came closer. "He's wearing city boots, and no spurs. Who can that be?"

Knuckles tapped at the door; the door, minus its latch, swung wide open.

"Quentin?" asked a strong voice. They both sat bolt upright. Quentin jerked a blanket out from under himself, wrapped it around Annie, then held her to cover his nakedness.

"Uncle Nick?"

"Of course. I'd left no message, so I thought you'd be expecting me. And congratulations! Brownell says Annie's to be my daughter...in the same way Quentin is my son," he added. Quentin's arms tightened about her. Uncle Nick pulled his watch from his vest pocket.

"A quarter past one. You best get dressed for the occasion. Although a wedding with the bride and groom in appropriate undress would be original, quite original. And honest. Everyone at a wedding is thinking of the wedding night."

Chapter Nineteen

Quentin grimaced at the dissolute face in the mirror. The reflection grimaced back, even more dissolute. His jaw and one cheek bore the mark of McCann's fist. The discoloration spread to his eye. He glanced down at his bare chest and arms. Nothing damaged there. He wondered how the other men in the fight had fared, those who had fought longer than he. No broken bones, he hoped. Half his mind concentrated on shaving. The other half he used to screw up his courage to question his uncle.

"Brownsville, Texas, then, is where we'll meet," said Uncle Nick. "Are you sure a month will be long enough for a honeymoon?"

"More than enough. She'll come on the survey, and that will be an extension of a honeymoon."

"She's a wonderful woman, Quentin. You're lucky."

He did not want to ask the question, but after Uncle Nick's remark in front of Annie, he had no choice. Sordid, he thought. How does one ask an uncle if he has violated one of the commandments? Quent cleared his throat, but at the last minute his resolution failed.

"One of the men on the drive, a cowboy the men call Broadbrim, he'd like a job on the survey. Says he's getting too old for trail drives."

"A steady man?"

"Steady, skilled. Quick to learn, I believe."

"Tell him to come. We'll need teamsters, and at least one wrangler for the horses and mules. I suppose you'll bring that boy you picked up south of Dodge."

"Yes," Quent said absently, rinsing the razor. He paid special attention to the area around the great bruise. It hurt to shave his jaw.

"Uncle Nick?" he blurted out. "Are you my father?" He turned at that instant, saw his uncle's happy face dissolve into a bleak mask. "Are you?" he asked, certain now. He clenched his teeth and tensed his muscles against the truth.

His uncle bit his lips. Uncle Nick, never at a loss for words, seemed completely overcome, unable to speak!

"I don't know," he finally said.

Quent had expected a flat negative, whether it was truth or lie. Uncle Nick would certainly say no. This horrifying admission damned his mother's reputation as much as a yes.

"Please, Quentin, I don't wish to lie to you, not when we have plans for the future. But I told her I'd never speak of it."

"What would you never speak of?" he asked harshly. "That you and my mother... Adultery... My father..." The words no longer made sense. He dropped the razor in the basin of tepid water.

"Shut up!" gasped Uncle Nick. "You don't know what you're saying. You do not speak of dear Leona in that tone of voice!"

"What else am I to say?" Quent asked, his voice unsteady, abashed by the storm of emotion he had generated.

"Shall I tell you the truth?" his uncle asked gently. "At this time, considering the circumstances, I think she'll forgive me if I speak the truth."

"If you can bring yourself to it," snarled Quent. He immediately felt even greater shame. The man was his uncle, and an elder, and deserved some respect. "I'm sorry. I shouldn't have—"

"Sit down. We don't have much time, so I'll leave out the details of no great importance. Your father is eight years older than I. You know that. He established himself in the law and married long before I left for college, let alone entered into the business world. In the summer of '58, just out of Harvard, I visited him in New York, excited by the possibilities of the railroads. Someday I'll explain the complexities of the deal that had been offered me, but for now I'll just say your father disapproved of everything I told him. We quarreled and I left, insulted and hurt at things he had said."

"I know what he said. The same things he said to me years later about being in trade and speculation."

"Exactly. I waited several days in New York, uncertain, not knowing what to do. Perhaps getting involved in this speculation *would* bring shame upon the family. Perhaps I should study law, live up to the expectations of my father and my brother. Your mother and your brothers and sisters were on Long Island, where they spent the summer. Your father had mentioned, before we quarreled, that he planned to join them for a week. Some days passed, but I made up my mind—I'd pay heed to Claude's warnings, start studying law in the autumn. I went to Long Island to apologize, to make up the differences between us, for brothers should not quarrel."

Uncle Nick had been standing stock-still, not even moving his hands. Now he advanced to where Quent sat on the edge of the bed and lowered his voice.

"He was not there. Some important case had kept him in town. Leona, your mother, said she expected him the next day and that I should wait for him. That night..." He coughed and swallowed hard. "The night before, there had been a magnificent show of falling stars. Your mother asked, after the children were abed, if I would accompany her to see if the display might repeat itself. We walked to the shore, then east, to the copse of trees. Is the bench still there?"

"Yes." *Great Caesar! Not even in bed! On a bench, in the open!*

"She had not bothered with a shawl, as the day had been quite warm. But a breeze blew from the Sound. I put my arm about her shoulders... and neither of us knew how it happened, but on that bench..." He turned away. Quent closed his eyes, sat very still.

"You must not blame her, Quentin. Claude had neglected her shamelessly that summer. Nor can the blame be laid at his door, for he was at that time stepping to the forefront of his profession. He thought of the future, particularly the future he might offer his children." He coughed again, walked to the window and pretended to study Temptation's dusty alleyway. He turned and met Quent's stare.

"The next morning, she and I talked quietly on the porch. No one, children or servants, could possibly have overheard us. We determined that I should go away, that neither of us would ever speak of what had passed between us. I left, I did not apologize to Claude, I did not study law and take my place in the firm. Instead, I went to Missouri, to join the men who contemplated the first Pacific railroad." He closed his mouth tightly, glared, daring Quent to dispute any part of his statement.

"And then?" asked Quent, feeling the story incomplete.

"What's to say? Months later I received a letter from a cousin—Claude, naturally, did not make any contact, thinking silence would bring me to my senses. This cousin wrote casually that Leona had given Claude a fifth child. I remember sitting in a tent in the midst of the railroad camp, counting the weeks between the two dates, and knowing. Rather, not knowing. For certainly Claude had come frequently during the rest of the summer, and doctors assure me it is very seldom exactly nine months. What's the chance of one incidence causing... a child?" he added faintly.

"When did you marry Aunt Millie?" asked Quent, curious to know if it had been a double adultery.

"Not until more than a year after you were born. When my railroad stocks began to accumulate and my activity on the western roads brought me some attention. It was then, for Claude could not afford to alienate Millie's relatives by absenting himself from the wedding, that I first saw you.''

''And?''

''I knew in my heart,'' he said simply. ''My heart has always known.''

''And no one else guessed? We're so much alike.'' Uncle Nick bent to look in the mirror, studied his face, then looked back at Quent.

''I'm your uncle. Always remember that. Your father was a towhead as a youngster. His hair darkened as he aged. You could well be his son. But after seeing you, I made it my business not to be too much about. I felt Leona's pain in my presence, so I avoided the family. Not that Claude was pleased to have me as a guest.''

''No, he often spoke ill of you.'' Quent went to the window in his turn, looked down on the dusty path below, the few straggling houses between the hotel and the limitless plains. ''My mother,'' he muttered. ''My own mother.''

''Don't be foolish,'' snapped his uncle. ''Has it never happened to you? The first caress, the first touch, innocent, without meaning, then the great rush to fulfillment that cannot be gainsaid. It is not men alone who experience it, I assure you.''

Quent thought of Annie, in Davy Lampman's arms. Had it been like that? And then the night on the platform of the car in Ogallala. And by the buffalo wallow.

''I have felt it,'' Quent said, ''but I *did* stop.''

''With Miss Annie?''

''Yes. At Ogallala. And later.''

''I suspected. Well, you contained yourself because you had a much finer upbringing than I. Throughout your life, I took care never to interfere, although I often disagreed with what Claude set out for you. That ridiculous private school, with games played on tended fields, when you should have been tramping through the woods with a pack on your back. Polo ponies and races, when you should have been riding a rough horse, leading a pack mule. Do you realize, when you were younger, we might have gone on a buffalo hunt together? But now it's too late.''

''I would have loved your alternatives,'' said Quent happily. ''Why didn't you make a few suggestions?''

''To even suggest was to admit what I'd done. What Leona had done.''

He could not see Uncle Nick clearly, because his eyes had filled with tears.

''You must get dressed,'' said Uncle Nick, consulting his watch.

Quent threw his arm lightly over Uncle Nick's shoulder. ''Thank you,'' he said huskily. ''Thank you for everything.''

''I must ask that you never mention this,'' said Uncle Nick. ''It is no certainty. Speaking of it might bring hurt to people we both love.''

Quent stepped into his trousers; the barkeep's wife had pressed them into a semblance of acceptability. ''Of course not. It is between us.''

He picked up his undershirt, then his shirt. Uncle Nick held his studs.

''It happens in the best of families,'' he said with assurance. ''And the true father is the man who provides the care. Even when a man knows, children are easy to love.'' Quent stopped, one stud half in, half out.

''Annie has a child,'' he whispered.

''Miss Brownell?'' The eyebrows went up, the mouth opened in surprise. Quent took a deep breath.

''Do you know Cyrus Lampman?''

''Of course. He bids on the rails....''

''His son David made advances to Annie while she visited her uncle in Washington. His father refused permission for the marriage. Annie was not at school in Louisiana, but in a convent, where she secretly had the baby.''

Quent grabbed the final stud from his uncle, glared at him, challenged him. ''We will go there immediately after the wedding to find her son. She longs for the baby, and I cannot deny her any possible happiness.'' Uncle Nick stared at him, but it was not a stare of disapproval.

"Bravo,'' he mouthed, barely whispering. "Bravo!'' This time louder. He punched Quent's shoulder. "You are indeed the pirate's heir. When people ask, hold your head up and speak the truth. Shuck off the rules of polite behavior and stand up for what *you* know is right.''

Good advice. If he had done that in Washington... Why did he have the feeling he had just, right at this moment, grown up?

"I clean forgot to tell you, I found the Caribbean van Kelsons. In Jamaica. They call themselves Keelson. Alexander Keelson is a businessman of no small repute in Kingston, imports and exports. Of color, naturally, so you have cousins of a darker hue.''

"The pirate had three families,'' Quent marveled lightly. "Quite a man.''

"If my eyes and ears have seen and heard aright,'' said Uncle Nick slyly, "you popped your bride twice in a little more than an hour. A worthy descendent of the pirate.'' Quent knew he was growing red again. He looked in the mirror. The blush really did not show much, behind the bruise.

"Six hundred,'' said the barkeep firmly, pointing at the paper on the table. Linares studied it, then passed it around so Brownell, McCann and Perk could see the figures.

"The bridegroom started the fracas,'' the barkeep continued, "so I suppose he should pay some of it.'' Linares wondered if it might be possible to get whiskey here, in the dining room. Or was it impossible to reach any of the kegs in the destroyed saloon?

"McCann started it when he insulted a lady,'' snapped Perk. "A real man stood up for her.'' One of his eyes was swollen shut, and the knuckles of his left hand bled.

"You'll damn well wait until the devil drinks ice water before you'll get anything from me,'' snarled McCann, a bit indistinctly, since his mouth refused to open very wide. He dug around in his vest pocket, pulled something out and flung it across the room. The gold ring rolled a few feet, stopped against the leg of a table.

"Six hundred!" Linares ran a finger down the itemized list. "I've never paid more than three hundred for any of my men's diversions."

"The plate-glass mirror," the barkeep reminded him. "When the big black man threw McCann over the bar. And the mirror falling broke most of my glassware."

Linares swallowed hard. Young van Kelson certainly should pay a share of this. He had indeed started the fight. His uncle had wealth enough to pay the whole damn thing with nary a blink. Nicholas van Kelson was probably the only man in Temptation with a diamond in his tie tack.

A man in a black frock coat filled the doorway of the dining room. The preacher. What a farce this wedding had become, with the original groom rejected, the bride's father barely able to stand because he'd stumbled on a stray whiskey bottle. What the groom's face looked like, no one yet knew. At least there was no photographer in town, engaged to take a wedding photo that could only be an embarrassment.

Linares sneaked a quick glance at McCann, who sat with them only because he had a hard time staying on his feet. One side of the man's face ballooned. A fine spectacle his cowboys would make tomorrow morning on the train. They could all walk, that he knew, for they'd been conscripted to help clean up the mess in the saloon. He heard the tinkle of broken glass, a mutter of voices, an occasional laugh. He presumed it was the Tall X crowd laughing, since technically they had won the fight. Van Kelson was getting the girl.

Brownell finally noticed the preacher and struggled to get out of his chair. Linares got up, pulled the man to his feet.

"Good day, Mr. Brownell," the preacher began. Then his eyes lit on McCann and he drew back. "What's wrong, Mr. McCann? Have you had an accident?"

"Yes," snapped Brownell. "He ran into a plate-glass mirror."

"His injuries should be treated," said the preacher. "Lydia—" he spoke over his shoulder to a woman waiting at the door "—get water, rags, bandages. Mr. McCann must be seen to." He turned to Brownell. "I took the liberty of asking my wife to accompany me, for I didn't know if Miss Brownell had a lady to stand with her during the ceremony. Perhaps, in view of Mr. McCann's accident, you'd rather not continue with the plans for—"

"McCann's not the groom anymore. The groom's fine, except he has a black eye." The preacher looked doubtful.

"I was invited to unite Mr. McCann and Miss Brownell in the bonds of holy—"

"She's marrying the man who knocked her up," snarled McCann. "I don't want the slut." The preacher's mouth snapped shut.

The groom and his uncle stood framed in the doorway to the lobby. Both wore clawhammer coats and stiff shirts. By damn, the young one had a fancy stone in his tie tack! It glittered blue, like his eyes.

"Here he is," Linares said, turning the preacher about so he would not hear any more filthy words from McCann. The preacher's doubtful, serious face dissolved into surprise and awe.

"Which one?"

"The young one." Linares pushed the preacher to the door to make the introductions. While young van Kelson and Old Nick shook hands with the preacher, Linares retrieved the ring from the floor. He thrust it into the groom's hands, muttered, "I don't suppose you had time to take care of this."

Van Kelson examined the ring. "Inside it says 'Anne and Hugh, forever,'" he protested in a hissing whisper.

"I'm sure you'll replace it with something finer as soon as you arrive in a city," Linares said, letting himself be a bit sarcastic.

"Mr. Brownell," Old Nick called from across the room. "Your daughter is ready to come down. Are you able to meet her at the foot of the stairs? If not, I'd be very pleased to perform the duty."

"You stay away from Annie!" yelled Brownell, who had reclaimed his chair. "Here, Linares, help me up." Linares tugged on Brownell's arm. With his support on one side and the cane on the other, Brownell made it to the lobby, to the foot of the stairs.

Linares caught his breath. She stood above them, in a gown the color of a ripe peach, with the same changing flush and shading a peach shows when it has achieved perfection. She wore nothing on her head but a frill of the same color, high up in back. She smiled so broadly, even the most charitable observer would have had to describe it as a grin. Very unvirginal. Rather unbridal. The girl was not prostrate with nervous anticipation of her wedding night.

"You're beautiful, my dear," said Brownell.

"Because I'm happy, Daddy."

"Well, I'm not. I wanted you to marry a good cattleman, a man who could run a ranch. Not a damn Yankee tenderfoot."

"He's not a tenderfoot," she said.

"Mr. van Kelson," Linares began uncertainly, "has the beginnings of being a fine cattleman. He performed well on the drive...."

Brownell snorted. "Never got beyond riding drag."

"But it was he who bossed the building of the bridge. Bossed the crews of three herds, Perk tells me, and did it well."

"Very well," Annie echoed.

"Perk says he can't get a loop over a calf standing still."

"Not all men are as fine a roper as you, or McCann. There's room for a multitude of talents in Montana."

Linares let go of Brownell long enough to stick his head around the corner, to see that the groom and his groomsman, his uncle, stood expectantly before the preacher. The preacher's lady had returned from her mission of mercy and waited there, too.

"I think they're expecting us," he said.

Annie Brownell did not lean on her father's arm heading to her marriage ceremony. She supported him on one side, and Linares carried his weight on the other. McCann had somehow managed to get on his feet, for he was not in the room. Someone had called the cowboys from their cleaning chores. The Tall X crew stood bareheaded, smiling. Even Broadbrim had removed his oversize hat. Van Kelson's boy mule driver looked the best, for he had already received his pay and had visited the barbershop and the general store. The cut across his forehead rather distracted from the trim of his hair, as did the dried blood down his nose. He grinned a bit too broadly at his boss's triumph.

Linares watched the ceremony without paying attention. He should be proud, bringing two such handsome young people together. But he tamped down the pride, because he was not altogether sure he had been right in putting them in the way of temptation.

The path to Temptation. The trail to Temptation. Well, he thought, justifying himself, there probably *was* good to be said for young women who waited until the proper words were said before they hopped into bed. But Annie Brownell and her chosen man were certainly the least nervous couple he'd ever seen before a preacher.

Linares hated to disturb the wedding dinner, but he had to finish the book work and settle up with the men. And, needless to say, he couldn't work in the saloon. So in between the toasts of the wedding banquet he made out the warrants the cowboys could cash at the first town with a bank. He put their names on the train tickets to carry them back to Texas. Plus, for each, a little cash, so they could buy proper clothes and clean up here in Temptation.

Perk. Abner Perkins, the warrant read, the first one he completed, naturally, since the foreman had privileges. Then

Stack, Charles Chaden. He called the names as he finished their papers.

"Broadbrim."

"You made that out Alex Keelson, didn't you?" asked Broadbrim. Linares examined the man, could see not one sign of the fight on the broad face. Well, maybe a little swelling on one cheek.

"Keelson!" exclaimed Old Nick, springing up as if he'd heard a rattle under the table. "My good man, might you be from Jamaica?"

"No," drawled Broadbrim, shoving back his huge hat in lieu of removing it, "but my pa is."

"Is he kin to Alexander Keelson of Kingston—?"

"My great-uncle. I'm named for him. You see, these folks about here—" he waved his hand, taking in everyone in the dining room "—they figure my ma and pa was slaves before the war. But my pa was a free man of color who came from Jamaica to Galveston, where he bought cattle to send home. And my ma, she's from the Indian Nations, so she was no slave, neither. In those days there weren't no cattle drives north. Texas cattle was shipped by boat to the islands, and my pa saw to getting cattle loaded for Jamaica."

"Quentin!" yelled Old Nick. "This man is our cousin! His great-great-great—I don't know how many—grandfather was the pirate. Come, come, Mr. Keelson. Join the table. Annie, you must hear about Quentin's ancestor, the first Nicholas van Kelson."

Linares observed that Brownell blanched and the preacher and his wife shoved their chairs noisily away from the groom, who made room for Broadbrim. Fortunately, Annie smiled at her husband, and her husband clasped her hand beneath the table.

"Thanks for the invite," said Broadbrim, taking off his hat completely. "But now that I have my pay, I'd best mosey down the street and buy me a new outfit. I'm not suitable for a dinner party." He twisted the shattered hat in his hands, picking at the decrepit remains of the Mexican gold and silver. "Maybe I'll buy myself one of those fancy Stetsons," he added. "Then people might call me Mr. Keelson."

There was considerable silence after Broadbrim left the room. Linares respected the cowboy even more. Broadbrim had seen the discomfort and refused to embarrass van Kelson and Brownell. Too bad he couldn't use Broadbrim as a trail boss, but there were some people . . . Someone had to restart the conversation. Linares cleared his throat.

"Well, van Kelson, will you be in Texas next spring, ready to bring up another herd? You're qualified now."

Brownell coughed. "Well, maybe he'd be able to tag along in the drag."

"Thank you, Mr. Linares, but I don't meet your qualifications at all," said Quent.

"I'd hire you on right now," said Linares, astonished by the unwarranted modesty. "Not maybe as foreman, but you could handle swing, and learn to ride point."

"No, you see, Linares, I still don't understand. I can appreciate that you don't want greenhorns or boys on a drive, maybe not even the run-of-the-mill woman—" he smiled at his wife "—but it's still a mystery to me, why don't you allow one-eyed cows in your herds?"

*   *   *   *   *